THE LAST
CHANCE

THE LAST CHANCE

A novel by

DARRIEN LEE

Q-Boro Books
WWW.QBOROBOOKS.COM

An Urban Entertainment Company

Published by Q-Boro Books

Copyright © 2007 by Darrien Lee

ISBN-13: 978-1-933967-22-6
ISBN-10: 1-933967-22-6
LCCN: 2006936962

First Printing October 2007
Printed in the United States of America

10 9 8 7 6 5 4 3 2 1

This is a work of fiction. It is not meant to depict, portray or represent any particular real persons. All the characters, incidents and dialogues are the products of the author's imagination and are not to be construed as real. Any references or similarities to actual events, entities, real people, living or dead, or to real locales are intended to give the novel a sense of reality. Any similarity in other names, characters, entities, places and incidents is entirely coincidental.

Cover Copyright © 2006 by **Q-BORO BOOKS** all rights reserved
Cover layout/design by Candace K. Cottrell
Cover photo by Ted Mebane; Cover Model N'Akia
Editors: Alisha Yvonne, Camille Lofters, Candace K. Cottrell

Q-BORO BOOKS
Jamaica, Queens NY 11434
WWW.QBOROBOOKS.COM

Dedication

The novel is dedicated in memory to the late
Preston Holt, my dear, devoted cousin.

ACKNOWLEDGMENTS

First I would like to thank God for his faithfulness and everlasting love. Without his inspiration I wouldn't be where I am today. I want to thank my church family at Olive Branch Missionary Baptist Church under the leadership of Pastor Vincent Windrow and First Lady, Stacy Windrow for your continued prayers and for uplifting my spirit and soul.

I want to give a shout out to my entire family for keeping me in your prayers. I wish I could name you all individually, but you know who you are.

To the Women of Color Book club in Clarksville, Tennessee, I appreciate your encouragement and for the beautiful doll you presented to me. To Page by Page and Page Turners Book club members, I love you and thanks for that delicious dinner you treated me to in Baltimore. I can't wait to hang out with you guys again.

To Candace Cottrell, you nailed my cover once again. Thank you for designing a book cover image that captured my vision and for your hard work in making my novel a reality. A special thanks goes out to Cory and Heather Buford of Gateway Online Marketing, who keep my website up and running and for your creative assistance. More thanks go out to Alisha Yvonne, for helping me fine-tune this exciting novel.

To my dear friends and fellow authors, V. Anthony Rivers and J. Daniels, thanks for always being there for me. Your friendship is priceless. To authors, Allison Hobbs, Tina Brooks-McKinney, Shelley Halima, and Harold Turley II, thanks for keeping me motivated even as you travel down your own literary paths. We're in this thing together so keep up the great work. To author, Laurinda Brown, I have mad love for you, sis.

A special thanks go out to Mark Anthony, Sabine, and the entire Q-Boro staff for your diligence and hard work. I'm so grateful to be a part of a talented group of writers who support and promote each other with the up most respect. Mark, I want to send out an additional thanks to you for never being too busy to take my call. You've always made yourself available to listen, and I'm so appreciative that you have faith and confidence in me and recognize my literary gift. I want to let you know that I won't let you down.

To my special friends, Brenda Thomas, Tracy Dandridge, Sharon Nowlin, Buanita Ray, Robin Ridley, and Monica Baker. Thanks for giving me plenty of colorful material to write about. Remember, I'm always listening. To the literary divas, Angie Burum, LaTonia Davenport, Sherrie Davis, Sharon Sutton, and Renee' Settles and Venus Boston thanks for putting my novels first and being in my corner. Your love and support means so much to me. To Anita Arlene and the sisters of Delta Sigma Theta Inc. for allowing me to be a part of your Literary Jazz every year.

A special thanks goes out to my beautician, Ronda Gilbert, and to Melinda at Beauty 4 Me, you guys always make sure I'm looking my best at all times.

Lastly, to my husband, Wayne, and daughters, Alyvia and Marisa, I love you and lift you up with joy in my heart every second of every day.

Darrien Lee

PROLOGUE

Tonight was a night most people dreamed of but never got to experience. For twenty-seven-year-old Keilah Chance, it was just another day on the job. She was serving as the personal security agent for the daughter of one of Washington's most affluent families. Arhmelia Randolph, the seventeen-year-old daughter of Supreme Court Justice Malcolm Randolph and his wife Teresa, was attending the Sweet Sixteen party of the daughter of a hip-hop mogul, and her safety was of the utmost concern.

Keilah arrived with her client to screaming fans outside D.C.'s Renaissance Hotel in her silver Jaguar. Once she put the car in park and stepped out, the valet quickly took the keys out of her hands. Keilah walked around the vehicle and opened the door for her young client. When Arhmelia stepped out onto the red carpet, she waved happily to a sea of screaming teens. Dressed in a designer outfit by G-Unit, she looked much older than her seventeen years.

As they walked the red carpet toward the entrance to the hotel, Keilah kept a sharp eye on the crowd, especially the young men who fought to get a view of her clients as well as the who's whos in music and movies, who were also arriving.

Keilah's main focus was to blend into the crowd, so she dressed accordingly and didn't look a day over twenty in her outfit. Her hair fell midway down her back in spiral curls, and her makeup was flawless.

After ushering Arhmelia into the ballroom, Keilah took note of the elaborate decorations and huge, five-tier birthday cake. There was a table full of a variety of food and drinks for the teenagers with the music being provided by a famous DJ out of New York City. The crowd of nearly two hundred people danced to the up-tempo beat being played. Keilah made sure Arhmelia always stayed within a few feet of her, which meant she had to spend half the night on the dance floor. However, Keilah had no problem finding a dance partner.

The party was going to last until one AM, so Keilah made it a point to escort her young client out of the crowd several minutes prior to that. Outside, they waited for the valet to bring the car around. As they lingered, Arhmelia struck up a conversation with a young man who exited the hotel around the same time they did. He was also the same young man who'd kept asking Arhmelia to dance at the party.

As the couple held a conversation, Keilah made it a point to stand between them, and even though it invaded Arhmelia's privacy, it also kept her safe. Keilah needed to make sure the young man not only kept his distance from Arhmelia but that he didn't say anything threatening to her either. Arhmelia rolled her eyes and looked over at Keilah.

"Come on, Keilah. Can you give us a little privacy?"

Keilah gave Arhmelia a look to let her know it wasn't happening. She also kept a sharp eye on their surroundings as they stood outside in the open, waiting for their car. Just as the valet drove up with the car, Keilah saw the young man pull out his cell phone and ask for Arhmelia's telephone number. Arhmelia was about to recite her number to him when Keilah stopped her and then made her get inside the car.

"I'm sorry, but she's not allowed to give out her number to strangers. If you give me your number, I will see if she would like to call you later."

The young man looked at Keilah as if he was sizing her up, and then he cursed loudly at her. About that time, a group of people exited the hotel and walked in their direction.

A handsome man dressed in a designer suit and expensive jewelry walked over and said, "Keilah Chance! What a nice surprise."

Keilah smiled at the gentleman and said, "Hello Quentin."

As the gentleman walked closer, he looked at the young man and frowned. "I thought you said you were leaving?"

Keilah pointed at the young man and asked, "You know this kid, Quentin?"

He sighed and said, "Yeah, he's mine. Boy, I know you didn't disrespect this lady! What did he do?"

Keilah folded her arms and said, "This can't be Malik."

"Unfortunately, it is, Keilah."

"I haven't seen him in years. I had no idea," she replied.

Quentin shook his head and asked, "What did he do?"

With a raised brow she said, "Ask him."

Quentin turned towards the young man and slapped him hard on the back of the head. "I don't have to ask him, Keilah. I know you, and you wouldn't be upset if he didn't do something stupid. Look, I'm so sorry about this. If there's anything I can do to make this right, I will. You know we go way back, and I don't want this to hurt our relationship."

Malik made an irritated gesture and rolled his eyes. Quentin slapped him again and said, "Boy, you're in over your head! Don't you realize who you're messing with? This is Keilah that used to protect your mother. Now apologize to her like you got some damn sense," the man said.

Malik rolled his eyes again before mumbling an apology to Keilah. The flashily dressed gentleman smacked the young man on the back of the head again and yelled at him.

"I said apologize to her, and do it right!"

This time Malik apologized to Keilah as instructed before walking off down the sidewalk with his friends. Keilah and Quentin watched as the trio walked down the street. While Quentin's back was turned Keilah watched as Malik turned and pointed his finger at her as if it were a gun and simulated pulling the trigger. After they were gone, Quentin, known to the hip-hop world as Diamond, smiled at Keilah and extended his hand. Keilah smiled and shook his hand.

"I'm sorry about all of this, Keilah. I'm still working on the boy. He's still stuck in the streets."

"I really didn't know he was yours, Quentin. My client was all starry-eyed over him, so I figured he had to be somebody."

"Well you wasn't around Malik that much since he didn't go on the road with us, so you didn't see him that often." Quentin pulled Keilah to the side. "Are we still good?"

Keilah played with the large gold necklace around Quentin's neck, and then patted him on the chest. "We're good. Get Malik under control, Quentin, before he gets himself in a lot of trouble."

Quentin turned and walked toward his entourage. He looked back at her seriously. "I'm working on it, Keilah. You have a good night, and I'll be in touch."

Keilah opened her car door and said, "Have a great night, Quentin, and give my regards to your wife."

"I will," he answered.

Keilah got behind the wheel of her car and hurriedly buckled her seat belt.

Arhmelia looked over at Keilah and asked, "Do you know who you were talking to? That was Diamond, the singer."

Keilah adjusted her rearview mirror and looked over at the young woman.

"Yes, I know who he is. I've known Quentin Rivers for a couple of years. I used to work for him, but I didn't realize that was his knucklehead son acting a fool."

"I can't believe you used to work for Diamond."

"Well, actually I worked for him to protect his wife," Keilah revealed.

"Wow, that had to have been exciting, Keilah."

She looked over and Arhmelia and said, "It had its moments, but Quentin really needs to get control of his son before the kid gets into a lot of trouble."

"Didn't you see how cute Malik was?"

"They're all cute at that age, and dangerous, Arhmelia. And another thing: You don't give your number out to strangers. I don't care who they are. If they're interested in you, they'll be happy to give you their number just as well. You young women are too careless these days, and you put yourselves at risk when you act like that."

Arhmelia buckled her seat belt. "But that was Diamond's son. He's so famous."

Keilah pulled out into traffic and headed out of the city. "I don't care about that. What I do care about is getting you home safe and sound, Arhmelia."

Arhmelia fumbled with the radio without responding as Keilah kept an eye on traffic.

"So, did you have a good time?"

"Yeah, it was cool. I saw you dancing your butt off."

Keilah giggled.

"I had to in order to keep up with you. Thanks to you my feet are killing me."

Keilah chuckled as she adjusted her rear view mirror.

"I have to give it to you, Keilah. You can dance. I like hanging out with you even though you cramped my style tonight."

"That's my job, sweetheart."

About that time, a dark-colored SUV pulled up on the passenger side of Keilah's Jaguar. She looked over and watched as the window lowered and the barrel of a gun pointed directly at them.

"Get down," Keilah shouted as she pushed the young woman's head down in the car. She swerved away from the vehicle.

Shots rang out. Arhmelia screamed.

"Hold on, Arhmelia!" Keilah yelled as she fought to maintain control of her car.

Keilah could hear the bullets as they hit her car, shattering the back window. She reached inside her jacket pocket, pulled out her gun, and started shooting back at the assailants as they once again pulled up beside her car. Arhmelia continued to cry and scream as Keilah exchanged gunfire with the occupants in the vehicle.

Meanwhile, in Dennison, California, Luke Chance was in the process of ending his night. He finished up signing some paperwork that his assistant had put on his desk earlier in the day. After working a ten-hour day, he was anxious to get home to his wife and children. Just as he stood to turn off his computer, a sharp pain shot through his head. He grimaced and sat back down in his chair. As he closed his eyes and rubbed his temple, a vision of Keilah flashed in his mind. He opened the top drawer of his desk and pulled out a bottle of Zomig, a medicine prescribed to him by his doctor for his sudden migraines. For some reason, he seemed to always get severe headaches when something was going on with Keilah. It started when she was thirteen and first got her period. Ever since then, he'd been able channel all her stress and anxiety, no matter where she was or how hard she tried to hide it.

Luke was Keilah's oldest brother. At forty-six years old, Luke had all the answers and was the father figure to his family. Being mild mannered and extremely understanding were his best traits. He was also an attractive man with physical characteristics that could easily qualify him as a male model. He wore his hair closely cropped, had a thin mustache over his upper lip, and had long, sexy eyelashes.

After popping the tablets into his mouth he drained the bottled water that was sitting on his desk. He looked at his watch and then at their family portrait on the wall. It was one o'clock in the morning in D.C., and even though his head was still throbbing, he had a strong urge to call her. He pulled out his cell phone and dialed her number. Four rings later, it went to her voicemail.

"Hey, Keilah, it's Luke. I know it's late, but I was sitting here thinking about you. I'm on my way home from the casino, but give me a call. I don't care what time it is. I love you."

After hanging up, he leaned back in his chair and closed his eyes. Luke was anxious for his migraine to subside and for Keilah to return his telephone call. He just prayed that whatever she was mixed up in, she was OK.

Back in D.C., Keilah's vehicle did a 360 and then faced the SUV as it approached them on I-395. Keilah opened her car door and pulled out a second gun. She unleashed a series of gunshots directly into the front window of the truck, causing it to crash into a lamppost. Keilah could see smoke rising from under the hood of the SUV, but there was no movement inside it. She wasn't sure if she'd hit anyone and had to be ready in case the occupants rushed her. As she kept her guns aimed on her assailants, she glanced into her car and yelled, "Arhmelia, are you hurt?"

The young woman screamed and cried without answering. Keilah frantically felt around on Arhmelia's body and yelled again. "Are you hit?"

Arhmelia leaned against Keilah and sobbed. "No. I want to go home. I want my momma and daddy."

Keilah looked back over at the SUV and in a panic yelled, "Hold on, Arhmelia. I have to call the police, and as soon as they get here, I'm going to take you home. OK?"

She kept her gun aimed at the SUV as she grabbed Arhmelia by her jacket and pulled her out of the driver's side door. She made Arhmelia squat down behind the Jaguar for protection in case the occupants of the car started shooting again. Arhmelia whimpered as Keilah spoke to police over the phone. Within seconds, several cars arrived with lights and sirens blazing.

Keilah could now relax. Arhmelia, on the other hand, was still visibly shaken. While officers questioned Keilah and checked her identification, she noticed a familiar officer walking in her direction. Other police officers pulled Arhmelia to the side so they could question her. Once they found out who her parents were, they quickly pushed the media back to protect her identity.

"I see you're still at it, Keilah," Officer Jackson said as he laughed.

"Don't start with me, Jackson. I've had a long night. Did I hit any of them?"

He pointed to an awaiting car and motioned for her to follow him. "No, you didn't, which means you must be losing your touch. I do need you to come see if you can identify any of them."

Keilah looked into the backseat of the car where three young black men sat in handcuffs. Immediately she recognized one of the men as Diamond's son. She pointed at him and said, "The one in the middle was talking to my client outside the Renaissance Hotel as we were leaving that party.

He was trying to get her telephone number, but I stopped him. They way he looked at me let me know he didn't like it. After that I found out he was Quentin Brown's kid."

"Why doesn't that surprise me? I heard Quentin's been trying to straighten him out." Officer Jackson gave Keilah back her gun and identification. "Well, it's not going to be easy for Quentin to get his kid out of this mess."

"He was at the Renaissance, too. He made his son apologize, but it was obvious he didn't like his old man calling him out in front of everyone."

"Keilah, you were lucky tonight. Maybe you should think about a career change."

She fingered her hair before putting her hands on her hips.

"You sound like my brothers. I'm going to tell you like I tell them. Don't hold your breath. I like my job, and I'm good at it, so don't expect me to give it up anytime soon."

Jackson looked over at the three young men and laughed. "All right. Next time you might not be so lucky."

"No, they're the ones who might not be so lucky," she yelled as she pointed to the patrol car. "So can I take Arhmelia home now? I've already contacted her parents so they wouldn't be worried."

"You'd better let us take her. We're going to have to tow your car in as evidence. You're welcome to come along for the ride."

"Come on, Jackson," she pouted.

He threw his hands up in defense. "You know it's procedure, Keilah, so don't even go there."

She folded her arms and sighed. "What a night. I can't believe those young thugs tried to take me out over a phone number."

Officer Jackson touched Keilah's arm tenderly and said, "It was about respect, Keilah. They couldn't care less about the telephone number, but he could've been trying to get close enough for something more sinister. You probably saved that little girl's life tonight, and that's a fact."

She blushed and said, "I was just doing my job."

"I joke with you about it, but you really are good at what you do. I know you're making a lot of money, so when I retire, don't forget about me."

"By the time you retire, Jackson, my kids will be running my company."

He opened the car door for her and laughed. "Come on so I can get Arhmelia out of here before the media has a field day with this one."

Keilah got inside the car beside Arhmelia and put her arm around her shoulder to comfort her.

CHAPTER ONE

Keilah twirled around in her chair and looked out over the skyline. It had been two days since the shooting, and she welcomed the tranquility of her corner office, which was housed in a twenty-story building on the outskirts of the nation's capital. She was co-owner of one of the most successful private security agencies in D.C., and at five feet eight, she was not only beautiful, she was highly educated, tough, and an expert in martial arts, which aided in her success as a highly skilled marksman.

Her career was totally against the life her brothers had planned for her, but this was her life and she was going to live the way she wanted. She'd been protected by her brothers all of her life, now it was her turn to do the same for others. Her brothers meant well, but they could be extremely overbearing at times.

Keilah owned the Stone Chance Protection Agency with an ex-military police officer, Ramsey Stone. They had been introduced through mutual friends, and they hit it off immediately. Keilah and Ramsey always felt it was fate that brought them together because, oddly, they'd had the same vision for a business and their business plans were basically identical. Keilah and Ramsey had a lot in common, and they felt like they had known each other for years, even though only six years had passed. While Ramsey was rugged and personable, he was also very handsome and had a physique like an African warrior. People often mistook him for former-wrestler–turned-actor, the Rock, and as far as beautiful women, he was a magnet and loved every minute of it.

Their company was a huge success and they employed twenty to twenty-five former military officers, Special Forces, and police officers. They were blessed to have been involved in an only few incidents, which caused them to fine-tune their skills even more. They honestly believed their match was made in heaven, and Keilah and Ramsey knew they could trust each other no matter what.

While Keilah was still staring out the window, Ramsey casually walked into her office, sat down and straightened his tie. "Well, well, well. I heard somebody had a busy weekend."

Keilah looked at him and frowned. "Who told you? Jackson?"

Ramsey started laughing. "Who else? I saw him downtown yesterday. He told me you had a run-in with Diamond's kid and some of his partners."

Keilah picked up a folder and handed it to him. "I just finished the report. Here's your copy. It was wild, Ramsey."

"I bet it was," he responded.

Ramsey scanned Keilah's report as she gave him the play-by-play of what happened.

Keilah got up and walked around her desk to the bookshelf so she could replace a book. She looked very professional in her black suit. The jacket was about the same length as her skirt, which showcased her magnificent legs. Her hair was still long and curly, and it complemented her facial features.

"I could tell he had a lot of attitude, but I didn't expect him to take a shot at me."

Ramsey closed the folder and added, "Well, I'm not surprised. I've heard a lot about that kid trying to make a name for himself on the streets."

Keilah turned to Ramsey. "Well I'm not the one."

He chuckled and said, "You don't have to tell me. By the way, call Luke. He's worried about you."

"Dang! I forgot to call him back. When did you talk to him?" she asked.

Ramsey popped a mint into his mouth and said, "Yesterday."

She picked a piece of lint off her skirt. "You didn't tell him about this weekend, did you?"

"No, but he's not happy with you right now. He said you're terrible with returning phone calls."

Keilah sighed and stared down at her Jimmy Choo pumps, and so did Ramsey. "Nice shoes."

She smiled and said, "Thank you."

"Call your brother, Keilah. I told him I would give you the message."

"I will. I'm sorry he called you."

He winked at her and said, "No bother. We had a nice talk."

Ramsey was about six feet four and sinfully handsome. His erect posture and polite nature radiated a military background, and he was a valued asset to their company's success. Their friendship was unbreakable, and at thirty years old, he was still single, dating heavily, but a serious relationship was the last thing on his list. It wasn't hard for him to attract women with his winning smile and cinnamon skin. The diamond stud in his ear gleamed just as brightly as his smile, and his short wavy hair and dimples had women constantly swooning. It didn't hurt that he could rock a business suit like a model, and the navy suit he had on radiated confidence.

Ramsey opened the folder again and looked at the report. "Have you found out when the hearing is going to be for Diamond's son?"

"I'm going to call today. That kid almost made me put him in the morgue. Quentin told me he was working on getting his son's attitude in check, and I'm sure it's going to be hard for him to get him out of this mess."

Ramsey tucked the folder under his arm. "You're right. It might be too little, too late, and he messed with the wrong two women this time. I'm sure Arhmelia's dad is going to push this to the full extent of the law."

"Oh, no doubt, Ramsey."

Keilah walked back over to her desk and opened a drawer. She pulled out the newspaper and held it out to him. "We made the paper. I'm just glad our names were kept out of it, but I'm sure the entertainment magazines will have a field day with it once they find out how Quentin is connected."

Ramsey frowned as he read the article. He laid the newspaper on Keilah's desk. "Well, I'm glad you and Arhmelia weren't injured. That's what's important."

"You're right, Ramsey."

He walked toward the door but stopped and turned around. "By the way, you look beautiful today. I also like the way you're wearing your hair."

She blushed. "Thanks, Ramsey."

He looked at his watch and smiled. "Don't forget the planning meeting at ten o'clock in the conference room, and I have a spot reserved for us to do some target shooting this evening at six o'clock if you're up for it."

"Sounds good. See you at the meeting," she replied as she typed on her computer.

"Call Luke," he reminded her before closing the door behind him.

As soon as Ramsey left the room, Keilah picked up her telephone and returned Luke's call.

* * *

At the ten o'clock meeting, Ramsey and Keilah went over the event of the weekend as well as upcoming assignments. The meeting lasted for about two hours and once it was over, lunch was served. A nearby restaurant catered the lunch, which included avocado egg rolls, sirloin salad, quesadillas, calamari, and buffalo wings.

Keilah didn't eat nearly as much as everyone else so she finished lunch first. Before heading back to her office, she walked over to Ramsey who was refilling his plate. "Ramsey, when you finish lunch stop by my office. I want to talk to you about something."

Ramsey stacked a couple of buffalo wings and some calamari on his plate and then smiled. "Okay. I'll see you shortly."

Shortly for Ramsey was another thirty minutes, but he finally made it to Keilah's office. He loosened his necktie as he walked in. "What's up, Keilah?"

She looked up and saw him fumbling with his tie. "You look full."

He sat down then grabbed his stomach. "I overdid it as usual."

She printed out some reports and laughed. "I'm sure you'll work it off in the gym."

Ramsey could tell she was hesitating, but knowing her like he did, he knew she wouldn't hesitate long. He picked out a piece of peppermint candy from the dish on her desk and stared at her. "So, why are you looking like the cat who ate the canary? What's going on? What do you want to talk to me about?"

She finally looked at him. "I need a favor, and I know it's going to feel like it's coming out of left field but hear me out."

"Sure, what is it?" he replied.

"Well, you know me and Trent broke up about four months ago, and since then, I just haven't been lucky enough to meet anyone else," she explained.

Ramsey curiously listened to her. Keilah had become somewhat of a workaholic since her relationship with Howard University Professor, Trenton Daniels soured. Trenton was a decent guy. He just couldn't handle Keilah being a bodyguard. Trent and Keilah dated heavily for about ten months after meeting in Union Station one Saturday afternoon, and after several efforts to make their relationship work, they decided it was best they parted ways.

Ramsey sat up in his chair and said, "Keilah, sadly it's going to take a real man to be able to deal with this line of work. The crazy thing is that women I meet find it exciting when I tell them what I do, but for some reason, men are intimidated when they find out about you and the other women in this business. Don't worry about it though. You'll find the right guy."

"I hope you're right, Ramsey, but in the meantime, I still need a favor," she reminded him.

"Okay, what is this favor? You know I'll do anything for you."

Keilah hesitated again. "Before you agree, you need to hear me out."

He laughed and said, "All right."

"Ramsey, I know you have a lot of lady friends you see on a regular basis, and I don't want to cause a problem with your routine, but I was wondering if you would put me on your list until I can get out of this rut."

Ramsey was in the state of shock. He stared at her as he sat frozen in his seat.

There was no way she could be asking him what he thought she was asking. Or could she? He cleared his throat. "Excuse me?"

"Look Ramsey, I'm just going to say it. We're both adults and should be able to handle this temporary arrangement with some maturity. I haven't had sex in about four months, and there's only so much that a battery operated device can do for me. I need some skin-to-skin contact really bad. So do you think you can help me out while I'm in this dry spell or not? No strings attached. I promise."

Ramsey couldn't believe his ears. He couldn't do anything but sit there and stare at her while he let her proposal sink in. "Wait a minute. Something must be wrong with my hearing because I know you didn't just ask me what I think you asked me?"

Keilah sort of giggled. She'd never seen Ramsey so at a loss for words. "Come on, Ramsey. You know what I'm asking. I've seen that case of condoms in your closet so stop acting so innocent. We're friends, and a little extra-curricular activity on the side won't hurt anything."

Ramsey burst out laughing. "Are you serious?"

"Yes, I'm serious. What do I have to do to convince you that I am?"

Ramsey laughed again. "Where the hell is this coming from? Why me?"

Keilah walked over and sat on the edge of her desk in front of him. This gave him a bird's eye view of her magnificent legs, which he didn't hesitate to take advantage of.

"Ramsey, we're best friends, remember? We know each other like a book so that means you know I'm not going to sleep with just anybody."

He leaned back in his chair and crossed his legs in disbelief. "So what you're saying is you want us to be sex buddies?"

She giggled again. "If that's what you want to call it—yeah. I just want to have someone to hang out with until that special someone comes along for me."

"You and me having causal sex together is not hanging out, Keilah."

"Ramsey . . . come on. I trust you, and I know we can do this without any emotional ties."

He straightened his tie. "I'm already emotionally tied to you. We've been tight for a long time, and I care about you. I don't know if I want to jeopardize that, Keilah."

See looked him directly in the eyes. "So, is that a yes or no?"

Ramsey laughed nervously. "You act like you're asking me to change your tire or something and you want me to answer you now?"

"Well, yeah."

He put his hands over his eyes and said, "This is crazy."

She leaned down and removed his hands from over his eyes. "Ramsey, all you have to do is relax and have fun with me like you do with all the others," she said, trying to convince him. "It won't mess up our friendship if you would just think of it as a little business arrangement. You know, like in that movie, *Pretty Woman* with Richard Gere and Julia Roberts."

Ramsey couldn't help but laugh out loud. He remembered that movie very well, but they weren't strangers like the characters in the movie. "It seems like you've given this a lot of thought."

Keilah slid down off her desk and walked over to her window and looked out. Ramsey joined her at the window in silence. "Yes, Ramsey, I've given it a lot of thought, and like I said, I know I can trust you to do it and not get all mushy on me."

"What about Trenton? Why can't you ask him? It's not like you haven't slept with him before," Ramsey replied.

She turned and softly tugged on his ear. "Are you listening to me? I said I don't want any emotional ties and sleeping with Trent will only be a setback for me. Besides, I wouldn't want to give him the satisfaction in knowing I'm not in a relationship right now. He told me I'd never be able to find a man who would put up with me being a bodyguard," she explained.

Ramsey played with his necktie. "Well, Trenton's a fool, and so is any other man who spits out that bull."

Keilah hugged his waist. "Thank you, Ramsey."

He put his arm around her and said, "I hope you know what you're asking for, Keilah, because this is some weird shit. But, I am a man, and you know it's not in our nature to turn down sex, especially from someone with attributes like yours."

She playfully pushed him away. "Please. Men do stuff like this all the time. Besides, are you going to stand here and tell me you've never fantasized about us?" she asked with a mischievous grin on her face.

Ramsey looked like a deer caught in headlights. Of course he'd thought about it, but he knew that was a line he never wanted to cross with her. He threw his hands up in the air and said, "I plead the fifth."

She turned to him and boldly said, "Kiss me."

"What?" he asked as he turned toward her.

"Kiss me," she asked again. "I want to see what I have to look forward to."

He frowned and stepped away from her. "I'm not kissing you in here."

She laughed at Ramsey's uneasiness. "You're not going to act like this when we hook up, are you?"

He looked at her. "No . . . I don't know. Look, Keilah, this is a lot to take in at one time, but if I agree to this crazy arrangement, I expect you to keep it just between us. I don't want your brothers, your friends, or anyone knowing anything about it."

She softly answered, "Agreed and just so you know, my brothers know only what I want them to know. Besides, I hate them being in my business, so they're the last people you need to worry about. Now as far as your harem, I'm sure you are going to have to juggle your schedule a little bit, especially with high maintenance Andria, huh?"

"I see you have jokes."

Keilah was right on the money about Andria, and Ramsey knew it. Andria was spoiled and selfish and would pout immediately if she felt like Ramsey wasn't spending enough time with her. She was the daughter of Secretary of Defense, General Thomas Kirkland Rockwell better known as General T. K. Rockwell. At twenty-eight years old, Andria was as sexy as they came and just happened to be a former client of Ramsey's. When Andria got too attached to him, he had one of his female employees take over his assignment.

"You know I'm right, Ramsey," she reminded him.

"Whatever, Keilah. Now listen. If I go along with this indecent proposal, when do you expect it to start and how long do you expect your drought to last?"

She reached over and took his hand into hers. "How about tonight? I'll cook us some dinner, and you can bring the wine. As far as how long it's going to last, well that's up in the air. Come on, Ramsey, can't you do this for me? You know I have a strong sexual appetite and how I've made it this long is beyond me."

He gave her hand a squeeze and turned and walked toward the door. "I hope you know what you're doing because I see disaster written all over this."

"No way. We're going into this with our eyes wide open and cards on the table," she replied.

Ramsey was still somewhat stunned by Keilah's request as he opened the door. Before walking out, he gave her with a serious look. "Keilah, I'll be there, but I can't tell how long I'm going to be able to do this."

She smiled. "Thanks, Ramsey. I love you," she responded with excitement.

"Forget you, Keilah," he yelled back before closing her door behind him. He could feel his heart beating wildly in his chest as he walked down the hallway to his office. When he walked by his secretary, Sherrie, she stopped him.

"Ramsey, I have a couple of messages for you and your mail."

"Thanks, Sherrie," he replied as he took the messages from her. "By the way you look very nice today."

She looked at him curiously. "Thank you. Ramsey, are you okay? You don't look so hot."

He smiled. "I guess it was those avocado egg rolls we had for lunch. I'll be fine, but thanks for asking."

She sat back down and pulled a bottle of Maalox tablets out of her desk. "Here. Take a couple of these. They'll make you feel better real quick."

Ramsey took a couple of the tablets and popped them into his mouth. "Thanks, Sherrie."

"You're welcome."

Unbeknownst to Sherrie, the avocado egg rolls were not the source of Ramsey's anxiety. Keilah had done this to him all by herself. Once inside his office, he laid everything on his desk and sat down. As he leaned back in his chair and closed his eyes, he did everything he could to make sense of the night ahead of him. "What the hell have I gotten myself into?"

After Ramsey left her office, Keilah sat there in deep thought, anticipating her night with Ramsey. He was about as fine as they came. She realized it was going to be a little weird the first time, but after they get through their first night, it should be smooth sailing.

CHAPTER TWO

Oddly, the day seemed to fly by, and because Keilah wanted dinner to be just right, she took off early from work. At home, she cooked chicken breasts smothered in a creamy wine sauce and flavored rice, and then in olive oil she sautéed broccoli, squash, and zucchini to create a vegetable medley. After she put the finishing touches on dinner, she took time to set the table and light some candles. Seconds later, the doorbell rang, startling her. She took one last look in the mirror, and then opened the door.

"Hey, Ramsey. You're right on time," Keilah said with a huge smile on her face.

Ramsey stepped inside the foyer. "I meant to get here earlier so I could help you with dinner."

Keilah closed the door. "That's sweet of you, but dinner is ready to serve."

Ramsey's cologne immediately sent goose bumps over Keilah's body. He always did smell heavenly, but tonight his scent was even more noticeable. He was neatly dressed in a pair of relaxed jeans and a light blue, button-down shirt.

The couple walked toward the dining room where Ramsey sat one of two bottles of wine on the table. Keilah kept walking, and Ramsey joined her seconds later.

In the kitchen, he found Keilah attending to their dinner. He opened the refrigerator and put the other bottle of wine and a can of whipped cream inside the refrigerator.

Keilah laughed and asked, "What did you put in there?"

He closed the refrigerator and smiled. "You'll find out in due time."

She giggled because she'd seen exactly what he'd placed inside her refrigerator. Ramsey walked over to the oven and opened it up. "Mmm, this smells good. What is it?"

Keilah turned to him, playfully smacked his hand, and closed the oven door. "Chicken, now take this dish and put it on the table, nosey."

"Can't I at least get a hug first?" he asked.

Keilah sat the glass dish down on the counter and wrapped her arms around his neck. Ramsey hugged her tightly, lifting her off the floor. "I feel better now."

"You're so silly," Keilah said as he placed her back on her feet.

She handed the vegetable dish to him and followed close behind with the chicken and rice. She sat the items on the table and then joined him. Ramsey opened the wine and filled their glasses.

"You can go ahead and sit down, Ramsey. I'm good."

"A gentleman never sits before a lady," he replied.

Keilah giggled. "I forgot you were so well bred."

He smiled and held out her chair for her. He watched Keilah as she placed her napkin in her lap. She was stunning. Tonight should be easy for him, but he was beginning to wonder if they would get through dinner, the way her jeans were hugging her apple-bottom hips. The short top she had on revealed her fit abs and the diamond stud in her navel.

She looked over at him and smiled. "Do you want to say grace?"

"Sure. Take my hand," he said in a soothing voice.

Ramsey proceeded to bless their food before digging into the appetizing meal.

"Keilah, you've outdone yourself. This is delicious."

She blushed. "This is nothing. I threw this together with hardly any effort."

He took a sip of wine. "Well, you did good."

The pair chatted about work, family, and issues in the news as they finished dinner and cleaned up the kitchen. Ramsey opened up the second bottle of wine and Keilah pulled an apple crumb cake out of the oven.

Ramsey smiled. "I don't know if I have room for dessert."

"Just try a little piece, Ramsey." She took her fork and held a small piece of cake up to his mouth.

He tasted it and said, "This is good, but I can't eat a whole piece."

"No problem. We can share."

He handed her a glass of wine. "I can do that."

They made their way into the family room and sat down on the sofa. Ramsey picked up the remote and turned on the TV. "Do you mind?"

Keilah curled up next to him on the sofa. "No, go ahead."

"Thanks. I just want to see the last quarter of the game."

She drank some more of her wine. "You know I don't mind."

Ramsey sat there transfixed by the TV screen for nearly twenty minutes. Neither one of them ate the rest of the cake. He finally looked over at Keilah, who hadn't moved or spoken since he started watching the game. He reached over and patted her softly on the thigh. "Are you asleep?"

She squirmed slightly. "No, just resting my eyes."

Ramsey turned off the TV and stood. He held his hand out to her. "Come on so I can put you to bed."

She looked up at him and smiled. He pulled her up into his arms and held her there for a second. Keilah pressed his face against his warm neck and let out a soft moan. He kissed her on the forehead and led her upstairs. Once in Keilah's bedroom, Ramsey cupped her face and kissed her tenderly on the lips. "You know you're crazy, right?"

She started unbuttoning his shirt, and within seconds, she had it off his shoulders. "Yeah, I know, but if I wasn't a little crazy we wouldn't be working together, would we?"

Ramsey's heart started beating wildly in his chest once again, and he felt like his body was on fire. Just having her hands caressing his flesh was driving him out of his mind. Once they got skin to skin, he had no idea what he would do. Keilah kissed him on his chest and his rock-hard abs. Ramsey flinched and sucked in a breath the moment her soft lips came in contact with his body. Keilah looked up into his eyes. "Are you okay?"

"I don't know," he replied. "You're sort of doing a number on me."

She smiled and took a step back. "If this is going to be too much for you, Ramsey, you're free to leave."

A huge lump formed in his throat. He'd never punked out of sex with a beautiful woman, but Keilah was no ordinary woman.

"I'm not leaving," he replied.

"Are you sure? Because you seem a little tense."

"Can you blame me?"

She wrapped her arms around his waist once again. "Ramsey, I've never felt as comfortable and relaxed with any man as I feel with you."

That was the last confirmation he needed. The next few minutes were a blur. He kissed her greedily, backing her over to the bed where they tumbled onto the comforter. Ramsey quickly removed her clothing, leaving her lying before him in next to nothing.

She giggled. "I guess this means you've gotten rid of the butterflies in your stomach?"

He leaned down and kissed her firmly on the lips. "Yeah, baby. I'm fine."

She smiled, cupped his face and kissed him slowly, slipping her tongue inside his mouth. "Ramsey, whatever you do, don't hold back."

"Don't worry, I won't," he proclaimed as she covered her full breasts with his hand.

He could feel the hardening of his lower region pressing against his jeans as he ran his tongue lightly over her brown peaks. Keilah closed her eyes and breathlessly whispered, "Oh, Ramsey."

The sensuality of her voice excited him. He anxiously unzipped his jeans as Keilah pulled back the comforter. She studied him closely as he lowered his jeans and boxers. What she saw was nothing short of magnificent.

"Now I see why you have so many women," she said as he climbed back into bed next to her. He laughed. Keilah couldn't resist touching him, causing him to gasp. "You brought condoms, didn't you?"

He gritted his teeth. "They're in my pocket."

She rolled over, opened the nightstand, pulled out a handful of condoms and tossed them on the bed. "Don't worry about it. I got you covered."

He picked one up. "You sure are prepared."

She tossed her hair over her shoulder and took the small package out of his hand. "Do you want me to do it?"

"No, no, no. If you touch me one more time, all of this is going to be in vain."

She laughed and wrapped her arms around his neck and kissed him again. "Thank you, Ramsey."

He winked at her before flipping her on her back. Her giggles filled the room as he kissed her beginning at her neck and ending at the diamond stud in her navel. He removed her lacy thong and immediately cupped her hips, burying his face between her thighs. Her giggles were instantly reduced to heavy breathing and soft moans. It didn't take long for Ramsey to make Keilah's eyes roll back in her head. She didn't know what Ramsey was doing to her, but whatever it was, it had her whole body trembling uncontrollably. "Ramsey . . . Ramsey . . ." she whispered over and over again.

He stopped long enough to apply the condom before positioning himself between her long brown legs. As he stared down at her, he couldn't help but sample her stiff nipples once again. Keilah arched into him as he devoured each one of them, sending shivers all over her body. His kisses were heated and passionate as he pushed his stiff manhood into her moist body. Keilah let a loud moan as he placed her legs over his shoulders, allowing him deeper access to her moist chasm. They moved rhythmically against each other and to the beat of their hearts. Ramsey felt his body sizzle as he thrust harder and deeper. Submerged in ecstasy, Keilah deliriously pleaded for mercy and begged Ramsey for more all in the same breath. Her confusion sent electricity through his body until he felt his own body shuddering with exhilaration. He felt his soul spiraling out of control and knew his sensual demise was close. However, he wanted to prolong their gratification as long as he could. Ramsey continued to kiss Keilah feverishly until his name tore from her lips as she climaxed hard against his large frame. His release caused his body to stiffen before he let out a groan of contentment. With sweat dripping from their bodies, Keilah and Ramsey continued to kiss and snuggle until the rhythm of their breathing was back to normal. He rolled over onto his back and pulled her on top of his chest. She kissed and licked the tattoos on his biceps and said, "Now that wasn't so bad, was it?"

He palmed her hips and pulled her as close to him as he could. Making love to Keilah was heavenly. So to try and stay cool, he simply replied, "It was perfect, Keilah."

CHAPTER THREE

Three months had passed, and things were going great between Keilah and Ramsey, as was their business. On this day, she twirled in her chair and stared out the window of her office. As Keilah sat in her office, her thoughts were interrupted by the buzz of her telephone. She reached over and answered it. "Stone Chance Protection Agency. K.C. speaking. How may I help you?"

"K.C.? When did you start calling yourself K.C.?" the deep, male voiced asked.

Keilah smiled hearing her brother, Genesis's voice. There was a ten-year difference between Keilah's age and her brother's. At thirty-seven years old, he was the gentle and compassionate one. He was also the one who fell in love the easiest and usually the hardest. Most of the women he came in contact with considered him a heartthrob because of his gentle and loving nature. Being very tall and handsome didn't hurt either. When Keilah was a little girl, a lot of the women would try to befriend her in an attempt to get closer to him; however, Genesis always saw through them. He had dark, wavy hair and smooth, cinnamon skin. He had a pair of dimples that showed up even when he wasn't smiling.

"I just started trying K.C. out for business purposes. What's up, bro?"

"Nothing much. I'm at the office, so I thought I would check in with you and see how you're doing. Luke told me he talked to you not too long ago."

"Yeah, we talked, but first he got onto me for taking two days to return his telephone call, then we had a nice conversation. I'm doing great though. How's everyone there?" she asked.

"We're all good, just busy. Other than that, we're cool."

Keilah turned back around to her window and said, "That's good to hear. I'm also glad business is doing well, too. Has anybody hit a big jackpot lately?"

"Since you mention it, a sixty-two-year-old lady hit for three hundred thousand two weeks ago."

"That's nice."

"Yeah, she just retired too. So, when are you coming home for a visit?" he asked.

"I don't know. Things are pretty busy right now, so I probably won't be able to see you guys until sometime after the holidays."

"Do you realize how far off that is, Keilah?" Genesis pointed out.

"Yes, I'm aware of it, and I'm sorry, Genesis, but it can't be helped."

"What happened to your 'family first' motto?"

Keilah's blood pressure instantly shot up. "Stop trying to put a guilt trip on me. You know I wish I could see you guys more often, but I can't, so you're going to have to deal with it."

Genesis chuckled and said, "That's cold, Keilah."

"No, it's not. It would be nice if you guys would fly here to see me sometime instead of always expecting me to come out there."

Genesis knew he had struck a nerve with Keilah. She was known to have a quick temper and saying she was angry was an understatement.

"Keilah, I didn't call to fight with you. I was just calling to see how you were doing and to see if you needed anything. We miss you."

Keilah took a breath to calm her nerves. "I miss you guys too, Genesis, but you have to understand I have a business to run just like you guys and I'm needed here."

"I know. Seriously, though, we have some family business we need to take care of on the twelfth of September, and all of us have to be here and accounted for in order for it to be settled."

"Does it have anything to do with the opening of the second casino?"

"Yes, but there's some other stuff we have to take care of as well."

"I'm sorry, Genesis, I can't. That's not going to work into our schedule here, so you guys are going to have to postpone it for a while," she explained.

"It can't be postponed, Keilah. You have to come, and that's all it is to it."

"I can't, so if there's some paperwork that I need to sign you, guys need to FedEx it to me so I can sign it and get it back to you. That's the only option I can offer you right now."

Genesis looked at his watch and said, "Look, I have to run. I'll give Luke your message. Be safe and I'll call you this weekend. I love you. Tell Ramsey I said hello."

"I'll tell him, and I love you too. Tell everyone I said hello."

"Good-bye, Keilah."

"Good-bye, Genesis."

After hanging up with Genesis, Keilah thought about what it was like growing up in the Los Angeles suburb of Dennison, California. She also remembered just how much pain and suffering her family had endured over the years. It all began a little over seventeen years earlier, but to Keilah it seemed like it was only yesterday.

Seventeen Years Earlier . . .

Ten-year-old Keilah had lost count of how many times her brothers had had to pull her down on the floor to prevent her from being hit by flying bullets. This night was no different in Dennison, California, a small but booming suburb outside of Los Angeles. Broken glass fell on her small body. She screamed as her twenty-seven-year-old brother, Roman, grabbed her and threw her down the laundry chute, which led deep into the basement. Keilah screamed all the way down until she fell into the large laundry cart at the bottom of the chute. She quickly climbed out and hid inside the special room her brothers had made for her under the stairs. She used to think it was a game, but as she grew older, she began to understand that this was just a hazard of the environment, as always.

She kept a portable CD player in the small opening so when the bullets started flying, she could drown out some of the noise with her favorite CD. Unfortunately, things got even more intense when the neighbors started shooting back at the perpetrators. That's when she started praying extra hard. She prayed for the madness to stop, for her brothers, and lastly, she prayed to finally get away from it all. Keilah knew she wasn't allowed to come out of the special room until one of the brothers came to get her, and if things ever went bad and no one came for her, they had a Plan B so she would know exactly what to do. Keilah prayed that she wouldn't have to sneak out of the basement and run down the block to Mrs. Mattie's house so she could call the police and their aunt in Virginia. Mrs. Mattie was a retired school teacher who had befriended the family after their mother passed away. She took a special liking to Keilah, which made her the obvious choice.

It was only minutes, but it seemed like hours before Roman came and pulled her from the small space under the stairs. Keilah hugged him tightly as a trail of tears ran down her face.

"Is it over, Roman?"

He inspected her small body to make sure she was not injured before picking her up in his arms.

"Yes, it's over. Are you hurt?" he asked.

"No, just scared. Why does this keep happening?"

Roman pinched her cheek lovingly. "It's just some stupid people who don't have anything better to do than shoot up other people's houses."

She looked at him with her tear-streaked face. "But why?"

Roman quietly sat Keilah down on the stairs next to him.

He sighed and said, "Baby, there are some people in this world who would rather take what they want instead of working for it, and then there are others who try to intimidate people to make them afraid."

"What does 'intimidate' mean?"

Roman smiled and said, "It's like being a bully."

"Oh," Keilah replied.

Roman was the most serious out of all of the brothers. He rarely smiled, but he had a soft side that he revealed on certain occasions. Keilah was very good at putting a smile on her brother's face, and she was thankful he shared her love for reading. They would go to the bookstore and library and spend hours reading mysteries and adventure novels. They inherited that trait from their mother, who never went to bed without reading a few pages from some type of book.

Roman stood nearly six feet three inches, and appeared to be all legs. He wore a short Afro and had a neatly trimmed goatee to match. His dark brown skin tone matched his dark brown eyes and he always smelled wonderful. One of his habits was to never leave the house without making sure he was neatly groomed and had applied one of the expensive colognes he owned.

Genesis opened the door to the basement and saw the two standing on the stairs.

"Keilah, are you okay?"

Smiling up at him, she answered, "I'm fine, but I'm hungry."

"Come on up so I can fix you something to eat."

"OK," Keilah replied.

After Genesis closed the door, Roman looked down at her. "Things are a little hot around here right now, Keilah. Somebody's shooting or robbing somebody almost every night. It might be a good idea if you go stay with Aunt Rosa in Virginia for a while."

"No, Roman. I don't want to leave. Momma wanted me to stay with you guys."

Roman ran his hand over his head in frustration. "I know what Momma said, but she's not here anymore, so it's our decision, and I say it's not safe for you to be here. You remember what happened to that four-year-old boy who lived down the street, don't you?"

"Yes. He got shot and died," Keilah said solemnly.

Roman leaned down closer to her. "I will not let that happen to you, and if I can prevent it, I will. Going to live with Aunt Rosa is the only option until we can get another house and move away from here."

"I'll be careful, Roman, I promise," she pleaded. "Please don't send me to live with Aunt Rosa. She lives too far away."

He stood there staring at his sister. Yes, their Aunt Rosa

lived across the country, but it was the only thing for them to do to keep her safe.

"Let's get you upstairs because it's past your bedtime. I'll talk to our brothers and see what they think about it, but I believe they're going to agree with me, Keilah."

They climbed the stairs and joined the rest of the family in the kitchen. After Keilah received hugs all around from her brothers, Genesis handed her a grilled cheese sandwich and a glass of milk. While she ate her sandwich, Malachi and Luke swept up broken glass and inspected damage to their house. Malachi looked over at Keilah and whispered to Luke.

"Man, that was close this time. We can't stay here. We could've been killed."

Luke scooped up the glass and dumped it inside the garbage can. "Yeah, and if Keilah had gotten so much as a scratch I would be out looking for their asses right now."

Malachi stopped sweeping for a minute. "Things have gotten out of control. We need to look for another house."

Luke thought for a second. "I guess you're right, especially since we can't watch Keilah twenty-four seven."

They looked over at Keilah as she enjoyed her grilled cheese sandwich. Roman joined them and Genesis followed close behind, keeping within sight of their sister. Roman folded his arms and looked his brothers in the eyes.

"This thing is getting out of hand. This is about the fourth time in two weeks that somebody decided to be ignorant and start shooting around here. I think we need to send Keilah to live with Aunt Rosa for a while.

Malachi replied, "I'm all for it."

Younger brother Malachi had the quickest temper of the brothers. At twenty-five years old, he was also the only one who wasn't in a relationship with anyone special. He wasn't able to stay with a woman too long because he suffered with trust issues. He was very jealous of the women he dated, which usually ran them off after a few weeks. He was handsome and was the sibling who looked most like their father. With his light complexion and gray eyes, he favored Motown singer Smokey Robinson, which made him draw a lot of attention from the ladies. Brothers Roman and Genesis did their best to help Malachi overcome his insecurities with women, but they had been unsuccessful.

Genesis, on the other hand, was in a serious relationship with a college senior at a nearby college. His brothers hoped things would work out with the relationship, but tried to prepare him for the worst case scenario.

Genesis looked his brother square in the eyes as they continued to talk about Keilah's well-being.

"I disagree. I don't think Keilah should be shipped off across the country. She's our responsibility and that should be the last resort."

"You're crazy, Genesis," Malachi yelled.

Luke looked over at Keilah, who was watching her brothers have their little meeting. She figured they were discussing her and prayed they would let her stay with them.

Genesis shook his head. "I'm not crazy, and I seem to be the only one thinking sensibly. Do you have any idea what it will do to her if she's that far from us?"

Luke raised his hands to calm the brothers. "Calm down you two. We're all under a lot of stress, but fighting amongst each other is not going to help anything."

Luke was the negotiator and peacemaker among the family. He should've made a career in the legal system, because he was just that good. Luke was serious about staying fit and worked out constantly, which gave him a set of six-pack abs that appeared to have been sculpted into his body. All of the Chance brothers were tall and stood only within an inch of each other, but Luke was the tallest at six feet five inches.

"Listen, we all agree that Keilah needs to be somewhere

safe. Hell, we all do, because I'm not trying to catch a bullet in the head for nobody. We just need to calm down and think this thing through. We're all Keilah has left since Momma and Daddy died, and we need to understand how sending her to Aunt Rosa will affect her emotionally."

Malachi sighed and leaned against the wall. "I guess you're right."

Luke turned to his brothers and softly spoke. "Well, it's past time for us to start looking for a house somewhere else anyway. We've outgrown this place and need to move somewhere safer where Keilah can play like a normal kid. Roman, are you going down to the library tomorrow?"

"Yeah, I have some books to return."

"On your way, stop by that real estate office on Second Street. They usually have new listings in the window. See if they have anything in the Barclay community. Check it out. Momma always dreamed of living over there. We should have enough money in our reserves to buy a house. Genesis, see what you can come up with. If all goes as planned, hopefully we can move out of here by the end of the month, if not sooner."

Malachi asked, "But what about the casino? We're supposed to be saving our money for that."

Luke replied, "That will have to hold for a minute until we get settled. It shouldn't take long."

Genesis looked over at Keilah and then whispered, "I'll do whatever it takes to get out this neighborhood."

"Then it's agreed," Luke announced. "Keilah will stay with us. We just have to work longer and harder to make things happen."

The four brothers mumbled, "Agreed."

Genesis walked over to Keilah and ran his hand over her hair lovingly.

"Looks like you're staying put, kiddo."

She smiled and said, "Thanks, Genesis."

A few weeks later, the family moved from their childhood home and into a much nicer and safer neighborhood. The move was going to be bittersweet for all of them. Their house was still adorned the décor their mother had chosen before she passed away of breast cancer. Changing it had never crossed any of their minds, and keeping it made them feel like a piece of her was still there. Now that they had decided to move, change was inevitable and wasn't going to be easy. Their father had been murdered not far from their home. They police never found out who killed him, and the case was now in their cold case files.

CHAPTER FOUR

Present Day

Those were some of the unpleasant memories Keilah had of her childhood as she sat at her desk. It wasn't until her telephone rang again that she snapped out of her trance.

"Keilah Chance speaking. How may I help you?" she answered.

"Hey, Keilah Chance. What's going on?" the male voice asked.

"Hey, Keytone, I haven't heard from you in a while. Where have you been hiding?" Keilah asked.

"I've been staying busy as usual. How's life treating you?"

She rubbed her tired eyes and said, "Hectic, of course. Have you seen my brothers lately?"

Keytone laughed. "Oh yeah, I see them all the time. They still hate me, but it's cool. We go way back and they can't seem to let the past stay in the past."

"What happened between you and my brothers, Keytone?" Keilah asked.

He laughed and said, "I really don't know. Why don't you ask your brothers?"

"I have, but they won't tell me."

Keilah remembered her brothers telling her that back in the day, after their father abandoned them, they made a lot of money working for Keytone. When their father returned, the money was too good for them to give up right away. The money they made allowed them the opportunity to help their mother, who was trying to make ends meet. Keytone was considered the neighborhood hoodlum, and all Keilah's brothers would ever tell her about him growing up was that he was bad news and to never associate with him. Unfortunately, she was grown now and she knew something about Keytone they didn't.

"Maybe one day you can hypnotize them and find out why they hate me so much, because honestly, I don't have a clue," Keytone revealed.

Keilah giggled and leaned back in her chair. "Now that's funny. Hypnotize my brothers? That will be the day. I do know that would freak out if they knew I was talking to you and letting you come visit me."

"You got that right," Keytone responded. "Keilah, I'm so glad you're in my life. I've had so many bad things around me for so long, it's nice to have someone good in it."

She blushed and tapped on her desk with her ink pen. She looked at her watch and sat up in her chair and said, "That's so sweet of you to say, Keytone. Oh! Look at the time. I have to go. I'll call you this weekend."

"All right, Keilah, be safe and take care of yourself and I hope to get out there to see you soon."

She stood up and said, "Sounds good. Good-bye, Keytone."

Keilah hung up the telephone just as Ramsey stepped inside her office. "Good afternoon, Miss Chance. I stopped by to see if you would be free for lunch."

Seeing Ramsey put an instant smile on her face, welcome after reminiscing about her eventful childhood.

"Well, let me check my appointment book and see," she joked. "How's your day going so far?"

His baritone voice chuckled. "OK, but my eyes started getting crossed from going over all these reports."

"Do you want me to do it for you?" she offered as she pulled her purse out of her desk.

He waved her off and said, "Nah, I just need a break to rest my eyes."

Keilah walked over to him and straightened his tie. "I bet you do. And you'll be happy to know that I'm free for lunch, Mr. Stone."

He smiled and replied, "Good. I hope you're hungry."

"So, where are you taking me?" she asked seductively as he put his hand on the small of her back.

"You'll see," he answered mysteriously.

Keilah turned to Ramsey as they walked down the hallway, and whispered, "Guess who I just got off the phone with?"

"Who?" he asked curiously.

"Keytone," Keilah revealed. "I haven't heard from him in a few days. He said he'd been busy but hopes to fly out here to see me as soon as he can."

Ramsey picked a piece of lint off her collar and laughed. "I bet he has been busy . . . breaking kneecaps. Man, I would love to be there when you tell your brothers about Keytone."

Keilah stepped inside the elevator ahead of Ramsey. She put her hand over her heart and said, "Ramsey, I know I'm going to have to eventually tell them about Keytone. I mean they deserve to know, but I'm afraid of how they're going to react. They have a history."

Ramsey buttoned his jacket and gave Keilah's hand a squeeze. "Don't stress over it, Keilah. When the moment's right to tell them, you'll know it."

The elevator doors opened. The couple stepped out into

the lobby, and Keilah softly said, "I hope you're right. Stone."

Lunch with Ramsey was quiet except for the occasional small talk about things going on in the news and at work. They hadn't seen much of each other over the past week because of their work schedules. Their little arrangement was still working out between them, but Ramsey had run into a slight problem with Andria. She couldn't understand why he didn't have time for her anymore, but the truth was that he was trying to reduce the number of women he was dealing with anyway, including her. He actually looked forward to spending his evenings with Keilah and wasn't missing the other players in the game at all. One reason was that Keilah wasn't full of drama and didn't nag him for attention like the others did. They got together after work when they could. Both of them had to spend long hours at the office because of new clients and new hires. Since their business was going through this transition, more of their time was needed at work to smooth things out

"Keilah, did you hear what I said?" Ramsey asked with a frown

Snapping out of her daydream she answered, "I'm sorry. What did you say?"

"I said it's going to be nice managing the company more than being in the field once things settle down. I mean, I still want to do some of the jobs on occasion, but I like training the new guys," he admitted.

"Well, you're good at everything, so whatever makes you happy makes me happy," she said before taking a bite of her salad. "Listen, Ramsey, Genesis called and said they needed me to come out there to take care of some family business."

"What's going on?" he asked.

She shrugged her shoulders. "I don't know the details, but I think it has something to do with the opening of the second casino. Is this going to be a problem? If it is, I can tell them this is not a good time and they'll just have to postpone everything until I can fly out there."

He sighed. "It's going to be a big problem. I won't get to see you for a couple of days, but I guess I'll live."

She smiled. "That's so sweet. Thanks, Ramsey. I don't like leaving when we're so busy, but I shouldn't be gone but a couple of days. I'm just glad it's after I go to that dinner with Arhmelia's mother. I would hate to send a replacement after confirming with her."

"You're right. You've made quite an impression on the Randolph family, and we've gained five major new clients because of them. There's no way you can cancel that detail," he pointed out.

Keilah pushed her salad to the side. "They're good people, and I've become very fond of Arhmelia. She's calmed down a lot since the shooting. I noticed she was trying to get a little rebellious with her parents at one time, but not anymore."

He took a sip of tea. "It's sad it takes something like a near-death experience to wake up some of these teens. But back to you; I think I can handle things while you go out to Cali to see your brothers. Family first. Remember?"

"I remember," she replied.

"With that settled, can I ask you something?"

"Sure," she answered.

"What would you do if I kissed you right now?"

This stunned Keilah. Ramsey was the one who wanted to keep their secret relationship on the down-low. Now for him to want to kiss her in public was out of the ordinary.

"What did you ask me?"

He leaned forward and licked his lips. This sent shivers over Keilah's body, because she'd come quite familiar with his luscious lips.

"You heard me. What would you do if I kissed you?"

Keilah picked up her napkin and wiped her mouth. "Here?"

"Yes, here," he softly replied. We've been working apart so much lately, I miss you."

"I thought you wanted to keep our little arrangement just between us?"

"I do, but right now, it would make my day if I could get a kiss."

Keilah smiled and folded her arms. "Have I spoiled you, Ramsey Stone?"

He winked at her and said, "Of course you have. We've been going at it for about three months now. I've gotten used to you, Keilah, and now that we haven't seen each other for over a week, I guess you can say I've gotten a little delirious."

Keilah looked around the room. "What if someone sees us?"

"We're partners. Remember?" he reminded her. "I have a right to show you some affection."

"So you're talking about a little peck on the lips. Right?" she asked.

He leaned forward and smiled. "No, I'm talking about a slow, wet, hot kiss."

Keilah closed her eyes briefly before responding. "You're not serious. You have too many women circulating, and I don't think you'd risk having one of them make a scene if they saw us. Besides, you were the one so adamant about keeping everything secret."

He put his hand up in defense. "I know what I said, Keilah. So are you going to kiss me or not?"

Keilah studied Ramsey and then asked, "Right here? Right now?"

He smiled. "Right here. Right now. And if you don't hurry up, I'm the one who's going to make a scene."

She blushed and lowered her head without responding.

"Don't make me get up, Keilah Chance," he teased as he scooted back in his chair.

Her flesh became hot at the thought of him pulling her out of her chair and kissing her in front of everyone.

"OK . . . OK . . . just wait a second."

He laughed. "Wait a second for what? You have three seconds to kiss me, or I'm out of my chair."

In that instant, Keilah leaned across the table and kissed him. His kisses made her stomach quiver with excitement, and for a moment she forgot where she was until she heard the people at the next table applauding them.

Ramsey pulled back slightly and whispered, "You taste so good." Keilah blushed again before he kissed her once more. "I guess we'd better stop before they start hosing us down."

Keilah giggled. "I guess you're right, but that was very nice."

"I'm glad you enjoyed it."

The waiter walked over to their table to see if either of them wanted to order dessert. Keilah waved him off while Ramsey ordered a slice of caramel pie. As soon as the waiter returned with the pie, Keilah slid her foot up Ramsey's thigh. His kiss had ignited something, and now she was the one simmering inside. It had reminded her just how much she'd missed feeling his skin against hers over the past week.

He froze and stared at her. "You'd better stop, Keilah, before you make me ravish you on top of this table. You're playing with fire," he warned her.

Keilah giggled. "You're the one who started the launch sequence with that kiss. Besides, I know you don't want to risk wrinkling that thousand-dollar suit of yours, Stone."

Ramsey sat his fork down, and then looked at his watch before looking at Keilah. "Don't underestimate me, Miss Chance."

She leaned forward and whispered, "Are you challenging me, Stone?"

Ramsey cleared his throat and laughed. "What time do you have to be back to the office?"

She pulled the cherry out of her drink and placed it seductively on her tongue. "Whenever I feel like it."

That was all Ramsey needed to hear. "Let's go."

"Go where?" she asked curiously.

Without responding to her, Ramsey motioned for the waiter to bring the check so they could leave. He hurriedly paid it and told the waiter to cancel his dessert order. He grabbed Keilah's hand and nearly dragged her out of the restaurant and into the Remington Hotel across the street. It would be two hours before they would exit. The week apart had taken a toll on both of them, and neither could go another hour without quenching their desires for each other.

Exhausted, but satisfied, the pair made their way back to their office to hopefully get some work done. Unfortunately, work was the last thing Ramsey could concentrate on once he returned to his office. He could still feel Keilah's lips and hands on his body, and it gave his skin a tingling sensation.

"Ramsey, can I get your signature on this form?"

He was so deep in his thoughts he didn't hear or see Keilah come in. She closed the door and walked over to his desk and handed him the form. He looked up at her and smiled as he picked up the form and read over it. Keilah walked around behind his desk and look out the window. "Ramsey Stone, I think you have a better view than I do."

He twirled around in his chair and scanned her body up and down. Ramsey's eyes took note of her fabulous legs and firm, curvy backside. "I disagree with you."

She turned around and found him undressing her with his eyes. She pointed her finger at him and said, "Behave, Stone. After what we just did, you should be content."

He set the form down, leaned forward, and caressed her thigh as he slowly eased his hands under her skirt. Keilah giggled and pushed his hands away. "What is going on with you, Ramsey? You act like you want us to get caught."

He stood up and walked over to his door and locked it. He walked toward her and whispered, "Maybe I do."

Seconds later he had her in his arms. His kisses seared her lips. Keilah breathlessly panted, "Ramsey," as his large hand disappeared under her skirt and slipped down inside her lace undergarments. He looked into her eyes and noticed their glazed appearance. He smiled, and just as he started to unbutton her blouse, Sherrie buzzed through on his telephone.

"Ramsey, I have Miss Rockwell here to see you."

"Damn!" he cursed before reaching over to pick up the telephone. "I'm in a meeting with Keilah right now, Sherrie. Take her into the break room. I'll be out in a minute."

"Will do," Sherrie replied.

When Ramsey turned back around, Keilah was buttoning her blouse and straightening her skirt. He sighed and said, "I'm sorry, Keilah."

"You have no reason to apologize to me, Ramsey. Just bring that form back to my office once you look it over and sign it."

As she walked past him, he took her hand into his and said, "I'll catch up with you later. OK?"

"No rush," she replied casually, as if nothing just happened between them. She unlocked the door and exited his office. Ramsey let out a loud breath and gathered himself before heading out to break room to see what drama brought Andria into his office unannounced.

Keilah walked past the break room on her way back to her office. Andria spotted her and called out to her. "Keilah, how are you?"

Keilah rolled her eyes before turning around to face Andria. "I'm fine, Andria. How are you?"

Andria put her hands on her hips and whispered, "I would be doing better if Ramsey wasn't working so much, if you know what I mean."

Keilah folded her arms and said, "I'm sure you can find something to keep you occupied until he has more time for you. We *are* trying to run a business."

"I know you are, but I'm sure you've heard the old saying that all work and no play makes Ramsey a dull boy."

"I've heard something like that," Keilah responded. "Look, it was nice seeing you again, Andria, but I have work to do. I'm sure Ramsey will be here shortly. Have a nice rest of the day."

"Don't worry. If I have anything to do with it, I will," she replied mischievously.

About that time, Ramsey approached the two women in the hallway. Keilah turned on her heels and said, "Good-bye, Andria."

Ramsey watched Keilah as she disappeared into her office. Andria turned up her nose and said, "No wonder she don't have a man. She's cold as hell."

Ramsey thought to himself . . . *if you only knew*. In fact, Keilah was about as hot as they came. He frowned. "You need to mind your business, Andria. You don't know anything about Keilah."

She hugged his neck and said, "Don't get upset with me, baby. I call it as I see it. If she had a man, she wouldn't be so uptight all the time."

Ramsey removed her arms from around his neck, hustled her into the break room, and closed the door. "Maybe she's only like that with you. What are you doing here anyway, Andria?"

She rubbed her arm and said, "I didn't come here to get manhandled, for sure."

"Look, I'm sorry. You interrupted a meeting I was in, and I thought I asked you not to just drop by my office without calling first."

"What are you trying to hide, Ramsey? Are you seeing someone else?"

"I'm at work, Andria. What about that can't you understand? Damn!"

She grabbed her purse and said, "You're hiding something. You never have time for me anymore, and I want to know what's going on."

Ramsey walked over to the counter and poured himself a cup of coffee. He turned to her and said, "The world doesn't revolve around you, Andria, and just for the record, I belong to no woman. If you can't handle that, or respect my job or my schedule, I'm sorry. Maybe you should just move on."

She swung her purse on her shoulder and said, "Maybe I should."

Ramsey took a sip of coffee and casually replied, "That's on you."

She angrily walked out of the room without responding. Ramsey finished off his coffee and headed back to his office to finish his day's work.

Later that night, Keilah was awakened by a strange noise radiating from downstairs. She sat up in bed and listened as she heard even more unidentifiable noises. She climbed out of bed, dressed only in boy shorts and a cami, and grabbed her cell phone off the nightstand. Easing over to her walk-in closet, she slid into a pair of sweatpants and tucked her cell phone inside her pocket before picking up her shotgun. Trying not to make any sound, she slowly cocked the gun before making her way out into her hallway. Once again, she heard a noise that sounded like breaking glass. It was obvious to Keilah that someone was in her house, but what troubled her was how they got past her alarm system. Once in the hallway, she made her way to the spare bedroom next door to hers and quietly stepped inside. She wasn't about to go downstairs and walk into the middle of an ambush. Instead, she decided to let whoever it was come to her.

As she stood just inside the door of the bedroom with door barely cracked, she noticed two dark figures slowly climbing the stairs. When they reached the landing, she could see there was something in their hands. She could also hear them whispering to each other as they entered her room. Keilah carefully maneuvered back down the hallway to her bedroom. When she stepped inside the door, she aimed the shotgun at the two figures, who were going through her nightstand and dresser. She turned on the light and found two men wearing ski masks standing in her bedroom.

"Don't you move an inch," she instructed them.

One of the men turned to Keilah, raised his handgun and fired at her. Keilah ducked with the bullet barely missing her head, and then she returned. The force of the shot knocked the main assailant against the wall, leaving him sprawled on the floor, lifeless. The second man raised his gun as well and attempted to shoot at Keilah; however, she shot first. The man lay on the floor, screaming, "You bitch!"

With her shotgun still aimed at him, she walked closer and kicked the gun away from his hand. "This bitch just shot your ass too, huh?" she said.

The man continued to curse Keilah as he writhed in agony. With her shotgun still aimed at them, she pulled out her cell phone and called the police.

Officer Jackson was dispatched as soon as the call came in. He turned on his siren and became extremely nervous when he realized whose address he was responding to. Approximately five minutes later, he entered the foyer and found Keilah being interviewed by detectives. When Keilah saw him, she stood and gave him a hug. "Hey, Jackson."

"What happened, Keilah?" Jackson asked.

"Some guys broke into my house and I shot them."

The detective interviewing Keilah asked, "You two know each other?"

Jackson replied, "Keilah and I have been friends for a couple of years. So who were the perps?"

The detective looked at his notepad and said, "Malik Rivers has been transported to the hospital with non life threatening injuries, but Darrius O'Neal was DOA."

Keilah lowered her head in disbelief. Jackson looked at her and said, "I can't believe that kid came after you."

"I can," Keilah replied. "Jackson, can you call Ramsey for me?"

"Sure," he answered as he stood and walked outside to call Ramsey.

The detective asked Keilah to explain the circumstances around her first altercation with Malik. Once she finished, the detective asked Keilah if she had somewhere else to stay for the night since her house was now a crime scene. She nodded, and the detective motioned for an officer to accompany her upstairs to gather her belongings.

By the time she packed a week's worth of items and made her way back downstairs, Ramsey was waiting for her in the foyer. Jackson had already filled him in on the shooting, and when Keilah's eyes met Ramsey's, his heart skipped a beat. As traumatic as the shooting was, Keilah didn't seem to be shaken one bit. When she reached the bottom of the stairs, Ramsey took her garment bag and suitcase out of her hand and asked, "Are you OK?"

She lowered her head and said, "I took someone's life, Ramsey."

He pulled her into his arms. "I know, but from what Jackson told me it was you or them."

She nodded and then turned to Jackson. "Can you make sure my house is secured when everyone finishes the investigation?"

Jackson gave Keilah a hug and said, "I'll take care of it. I'll give you a call when you can get back in."

"Thanks, Jackson."

Ramsey shook Jackson's hand before leading Keilah out the door to his car.

Keilah ended up staying with him for a week. During that time, Ramsey arranged for Keilah's house to be cleaned before she moved back in. She was also notified that her shooting was classified as justifiable homicide and that she had acted in self-defense.

Over the course of the next few days, Quentin repeatedly tried to contact Keilah, but Ramsey intercepted the calls, reminding Quentin that they weren't allowed to talk to him about the case and that all calls would have to go through their lawyers. Quentin assured Ramsey that he was only calling to offer her his apology to her on behalf of his son and to make sure she was OK. Ramsey told Quentin that he would pass on the message to Keilah, but wouldn't be able to talk to him about the case. Quentin agreed and apologized once more before hanging up the telephone.

In the days following the incident, work went on as usual at the Stone Chance Protection Agency over the next two weeks. Keilah seemed to have shaken off the incident and continued to conduct business around the office as usual. She and Ramsey continued to train their new hires and adjusted their work schedules to accommodate even more new clients. With the overload of work, the couple found time to get together when they could, and when they did, it was just as explosive as it had been even before the shooting. Most people would have a hard time readjusting to life after such a traumatic event, but Keilah never seemed to let it affect her. In any case, the situation didn't rattle her, and life went on as usual.

Ramsey seemed to be content with life himself and being with Keilah. He hadn't heard from Andria since their altercation, and he wasn't losing any sleep over it either. She was one less irritation he had to worry about.

On this day, Keilah stuck her head in Ramsey's office before leaving for the day. "Hey, Stone. Somebody has a birthday tomorrow, huh?"

He looked up at her and frowned. "Keilah, I'm warning you now. Don't do anything crazy."

She waved him off and said, "Stop whining. It's your birthday and you can't tell me what not to do. Besides, I'm not the one you should be worried about. I'm sure Andria has something planned for you. I only stopped by to let you know I was headed out for the day."

He yawned and said, "I haven't heard from Andria and I doubt I will."

"Don't underestimate her, Ramsey. You know she's notorious for showing up when you least expect her to."

"You're right about that. Now enough about my birthday and Andria. Tonight's the big night with Teresa Randolph at the Breast Cancer Awareness dinner, huh?"

She walked farther into his office and said, "I guess. What are you going to do tonight? Big date, or are you and Bradford going to hang out?"

Bradford was a dear friend of Ramsey's who had served with him in the military as a military policeman. He was now working at the Pentagon, and like Ramsey he was still single but dating heavily.

"No, I'm going home. I'm tired from working these twelve-hour days for the past few weeks," he admitted.

"You got that right," she replied as she turned to walk out of his office. "If it wasn't for this dinner, I would be crashing with you."

Ramsey stood up and came around to the front of his desk and leaned against it. "Keilah, come in here for a second."

She walked into the office and closed the door behind her. "What's up?"

"I've been told to pass on a message to you, but I wasn't sure I wanted to."

Keilah looked at him curiously and asked, "From who?"

"Ron Davenport."

"Ron Davenport? What kind of message?" she asked as she studied Ramsey's facial expression.

"He wants to ask you out."

She walked closer to Ramsey and giggled. "Well, I hope you told him I don't date clients."

"He's not a client anymore." Ramsey replied as he stared directly into Keilah's eyes. He wanted to see if there was any indication that she was the least bit interested in Ron Davenport, who had become a good friend to him.

Keilah thought for a moment before responding. "It doesn't matter. He's been a client, and that's one of my rules. You know that, Ramsey."

He stood up and said, "I'm just the messenger, Keilah."

She nodded and said, "I know you are, but you should've told him as soon as he brought it up."

"It wasn't my decision to make. Besides, you could've changed your rules for all I know."

She smiled and said, "Well I haven't, and while we're at it, add the rule that I would never date any of your friends either."

"Why not?" he asked.

She blushed. "Because of our closeness, Ramsey. It would be too weird."

He laughed and said, "And what we've been doing isn't?"

She walked closer to him and whispered, "I'm sorry, Ramsey. I didn't mean for this thing between us to go on as long as it has. I know you went along with it because you care about me. I don't want it to affect you and your relationships anymore."

He hugged her and said, "Don't worry about me. My relationships with those women are not serious."

Guilty tears formed in Keilah's eyes. "Maybe if it wasn't for me, you would finally get serious with one of them and get married."

He laughed again. "Looks like the pot is trying to call the kettle black. I'm a grown man, Miss Chance. I'm not confused about anything I've done with you or any woman, and as far as marriage, well you can forget that."

"So you're saying you're never going to get married?" she asked.

He winked at her and said, "All I'm going to say is don't hold your breath. Listen, you know how I am with women. I like too many flavors."

She lowered her head and said, "It was still selfish of me to ask you to do it in the first place."

He kissed her forehead and said, "We're cool, Keilah. I've enjoyed being with you, so stop stressing. I'll see you tomorrow. Have fun with Teresa Randolph tonight."

"Thanks, Ramsey. Good-night, and get some rest."

"Good-night, Keilah."

CHAPTER FIVE

After a couple of hours of beauty treatment at the salon to get her hair and nails done, Keilah headed to the Randolph house to pick up Teresa Randolph for the dinner. The agency had invested in several luxury limousines so they could drive and transport their clients to ensure their safety. This also gave the agency the opportunity to scan the vehicles for any devices that could cause harm or invade the privacy of their clients.

As the limo pulled through the gates of the mansion, Keilah checked her appearance in the mirror and the firearm in the holster around her thigh one last time. The black, beaded gown she had on hugged her curves in all the right places, but still concealed the dangerous weapon she hid underneath. Her partner, who was working undercover as the driver, came around, opened the car door for Keilah, and held her hand as she stepped out. When she rang the doorbell, she was stunned to come face to face with a tall, handsome gentleman dressed in a military uniform. His broad shoulders and erect posture radiated discipline, and his dark, chocolate skin and thick mustache made Keilah's heart thump against her rib cage. The tall stranger with his pearly white teeth and beautiful smile instantly took her breath away. He held his hand out to her and said, "You must be Keilah Chance."

"I feel like I'm at a disadvantage. You know me, but I don't know who you are," she admitted as she walked through the door.

He smiled. "Come in, Miss Chance. I'm Michael Monroe, Teresa's nephew."

Arhmelia appeared at the top of the stairs and yelled, "Hey, Keilah."

"Hi, Arhmelia," Keilah greeted her.

Arhmelia slid down the banister to the foyer, which caused Michael to grimace. "Arhmelia, if your mother had seen you do that, it would've given her a heart attack."

"Oh, Michael, I do it all the time. Chill out."

"Whether you do it all the time is not the issue, Arhmelia. I just know Aunt Teresa wouldn't approve of you doing it," he explained to her.

Arhmelia rolled her eyes. "So, Keilah, I see you've met my cousin."

"Well, not officially," she replied.

"Well, let me introduce you guys," Arhmelia said as she saluted Michael playfully. "Michael, this is Keilah Chance of the Stone Chance Protection Agency. Keilah, this is Major Michael Monroe, my cousin and major pain in the—"

"Arhmelia!" Michael yelled.

Arhmelia's antics caused Keilah to giggle.

Michael sighed. "Keilah, I'm sorry my cousin is so energetic tonight."

Keilah held her hand out to Michael. "It's okay. Arhmelia and I are old friends. It's nice to meet you."

"Likewise," he said softly as he took her hand into his and kissed the back of it. Keilah tried her best not to appear shaken by the sensation of his lips on her skin but she was unsuccessful. Michael immediately noticed the effect he had on her and smiled at her as he released her hand.

Arhmelia rolled her eyes and mumbled, "That was so lame, Michael."

Michael frowned. He turned to Arhmelia and asked, "Isn't it past your bedtime?"

"No, Michael, I go to bed when I want to. Thank you very much. Hey, Keilah, guess what?" Arhmelia asked, waving Michael off.

"I have no idea. Why don't you tell me?" Keilah asked.

"I'm on the honor roll this semester, and I think Daddy's going to get me a new car."

Keilah patted Arhmelia on the back. "Congratulations. I'm so proud of you."

Michael interrupted them. "That is good news, Arhmelia."

"Thanks, Michael," she replied.

Michael turned his attention back to Keilah. "So, Keilah, you're a bodyguard?"

Keilah held her hand up and said, "Guilty as charged."

"How could someone as beautiful as you be in that line of work?"

Arhmelia turned her back to Michael so he couldn't see what she was doing. She pretended to gag her throat with her finger in response to Michael's flirtatious comment. "Give it up, Michael."

He frowned and turned to Arhmelia. "Don't you have some homework you need to be doing or something?"

Arhmelia turned to walk back up the stairs. "Not really, but I know when I'm not wanted around. Keilah, don't believe a word he says."

"Good-night, Arhmelia," Michael said with a raised tone of voice.

Keilah giggled. "She's a sweetheart."

"She's a brat," Michael replied jokingly. "Seriously though, I love her to death. She's a good girl, just a typical teenager."

"Now that I can agree with you on," Keilah said.

"I am so sorry. Arhmelia's silliness distracted me. Won't you come sit down until Aunt Teresa decides to grace us with her presence?"

Keilah looked at her watch. "Thank you, but I'm sure she'll be down in a second. I know she hates to be late to anything."

Michael leaned over and whispered, "You must know my aunt very well."

Keilah blushed. "I must say I do."

About that time, Teresa descended the stairs, dressed elegantly in a pink chiffon Vera Wang gown. "Keilah, I'm sorry I'm late. I see you've met my nephew."

"Yes ma'am, I have," Keilah answered.

"Now, we've been through this before. It's Teresa, and I won't have you addressing me any other way. Understood?" Teresa fingered her hair in the mirror. "By the way, I love that dress. You look stunning. Doesn't she, Michael?"

He stared at Keilah and said, "Without a doubt. I need to be scolded for not pointing that out when you first walked in."

"It's okay. Thank both of you, and I must say you both look very nice as well," she replied.

Teresa turned to Keilah. "That's why I love you so much. Michael, could you get the door for us please?"

Michael opened the front door for the ladies to exit. Keilah was shocked when she noticed that Michael was following them out to the car. The driver opened the door for them, and Teresa slid inside the vehicle. Keilah climbed in after her, with Michael following close behind. She turned to him. "Michael, I didn't know you were joining us."

Teresa patted Keilah on the thigh. "I'm sorry, Keilah. When I found out Michael was already going to the dinner, I invited him to ride with us. That's not a problem, is it?"

"No, it's not a problem, but I like to know anytime there's a change of plans," Keilah informed her.

Teresa looked over at Michael. "See, this is the kind of woman you should be looking for instead of those women you . . ."

"Aunt Teresa, please," he begged.

Keilah turned away to conceal her laughter.

Clearly embarrassed, he said, "Keilah, you have to excuse my aunt. She has the tendency to speak before she thinks."

"Hush up, Michael. You know I'm right. You need to settle down. I'm sure Keilah's not treating her body like the devil's playground."

Keilah lowered her head in embarrassment. Was Teresa Randolph a psychic or something? "Teresa, I'm sure Michael is nothing but a gentleman and only dates the finest women in town. So surely he'll settle down when he finds the right woman," Keilah replied.

"I hope you're right, Keilah," Teresa said as she reached over and grabbed a bottle of champagne. "Open this for me, Michael."

Michael took the bottle out of her hand and opened it. Teresa held out her glass so Michael would fill it. He turned to Keilah and asked, "Would you like some?"

She waved him off. "I'm on duty. Thanks anyway."

"I'm sorry. I forgot. It's hard to look at you and see you for anything else but a very attractive woman," he said, flirting.

Teresa looked at Michael and then over at Keilah and smiled, hoping her prayers would be answered.

The evening went off without a hitch. Michael couldn't take his eyes off of Keilah, and she felt him staring at her all night long. Even at dinner, as they enjoyed a delicious meal of chicken breasts with chipotle orange sauce, steamed vegetables, and roasted potatoes with lemon, oregano, and garlic, Michael couldn't restrain himself from staring at her. Her beauty had him awestruck and since she was a bodyguard, it excited him to the point that it affected him physically. It was a sensual turn-on for him, and he was glad they spent most of the evening sitting so he could conceal how much she aroused him.

Keilah did her best to be relaxed and cordial while discreetly protecting Teresa Randolph. However, Michael was making it difficult for her to stay focused. He was so handsome, and his personality impressed her even more.

"So, Michael, do you live in D.C.?"

He took a sip of champagne and smiled. "Yes, but because of my job I spend a lot of time in Iraq."

Keilah frowned. "That has to be scary."

He leaned over and whispered, "I doubt it's as scary as what you have to deal with."

She smiled and said, "You have a point, but it still has to be very tense over there."

"It is, but everyone is highly trained, which makes our job a little easier."

Keilah shook her head and solemnly said, "It's a shame so many of our men and women are losing their lives over there."

"It is but they know they have a job to do, and unless you're military it's hard for others to understand the mission."

"Maybe so. It's still a sad situation all around. I just wish our troops could come home."

He smiled and said, "So do a million or so other Americans."

"So I've heard," she replied.

"So, Miss Chance, what do you do for fun?" he inquired.

"I have no limits, Mr. Monroe. I'm an adventurous woman," she revealed.

He sipped his champagne once more and said, "That's good to know, because I'm an adventurous man."

She blushed. "I guess that remains to be seen, huh?"

He tilted his head and smiled. "Excuse me, Miss Chance, but are you asking me out?"

Keilah looked away and said, "Maybe."

"That is very flattering, Keilah, but you didn't give me a chance to ask you out first. I was planning to make my move before the night was over."

She turned to him and asked, "Why wait? I'm sitting right here."

Michael could already see that Keilah was going to be different from any woman he'd ever known, and his craving for her was getting stronger. He leaned close to her ear and whispered, "Miss Chance, I would be honored if you would allow me to take you out for an evening of fun or whatever."

His warm, sweet breath caressed her ear and sent shivers over her body. She turned to him and said, "I would love to go out with you, Major Monroe."

"Good, now may I please have your number so that I may call you to make the proper arrangements?"

Keilah reached inside her purse and handed him a business card. He took it and tucked it into his pocket for safe-keeping. "Thank you, Keilah. You'll be hearing from me very soon."

"I look forward to it, Major."

Needless to say, the evening ended on a high note for Keilah with the anticipation of what she hoped would be an exciting date with Major Michael Monroe.

It was after midnight when Keilah finally made it home. She slowly made her way to her bedroom and turned on the lamp on the nightstand. Almost immediately, she noticed the blinking light on her answering machine. As she played back her message, she unzipped her gown and laid it across the chair. She fell across the bed in her black lace thong and matching strapless bra and listened to her message. The only message she had was from Ramsey.

"Hey, Keilah, I hope everything went well tonight. Send me a text so I'll know you made it back home, OK? Goodnight, and I'll see you tomorrow."

Keilah picked up her cell and sent Ramsey a text message as instructed. Her conversation with him earlier opened her eyes to what she'd been doing to hold back herself and Ramsey. Meeting Michael tonight confirmed to her that it was past time for her to move on with her life and stop using Ramsey as a crutch. He would always have a special place in her heart, and she would always love him because of his unselfishness nature. His birthday was tomorrow, and she'd plan to do something wild and seductive for him. Ramsey never wanted her to make a big deal over his birthday, but since it was the end of their special time together, she wanted it to be a birthday he would never forget.

As she rolled over onto her back and closed her eyes, she immediately got a visual of Michael Monroe. The thought of him made her lower region throb, and she couldn't help but to touch her body in her most intimate spot, causing her to gasp. Michael was dignified, handsome, educated, and single, and if the way he had stared at her was any indication of how he felt about her, exciting things could be in the forecast with Major Monroe. Shaking his image out of her head, she got up, showered, and crawled under the soft sheets of her bed, succumbing to sleep within minutes.

CHAPTER SIX

The next morning was Ramsey's birthday, and Keilah left instructions for Sherrie to decorate his office with a few balloons and to put a small birthday cake on his desk. She arrived early at the office and gave Sherrie strict instructions to call as soon as Ramsey arrived.

Around ten o'clock, Ramsey waltzed into the office with his cell phone to his ear. He was talking to Ronald Davenport. As he passed Sherrie's desk, she handed him his messages. He mouthed *thank you* to her before entering his office. As soon as he stepped inside the door, he frowned when he saw the balloons, the confetti, and the cake on the desk. Since he was on a business call, he was unable to get off the phone and reprimand the culprits. He knew it was between Sherrie and Keilah or both. Continuing to talk on the phone, he sat down at his desk and turned on his computer. Once his computer screen was up, he pulled some files out of his desk and opened them. Sherrie walked into his office with a mischievous smile on her face, then set a large cup of coffee on his desk. Ramsey covered up the mouthpiece on his phone and whispered, "You're in big trouble, lady."

Without responding, Sherrie just smiled and exited his office. Seconds later, Keilah walked in and closed the door behind her. Ramsey glanced up at her and noticed she was wearing a trench coat. She walked over to his desk and flashed him.

He yelled, "Sweet Jesus! Ron, I have to call you back."

"Is something wrong?" Ron asked.

Lying, Ramsey said, "I just spilled my coffee all over my desk."

Ron laughed on the other end of the telephone and said, "No problem. I have a few calls to return anyway."

"Thank you, Ron. I'll call you back within the hour."

He hung up the telephone and said, "Damn, Keilah. What are you trying to do to me?"

Keilah stood before him in a black lace Victoria's Secret bra and panty set with matching garters and sheer black stockings. She seductively replied, "Happy Birthday, Ramsey."

He walked around the desk so he could get a closer look at her sexy ensemble. Pulling her into his arms he said, "I can't believe you came in here nearly butt naked. Did you lock the door?"

She snuggled up to him. "Yes, it's locked. I wanted to do something you would remember for your birthday, since you're such a party pooper."

"Hell, I almost fell out of my chair," he teased. "You know you can't do stuff like this to me at work. Seriously, this was cool, and those Victoria's Secret models have nothing on you because you're wearing that lingerie."

Keilah cupped his face and kissed him. "Thank you, Ramsey."

"For what?" he asked as he glanced down at her cleavage.

She kissed him again and said, "For everything. And just so you know, I have a big night planned for you, so don't eat too much today."

He caressed her thigh and said, "You don't have to do that."

"I want to, Ramsey, so let me. OK?"

Ramsey licked his lips. "You're killing me, Keilah. Besides, I thought we were through."

"Don't say it like that. Besides, today is your special day, so let's enjoy it and not think about that. Deal?"

He smiled and said, "Deal. So is this what I have to look forward to tonight?"

"I'll never tell," she teased.

"Are you saying you're going to make me wait until tonight?"

She stepped out of his arms and tied the belt on her trench coat. "A couple of months ago you wouldn't even kiss me in here, so I know you're not going to do anything else."

He stepped to her, backing her against the wall. "That was then and this is now. Don't play with me, woman. You've started something, and now I'm going to finish it. I don't care what you say."

He sprinkled Keilah's neck with gentle kisses, causing her eyes to flutter as soft moans escaped her lips. "You're making this real hard for me, Ramsey."

Ramsey trailed kisses from her neck down to her cleavage. "Join the club."

She wrapped her arms around his neck and whispered, "So what do you want to do?"

He pressed his forehead against hers and then kissed her greedily on the lips. "You should be able to tell. I know you feel it."

Keilah giggled. "Sherrie might hear us, and then what?"

"Damn. I forgot about Sherrie and her bionic ears," he said as he continued to caress Keilah's hips.

"Ramsey," she whispered. "Are you OK?"

He released her and went and sat down on his leather sofa. He leaned his head back and closed his eyes. Keilah let her coat slide off her shoulders before joining him on the sofa.

"Keilah, please, don't touch me right now. I have to calm down and get myself together."

Keilah could see the agony on Ramsey's face and in his lower region as she caressed him. She kissed him on the cheek and whispered, "I got you, partner. Happy Birthday."

Before he could respond she unbuckled his belt, unzipped his trousers and dipped her head toward his lap. In mere seconds she covered him with her soft, rose-colored lips. Ramsey felt like he was frozen in time, in shock, unable to move. Keilah had just taken their liaison to another level as he felt her warm mouth devour him. She was torturing him while she savored the sweetness of his body. Ramsey gritted his teeth and ran his hands through her soft curls as he watched her set his soul on fire. His moans of satisfaction sent her into overdrive and him spiraling out of control. He knew his body was going to betray him at any minute. "Keilah, please," he begged.

His pleas caused her to move even faster over him. "Keilah," he begged again with a slight elevation in his voice.

She looked up at him as she slowed down momentarily. The tears she saw in his eyes and the pulsating vein in his neck was her signal of triumph. She quickly retrieved a condom from her coat pocket and walked back over to Ramsey. He looked up at her and smiled. "You're not serious, are you?"

She proceeded to applied the condom without hesitation. Glancing up at him she seductively asked, "Why stop now?"

What about Sherrie?" he asked.

"I won't scream if you won't," she teased as she straddled his lap and allowed him to glide with ease into her moist flesh.

Ramsey wasn't able to guarantee his silence as he gripped her hips and assisted her as she gyrated her body against him. They never lost eye contact as they pleasured each other. The moment Ramsey felt Keilah's body stiffen, he knew she was there and so was he. She fell against his chest and grunted, "Oh, baby."

Ramsey had to use every fiber of his being to keep from screaming out her name. How he succeeded, he would never know. Keilah looked down at him and smiled. He kissed her once again, continuously sucking her tongue into his mouth.

"I can't believe you did that, Keilah."

Keilah giggled and climbed off his lap. "I wanted you to remember this birthday and to thank you properly for making me feel so good these past few months."

"Well, you're right about one thing. I'll never forget this birthday."

She hurriedly put on her trench coat while he zipped up his pants. When she got to his door she turned and said, "Have a nice day, Ramsey, and meet me at my house at seven tonight for dinner."

He slowly made his way over to his desk. "I'll be there. Now go put on some clothes."

Ramsey could hear Keilah giggling as she walked down the hallway.

Later that night, Keilah and Ramsey celebrated his birthday in a simple fashion. Keilah treated him to a first-class dinner at D'Acqua restaurant and then they went back to her house to watch the movie, *Diary of a Mad Black Woman*. Unfortunately, neither one of them were able to stay awake to see the end of the movie. Instead they fell fast asleep in each other's arms on Keilah's sofa.

What they'd done in his office earlier that morning was a birthday Ramsey would never forget. Keilah cared deeply for Ramsey, but had decided that if she wanted to take a chance with Michael Monroe, she couldn't date him and still be sleeping with Ramsey.

* * *

The next morning, the pair got up early and teamed up on an assignment with two of their newest employees to observe and to assist them on a detail. They had to protect an abortion clinic doctor and her children as they attended an outdoor book festival on the grounds of Potomac Park. Keilah bought a bag of popcorn and shared it with Ramsey as they walked around the park, blending into the crowd.

"Keilah, I want to thank you again for an awesome birthday."

She popped a few kernels of popcorn into her mouth and said, "You're very welcome. Listen, Ramsey, I need to talk to you about something."

He adjusted his sunglasses and asked, "What's up?"

"I met someone."

"You did? When?" he asked as he found them a seat on a nearby bench. From this angle they were still able to observe their employees and their clients.

"I met him the other night when I took Teresa Randolph to that Breast Cancer Awareness dinner."

He smiled and asked, "Who is it?"

"Teresa Randolph's nephew, Major Michael Monroe."

Ramsey looked out over the crowd and repeated, "Major Michael Monroe, huh? Why haven't you mentioned him before now?"

"I don't know," she responded.

"What is he like?"

Keilah smiled. "He's nice, Ramsey. In that short time I was around him, I felt like I've known him for years."

"I see. So he has no problem with you being a bodyguard?"

She ate more of the popcorn and said, "No, he said he found it quite fascinating."

Ramsey didn't respond. Instead he spoke into his hidden

transistor to instruct his employees to move into closer proximity to their clients. Keilah handed the bag of popcorn to him so he could grab a few kernels. When he handed it back to her he asked, "Do you think Mrs. Randolph set you up?"

With a smirk on her face, Keilah replied, "It was so obvious, Ramsey, but I'm glad she did it. Michael has the warmest smile."

He looked over at her and observed her facial expression. It was evident that Keilah was smitten with this mysterious man.

They stared at each other for a moment. Keilah felt something tugging at her heart. She broke the silence as she looked away and put her hand over her heart. "You know I have you right here, don't you?"

"I know," he answered. "I feel the same way."

"I'm really going to miss snuggling up next to you at night, Ramsey. You've spoiled me."

Ramsey stopped a passing vendor to purchase a couple of sodas. He glanced over at her and said, "I'm going to miss you, too, especially the way you snore."

"I don't snore!"

He laughed. "Yes, you do."

She laughed along with him.

Ramsey put his arm around Keilah's shoulders and gave her a loving hug. "It's been a wild few months, huh?"

Keilah blushed. "Yes it has, but I wouldn't trade it for anything. You're a passionate man, Stone."

He chuckled. "Thank you, Keilah. You're packing some heat yourself. "

"Thank you," she replied softly. "You have a special place in my heart, Ramsey Stone."

He removed his arm and stared into her eyes. He did his best to swallow the lump in his throat. "Right back at you. I hope this guy has everything you're looking for."

Keilah smiled and said, "Me too."

Ramsey ate a little more of the popcorn as Keilah glanced over in the direction of their client. The smile left her face when she noticed a woman with something in her hand moving slowly in their direction. She stood and said, "Ramsey, look at that woman in the black T-shirt. What does she have in her hand?"

Ramsey also stood. "I can't tell, but from here it looks like a thermos. Let's move closer."

Ramsey and Keilah moved closer and watched the woman as she stopped to look at some books. He watched her eyes as she glanced over at their client before moving to the next table, which brought her closer to them. Ramsey spoke into his transistor. "Heads up, guys. There's a lady in a black T-shirt moving in from the southwest corner who looks suspicious. We're maneuvering in from the south and west for support."

Before Ramsey could say another word, Keilah was already within ten feet of the suspicious woman. It was then she noticed that the woman had unscrewed the top of the thermos. Seconds later, the woman screamed out some type of gibberish and made an aggressive move toward their client. The crowd scattered as Keilah tackled her with ease. The woman was still screaming as she struggled to get away, but she was unable to because Keilah put her knee in the woman's back and pulled her arms around behind her. She held her there until Ramsey arrived with handcuffs to retrain her. The Stone Chance Protection Agency employees hustled their client and her children away to a safe area while Ramsey and Keilah dealt with the assailant. Ramsey kicked the thermos away from her hand as police officers hurried over to them. They immediately handcuffed the woman, who was screaming anti-abortion slogans. A second police officer picked up the thermos carefully and realized it had what appeared to be blood inside it. As the woman was placed in a police car,

Ramsey and Keilah showed the officers their identification. Ramsey asked, "Do you know what was in the thermos?"

The officer said, "It's probably pig's blood. A lot of those anti-abortion protesters use pig's blood to throw on abortion doctors. You guys did a good job."

Keilah knocked grass off her pants leg and said, "Thank you, officer. Do you need to interview our client before we take her home? I'm sure her children are pretty shaken up."

"Just briefly, and then you can be on your way," the officer said before shaking Keilah and Ramsey's hands.

Ramsey and Keilah walked with the officers over to their client and their employees. Once there, they congratulated their employees for a job well done in protecting the client. Once the officers finished interviewing the doctor, they were allowed to leave. On the way back to Ramsey's car, he looked over at Keilah and laughed.

"What are you laughing at, Stone?"

He unlocked the doors on his truck and said, "You."

She put her hands on her hips and asked, "Why?"

He opened the truck door for her and said, "Because you can be scary at times. You took that woman down so fast, I didn't have time to blink."

"She was making her move, Ramsey. What was I supposed to do?"

He laughed again. "You did your job, Keilah. All I know is she's going to be sore as hell in the morning."

Keilah climbed into Ramsey's truck and smiled. "Oh well. She brought it on herself."

He started the engine and put it in drive. "You're right about that."

Ramsey pulled away from the curb and headed back to their office to do paperwork on the incident.

CHAPTER SEVEN

A few days later, Ramsey got the chance to meet Major Michael Monroe in the flesh when he showed up at their office with two dozen pink roses for Keilah. Ramsey couldn't help but notice how distinguished he looked in his military uniform.

"May I help you?" Ramsey asked.

The major extended his hand. "Good afternoon. I'm Michael Monroe, here to see Keilah Chance."

"Oh, yeah, you're Teresa Randolph's nephew. Keilah told me she met you at the charity banquet," Ramsey stated as he shook the major's hand.

"Guilty as charged. And you are?" Michael asked.

"Ramsey Stone. Keilah and I run the company together."

"It's nice to finally meet you. Keilah speaks very highly of you."

"Likewise," Ramsey replied as he signed some papers and handed them back to the receptionist. "Nice flowers. Does Keilah know you're here?"

"I just stepped off the elevator when you walked up. Your receptionist was just about to announce my arrival."

Ramsey shook his hand once more before walking away. "Well, I know for a fact she'll love the flowers. I'm sure she'll be right out. It was nice meeting you. Give my regards to your aunt and uncle."

"I will," Michael replied.

When Michael was out of earshot, Ramsey mumbled, "Toy soldier."

An hour or so later, Ramsey walked into Keilah's office pretending not to know anything about the flowers. "Who sent the flowers?"

She looked up and smiled. "Michael brought them by this morning."

Ramsey walked over to the flowers and picked up the card. "May I?"

Keilah glanced up at him and said, "Sure, go ahead."

Ramsey unbuttoned his jacket and sat down. He pulled the card out of the envelope and started reading aloud. "'Thank you for being such a beautiful distraction Saturday evening. I hope to get a chance to know you even better. Yours truly, Michael Monroe.'" He turned his attention to Keilah. "Well, well, well, Miss Chance, I see that Major Monroe is making all the moves to win your heart."

Without looking up she said, "Very funny, Ramsey."

Ramsey sat the card on her desk. "So you really like this guy, huh?"

She tilted her head. "So far, so good. We've been talking on the telephone to try to get to know each other better."

Ramsey scratched his head and then asked, "You haven't told him what you're worth, have you?"

She looked up at him and smiled. "Of course not. I learned not to do that a long time ago. I want to be loved for me, not for my money."

Ramsey got up and walked toward the door and said, "Take it slow, Keilah. I don't want to see you get hurt again."

"Don't worry, I am," Keilah said as she picked up her pen and started writing.

Ramsey turned to Keilah and said, "I have a detail to do this evening if you're looking for me."

She frowned and pulled up his itinerary. "When did you add this one?"

"About two hours ago. I'm doing a favor for Ron Davenport."

"I see," she responded. "Well, have fun."

"I'll holler at you later. Keep me posted on G.I. Joe," he teased.

She giggled. "I will. He invited me to dinner tonight, so if you're looking for me that's where I'll be."

"Oh, really?" Ramsey asked.

She nodded mischievously and tapped her pen on her desk. "Really. Be careful tonight and text me when you get home."

"Will do, and before I go, the lawyers called and said Malik Rivers pled guilty. He got fifteen years, so you can put that chapter behind you."

"You think?" she asked.

"Quentin gave me his word."

"If you say so, because the next time, there won't be any survivors," she announced.

"I understand," he replied before closing the door behind him. He wasn't ready to let go of his intimate moments with Keilah, and deep down he prayed that Major Michael Monroe would disappear just as quickly as he'd appeared.

R amsey followed Ron's directions and picked up a young man who appeared to be in his early twenties from an apartment complex not far from the campus of Howard University. His name was Martez, and he was scheduled to testify against a fellow student by the name Jazera, known around campus as "Jazz," who'd been selling drugs with Martez on the campus of Howard University. Martez wanted out and agreed to testify against his partner for immunity, or at least a lighter sentence. Martez was the nephew of a friend of Ron Davenport's and the young man he was going to testify against had ties to a prominent family in Chicago. Today, they were headed to a college football game, which would be challenging for Ramsey because of the huge crowd.

"So, Mr. Stone, I guess you know about the trial coming up, huh?"

Ramsey pulled into the parking lot of the stadium and put the car in park. "It's my job to know everything about my clients."

"Don't you want to know why I did it?" Martez asked.

"It doesn't matter to me. I'm here to do my job, period," Ramsey replied.

"Cool," Martez replied as he opened the car door.

Ramsey grabbed his arm and said, "Let's go over the rules again."

Martez sighed and listened as Ramsey reminded him of the dos and don'ts. Once he was finished, he said, "Do you understand everything I just told you, Martez?"

"Yes, Mr. Stone, I understand. Just try not to look so obvious. I don't want my friends to know."

"They might not have a choice. Listen, son, there's a reason your parents wanted me to protect you. It's obvious they're a little more concerned about you testifying against that other kid than you are."

Martez scratched his head and said, "All right. I'll do what you say."

Ramsey climbed out of the car and said, "As long as we have an understanding, we have nothing to worry about."

The pair walked toward the gates and into the stadium to watch the football game.

During the football game, Martez and his friends sat together while Ramsey sat on the bleachers directly behind them so he could have a bird's-eye view of the crowd and any suspicious movement.

After the ball game, Martez and his friends attended a victory party at a local nightclub. Ramsey wasn't too excited about the setup because the nightclub had limited parking and dim light, and it was packed to capacity. The room was full of gyrating young adults and Ramsey found himself constantly getting propositioned by college-age females. A couple of them even stuffed their telephone numbers into the palm of his hand with the request that he call them later. Ramsey couldn't do anything but laugh, but took pleasure in admiring their beauty and physical attributes.

Hours later, Martez still seemed to be having a great time dancing with his friends. Ramsey had even found him getting up close and personal with a young woman who wasn't in his original group of friends from the ball game. The young woman danced, rubbed, and ground her body repeatedly against Martez as they danced to the rhythm of the music. Ramsey frowned, walked over to Martez, and asked him to step away for a second so they could talk.

"What's up, Mr. Stone? You're blocking my flow."

Ramsey leaned down to the young man's ear and said, "It's time for us to go."

Martez looked at his watch and said, "It's only one AM."

Ramsey frowned and said, "I know what time it is, and the deal was that I would have you home by two AM, so let's go."

Martez glared at Ramsey and then said, "Let me go tell that honey good-bye. I'll be right back."

Ramsey held up his fingers up and said, "You have two minutes."

Martez pushed through the crowd and over to the young woman. Ramsey watched as Martez spoke into her ear. The woman smiled, took his cell phone out of his hand, and appeared to be keying her telephone number into it. Martez kissed her on the cheek and made his way back over to Ramsey. "OK, Rambo, I'm ready."

Ramsey didn't find Martez's comment regarding Rambo funny. He grabbed him by the collar and pulled him through the crowd and out the door. Once outside, he looked at Martez and said, "I see you have a sense of humor."

Martez laughed as they turned the corner and walked across the street to Ramsey's car. "I'm just trying to get you to lighten up, Mr. Stone."

"I'm working, Martez. I lighten up when I'm off duty," Ramsey pointed out to him.

Ramsey deactivated the alarm on his car as they approached it. It was at that time that two men stepped out of the shadows. One had a gun, the other a knife. The man with the gun said, "Give up the money."

Martez put his hands up and said, "We don't have any money."

The second guy said, "Don't make me cut you. Now give me your money."

Ramsey eyed the two men and then quickly reached into his back waistband and pulled out his gun, shooting the man with the gun in the shoulder. The gunman fell to the ground in agony as the man with the knife lunged at Martez and screamed, "This is from Jazz!"

Ramsey pushed Martez out of the way and grabbed the man's wrist. He twisted his arm, causing him to scream out in pain until he dropped the knife on the ground. Ramsey looked down at Martez and yelled, "Go back into the club!"

By that time, a group of people coming out of the club saw Martez running frantically toward them screaming, "Call 911!"

Ramsey kicked the man in the face, knocking him over the hood of a car. He glanced back over the man he'd shot and saw that he was still squirming around on the ground.

Ramsey picked the guy up who originally had the knife and slammed him head first into the driver side windshield of a car, shattering it, which knocked him unconscious. Ramsey then turned his attention to the man he'd shot and grabbed him by the foot. He drug him around to the front of his car and said, "Next time, tell your boy to send more people."

Someone from the group of people who heard the commotion called the police and within seconds, D.C. police were on the scene taking a report.

Keilah met Michael for dinner later that night. She wore a lavender suit with matching shoes, and as soon as she walked into the restaurant, Michael stood and greeted her with a tender kiss on the cheek. "Keilah, you look beautiful."

"Thank you," she replied as he held out her chair for her. Michael was dressed in full uniform, and he looked so handsome.

He sat down across from her and said, "Keilah, I'm so sorry I couldn't pick you up for dinner. My meeting ran over longer than I thought it would, and our reservations were for seven."

She placed a napkin in her lap and said, "Stop apologizing, Michael, it's OK."

The waiter approached their table and showed Michael a bottle of champagne. Michael looked over at Keilah and asked, "Do you approve?"

Keilah nodded in agreement. The waiter turned over their glasses and proceeded to pour two glasses of champagne. Before walking away, he handed both of them menus and said, "I'll give you a few minutes to look over the menu, and as soon as you're ready, I'll be happy to take your order."

Michael smiled at the waiter and said, "Thank you."

Once the waiter was gone, Michael held his glass up to Keilah and said, "To new beginnings."

"To new beginnings," Keilah repeated.

The pair sipped their champagne. Keilah took a longer sip before setting her glass down. She felt a little nervous. Michael was staring at her so much that she could see the candlelight flickering in his eyes. "Keilah, you have a unique name."

She smiled and said, "Yes, my mother got it from the Bible."

"Keilah is a city in Judah, right?"

Impressed, Keilah smiled and said, "That's right. How did you know?"

He took another sip of champagne and said, "I was born and raised in the church so I picked up on a few things."

Keilah blushed. "So I notice. Actually, my mother gave all of us names from the Bible."

"Really? How many brothers and sisters do you have?" Michael asked.

I have four older brothers. Luke, Roman, Malachi, and Genesis."

Michael smiled and said, "I see what you mean. Your parents gave all of you some strong biblical names."

"Thank you, Michael."

He picked up the champagne bottle and refilled Keilah's glass before refilling his own. "So you're the baby of the family and the only girl?"

"Unfortunately, I am. It has it rewards, but my brothers are terribly overprotective of me."

"I wouldn't expect any less. If I had a sister, I would be the same way."

She laughed and said, "I understand, but you don't know my brothers. They can be quite extreme."

He frowned and asked, "Why?"

Keilah smiled and said, "My brothers are ten-plus years older than I am. They basically raised me, so I think they look at me as not only their sister but their child as well."

"I see," Michael replied.

The waiter returned to the table interrupting them. "Sir, are you ready for me to take your order?"

Michael nodded at Keilah and she recited her order to the waiter. Michael gave the waiter his order as well before returning to his conversation with Keilah.

"Having older siblings can be difficult, and in your case I can see how it can be a little overwhelming. Are your parents able to make them ease up on you a little bit?"

Keilah lowered her head in silence. Michael immediately noticed her withdrawal from the conversation. "Keilah, are you OK? Did I say something wrong?"

She looked up at him with tears in her eyes. She waved him off and said, "It's not you, Michael, I'm sorry. You see, my mother died of breast cancer when I was ten years old and I never knew my father. He was murdered before I was born."

Michael reached across the table and held Keilah hand to comfort her. "I'm so sorry, Keilah. I didn't mean to pry or upset you."

"I'm fine, Michael. Enough about me, tell me something about you."

"What do you want to know?" he asked.

"How old are you, Michael?"

"Thirty-five. What else do you want to know?"

"Have you ever been married or had any children?"

He sipped his wine and said, "No on both questions, Miss Chance. Now answer a question for me?"

"OK," she replied.

With a gleam in his eyes, he asked, "Do you want children?"

"Of course I do, and since I was raised in house full of men, I want at least two girls."

"How many children do you want to have?"

Keilah blushed. "I don't know. I guess at least three. Now it's my turn. Do you want children?"

Michael smiled and softly said, "Yes, and as soon as possible. Whoever I choose as the mother of my children would have to start right away."

Keilah frowned and said, "I see you're on a mission."

He took a sip of champagne and said, "Most definitely. My mate would also have to be beautiful, intelligent, educated, and in excellent health."

Keilah didn't know what to think of Michael's requirements. He actually spoke as though he was looking for a baby machine instead of a wife, so she decided to ask him.

"What about a wife, Michael? Aren't you looking for a wife too?"

He shifted his position in his chair and took a long sip of champagne. He sat his glass down and smiled. "Of course. Now, do you have other questions?"

Keilah giggled. "As a matter of fact, I do. Do you have any brothers or sisters?"

He raised his glass to her and said, "Luckily for me, I'm an only child."

"It's not so bad having several siblings. I loved growing up in a big family. What about your parents? Are they still alive?"

"My father's deceased, but my I still have my mother. She's in an assisted-living facility in Virginia. My mother and Aunt Teresa are sisters, but my mother is much older. Her health is not so good right now, but she's a tough old lady."

Keilah played with the bouquet of roses in the center of the table. "Were you close to your father?"

"I was. He was a career military man as well."

"Like father, like son," Keilah said.

"I do. Losing someone you love is never easy, Keilah. Now, let's change the subject. This is supposed to be a happy occasion. Agreed?"

Keilah smiled. "Agreed."

Michael and Keilah went on to enjoy a wonderful dinner and livelier conversation. Michael filled her in on his family, education, and military background. They didn't discuss past relationships, but the couple did share with each other their interests and hobbies before bidding each other good-night.

That was the first of many dates between Michael and Keilah and with each date, they grew a little closer together— much to the approval of Teresa Randolph and the disapproval of Ramsey. He was still skeptical of the relationship between Keilah and Michael, but he kept his opinion to himself. He missed Keilah terribly. Even though he was actively dating two other women, they could never measure up to the woman Keilah Chance was.

Three weeks into Keilah's relationship with Michael, she had to cancel a date with Michael to work late with Ramsey. Michael was disappointed but understood her responsibilities.

Ramsey met Keilah at her house after picking up dinner on the way. He handed her a container of food and tried to set things up in her kitchen, but before he could get everything out of the bag, Keilah said, "Bring everything into the living room. I have the files in there."

"Slow down, Keilah, before you choke," Ramsey joked as he followed her into the living room.

She looked over at him and smiled. "You don't understand. I am starving."

He sat down on the sofa and opened his plate. His eyes widened as he viewed the baked chicken, macaroni and cheese and green beans. When he looked over at Keilah, her plate was nearly empty.

"Why didn't you eat lunch?" he asked. "You know you get a little crazy if you go too long without eating."

She wiped her mouth and said, "I know, Ramsey, but I didn't get hungry until around two o'clock, so I just ate a breakfast bar. Besides, I thought I was going to be eating dinner by six o'clock, remember?"

He shook his head and said, "Poor baby. Listen, I have to go to court next week for that shooting incident at that club."

She giggled as she got up to throw her empty container in the garbage. "Did that kid really call you Rambo?"

"Yes, he did. I wanted to smack him," Ramsey replied as he admired her heavenly figure. She was dressed in a short, navy blue skirt with a light blue silk blouse. When she returned to the room she caught him staring at her. She smiled as she sat down next to him and opened her laptop.

"What are you staring at, Stone?"

"You," he answered casually as he took a bite of his food. "You look good . . . I mean happy."

She opened a folder and without making eye contact, she said, "Thanks, and good luck in court."

"So, Miss Chance?"

She looked over at him again. "So what, Mr. Stone?"

"Are you happy?"

She thought to herself for a moment. "I'm good."

He frowned and sat her fork down. "What does that mean?"

"It means I like Michael very much."

Still frowning he asked, "That's it?"

Keilah tilted her head and look at Ramsey. "What do you really want to know, Ramsey?"

Ramsey had the weirdest expression on his face, which was a cross between angry and confused. He stood up, removed his tie, and unbuttoned a few buttons on his shirt, then looked down at her. "I want to know if you're happy with this guy. Is he treating you good? Taking care of you?"

Keilah blushed. "Michael is a gentleman, Ramsey. He's tender, attentive, loving, and compassionate. What can I say? I guess you can say I am happy."

"You guess? Either you are or you're not, Keilah."

She reached over, took his hand, and caressed it. "What's really on your mind, Ramsey?"

At that moment, Ramsey realized that Keilah could see right through him, but he wasn't about to give her the satisfaction of confirmation. He pulled his hand away. "Never mind, Keilah. Forget I asked."

"Are you upset with me about something, Ramsey?"

He stood up and took his food into the kitchen without responding. When he returned, Keilah was standing with her hands on her hips. "Talk to me, Stone."

He ignored her, sat down on the sofa, and picked up a folder. She sat down next to him, snatched the folder out of his hand, and laid it on the coffee table. "I said talk to me."

Keilah's perfume caressed his nostrils, and his skin was starting to heat up. He tried his best to ignore her, but she continued to try and force him to open up to her. Ramsey was winning his battle until Keilah cupped his face and made him look her directly in the eyes. The warmth and softness of her hands on his face made his body heat up several degrees. Keilah caressed his cheeks and then tenderly kissed him on the lips. In that instant, Ramsey's hands were everywhere on Keilah's body.

"Ramsey," she panted as she clung to his body.

His kisses were electrifying her as he tore open the front of her blouse and unhooked her bra. Ramsey only stopped kissing her so he could consume her nipples. Keilah cried out louder as he licked and kissed her rigid peaks before moving lower. Keilah sat up momentarily only to rip Ramsey's shirt off his chest so she could have access to his toned abs. The minute her lips came in contact with his skin, he trembled with anticipation. The couple worked so feverishly with each other they didn't realize they were about to roll off the sofa. The moment they hit the floor, Ramsey pulled off her skirt and tossed it across the room. All that was left was her navy thong, which was no match for his muscular hands.

"Wait," she begged. "I want to undress you."

Ramsey swallowed hard as Keilah unbuckled his belt and

lowered his pants and briefs. The moment his clothes were free he parted her legs and dipped his face between her thighs. Ripples of heat and desire radiated throughout her body. She writhed and moaned, knocking the mounds of folders and her laptop off the coffee table and onto the floor. Ramsey devoured her until her body quivered and she begged for mercy. "Ramsey . . . my God . . . please."

He towered over her and whispered into her ear. "I'm trying to, sweetheart."

Keilah's eyes fluttered as she wrapped her arms and legs around Ramsey's powerful frame. He was inside her in one swift motion and their bodies went up in flames. The rhythm of their hips was full of vigorous and searing passion as Ramsey plunged deeper into her abyss. She ran her tongue across his neck and kissed his ample lips until she felt his body stiffen. Keilah could see the veins in his neck as he struggled to hold his composure, but the moment she stuck her tongue in his ear, he lost it. The instant she felt him release his essence, she climaxed and screamed out his name like she'd never screamed it before.

CHAPTER EIGHT

In Dennison, Luke walked into their casino office and found Genesis working hard on the computer. Luke looked suave and debonair in his gray designer suit.

"Hey, bro."

Genesis glanced up and said, "Hey, Luke. Why are you so dressed up today?"

"I have a meeting with some potential vendors. How has everything been going today?" he asked as he took his jacket off and hung it in the closet.

Genesis rubbed his eyes and said, "Fine. I've just been going over the payroll."

Luke opened the small refrigerator, pulled out a bottle of apple juice, and took a sip. "Have you talked to Keilah any more about coming out here?"

"She said she couldn't come home until after the holidays."

Luke frowned and said, "That's some bull."

"I'm just telling you what she said."

Luke sat down in the leather chair in front of the desk and

pulled out his cell phone. "Did you tell her about the grand opening for the new casino?"

Genesis stood up and stretched his long limbs. "Yeah, I told her, but not in any detail."

Luke dialed Keilah's number and loosened his necktie as he waited for her to answer.

In the meantime, Keilah was still trying to recover from her recent sexual encounter with Ramsey when her phone rang. Ramsey helped her off the floor and gave her a playful pat on her bare backside before he started gathering his clothes. Keilah hurriedly slid into his dress shirt and answered her telephone. "Hello?"

"Good evening, baby girl."

Keilah smiled and said, "Hey, Luke. What's up?"

He didn't waste any time tearing into her. "What's this nonsense I hear about you not coming home until after the holidays? What's going on? "

Keilah sat down on the sofa and watched Ramsey get dressed. "It's not nonsense, Luke but—"

Luke interrupted her. "What's keeping you there? Can't Ramsey handle things for a couple of days?"

She rolled her eyes. "Ramsey's very capable of handling things by himself, but he shouldn't have to. We're stretched thin enough as it is and sometimes you guys act like my business is not as important as yours."

Ramsey glanced over at her briefly upon hearing his name, then started gathering up all the items Keilah had knocked on the floor as they made love.

"That's not true, Keilah, but if you guys are stretched so thin, you need to look into hiring more people. This is our grand opening and it's important to the entire family."

"I know it's important, Luke, but my employees still have to be trained, and it takes time. Ramsey can't do that by himself, and I won't ask him to."

Luke looked at Genesis and shook his head. Keilah was

being just as stubborn with him as she was with Genesis. It was difficult for them to realize that she was just like them: full of passion about her job.

"Just run it by Ramsey. I'm only asking for a couple of days, Keilah."

Keilah held the telephone in silence for a moment. Even though Ramsey had given her his blessings on her trip home, she wanted to make Luke simmer for a few more days. "I'll see what I can do, but I'm not going to promise you anything."

"Good. Now get back to me as soon as you can, because I can't stress to you enough how important this is to the family."

Keilah scooted over closer to Ramsey on the sofa and massaged his neck as he powered up her laptop. Her subtle gesture weakened him once again. He whispered, "You'd better stop."

She smiled and continued her conversation with Luke. "I'll let you know. Tell everyone I said hello."

"I will," Luke said. "I have to run to a meeting now, but call me back after you talk to Ramsey. I love you, and be careful."

"I love you too, Luke. Good-bye."

"Good-bye, Keilah."

Keilah hung up the telephone and stared at Ramsey. He glanced over at her. "May I help you?"

She started massaging his neck again. "How did you know I needed a fix?"

"I didn't," he replied. "Besides, I figured you and G. I. Joe had been burning up the sheets."

She moved her massage from his neck to his back. "No, we haven't slept together yet."

Ramsey was relieved and surprised by her admission. "You haven't slept with him? Why not?"

Keilah sighed and lay back on the sofa. "I don't know why,

Ramsey. Things have gotten pretty hot between us, but he always stops himself at the last moment."

Without looking at her he replied, "What's wrong with him?"

She buttoned Ramsey's shirt and said, "I don't know. He keeps telling me I'm the one and that he doesn't want to mess things up."

Ramsey frowned as he typed on the laptop a little more. "The one? He's moving a little fast isn't he? Besides, I thought you two hadn't had a lot of time to hang out together, and now he's calling you the one?"

"We have had some time together, just not like it should be, and when we do get together it's only for an hour or two and then one of us has to run off to an assignment, meeting, or whatever."

"That's too bad. You both have demanding careers, so that will probably be the norm with you guys," Ramsey pointed out.

Keilah stood and gathered up her clothing. "You're probably right, Ramsey, but a girl can hope for better, can't she?"

"Of course," he replied as he watched her and thought she'd never looked sexier than she did at the moment in his dress shirt. Keilah smiled when she caught him staring at her once again. "Ramsey, are you upset with me about something? You seemed a little tense earlier."

He shook his head and said, "No."

"You might not be now, but you were acting like you were before we made love. Maybe you needed a fix more than I did."

Ramsey stopped typing and ran his hands over his face. He smiled and said, "I'm cool, Keilah, and I'm sorry I gave you that impression."

"Are you sure?"

He walked over to her and kissed her on the cheek. "I'm sure."

Keilah watched his movements as he pulled a folder out of

his briefcase. She knew something was going on with Ramsey but realized he wasn't going to tell her. He sat back down and opened the folder. "Are you ready to get to work now?"

She giggled. "Yes, boss, but can I change clothes first?"

"No, because if you go upstairs you'll find something to distract you and I'll be down here working all by myself. Besides, you look hot in my shirt so keep it on."

She giggled again, sat down beside him, and started working on their project. Little did Ramsey know just sitting next to him was distraction enough for Keilah. He was gorgeous, and every few minutes the scent of his cologne on the shirt made her mind wander back to their earlier lovemaking session making it hard for her to stay focused on the work at hand.

The couple worked into the wee hours of the night. Keilah eventually fell asleep on the sofa while Ramsey continued to work on the fuel of a couple of Red Bull energy drinks. There were supposed to be taking turns napping, but Keilah just couldn't keep her eyes open any longer. Ramsey looked at his watch and rubbed his eyes. It was one o'clock in the morning, and he was exhausted from putting in a seventeen-hour day. He turned off the laptop and yawned. When he looked over at Keilah, she was still sound asleep and had the face of an angel, even when she snored. Ramsey decided to call it a night, so he turned off all the lights in the room before picking Keilah up off the sofa. He carried her up the stairs and into the bedroom, placing her under the warm sheets. He found it difficult to hold his eyes open any longer, so he removed his clothes and climbed into bed beside her. Keilah stirred slightly in her sleep as he pulled the comforter over them. Keilah spooned her hips against his body, snuggling close to him. Ramsey wrapped his arms securely around Keilah, but before falling asleep he whispered softly in her ear, "I love you, Keilah Chance."

As soon as Ramsey closed his eyes, Keilah slowly opened hers. She stared into the darkness after hearing Ramsey's breathless confession. She laid there listening to rhythm of his heartbeat for several minutes before succumbing to sleep once again.

The next morning, Keilah decided not the tell Ramsey she overheard his loving confession. For one, she didn't know if it was a sleep-deprived utterance or if he really meant it. They'd told each other they loved each other before, but there was something different about the way Ramsey said it this time. They were in a compromising position and it sounded like he meant it in the most intimate way. She had to admit to herself that her heart thumped hard in her chest when she heard his loving words, and it also opened her eyes to things she'd been in denial about for several months now. Until she had a better understanding of what was really going on, she decided to go on with her life as usual, so she got dressed and went in to work like she normally did. Ramsey had to drive home to get dressed before heading out on an assignment with a new agent.

When Keilah got into her office, the first thing on her list was to call Luke and put him out of his misery and let him know she would be coming home on the twelfth of September. Needless to say, he was very happy with the news. She also reluctantly mentioned to him that she would be bringing a friend along for the trip in the form of Major Michael Monroe. She figured now was a better time than any for her brothers to meet Michael, and it was best they didn't know much about him ahead of time. Otherwise they would gang up on her as soon as she stepped off the plane. All she told Luke was that Michael was a thirty-five-year-old, single, career military man. Luke wasn't happy at all about the age difference, but decided to wait until he was face to face with Keilah and Michael before engaging in any more conversation about the new man in her life. Keilah prayed the trip home would give her the opportunity to sort out everything, especially her true feelings, before things progressed and possibly got complicated.

Ramsey wasn't happy at all when Keilah told him she was taking Michael home with her to meet her family. His only comfort was the fact that he knew her brothers well and found solace in knowing the Chance brothers would interrogate Michael to the fullest. If they felt like he wasn't on the up and up for any reason, they would make Keilah end the relationship before it had a chance to get started. That, he was sure of, and he prayed things would play out just like he hoped.

CHAPTER NINE

The Lucky Chance Casino had been the Chance brothers' pride and joy for almost seven years. It was the only one of its kind in the area, and business was booming. Because of this, everyone wanted a piece of the action. The Chances vowed to keep their business only in the family without allowing outsiders to penetrate their sanctuary. Because of their success, gangs and other undesirables were trying hard to muscle their way into the business. Opening the a new casino was going to be even more profitable because it would not only be named after Keilah, but it would be for her and her heirs. The brothers had decided to call it the Special K Casino, and they hoped to keep it a surprise until the grand opening. The decor would have a more feminine touch to it, and some of the amenities were a spa, beauty salon, and nail shop off from the main floor and a designer shoe store and boutique on the second floor. They wanted to cater to female patrons by providing them with things near and dear to their heart. The Chance brothers made sure all the businesses would be available to their customers twenty-four hours a day.

* * *

It didn't take long for the twelfth to roll around, and Keilah was due to arrive within a few hours. Malachi and Roman were overseeing the finishing touches on the interior decor of the casino while Luke and Genesis conducted final interviews on the last group of prospective employees. They had to be careful and run background checks, because they didn't want anyone working for them who could possibly allow the underworld to infiltrate their establishment. Keilah would be arriving later, and they wanted everything to go as planned.

Malachi pulled his direct-talk telephone from his pocket and said, "Roman, what time will the delivery trucks be here with the spa equipment?"

Roman looked at his watch. "They should be here by two and the liquor warehouse will be here around three. I have to go check on Keilah's gift, but I'll back in about an hour."

"Cool, make sure everything's set. I would hate to have to pull my nine on them," Malachi responded.

Roman shook his head and tucked his phone inside his pocket.

Keilah's gift was going to be extra special, and the brothers hoped it would be just enough to convince her to stay in town permanently. They hated that she lived so far away. She was their baby sister, and even though she was an adult, they felt like they still needed to keep a closer eye on her.

Luke made notes on the clipboard as he spoke with a female employee. "Ronda, this job is going to be hectic at times, but rewarding in salary. Are you up for it?"

She smiled nervously. "I sure am. I have a lot of patience and actually enjoy working with an enthusiastic crowd, Mr. Chance."

He looked up at her and took note of her confidence.

"Please, call me Luke. We want to keep things on a first-name basis; however, this is a business, and we expect our employees to conduct themselves as such."

The young lady crossed her legs slowly. "I wouldn't expect it to be any other way, Mr. Chance."

He smiled. "It's Luke, remember?"

"I'm sorry. It's going to take me a while to get used to calling my bosses by their first names," she replied with a smile.

"We want to make sure your career here with us will be a pleasant one. Are you sure this isn't going to interfere with your classes at the university?"

"Not at all, sir."

"Well, if you don't have any other questions, all that's left is for me to welcome you aboard," Luke said as he stood up and extended his hand.

Ronda stood and happily shook his hand. "I'll see you on Monday, Luke," she replied.

"Have a good day."

Luke turned and watched a nice pair of legs walk out of his office. He was going to have to remember how young she was and the fact that he was a happily married man. Ronda Gilbert was the last name on his list. He knew Genesis was still interviewing in his office so he walked over and tapped on the door.

"Come in," the deep voice replied from the other side.

Luke opened the door and greeted the man Genesis was interviewing. Luke shook the gentleman's hand and said, "Excuse me for interrupting."

"It's okay, sir," the young man answered.

Luke looked over at Genesis and held his hand up to his ear. "Hit me up on the phone and let me know when you're done. I'll be out on the floor for a while, and then I have to pick Keilah up at the airport in a couple of hours."

Genesis leaned back in his chair. "I will."

* * *

Keilah held onto Michael's hand as they sat side by side on the airplane. Since their morning had started so early, Michael was taking the opportunity to catch up on sleep. Keilah was too excited to sleep. She hadn't seen her brothers in a long time and was anxious to see them again. Tears formed in her eyes just at the thought of them. She wiped her eyes and turned and looked out the window at the clouds floating in the blue skies. It was then she remembered how protective they were, and because of that, she wasn't allowed to have many friends. When they were younger, their fear was that someone would try to hurt her to get back at them.

The reason the Chance brothers weren't always on the up and up was that they indulged in the sale of street pharmaceuticals to help their mother after their father ran out on them. It took their mother a while to find out what they were involved in and by the time she did, they were deep into it. She thought they were working reputable jobs, but gossip from neighbors told her otherwise. It wasn't until she saw it for herself that the reality sunk in, and it broke her heart. She'd raised her sons in the church, so they knew right from wrong. In a way, she felt guilty that her sons felt they needed to resort to illegal activities to help her, but the real blame fell on her husband, who had abandoned them.

Keilah shook those awful thoughts from her head just as the captain of the airplane spoke over the intercom.

"Ladies and gentlemen, this is your captain speaking. If you would look to the right, you can see the Grand Canyon and the Colorado River."

The captain's voice woke Michael up from his nap. When he looked at Keilah he could see the sad look on her face. He sat up and gave her hand a squeeze.

"What's wrong, Keilah?"

"Oh, nothing much. I just have a few things on my mind." Michael kissed her gently on the lips. "Is it anything you want to talk about?"

She smiled as she wiped her eyes. "No, I'll be fine. Thanks for asking though."

Keilah and Michael had gotten very close over the past month . . . very close. They finally took their relationship to the next level and made love. Actually, they made love almost every night that first week, and it had been great.

Michael kissed Keilah again. "Do you want me to get you something to drink?"

"No, I'm going to try and grab a nap before we land because I know my brothers are going to have us on the go as soon as our feet hit the ground."

"I'm ready if you are," he joked. "I hope they like me."

Keilah linked her arm with his, laid her head against his shoulder, and sighed. "I'm sure they will, Michael."

"I love you, Keilah."

She sat up and looked at him. "You do?"

"Of course I do. You make it easy. Besides, I told you not long after we met that you were the one, remember?" he explained.

Keilah didn't know how to take Michael's comment. How could he be in love with her in the short time they'd known each other, and why did he keep calling her "the one?"

Michael leaned his head back against the seat and closed his eyes. Keilah didn't know how to respond to Michael. Yes, they'd had a passionate four weeks, but sex was her favorite pastime. Surely he hadn't fallen in love already. Or had he?

It wasn't long before the airplane touched down in sunny California. As they taxied toward the terminal, Keilah touched up her makeup and smoothed down her hair.

Michael looked over at her and announced, "You can't improve perfection, Keilah."

"You're biased, Michael, but thank you. So are you ready?"

He patted her thigh and said, "Stop worrying, Keilah. If I can handle Iraq, I'm sure I can handle your brothers."

Keilah put her compact back in her purse and shook her head. "You don't know them, Michael. They can be very unreasonable."

He leaned over and kissed her cheek. "We'll be fine. You'll see."

"I hope you're right," she replied as she put on her denim jacket. Keilah was sporting a pair of designer jeans, a jacket, and a cranberry colored tank top. Michael also wore jeans with a tailored pink button-down shirt.

The plane finally stopped at the terminal, and passengers quickly filled the aisle. After several people filed by, Michael saw a chance for them to exit the plane. He took Keilah by the hand and escorted her out of the plane and down the tunnel. As they walked arm in arm, Keilah stopped and turned to him.

"Michael, before we go any further, I want to thank you for coming home with me so my family could meet you."

He pulled her into his arms and kissed her on the lips. "I'm glad you invited me, because I wanted to meet the men who raised my number-one woman."

Keilah smiled. "Number one, huh? That's sweet, Michael."

He kissed her again, this time a little longer on the lips. "No, that was sweet, and if you keep that up, we're going to be spending the entire weekend in bed."

"I doubt my family will let that happen, Major," she replied as she pulled out her cell phone. "I need to call Ramsey to check in and let him know we got in OK."

"Go right ahead," Michael replied. "I need to use the rest room anyway."

Keilah sat down at a nearby table. She dialed Ramsey's number, and he immediately picked up.

"I was wondering when you was going to call. I guess you're on the ground, huh?"

Smiling, she said, "Yeah, we just got here."

"So how are things going so far?" he asked.

Keilah toyed with a small menu on the table. "We haven't made it to the front of the terminal yet, so we haven't seen anyone. Michael's in the rest room right now, so I wanted to call and check on things."

"It's a normal day around here, no big deal. I miss you already, though," he admitted.

"Well, I'm going to let you in on a little secret, Stone. I miss you too."

Ramsey held the telephone in silence for a moment. Actually, he was gripping it tighter than he realized he was. "What's really going on, Keilah? Why are you with this guy?"

"Excuse me?" she asked. "What do you mean?"

"You know what I mean," he replied with an irritated tone. "Are you trying to prove something to yourself?"

"No, I don't know what you mean," Keilah answered with a slightly elevated voice. "Why don't you tell me?"

Ramsey could have kicked himself for blurting out a hint of his true feelings, but the jig was up now. "It's so obvious, Keilah. Stop acting like you don't know."

"Know what, Ramsey?" she prodded.

Just as Ramsey was about to tell her everything, Michael exited the rest room. Keilah let out a breath and stood up. She'd almost gotten Ramsey to confirm the words she wanted to hear him say so badly, but since Michael had reappeared, now was not a good time. "Look, Ramsey, Michael's back, so when I get a chance I'll call you later so we can finish this discussion. OK?"

Without responding to her, he said, "Have a nice visit with your family, Keilah, and tell everyone I said hello."

"I will," she said before hanging up the telephone.

"Is something wrong at the office?" Michael asked.

She pulled her purse on her shoulder and smiled. "No, everything's fine."

"Good. Are you ready to go?"

"Lead the way," Keilah suggested as they made their way through the terminal and into the lobby of the airport. It was there, Luke spotted his very grown-up-looking baby sister and her new friend.

He mumbled, "What the hell? He looks older than I am."

Keilah spotted Luke and ran over to greet him. She jumped into his arms and hugged him.

"Luke, oh my God . . . I've missed you guys so much," she yelled.

He held her tightly in his arms. "The same goes for you." Luke set her on the ground and extended his hand to Michael. "I take it you're Michael Monroe?"

Michael shook Luke's hand. "I am. It's nice to finally meet you."

"The pleasure is all mine," Luke replied.

"Luke, wasn't it sweet of Michael to come out here for the grand opening with me?" Keilah asked.

Luke playfully nudged Keilah. "I guess, but I would rather you had brought him on a weekend we weren't so busy."

She nudged him back. "What difference does it make?"

"It doesn't matter, sis. I'm just glad you're home. Let's get your luggage so we can get out of here and over to the house."

As they walked together, Keilah cleared her throat before speaking. "Just so you know, we're staying in a hotel while we're in town."

Without making eye contact or breaking his stride, Luke replied, "No, you're not."

"Yes, we are. I want some privacy, and that's something we can't have at your house," she said adamantly.

Luke turned to Keilah with a frown. "What kind of privacy do you need? Was this his idea?"

Just as Michael was about to defend himself, Keilah put her hand up to stop him. "Let's get this shit straight right now, Luke. I am grown, and Michael and I are dating. So I don't need him or any man speaking on my behalf. I didn't come here for you guys to start trippin'. I came here to visit my family and to have a good time. If you don't do anything else this weekend, respect my wishes, please. Now I think you owe Michael an apology."

Luke looked down at the floor and shook his head. Keilah was a true Chance and wasn't a pushover for anyone, not even him. He looked her in the eyes. "Keilah, I don't want to fight with you. Maybe I shouldn't have been so forceful . . ."

"Maybe?" she questioned. "If you guys can't handle something as simple as allowing us to stay in a hotel, Michael and I will be on the next plane smoking back to the East Coast. Do you feel me, Luke?"

Luke started laughing. He pulled her into his arms and hugged her. "I'm sorry, Keilah. No matter how hard we try, it doesn't get any easier when it comes to you. I'm not going to make any promises, but I'm going to try to chill out a little."

"Sounds good, and I hope Sabrinia has dinner ready, because I'm starving," she said.

"You're out of luck today, because Malachi is the cook."

Keilah frowned. "Malachi?"

Without reiterating, Luke laughed as they continued to walk through the airport. They collected their luggage and exited the door.

CHAPTER TEN

It didn't take long for Luke to get to his neighborhood. Before coming to the house, he took Keilah and Michael by their hotel so they could check in. He knew that his brothers were going to have the same problem he did with Keilah staying in a hotel, but they all were going to have to live with it for the weekend. When he pulled up to the security gate, Keilah noticed what appeared to be elevated security, bearing sidearms.

She sat up and asked, "What's with all the guards being strapped, Luke?"

He didn't answer her as he rolled down his window and showed identification in order to enter the gated community.

As the gate was lifted, Keilah asked again, "What's with all the extra security?"

He looked at her from the rearview mirror. "Just some of the fringe benefits of living out here."

She knew Luke was lying. She was in the security business, and armed guards patrolling the community wasn't something she'd seen on her last visit home. If Luke wouldn't tell her, she was sure she could get the truth from Genesis.

By the time Luke pulled into his driveway, he could see that all of his brothers and their families had arrived. As soon as Luke put the truck in park, Keilah stepped out it.

"That better be barbecue I smell," she said.

Luke and Michael climbed out and laughed as they watched Keilah head straight for the backyard. Within seconds they heard joyful screaming.

Michael turned to Luke and said, "Luke, I hope you guys go easy on Keilah while she's here."

Luke folded his arms and asked, "Why is that?"

"Well, she was a little upset on the plane ride here. I woke up and found her crying. When I asked her what was wrong, she mentioned she was thinking about her mom. I'm sure you know Keilah is tough as nails for the most part, but she also has a fragile side, and I don't want to see her hurt. She loves you guys, and she tries so hard to please you."

Luke frowned. "I appreciate what you're saying, Michael, but I don't think you've known our sister long enough to have much of an opinion about her nature, and if anyone knows how fragile Keilah is, we do."

"Then cut her some slack. You and your brothers raised her into a fine young woman, and it shows if you guys would just open your eyes."

Luke stared at this man who had invaded Keilah's life. What the hell did he know about Keilah? One thing Luke did was respect Michael for defending her. Maybe he wasn't so bad after all.

"I'll take that under advisement, Michael. Now, come on so you can meet the rest of the family and get something to eat."

By the time Luke and Michael reached the backyard, Keilah had already hugged and kissed everyone and was now eating. She had her two-year-old niece on her lap and was chewing on some ribs. She made eye contact with Michael, smiled, and then set her niece down just before walking over to him. Malachi and Genesis watched as Keilah hugged and kissed Michael and then started introducing him to the family. She eventually made her way over to them and with teary eyes gave them huge hugs and kisses. Afterwards she introduced Michael to them and shared a brief conversation before finishing her introductions. After they walked off Genesis whispered, "So, what do you think of the new boyfriend?"

Genesis laughed. "I guess he's all right. What do you think?"

Malachi turned the hot dogs over on the grill. "I don't know. Look at her. She's glowing," he started.

"She's not glowing," Genesis said. "That's from the heat."

Malachi was staring at Keilah and Michael so hard he nearly burned the hot dogs. "I don't like him."

Genesis sampled one of the hot dogs and laughed. "You don't even know the man."

"I still don't like him," Malachi repeated.

Genesis laughed and said, "You don't want to go toe to toe with Keilah, bro. You remember how long it took her to start talking to you again after you pulled that gun on her ex."

Malachi took a sip of beer and grunted. "I'm not worried about Keilah. She can't whip my ass."

Genesis laughed out loud and bit into the hot dog again. "I don't know, bro. Keilah has gotten pretty tough over the past few years."

"I don't care how tough she thinks she is. I'm not letting her hook up with some buster just because she thinks he's cute."

At that time, Keilah walked back over to them and smiled. "Can a sister get some more love from you two or what?"

Genesis pulled her into his arms first, hugging her and kissing her lovingly on the forehead. "Welcome home, sis. You don't come home enough. Six months is too long."

"I know, I know, I'll try to do better. You guys know where I live, too."

Genesis hugged her again and said, "You're right."

She looked at Malachi, who was in the process of turning the ribs. He put his tongs down and wiped his hands on his apron. "Hey, Boo. I'm really glad you're home. Talking on the telephone and e-mailing is not the same."

She wiped a lone tear off her cheek and smiled. "When did you start wearing dreads, Malachi?"

He picked up the tongs to attend to the ribs. "I've had them for a while now. You like?"

She smiled. "I do. They really look good on you."

He blushed upon hearing her compliment. "You look good too, girl. D.C. agrees with you."

"Thank you, Malachi. Genesis, you're looking good too."

"Thanks, sis," Genesis replied.

"Did you guys see Michael?" she asked.

Malachi sighed. "So that's your new interest, huh?

She took a sip of her soda and said, "For the moment."

Genesis and Malachi both rolled their eyes. Malachi asked, "Why did you bring him home with you? We wanted this to be a family occasion."

She walked closer to him, folded her arms and firmly replied, "I had hoped you guys would want to meet him."

Malachi held the tongs up and said, "That's one thing you're right about, but I'm going to tell you now, I don't like dude."

She put her hands on her hips. "Malachi, don't start. Besides you hate everybody."

"I don't hate everybody, just the men you date," he revealed.

She folded her arms and walked closer to Malachi. "He's a nice guy, Malachi, so do me a favor and don't embarrass me."

Malachi brushed some barbecue sauce onto the ribs and laughed. He looked at Keilah and said, "If he does or says anything out of line or disrespects you in any way, I'm going to be all over him, Keilah. You know me, which means you know I don't play."

"Like I said, he's a nice guy so you don't have to worry about him disrespecting me. I want Michael to have a good time while he's here. Don't mess that up for me. OK?"

He smiled mischievously. "I'm not going to make any promises, sis. Why are you so worried about us meeting him anyway? It's not like you're getting ready to marry him or something."

Keilah saw an opportunity to have a little fun with her brothers. She looked them directly in their eyes, smiled, and then turned on her heels and walked away without admitting or denying anything. Malachi almost dropped the ribs.

"Did you see that, Genesis? What the hell is wrong with her? I know she's not about to marry that dude. She barely knows him. Keilah," he called, "get back over here."

Keilah looked back at them and waved mischievously.

Genesis sipped his beer and said, "Dang, bro. Keilah is tripping. I hope she's not foolish enough to get married yet. She's too young."

Malachi removed the ribs from the grill and dropped them in the pan, one by one. "She's not crazy. Keilah needs a man that can handle her attitude. You know . . . someone like . . ."

Genesis cut him off saying, "Like you?"

Malachi's eyes got blood-red. "Someone's that's not a punk."

"Call him what you want to, Malachi, but I think Keilah really likes this guy. Besides, he couldn't have worked his way up through the military ranks being soft."

"Whatever," Malachi responded.

Before Genesis walked away, he laughed at Malachi's obvious irritation.

"You'd better get used to it, because Keilah's not going let you or any of us tell her who she can kick it with, regardless of what we say."

"Shut the hell up, Genesis, and get those bad-ass kids of yours, Luke's, and Roman's out of the pool, and tell everybody the food is ready," Malachi announced.

Genesis chuckled at his brother's colorful antics, walked over to his family members, and made the announcement. He then gave Michael a friendly greeting so Keilah would know he was on her side. He realized a long time ago that they were unable to stop her from growing up into an independent, strong, and beautiful woman.

Keilah was excited to see her sister-in-laws and all her nieces and nephews. Malachi was still the only one unmarried, but he had been in a relationship with the same woman for over three months, which was an accomplishment in itself.

As things wound down, Keilah announced that she and Michael were tired and ready to get back to their hotel. That's when the brothers really started making noise.

"Look, I'm not fighting this battle tonight because I'm too tired," Keilah said. "We're staying in a hotel, and that's final. OK?"

The brothers couldn't do anything but mumble among themselves. Their wives loved to see their husbands being handled by their baby sister. She was the only woman who could bring them to their knees.

Luke walked over to Keilah and dropped a set of keys in her hands. "If you're determined to have your privacy, take my Infiniti so you guys will have some transportation," he said.

"You don't have to do that, Luke. We were going to rent a car," Keilah replied.

"No need. Now take the truck, Keilah," Luke answered with an elevated tone.

Keilah backed down and kissed him on the cheek. "Thanks, bro."

As Keilah and Michael headed toward the garage, Luke yelled, "Meet us at the casino at noon tomorrow so we can take care of business."

"I will," Keilah answered.

Michael waved and said, "Good-night everyone."

In unison, they replied, "Good-night.

B ack at the hotel, Keilah fell backwards on the bed in total exhaustion. She'd forgotten just how draining dealing with her brothers could be. Michael lay down next to her and asked, "Is everything cool with you and your brothers?"

She turned to face him. "Yes. They just have to be reminded that I'm over twenty-one from time to time."

"Good. Now how would you like a nice hot bath?"

She caressed his shoulders and whispered, "I'd like that very much, sweetheart."

"I'll be right back," he replied before walking into the bathroom.

"OK. I'll call room service and get them to bring up some wine," she announced. She picked up the telephone and ordered two bottles.

After hanging up the telephone, Keilah lay there thinking about the conversation she'd had earlier with Ramsey. She wished she could've had the chance to call him back. but now it was too late. Hopefully she would get a chance to talk to him tomorrow. In the meantime she would make the most of her night.

Michael called from the bathroom just as there was a knock on the door.

"Keilah, the water's ready," he said.

"I'm on my way. Let me get the wine first," she replied as she scooted off the bed. Keilah opened the door and allowed the waiter to enter with a large silver bucket full of ice and two bottles of wine. She directed him over to the table and tipped him generously before opening the door for him. She kicked off her shoes, grabbed the wine and two glasses, and then joined Michael in the steamy bathroom.

Malachi drove his Mercedes Benz down the expressway feeling bad that he hadn't smoothed things over with Keilah before she left the cookout. He now realized that if she ended up married to Michael, he was going to have to tolerate him whether he liked him or not. With all these thoughts running through his head, he knew he wouldn't be able to sleep unless he made amends with her.

Luke told him which hotel they were staying in, so he picked up his cell and dialed her number. When her voicemail came on, he spoke into the phone. "Yo, Keilah, this is Malachi. I need to holler at you, so I'm getting ready to swing by your hotel. See you shortly."

What Malachi didn't know was that Keilah's cell phone was in the bottom of her purse, and she didn't hear it ring. Their tranquility would soon be interrupted, but in the meantime, Michael massaged Keilah's body with expertise. Keilah sighed as Michael's large hands explored every inch of her body. She straddled his lap, causing Michael to lose touch of his senses. She heard him groan as she pressed her body against his. "You like that, don't you?" she teased.

He pulled her hips closer to him. "You know I do."

Michael loved the way Keilah's soft lips tasted, and he never wanted to lose that feeling. Things were heating up even more as she leaned back so Michael could have total access to her voluptuous breasts. He ran his tongue over her nipples and feasted on her. Seconds later, he pulled back. "What was that?"

"What was what?" she asked.

Michael sat there quietly for a moment then said, "Shhh . . . listen."

Keilah playfully nibbled on his ear and kissed his neck. "I don't hear anything."

"Is that someone knocking on the door?" he asked.

Keilah was all over him. She breathlessly said, "I didn't hear anything, Michael."

"Wait. There it is again," Michael said as he eased Keilah off his lap so he could climb out of the tub.

"Michael, whoever it is will go away if we ignore them," she pleaded.

He wrapped a towel around his waist. "It could be the front desk. You wouldn't want them to find us like this, would you? Stay here. I'll see who it is."

Keilah leaned back in the bubbles and closed her eyes as she drained the last of the wine out of her glass.

Michael walked over to the door, looked through the peephole, and let out a breath as he opened the door. "Hey, Malachi. What's up?"

Malachi's eyes widened and turned blood-red, seeing Michael standing before him nearly naked. He could only imagine what he had just interrupted between Michael and Keilah. With an obvious scowl on his face Malachi asked, "Where's Keilah? I called before I came over."

Before Michael could answer him, Keilah walked into the room with a large white towel wrapped around her body looking very agitated. "Malachi? What are you doing here?"

Malachi walked into the room, allowing Michael to close the door behind him. "I left a message on your cell phone."

She sat down in a nearby chair and crossed her legs. "Well,

I didn't get it, and what is so important that it couldn't wait until tomorrow?"

Malachi got even more disturbed as he noticed suds sliding down both of their legs. He had to shake the images from his mind and remind himself his sister was a grown woman.

Michael tugged on his towel to keep it from falling off. "I'll give you guys some privacy so you can talk."

Malachi put his hand up and said, "No, this concerns you too." Keilah and Michael looked at each other in confusion. Malachi shoved his hands into his jacket pockets. "Look, Keilah. I know I haven't been the brother I should've been since you've been out on your own. I'm going to be honest with you and say I don't think any man will be good enough you, but I'm going to try and let you live your life and not interfere. Bottom line, I want to see you happy. You're my sister, and I love you regardless."

Michael walked over and shook Malachi's hand. "I appreciate that, Malachi. Keilah means a lot to me, and whether you guys want to believe it or not . . . I do love her very much."

Keilah smiled and then walked over to Malachi and hugged him.

"Thank you," she whispered. "Now if you don't mind, could you please get the hell out of here so we can get back to what we were doing?"

Embarrassed, Michael yelled, "Keilah!"

She clutched her towel, turned to him and winked seductively. "It's okay, baby. I'm a full blooded woman with needs and desires just like theirs."

Malachi grunted and turned toward the door. Keilah saw the agony in her brother's face and couldn't help but laugh out loud. "Malachi, I'm sorry. You know I enjoy messing with you guys."

Before going out the door, he smiled. "I am glad you're home, little sister. I'll see you guys tomorrow."

"Later," Michael replied as he closed the door behind him.

He turned to Keilah and leaned against the door. "Now that was interesting."

Without responding, she walked toward him seductively and removed his towel. She then let her own towel fall to the floor. Michael slowly scanned her curvaceous body and smiled. He sprinkled her shoulders and neck with light kisses.

"You're driving me crazy, Keilah Chance."

She held onto him tightly and nibbled on his ear. "Then what are you waiting on?"

Michael kissed Keilah all the way back into the bedroom until they fell upon the bed. "You're perfect, Keilah."

She giggled. "No, I'm not."

Michael stopped kissing her for a moment and looked at her seriously. "Yes, you are. You're the answer to my prayers in more ways than one."

"That's deep, Michael."

He started kissing her again. "It's the truth."

Keilah closed her eyes and let out a soft moan when Michael kissed lower. He felt her body tremble when he ran his tongue across her navel. "Do you like that, sweetheart?"

She withered and whispered, "You know I do."

He kissed her lips as he moved between her thighs. "Michael, wait a second."

Michael pushed her legs further apart. "But I want you now."

Keilah pushed him off of her body. "What is wrong with you, Michael? You know we don't have sex without a condom."

He caressed her thigh and smiled. "What's the problem? You're on birth control."

Keilah scooted off the bed and angrily picked her towel off the floor. "Stop acting ignorant, Michael. Getting pregnant is not my biggest worry."

Michael scooted off the bed and walked over to her. He wrapped his arms around her waist and said, "I'm sorry I took our relationship and you for granted, Keilah, but I will say this. I know I love you and I hope at some point you feel the same way about me. You're the one and I trust you."

Keilah couldn't believe what she was hearing. "Michael, we haven't known each other long enough for you to try something like that without discussing it with me. You can't just assume it's OK to have unprotected sex with me."

His kissed her on the cheek and said, "You're right. It's just that you make me lose control of my senses when I'm with you. Keilah, you're so sexy and beautiful that that a man would have to be a fool not to want to feel every part of you."

She stepped out of his embrace, walked over to the dresser and pulled her lingerie out of the drawer. As she got dressed she said, "That's flattering, but my life means more to me, and it should to you."

"OK, I see you're angry with me and I don't want it to ruin our night. I apologize."

Keilah climbed into bed and said, "Let it go, Michael. I'm tired. Good-night."

Michael stood there scratching his head before he slid into his pajamas. He'd messed things up with Keilah tonight but hoped to make it up to her tomorrow. "Good-night, Keilah."

Hours later Keilah tossed and turned as she lay next to Michael who had begun to snore. She found herself wide away and unable to sleep, so she eased out of bed, slid into her robe, poured herself a glass of wine, and walked out onto the balcony. The late night breeze caressed her skin and tousled her hair. She took a sip of wine and looked out at the sleepless city. As she stood there, she thought about her childhood once again and so many memories came back to her like a flood. One such thought was the curiosity she always had about the father. Her brothers would tell her just about everything she wanted to know about Joe Chance except the events surrounding his death.

Keilah poured herself another glass of wine, sat down in the lounge chair, and closed her eyes. There was so much she wanted to know about her father.

She sighed as she remembered one particular day when she was around eight years old. She'd cornered Genesis in the kitchen and quizzed him about their father.

"Genesis, tell me about my daddy."

He sighed with frustration as he open the refrigerator and sat the carton of orange juice on the bar.

"What do you want to know, Keilah?"

She pulled on his arm playfully. "I want to know everything about Daddy. When I asked Roman and Luke, they always say there's nothing much to tell."

Genesis tugged at her ponytail before reaching into the cabinet to pull out two small glasses. "They're right. There's not much to tell you. Daddy was in and out of our lives a lot, but he was a good daddy when he was here."

"Do you think he would've loved me if he hadn't died?"

Genesis poured the orange juice into their glasses. "Even though Daddy never laid eyes on you, he loved you, Keilah. He was in love with the promise of having a daughter one day, especially after having all of us. He just didn't live long enough to see just how beautiful and wonderful you are."

"Why did he have to die, Genesis?"

She was questioning him like an adult, and he didn't know how much information to reveal to her. "He died because there are people in the world who don't have respect for life, and they don't care who they hurt," he explained.

"Malachi said Daddy was gone a lot. Didn't Daddy want to be here with Momma? Didn't he love her? Why did he leave?"

Genesis sighed. Keilah was throwing a list of questions at him. "Yes, he loved Momma very much. He just had a hard time holding down a job, so he would leave us to go find work."

Genesis could see the sadness creeping into his sister's eyes. He picked her up and sat her on the barstool. "Keilah, Daddy was a good man, and I'm sorry you never got the opportunity to know him. You're a Chance, and we're survivors. We have to take care of each other. That's what's important."

Keilah hugged his neck and kissed him on the cheek. "Thank you, Genesis."

"You're welcome. Do you still have that picture we gave you of Momma and Daddy?"

She took a sip of her juice and nodded.

"Good. Then whenever you look at it, I want you to believe in your heart that Joe Chance was the kind of daddy you always wanted, OK?"

"I believe he was a good daddy like you, Luke, Roman, and Malachi."

Keilah's comment touched his heart and nearly brought him to tears. Genesis and his brothers tried to be the best fathers they could be for Keilah. They just prayed they made all the right choices for her so she would grow up to be a strong, educated, independent woman.

Keilah wiped away tears as she stood out on balcony of their hotel reminiscing about her childhood. She didn't expect her memories to upset her, but they had. She never doubted that her brothers had done a good job raising her.

However, she still couldn't help being saddened by the fact that she never got the opportunity to know her father and that she didn't have the chance to grow up with a mother. She stood up and finished off the last of the wine.

Feeling tense, she tried to massage her stiff neck. Seconds later, Keilah was startled when Michael's large, warm hands came in contact with her petite shoulders. He kissed the back of her neck and whispered lovingly to her.

"What are you doing out here all by yourself?"

She leaned back against his chest, allowing him to wrap her securely in his arms.

"I couldn't sleep, so I came out here so I wouldn't disturb you."

He gently massaged her shoulders and neck. "What disturbed me was waking up to find you missing from our bed. Keilah, I want to apologize again for being so presumptuous earlier tonight."

"Let it go, Michael."

He tilted her chin upward so he could see her eyes. It was obvious that she had been crying. Instead of questioning her, he kissed each eyelid and then her forehead. "I hope those tears are not because of me."

Keilah wiped a tear off her cheek. "No, I just have a lot on my mind."

"Well, I'm here for you if you ever want to talk about what's bothering you."

She closed her eyes and hugged his waist tightly. "Thank you, Ramsey."

He pushed her back and frowned. "Ramsey? Why did you call me Ramsey?"

Keilah was embarrassed, but she didn't panic. "I didn't mean anything by it, Michael. I was thinking about Ramsey because I didn't get a chance to call him back from earlier today. It's just a slip of the tongue."

Michael was still frowning. Keilah wasn't sure if he was buying what she was selling, but she remained calm.

"Just a slip of the tongue, huh?"

She smiled. "Of course. Ramsey was on my mind, and I just said his name instead of yours. It was an honest mistake."

Michael looked her directly in the eyes in silence. Keilah wished she could read his mind so she would know what he was thinking. He finally said, "Don't let it happen again."

As he walked back into their hotel room Keilah followed close behind. She couldn't believe what he'd just said. "Excuse me?"

Michael pulled back the comforter and climbed into bed. "I don't take well to my woman calling me by another man's name."

Keilah put her hands on her hips and said, "I told you it was a mistake, but if you want to make a big deal out of it, go ahead."

Keilah climbed into bed next to Michael and turned her back to him. Ramsey was definitely on her mind, but not for the reasons she explained to Michael.

"Keilah?"

She turned to face Michael and whispered. "Yes?"

"I know you would never let another man touch you while we're together, because if you did I don't know what I would do."

"It's been a crazy day, Michael. Let's just forget it and start fresh tomorrow. Deal?"

He kissed her tenderly on the lips and said, "Deal. Good-night, sweetheart."

"Good-night."

Keilah turned back over and let out a sigh of relief. She was glad Michael had interrupted her thoughts earlier about her father. It bothered her that their father's murder had gone unsolved for so many years. Somebody knew something, and she hoped to eventually find out who was involved because she wouldn't rest until she found out who was responsible for his death.

CHAPTER ELEVEN

The next day, Keilah and Michael met up with her brothers at their casino. While Keilah met in the conference room with her brothers, Luke gave Michael some complimentary poker chips to try his hand at the poker tables. Inside the conference room, the brothers had champagne chilling in a nearby bucket. There was a notebook positioned by each one of their seats, as well as a notepad.

Keilah walked in and jokingly said, "Dang. It looks like we're about to have a meeting with the president of the United States."

Luke closed the door and smiled at her. "We just might have to do that, sis."

Genesis, Malachi, and Roman chuckled as they took their seat. Luke sat at the head of the table since he was the oldest. He jotted down a few things before he began speaking. "OK, guys. Let's get this meeting started. First, I want say again how good it is to have our baby sister back home. Keilah, you're missed around here by not only me, but also the entire Chance family. You don't come home often enough, sis, so work on improving that next year."

Unified laughter from the brothers filled the room. Keilah tapped her pencil on the table and smiled without replying. Luke stood up and retrieved the champagne bottle, along with a handful of champagne glasses. He passed the glasses out to each of his siblings and began filling them with the bubbling liquid. After every glass was filled, Luke asked his brothers and sister to stand. He held his glass up and spoke softly.

"Today is a milestone for the Chance family. We've overcome some major obstacles in our lives and in this business. The Lucky Chance has prospered beyond any of our wildest dreams, and because of that we have been able to open our second casino. Keilah, you are our only sister, and we love you very much. It's because of our love for you that the grand opening wouldn't have been complete without you here. Welcome home, sis."

Tears filled Keilah's eyes as she took a sip of her champagne before setting it down on the table. Her brothers hugged and kissed her lovingly.

"I'm glad to be here with you guys, and I love you, too," she whispered as she wiped away her tears. Genesis handed her a handkerchief and kissed her on the cheek. "Thanks, Genesis. So, when can I see the new casino?"

Roman finished off his glass of champagne then wiped his mouth. "Not so fast, Keilah Chance. You can see the casino tonight when you step out on the red carpet. By the way, a limo will be picking you guys up at the hotel. This is going to be huge."

Keilah smiled and went into a slight panic. "I didn't know you guys were going all out like this. I need a dress, and Michael didn't bring a suit. We have to go shopping."

Malachi mumbled, "Just like a woman."

About that time, their attorney P.K. Sloan walked in. "Sorry I'm late. Traffic was hell on I-110."

"We were just getting started anyway, P.K.," Luke said. "You remember our sister, Keilah, don't you?"

P.K. walked over to Keilah and shook her hand. "Sure I do. It's good to see you, Miss Chance. Welcome home."

"Thank you, Mr. Sloan," she replied.

P.K. pulled a couple of documents out of his briefcase and said, "If you guys could help me out and sign these so I can make my next meeting, I'd appreciate it. I need to be back downtown in thirty minutes."

Luke said, "I think we can help you out."

"Thank you. Luke, these are the documents you wanted me to draw up. All I need is Keilah's signature, since you guys have already signed it. Keilah, just sign on the lines where your name is printed. This makes everything official."

Luke had had P.K. draw up papers giving Keilah sole ownership of the Special K Casino. They just hoped she wouldn't look at the forms too closely. Luke quickly scanned the documents and slid them over to Keilah. "Sis, before you run off to the mall, P.K. needs your signature on these for the casino."

She picked the forms up and asked, "What are these for?"

Luke took a sip of his champagne. "It's just a formality regarding ownership of the casino. They need a copy on file with all of our signatures. Yours is the only one missing."

Keilah quickly scanned over the paperwork as her brothers held their breath. Keilah didn't even notice their nervousness as she quickly signed her name on the dotted line. Her mind was on what kind of dress she was going to wear at the grand opening. The Chance brothers quietly finished off the rest of the champagne as Keilah signed the last document and closed the folder. She stood and handed the folder back to Luke, who passed it over to P.K.

"Do y'all need me for anything else?" Keilah asked as she grabbed her purse.

P.K. looked at the documents before placing them in his suitcase and said, "No, it looks like everything is in order. I think we have all we need from you, Keilah. It's good seeing you again."

Keilah shook his hand once more and said, "Thank you, and have a good evening. Well I'm out."

Luke said, "Have fun shopping."

"I will," she replied as she blew her brothers a loving kiss before walking out the door. "I love you guys."

The brothers blushed and smiled as Keilah rushed out the door to find Michael. Once she was gone, Luke turned to P.K. and his brothers. Genesis sat back in his chair and threw his pencil on the table. "Man, that was close. If Keilah had looked at those papers any closer, our surprise would've been ruined."

Luke opened the second bottle of champagne and sighed. "Keilah trusts us. I knew she wouldn't look at the paperwork too hard. Now, with that out of the way, Malachi, do you have all the security in place for tonight?"

"You'd better know it."

Luke turned to P.K. and asked, "Is this everything?"

P.K. stood and said, "Yes, that's everything. I'll get these on file right away."

"Thanks, P.K."

P.K. shook everyone's hand before hurrying out the door. He'd been their family attorney for over ten years, and he was very good at what he did.

After P.K. left the room, Luke went down his checklist and had each brother report on their assigned task in preparation for the grand opening. When they were finished, everyone except Luke exited the conference room and headed out onto the casino floor. As he sat there alone, he thought back over all their accomplishments and the long road they had traveled to get where they were.

* * *

Nearly thirty-years ago, Joe Chance and his friend Graham opened up a small but successful gambling house in the area. Luke and his brothers were busy trying to support their mother by working for Keytone. The brothers didn't want to get in deeper than they already were with Keytone. He gave them a huge offer, but they passed on it, much to his dismay.

Joe's partner, Graham, had inherited somewhat of a drinking problem, and within a year, it sent him to an early grave. After Graham's death, Joe tried to get his sons to work with him rather than Keytone to keep them out of trouble, but the money was too good for them to turn down. Luke and his brothers' plan was to work for Keytone for only a short time because they knew they were putting themselves in danger of getting robbed, killed, or arrested.

While Joe's gambling house was prospering, the boys wanted their own money to care for their mother and to establish their own business. Eventually, Joe convinced his wife to take him back so their sons would stop doing illegal jobs for Keytone. He also wanted to make amends for all the hurt he'd put on his wife and sons and start over as a family. In the end, Joe's sons gave in to their father and helped him open his first casino. It was small but became a huge success quickly, which had money rolling in for the Chance family. The casino profits were climbing fast, and Joe realized that with success also comes drama. All types of criminal elements—who saw the small casino as Joe did: a potential gold mine—tried to infiltrate the growing casino. With that in mind, Joe decided he needed a will in place to make sure his children would never be without financial security ever again. Joe felt like it was the least he could do after he abandoned his family in the past. Things were going great for the Chances, and it seemed that Joe was finally happy to have something go right in his life. He was able to take care of his family and have a business to call his own, but after about a year and a half, the unexpected happened.

One sunny afternoon, nineteen-year-old Luke Chance savored the smell of fried chicken as he walked down the street. The heavenly smell radiated from the smokestacks of Leroy's Chicken Shack. As he walked closer, he noticed a large crowd of people gathering on the next block. He also noticed a large number of police vehicles blocking the street as well. Curious, he joined the crowd of people to see what was going on. Making his way through the crowd, he pushed his way to the front and froze. The coroner was pushing a gurney with what appeared to be a body on it toward their vehicle. He couldn't take his eyes off it, and immediately his attention was drawn to the shoes sticking out from under the sheet. Almost immediately, Luke heard a familiar scream. It was his mother, and she was on the ground, distraught. Someone in the crowd had told Amanda the person killed was in fact Joe. Two detectives started questioning her even though it was obvious she was very upset. This angered Luke, because at the time, his mother was pregnant with Keilah, so he rushed to her side and to her defense.

"Ma'am, do you have any information on this homicide?" the detective asked.

Before she could reply, the officers were interrupted by a very angry young man.

"Leave my mother alone," Luke yelled.

Amanda was speechless at first, but when Luke embraced her she gathered enough strength to try and answer their questions. "It's okay, Luke," she said through sniffles.

"No, it's not okay. They can see you're pregnant."

The detective turned to Luke and asked, "Who are you?"

"This is my mother. Whatever you want to know, you can ask me," he stated boldly.

Amanda patted Luke on the chest and said, "No, Luke.

I'm okay. I can do this, and I need to know if that is your father."

The officer reached inside his pocket and pulled out a
notepad and pen. "In a moment, ma'am. What is your name?"

"Amanda. Amanda Chance. This is my oldest son, Luke."

Luke held onto his mother tightly and bit down on his
lower lip to keep it from trembling. He frowned and looked
the officers directly in the eyes. "Is that my daddy under that
sheet?"

The officer wouldn't look Luke in the eyes, and that was
all the confirmation he needed. His heart thumped in his
chest because he knew in that moment he had become the
man of the house.

The detective said, "Mrs. Chance, let me get you out of
this hot sun and off your feet. You'll be more comfortable in
my squad car."

Luke took his mother by the arm and led her over to a police car. He turned to the detective and said, "I need to know
if that is my father." He walked over to the coroner's van and
looked down at the gurney. The second officer joined Luke
at the van.

"Are you sure you want to do this, son?"

Luke stood there in deep thought for a moment before
answering. "I have to do it, officer."

The officer nodded at the coroner who reached over and
pulled back the sheet. Luke stood there, unable to move. It
was Joe, and whoever killed him wanted to make sure he was
dead. There was no way he could let his mother see Joe in
this condition. He had been beaten and shot multiple times,
and his throat had been slit. The officer finally spoke up and
snapped Luke out of his trance.

"Is that your father, son?"

Luke swallowed hard and nodded. He felt lightheaded, so
he bent over to try and get air into his lungs. He looked over
at his mother, who was still crying. The officer put his hand

on Luke's shoulder to comfort him. "Are you going to be okay?"

"Yeah. Who did this to my daddy?" Luke asked.

"We're working on it, son. We're interviewing anyone who could've been a witness, but right now it appears that robbery was the motive. When was the last time you saw your father?"

"Yesterday, around noon."

The officer asked Luke a few more questions before giving him his business card.

"Call me if you think of anything or need anything. We're going to do everything in our power to find out who murdered your father. I'm so sorry for your loss."

Luke took the card out of the officer's hand and tucked it inside his pocket.

"Thanks, man. Look, I need to get my momma home."

After giving the officer their address, he walked over to his mother and helped her out of the squad car.

"Come on, Momma. Let me take you home."

She looked up into Luke's eyes. "Is it Joe?"

"Yeah, Momma. It's him."

She fell against Luke and sobbed.

From that moment on, their lives were never the same. Amanda loved Joe very much in spite of his shortcomings. He'd become a much better father after he had started his business, and Luke believed that money was the reason he was killed, especially since his business was doing so well.

Sadly, neither Luke nor his brothers could ever get anyone on the streets to come forward and tell them who killed their father. It remained a thorn in their side for years. One thing he always told his brothers was that Joe didn't die in vain. Their father's death was the reason they were determined to make the family business the huge success Joe had always envisioned.

Luke's cell phone rang, snapping him out of his trance. He stood and answered the phone as he gathered his thoughts and the paperwork. He'd done enough reminiscing for one day and needed to go home and get ready for the grand opening.

CHAPTER TWELVE

Keilah found the perfect dress for the grand opening. It was a tea-length red halter dress with a plunging neckline. The three-inch-heeled Jimmy Choo sandals that adorned her feet made her appear even more statuesque than she was. Her hair was wavy and cascading down her back. As she sat there staring at herself in the mirror, she thought about Ramsey. Michael was in the shower so she picked up her cell phone and quickly dialed his number.

"Hello?" he answered

"Hey, Stone. What are you doing?"

"I'm getting ready to go to the firing range with some of the guys. What are you doing?"

She fingered her hair and said, "Getting ready to go to the grand opening of the new casino."

"That's great," he replied. "I'm sure you'll have a good time."

"Look, Ramsey, we didn't get to finish our conversation yesterday so I thought I would call and . . ."

Ramsey stood up, pulled his gun out of his desk, and put it

in his holster. "Now is not a good time. I'm on my way out, and so are you. We'll talk when you get back."

Keilah could feel the stress in Ramsey's voice. She looked toward the bathroom door. "Maybe you're right."

"Where's G. I. Joe?" he asked.

She solemnly replied, "In the shower."

"You don't sound very excited about tonight. You should be bouncing off the walls. This is a big deal for your family."

"I don't know what's wrong with me. I don't feel like myself at all."

Ramsey became somewhat concerned as he walked down the hallway to the elevator and pushed the button. "You're not getting sick, are you?"

"I don't think so."

Ramsey looked at his watch and said, "Well, don't overdo it tonight, and try to get some rest tomorrow, and maybe you'll feel better."

She played with the links on her diamond bracelet and said, "I hope so."

"Good. I can't wait to hear all about the grand opening. Now be careful, and I'll see you when you get back."

Keilah bit down on her lower lip and said, "Ramsey?"

He stepped inside the elevator and pushed the button. "Yeah?"

"You be careful too. OK?"

Just hearing Keilah's voice made Ramsey's heart swell. "I will. Tell the family I said congratulations."

"I will," she replied before hanging up the telephone. As she sat there, she didn't realize just how long she'd been on the telephone nor that she no longer heard the shower running. When she turned around, Michael was standing right behind her, which startled her. "Michael, I didn't hear you come in here."

He wrapped his arms around her waist and said, "That's obvious. How's Ramsey?"

"He's fine. Headed to the firing range," she informed him.

He caressed her cheek and said, "Enough about Ramsey. You look beautiful, Keilah."

"Thank you, Major. You're looking mighty handsome yourself. You dress fast."

"I have to in my business," he answered as he sat down on the edge of the bed and put on his shoes. He stood up and buckled his belt. Keilah made her way over to him and straightened his tie. He immediately ran his hands down her back, resting them on her hips. She looked into his eyes and smiled. "It's getting late, so we'd better get downstairs because the limo should be here at any minute."

Keilah walked over and picked up her purse. "I'm ready if you are."

Michael took one last look in the mirror and said, "Let's go, sweetheart."

The pair exited the room, and as soon as they entered the lobby, their limo pulled up in front of the hotel. Once outside, the chauffeur opened the door for them, and within seconds they were on their way. Keilah was unaware that she was in for the night of her life.

Ramsey and his friends, Ron and Bradford, made their way to the firing range. Once there, his friends noticed Ramsey's solemn mood.

"Why are you so quiet?" Ron asked as he looked over at Ramsey.

Ramsey put the clip in his nine-millimeter and said, "I didn't know I was."

Ron glanced over at Bradford, who was shaking his head. Bradford asked, "Is everything OK at the office?"

Ramsey looked at Bradford and frowned. "Why are y'all asking me all these questions? I'm fine. Now, are we here to shoot or gossip?"

Ron laughed as he put his goggles and earmuffs on for protection. "You have to admit, bro, that you're not your normal upbeat self. You're acting like you've lost your best friend."

Ramsey put his goggles and muffs on as well and said, "Maybe I have."

Bradford sat his gun down and folded his arms. "What's really going on, Ramsey? You can talk to us."

Ramsey took his earmuffs off and asked, "What did you say?"

"What's really going on? Did you and Keilah have a fight or something?"

"No, Keilah's in California visiting her family for the weekend."

"Does this have something to do with Keilah?"

Ramsey was beginning to get irritated with Bradford's questions. "What makes you think this has something to do with Keilah?"

Bradford picked up his gun and said, "It's just a hunch. So, does it have something do with Keilah? You told me she was dating some guy in the military. Is everything going OK with them?"

"I guess. I don't ask her anything about him," Ramsey replied.

Ron stepped in and asked, "Have you met him?"

"Yeah."

"So what do you think about him?" Ron asked.

"I don't like him. OK? Are you happy now?" Ramsey blurted out.

Ron picked up his goggles and said, "Is that's why you're in a funky mood?"

Ramsey didn't answer him at first. He sighed and said, "She took him to California with her to meet her brothers."

Bradford studied Ramsey's facial expressions and could see he was struggling with their questions. He calmly said, "Look, bro, I know you care about Keilah. Hell, you might even love her, but until you admit it to yourself, nothing's going to change. You and Keilah have been friends for years now, and if you want to take things to the next level with her, just talk to her before you lose out. Keilah's a fine woman and if you feel about her the way I suspect, then I know it has to be killing you seeing her kicking it with another man."

The threesome stood there in silence for a moment. Ramsey was the first to put on his earmuffs. Ron and Bradford slowly followed behind him. They went into their designated cubicles and started shooting at their intended targets. When their clips were empty, they pulled their cardboard targets in and inspected the results. All of them had done well, but it was Ramsey who had emptied his clip between the target's eyes and into the heart. Bradford took his protective muffs off and walked over to Ramsey's cubicle.

"Damn! That's some good shooting, Stone."

Ramsey inspected the cardboard piece and said, "Thanks, Bradford."

Bradford set his gun down and said, "Ramsey, I'm your boy and I know you better than anybody, so tell Keilah how you feel before she messes around and marry that guy or something. I'd hate for you to miss out just because you're stubborn and proud."

"What if she doesn't feel the same way I do?" Ramsey asked.

"You'll never know until you talk to her and find out," Bradford added.

Ramsey ran his hands over his face and then said, "I need to come clean and tell you guys something, and you better not repeat it."

"What is it?" Ron asked as he joined the pair.

Ramsey turned to them and said, "Keilah and I had a little thing going on for the past several months. It was supposed to be strictly physical, but things went a lot further than I expected."

"What do you mean it was supposed to be strictly physical?" Ron asked.

Ramsey sighed and said, "Keilah wanted me to be there for her during what she called her 'dry spell' until she met someone."

Bradford stepped forward and asked, "When you say 'be there for her,' you mean sexual, right?"

Ramsey put another clip in his gun and nodded.

"You lucky son of a bitch," Bradford replied. "No wonder you're acting so weird. You should've known you wouldn't have been able to walk away from a woman like her without getting caught up. I ain't mad at you, though, because I'm sure I would be acting the same way or worse, especially since she's dating someone else now. I don't have to ask you if she was off da hook, do I?"

Ramsey looked at his two friends and said, "No, you don't. She's the most amazing woman I've ever been with. Because of her, I'm even thinking about turning in my player's card."

Ron said, "I knew something was going on, because when I asked you to find out if Keilah would be interested in going out with me, you sort of frowned and squirmed in your seat. You're in love with her, aren't you?"

"I don't know," Ramsey answered with frustration.

"What do you mean you don't know?" Bradford asked. "A man always knows."

"I don't know," Ramsey repeated in an elevated tone.

Bradford stepped to Ramsey and said, "A woman like Keilah would get me to altar with no hesitation, and if you don't know whether or not you love her, something's wrong with you. All I'm going to say is if you're not sure about how you feel, you'd better figure it out and quick, because that soldier boy is pushing up on Keilah hard and fast. And you say he's out in Cali meeting the family? That's not good. You need to find out how she feels about you and fast," Ron admonished.

All of them put their goggles on. Ron patted Ramsey on the shoulder and said, "I'm rooting for you, bro. It'll work out, so don't worry."

"I'm rooting for you too," Bradford added.

All three of them dropped the subject, went into their cubicles, and reloaded their weapons for another round of target firing. After leaving the firing range, they went to a nearby restaurant for dinner before going their separate ways. When Ramsey got home he thought about everything that his two best friends had said to him. Maybe they were right and he should sit down with Keilah and find out exactly how she felt.

CHAPTER THIRTEEN

Genesis paced back and forth in the front of the casino lobby. The casino was full of patrons, and the guest of honor was running late. He pulled his phone out of his pocket, pushed a button, and spoke into it. "Roman, did you call Keilah's cell?"

"Yeah, she said they were on their way."

Genesis ran his hand over his head nervously.

"Hell, that was twenty minutes ago," Roman continued. "You know how long it takes Keilah to get dressed. Maybe she wanted to make a grand entrance."

"Whatever, y'all better get down here before she gets here."

"Chill, Genesis. We're on our way."

While Genesis waited for his brothers, he checked in with security. Minutes later, Malachi, Luke, and Roman turned the corner, and they all walked outside onto the red carpet to greet their beloved sister. Seconds later, her limo pulled up and came to a stop.

The brothers' hearts swelled with pride when they saw her step out of the car. She was absolutely beautiful and looked exactly like their mother. Roman had arranged for a videographer and photographer to capture the moment Keilah saw the casino. They were secure in knowing she wouldn't realize it was named in honor of her until the right moment. Michael stepped out of the limo and stood beside her. Both of them were taken aback by all the lights and flashing of the cameras. Patrons and spectators watched as the handsome Chance brothers met their sister on the red carpet.

"Oh, my God. This is beautiful. I had no idea it was going to look like this," Keilah said.

Luke kissed her, and with tears in his eyes, smiled. "Welcome to the Special K Casino, sis."

She tilted her head and looked at him in confusion. Luke pointed upward toward the marquee. Michael and Keilah looked up and saw the name of the casino in lights. Michael embraced her and pulled her close. "Baby, what an honor."

Keilah looked up at the glittering sign and tears immediately ran down her face. She jumped into the arms of her brothers with total excitement. "I don't believe you guys. I love it. Thank you so much."

Roman took her arm and twirled her around for the cameras. "You haven't seen anything yet, little sis," he said.

Luke put his hands up to get his siblings' attention and motioned for their wives to join them. "Wait, guys. There's something Keilah has to do before we go in, and we have to get pictures first. Come on, Michael. You stand next to Keilah."

Michael took his position next to Keilah, and the brothers stood behind them along with the women in their lives. One of the casino employees brought over a pair of gigantic scissors as two others stretched out a large yellow ribbon in front of the doors. Keilah did the honor of cutting the ribbon to officially open the Special K Casino. There was thunderous applause as the ribbon was cut, after which Keilah greeted the rest of her family members before walking through the doors.

Once inside, Keilah was again in awe. She immediately noticed the feminine touch to the décor. She turned to her brothers and dabbed her eyes with a handkerchief Michael had given her.

Luke smiled and gave her a loving hug. "You like?"

"I love it. You guys are amazing. I couldn't love you any more than I already do. I just wish Momma and Daddy could've lived to see this."

Malachi stepped forward and also hugged her. "Don't worry, sis. I have no doubt they're both looking down on us right now."

Genesis took a call over his phone and then interrupted them. "Hey, guys, everything's set up in the conference room."

"What about my tour?" Keilah asked.

Roman took her by the arm and led her toward an elevator. "First things first, baby girl."

They all piled into the elevator and watched as Luke slid a key into the special lock on the panel. Within seconds they stepped out onto a private floor above the casino. The entire family entered the room, which was filled with balloons, an assortment of food, and plenty of Cristal. Luke and Genesis popped a couple of bottles of the champagne and poured the clear liquid into everyone's glasses. Luke held his glass high and spoke softly.

"Tonight, we are one as a family, the way it was always meant to be. Tonight we reached another milestone by opening the Special K Casino in honor of our only sister, Keilah Chance. Keilah, we never doubted for one second that you would grow up to be a young woman who would touch the lives of many people; however, you have touched our lives more. That's why we wanted to show you our love by giving you the Special K Casino so you'll know just how much you mean to us. This casino is for you and your heirs, and we want you to make sure it is passed down for generations to come. Joe Chance had a vision for his children a long time ago that was on its way to becoming a reality when his life was cut short. We have been blessed to make sure his vision became a reality twice over. Tonight we raise our glasses to toast in honor of you and the memory of our father and mother, Joe and Amanda Chance."

There wasn't a dry eye in the room. Even the brothers found it hard to control their emotions. After comforting and congratulating each other, the family members enjoyed delicious chilled shrimp, mini quiche, and many other delicacies before Malachi and Luke gave Keilah the grand tour of her very own casino while Michael, Roman, Genesis and some of the other family members continued to celebrate upstairs.

The tour of the casino amazed Keilah beyond her wildest dreams. She was especially impressed that her brothers incorporated businesses within the casino that she loved as well as most women did. This was their ingenious concept to cater to female patrons, which in turn would bring in more male patrons. As they walked the floor of the casino, men and women alike praised the facility for its exceptional service and unique amenities. The men loved it because if the women in their lives were not into gambling, they could get pampered in the salon or spa, or shop in the shoe store or boutique.

As the group continued through the casino, they recognized some local entrepreneurs and professional athletes as they enjoyed the facility. They also noticed that some of the city's known street pharmacists were also part of the grand-opening crowd. Minutes later, they came face to face with the last person they wanted to see: Keytone and his two associates.

"Well, well, well, I see the Chance brothers have done it again. Congratulations," Keytone said as he held his hand out and waited for Luke to shake it.

Luke stared at Keytone and shoved his hands inside his pockets.

"Ah, come on, Luke. Can't you give your homeboy some love?" Keytone asked.

Malachi attempted to step forward, but Keilah discreetly grabbed his arm, stopping him. The last thing she wanted was to have her homecoming turn into an all-out brawl. Luke looked around before stepping closer to Keytone. "Keytone, this is a respectable business, and I won't have it tarnished by you or anyone like you."

"Come on, Luke. I'm just here to congratulate you on your new casino. You know we go way back. That has to count for something even though you guys ran out on me, but I'm willing to let the past stay in the past."

"I hope you mean that, Keytone," Luke responded.

Keytone looked over Luke's shoulder and spotted Keilah. "Keilah Chance, what a nice surprise. You're looking fabulous as ever."

Keilah stared back at Keytone and smiled. "Thank you."

He smiled and asked, "So, how's the bodyguard business doing?"

"It's doing well, Keytone," she replied with pride. "Thanks for asking."

Keytone smiled with admiration. "I'm sure you're good at what you do. It's not like you haven't had some great guidance from your brothers. But from where I'm standing, it looks like you're the one who needs guarding. You've grown up into a beautiful woman, Keilah, and I'm happy to see a hometown girl do well."

She lowered her head and blushed. "I appreciate that, Keytone."

Luke turned and noticed that Malachi was getting agitated with the conversation, so he felt he'd better hurry up and end it before things got out of hand. When the rest of the brothers along with Michael arrived on the scene, Luke knew he had to defuse the situation immediately.

"Look, Keytone, we all know Keilah has grown up, and

we're also proud of her accomplishments. I just want to make sure we understand each other, and I want you to stay away from her. Do you feel me?"

Keytone put a toothpick in his mouth and laughed. He was notorious on the streets, but he knew the brothers were just being protective and this wasn't the time to challenge them.

"I see you guys haven't changed a bit. Still treating little Keilah like she's a baby."

Malachi couldn't take it anymore. He stepped forward and yelled at Keytone. "Keilah has sense enough not to waste a minute of her time with someone like you."

Keytone shoved his hands into his pockets and laughed even louder. "You know, it hasn't been that long ago that you guys begged me for a job and I helped you guys out. You seem a little ungrateful to me, but that's okay. Look, I'm cool with you guys, but for some reason you have a problem with me. Now if you don't mind, the poker table is calling my name. Keilah, it's good seeing you again, and good luck with your business."

She nodded without speaking, and they all watched as Keytone and his associates made their way toward the poker tables. Malachi sighed as the rest of the Chance brothers, except for himself and Luke, dissipated into the crowd. Luke took Keilah by the arm and attempted to lead her across the room. "Come on, let's finish your tour."

She pulled away from him and looked at Malachi. "Why do y'all always have to embarrass me like that? Keytone was right. You guys act like I'm still a little girl needing your protection. I wish you would stop treating me like a child."

Malachi grabbed her by the shoulders and turned her toward him. "Keilah, Keytone is dangerous, and you can't take your eyes off him for a second. We used to work for him, so we know what we're talking about."

Keilah couldn't believe her ears. She pulled away from

Malachi and asked, "Have you ever heard of people chang-ing?"

Malachi and Luke were stunned. Malachi gave her a look that could kill. "Have you lost your damn mind? We know him better than anyone, and believe me, he hasn't changed."

"But what if he has, Malachi?"

Luke put his hands up to diffuse the situation. "Keilah, stop yelling. Look, you have to understand that we saw things, unpleasant things, when we were associated with Key-tone, and that's a life we don't want any part of ever again."

She folded her arms and let out a breath. "That was a long time ago, Luke."

Luke and Malachi stared at her in amazement. They were shocked to hear Keilah defend Keytone after everything they'd told her about him. Unbeknownst to them, she knew a different side to Keytone, a side that she had been familiar with since she was a little girl. Yes, she'd seen his police record and read the newspaper articles, but he had never been convicted of any of the things he'd been accused of.

Luke sighed and said, "Let's all calm down. This is sup-posed to be a happy occasion. Malachi, we'll keep our eye on Keytone like we've always done. Keilah, stop acting so god-damn defiant. We know you can take care of yourself, but don't for one second think you're invincible or that Keytone has changed his ways."

She lowered her head and sighed. "I'm sorry. I just hate to see you guys carry around so much anger for one person, and I don't mean to give you a hard time."

Luke took her by the hand and smiled. "Apology accepted. Now come on. Let's gamble and have some fun."

Malachi was still angry that Keilah would defend someone like Keytone, and just as he followed the pair around the corner, he noticed another familiar face looking their way. He tapped Luke on the shoulder to get his attention. "Luke, is that X and his crew?"

Luke stared across the room in the direction of the young man, then turned away. "Yeah, that's him."

Keilah followed Malachi's gaze curiously. "Who's X?"

As they walked off together, Luke sighed before responding. "His name is Xavier, but he's known as X on the street. His dad and Joe were friends, but he's just another thug trying to make a name for himself. He usually hangs out at a railyard on the outskirts of town. I think his family has some businesses out there."

Keilah looked back over her shoulder at the young man who held up his drink and winked at her from across the room.

It was nearly three AM when Keilah and Michael called it a night. It had been a night of fun and gambling, and now they were exhausted. They said their good-byes to the rest of the family and climbed inside the limo for the ride back to their hotel. Unbeknownst to the pair, their every move was being tracked.

Chapter Fourteen

The next morning, Keilah woke up extra early to get her workout in before meeting back up with the family. Just as she exited their hotel room, her cell phone rang.

"Hello?"

"Good morning, Keilah. I thought I would check in to see how everything went last night and to see if you were feeling better today?"

Keilah pushed the button for the elevator and smiled upon hearing Ramsey's voice. "It was beautiful, Ramsey, and for the record, I'm feeling much better. Thanks for asking."

"I didn't mean to call you so early, but I know how you like to work out, so I figured you were already up," he replied.

"You're right. I'm on my way down to the fitness room now."

"What did your brothers say about Michael?"

Keilah sighed and said, "They don't like anybody I date, Ramsey. Of course they feel like he's too old for me, but when you look at it, there's not that much difference in our ages."

"Who gave you the hardest time?" Ramsey teased.

Keilah giggled. "Do you have to ask? You know it was Luke."

Ramsey laughed. "Well, don't be so hard on him. You're like his daughter more so than his sister, and he only wants the best for you."

"I know, and I appreciate it so much, but my brothers definitely need to lighten up."

"Maybe they see something in Michael that you don't."

"That would make me blind as hell, wouldn't it?" she replied with a smile on her face.

"Keilah, I know you've only been gone for about twenty-four hours, but I miss you around here."

"That's so sweet of you and just so you know, I miss you too. I'm having a great time with my family—well, I am when I'm not arguing with my brothers over stupid stuff."

"Stop being a hard-ass, and listen to them. You know they mean well," Ramsey replied.

"I know, but they really know how to push my buttons."

"Tell me something I don't know. By the way, some of your regulars are missing you, too, and we picked up a few new clients. When you get back, we need a meeting to discuss scheduling assignments."

Keilah looked at her watch and said, "Sounds good. So why are you up so early?"

"I couldn't sleep," he admitted. "So I thought I would get some work done, and then I'm going to go work out myself."

Keilah stepped out of the elevator and walked through the lobby and down the hallway to the exercise room. She was so into her conversation that she didn't realize she was being followed.

"Yeah, I noticed you getting a little thick around the mid-section."

Keilah was joking with Ramsey, and he knew it. He had a rock-hard, chiseled body that she was very familiar with. Ramsey spent countless hours defining his body and was nowhere close to being out of shape. He stood and laughed. "Yeah, Keilah, just like you and your beer belly."

Keilah laughed at Ramsey's comment. "Seriously, I am so ready to get back to D.C."

"Don't rush back. Spend some time with your family. They love you, Keilah, and if they didn't care, they wouldn't be making fools of themselves like they do. Remember, they raised you, and you've been their responsibility for almost all of your life."

Keilah let Ramsey's words sink in and understood that they were right on the money.

"Thanks for bringing me back to reality, Ramsey."

"You're welcome."

"Oh, you know that grand opening of the second casino I was telling you about?"

Ramsey made himself a cup of coffee and said, "Yeah, what about it?"

"They gave it to me. It's called the Special K Casino."

He took a sip of coffee and then smiled. "Get the hell out of here. Are you serious?"

Keilah laughed with pride as she punched in a series of numbers on the treadmill and started jogging. "I was just as shocked as you are. You should've seen Michael's face."

Ramsey sat back down and turned on his computer. "I'm sure Michael was very impressed. Your brothers don't expect you to run it, do they?"

Keilah shrugged her shoulders and said, "Surely not. They know I don't live here anymore and that I have a business to run in D.C. Besides, there are enough of them to manage it without me."

"You're right, but you need to clarify that with them because you and I both know they've been trying to get you to move back home for some time now."

Keilah thought about what Ramsey said for a moment and realized he was right. "I'll talk to them about it later today."

Ramsey logged on to his computer and said, "So, where's your loverboy?"

Keilah smiled. "He's asleep."

Ramsey grimaced at the thought of Keilah and Michael together. "I guess you guys stayed up late celebrating, huh?"

"Something like that," she replied as she entered the fitness room and climbed onto the treadmill. "He had a good time."

"I bet he did. Well, I can't wait to check the casinos out. I know they're some of the best in the nation," Ramsey said.

"They are," she answered as she punched a series of buttons and started jogging. "So, Stone, have you heard from Andria yet?"

"Where did that come from?" he asked.

Keilah giggled. "I just thought I would ask since you're all up in my business. She was pretty angry with you the last time you were together, wasn't she?"

"Sort of," he admitted. "I haven't heard from her, but I have a strange feeling she'll raise her ugly head sometime in the near future."

"You and I both know she's nowhere close to being ugly, but I know what you mean. You're going to need my services one day just to protect you from some of those future stalkers you're dating, including Andria. You're very charming, Ramsey Stone. I know that from experience, and I also know you have the gift of pleasure that's hard for a woman to give up."

Ramsey raised one eyebrow and asked, "Is that so?" Had Keilah given him a clue to her feelings for him? Maybe he should test her.

"Oh, yeah. It's so. Seriously, Ramsey, be careful. Fatal attraction is real."

"If you were mine I wouldn't have to worry about stalkers, now would I, Miss Chance?"

Keilah's heart pounded hard in her chest. Ramsey was

playing a game of cat-and-mouse with her. "Don't be so sure, Stone, because if I was your woman and thought there was a chance that I had some competition, it would be on."

"If you were mine, you wouldn't have to worry about any other woman because no one can compete with you," he answered seductively.

A huge smiled appeared on Keilah's face. Ramsey was obviously flirting with her, and it sent shivers all over her body. "See, that's why I love you. You know exactly how to stroke my ego."

Now Ramsey's heart was beating wildly in his chest. He wanted to stroke more than just her ego, and he prayed she would give him the opportunity once again.

"Is that the only reason that you love me?" he asked softly.

Keilah continued to play the game with Ramsey, and then she realized it might not be a game. She decided to cut things off until she could analyze what was going on more closely. "Of course not, Ramsey. You offer so many other reasons for me to love you."

The pair was silent for a few seconds. Keilah felt like something major was getting ready to happen, and so did Ramsey. But just when he was about to get up the nerve to question Keilah about their relationship, she said, "Hey, partner, you're keeping me from getting my workout on. Can I call you back when I'm done?"

Ramsey scolded himself discreetly for letting another opportunity slip away. "I'll be here. Don't overdo it. You call your brothers extreme, but you're just like them."

With a smirk on her face, she replied, "Bye, Ramsey."

Ramsey stood and gulped down the first cup of coffee. "Good-bye, Keilah." After hanging up the telephone, he leaned back in his chair and exhaled. His conversation with Keilah had left him drained even though nothing was revealed. He slammed his fist down on the desk and immediately refilled his cup before he started working on his computer.

Keilah tucked her cell phone inside her pocket and put her iPod earplugs in her ears. The conversation she'd just had with Ramsey left her wondering about him, but she would wait until later to give it deeper thought. She was in a full sprint and now able to totally concentrate on her workout. After about thirty minutes, Keilah lowered the speed so she could jog for the last thirty minutes. Once she was finished, she stepped backwards off the treadmill, but she was blinded by something thrown over her head. She fought off her attackers fiercely and was somehow able to knee one of them in the groin. She could hear him moan in agony as he fell to the floor. The other man grabbed her, and Keilah did everything she could to get whatever was covering her head off. Before she could, one of the men tripped her, knocking her to the floor. He held her on the floor with the weight of his knee, making it hard for her to breathe.

"Stop fighting before you make me hurt you," her assailant yelled. Keilah could still hear the other man moaning on the floor beside her.

"Hey, man, get up so you can help me with her," the man yelled as he continued to keep Keilah pinned to the floor.

She knew she had paralyzed one of them with the hard kick to the groin. Now if she could just get this one off of her so she could do what she did best. She continued to struggle against the man until she was able to raise her leg and kicked him in the back of the head, which caused him to fall away from her.

"Dammit," he yelled. "Grab her."

Keilah crawled across the floor to get away so she could remove the item that was covering her head. This time she was successful and came face to face with two very large men. When they charged at her, Keilah grabbed one of the five-pound weights off a nearby rack and hurled it toward them, striking one of them in the head. The man yelled out in pain and was somewhat dazed as he dropped down to his knees.

"I see you like it rough. If that's the way you want it, that's the way I'm going to give it to you," the second man said as he lunged at her.

His efforts were all in vain, because Keilah kicked him so hard in the chest it caused him to stumble backwards and fall over a rack full of weight equipment. Keilah hoped the loud noise would alert security so they would come investigate or at least give her some backup. In the meantime, she was doing everything she could to keep the men off her. By the time she turned back to the first man, he had a gun pointed directly at her. "Chill, bitch, before you make me do something I'll regret."

Keilah realized she was at a disadvantage, at least until she was in a position to make a move. Seconds later, voices were heard coming from the end of hallway.

One assailant helped the other up and yelled, "We gotta go, man. Five-o is on the way."

The second man, still dazed, stumbled toward the doorway. Before walking out, the first man turned and said, "Tell your brothers this shit ain't over, and if they know what's good for them they'll take the deal."

Keilah was angry and confused by what just happened to her. By the time security guards made it to the exercise room, the men were gone. The guards attended to Keilah to make sure she was unharmed. Once they found out she didn't need medical attention, they questioned her about the assault, filed a report and called the police. She pulled her cell phone out of her pocket and dialed Michael's phone, and shortly he was by her side. He was frantic, but did his best to comfort her. Minutes later, local authorities arrived to accompany hotel security and the pair back to the fitness room so Keilah could give them the details of the incident. Once the authorities finished taking their report, they explained to Keilah that they would review the hotel's security tapes and do everything they could to find out who had assaulted her. After thanking them for their help, Michael escorted Keilah back to their room for a closer examination. He started with the obvious bruising on her neck.

"I'm fine, Michael. You don't have to fuss over me."

He ignored her as he inspected her neck and arms. "They could've killed you."

She stood and removed her T-shirt.

"What the hell happened to your chest?"

Keilah looked down and explained in detail how she got the mark on her chest. "One of the guys held me down with his knee."

Michael gently ran his hand over the area and let out a breath. He was doing everything he could to hold back his anger. "Sweetheart, maybe you need to have a doctor look at you. Does it hurt?"

"Just a little bit, but after a soak in the tub, I'm sure it'll feel better. I'll be okay. Don't worry, Michael, I'm used to getting bumps and bruises like this all the time."

Michael cupped her face and looked down into her eyes. "I don't care. This was different and not related to your job. You do know what I'll do to them if I get my hands on the people responsible for this, don't you?"

She wrapped her arms around his neck and nuzzled his neck. "I know, and it's sweet that you want to defend my honor. Those guys better be glad they grabbed me from behind."

Michael released Keilah so she could retrieve some clothes out of the closet.

"You know you need to call your brothers and tell them what happened."

She turned to Michael and nodded in agreement. "I

know, but what's crazy, Michael, is that one of the guys said something about how my brothers 'better take the deal' or something like that."

Michael frowned. "So this was about them and not a random act?"

She walked toward the bathroom and then turned. "That's what it looks like."

"Why didn't you tell the police so they could look into it?"

Keilah lowered her head. "I know I should've told them, but I want to look into things myself. Whoever did this probably followed us from the casino last night."

"So they attacked you just to send a message to your brothers?"

She threw a towel over her shoulders and said, "I don't know, Michael."

"If it's true, that's some bull," Michael yelled.

Keilah walked further into the bathroom, and Michael followed. Keilah sat on the side of the tub and started filling the tub with hot water and a few capfuls of bath gel. She knew exactly who could help her find out what this was all about. The problem was doing it without her brothers knowing.

"Keilah? Did you hear what I said?" Michael asked as he paced the floor. "Maybe we need to get back to D.C. before those thugs try something again."

She tested the water's temperature and said, "If you want to go back to D.C., go ahead, but this is my home, and when someone threatens me or my family, I'm not going to run away from it."

He folded his arms and said, "So I noticed."

Keilah looked up at him and saw the stress in his face. "Michael, I have to find out what's going on. If this thing is not handled delicately, my brothers will turn this city into a war zone until they find out who did this to me."

Michael knelt down in front of her and took her hands into his. "Can you blame them?"

She caressed his cheek and smiled. "You're so sweet, Michael, but we have a way of handling things in our family. But I appreciate you being here for me."

Michael kissed her cheek. "Like I said, I love you, Keilah. I'd do anything for you."

She stared at him. Could this man love her as much as he said he did even though they hadn't known each other very long? Maybe she had underestimated Michael Monroe and hadn't given him the benefit of the doubt. With Ramsey, she knew without hesitation that he loved her, probably more than she was willing to admit to herself. But he'd never spoken to her about marriage. Michael seemed to know for a fact that she was the one for him and would be ready to marry her at the drop of a dime.

"Michael, I can tell you're a good man, but I don't want you to get caught up in this."

Michael kissed her and gave her another loving hug.

"I'm already caught up in it. I'm just glad you weren't hurt worse than you were."

"Thank you. Now, get out of here so I can soak in these suds. When I get out, we can go find my brothers and tell them what happened."

He released her and walked toward the door. "OK, but don't stay in there too long."

She smiled and said, "I won't."

Michael closed the door behind him. Keilah removed her clothes, eased into the hot, sudsy water, and closed her eyes. She had a strange feeling that sent chills over her body, a feeling that her life was in store for some changes that would take her on a roller coaster ride. She whispered, "Hold it together, Keilah. You're a Chance, so act like it."

CHAPTER FIFTEEN

Xavier, better known as X, twirled around in his chair and stared at the two large men known on the street as Slim and Baby Dee. X, who was in his late twenties, had come a long way from being a hoodlum on the street corner. He had his eyes on bigger and better things, and at the moment his eyes were on Slim and Baby Dee. "You didn't hurt her, did you?"

Slim was first to speak up with his deep, bass voice. "She might have a couple of bruises, but it's her fault because she put up a struggle. Hell, X, she's in better shape than we are. That chick is no joke, and because of her, I might not be able to have any children since she kicked me in the groin. I can barely walk."

X, dressed in the latest Rocawear attire, frowned as he rose from his chair. He took his eyes off the men temporarily as he walked over to the window and looked down on the street below. "I thought you understood me when I said don't hurt her."

"We tried not to hurt her, X, but a couple of times she almost got away. We were trying to keep her from seeing our faces, but she got the pillowcase off her head anyway. She wasn't an easy take-down at all."

He turned to the men. "What you're saying is that she can identify you?"

"Well . . . yeah," Slim replied.

Xavier laughed. "She won't do it though. I know her type. If anything, she's trying to track you down on her own. What a woman. Never underestimate her because she's got the streets in her and can be deadly if she has to. You guys got off lucky. She makes her living being a hard-ass as a body-guard in D.C., and my sources tell me she's one of the best in the business."

Baby Dee and Slim stood silent as X made his way back over to his chair.

"Did you get a chance to deliver my message to her?"

Baby Dee spoke up this time. "Yeah, I delivered it."

X smiled and laid his nine-millimeter on his desk. "Good. I'm sure she's wondering what it meant, especially since there is no deal, at least not yet. Keep an eye on her. I don't know how long she's going to be in town, but I'm sure she won't leave until she finds out why she was targeted and what it has to do with her brothers."

Slim and Baby Dee turned to walk out of the room.

"Remember, I just want you guys to tail her for now," X re-iterated. "Oh . . . one more thing." The two men turned to him and waited for him to speak. X tossed a wad of money to them. "Here's a little something for your trouble."

In unison, Baby Dee and Slim replied, "Thanks, X."

Before they disappeared through the door, Baby Dee turned and asked, "What about her brothers?"

X eyed them with seriousness. "Let me worry about the Chance brothers."

The two men walked out of the room, leaving X with his thoughts. He was prepared to go to war if he had to, and he knew there was a possibility it could be fatal.

* * *

Across town as Keytone was preparing to step out his door, his telephone rang.

"Yeah?" he answered with an agitated tone.

"We need to talk. Can you meet me at Starbucks on Wilshire Boulevard in twenty minutes?"

Keytone smiled. "I thought you was warned to stay away from me?"

"This is serious, Keytone."

"OK . . . OK . . . calm down. I was just joking. I'll be there."

He stood, tucked his cell phone inside his jacket, and headed out the door.

Twenty-five minutes later, Keytone walked into Starbucks and made his way over to the table where his lovely companion was waiting for him. He leaned down and kissed her on the cheek. "Hey, sweetheart. What's up?" he asked.

Keilah frowned at Keytone as he sat down across from her with a big grin on his face.

"Don't 'sweetheart' me. Why were you trying to pick a fight with my brothers last night? You know they can't stand you."

He plucked a piece of lint off the arm of his jacket and smiled. "If I remember correctly, Malachi was the one getting all hostile. I was cool. You know me."

"You didn't help matters, Keytone, and you know it."

He leaned forward and touched her hand lovingly. "Well, at least I know one Chance sibling cares about me."

Keilah pulled her hand away from him and lowered her head without responding. Keytone studied her body language for a few seconds before speaking. "When are you going to tell your brothers our little secret?"

A slight panic came over Keilah, and her head jerked upward.

"I don't know, Keytone, but when I feel that bit of information needs to be shared with them, I'll do it."

Keytone raised his hands in defense. "I just asked, Keilah. Chill."

"Listen, I asked you to meet me because I know you're up on everything going on around here and on the streets. Have you heard anyone talking about making some type of deal with my brothers?"

"No, I haven't. Why are you asking?"

Keilah sighed. "Something weird happened to me this morning."

This got Keytone's undivided attention. "What do you mean?"

She folded her arms and struggled with her words. "I got jumped by two guys in my hotel early this morning when I was in the fitness room."

The smile on Keytone's face was immediately replaced with a scowl. He sat up in his chair. "You mean to tell me that somebody put their hands on you?"

She cleared her throat and nodded.

Keytone leaned forward and angrily yelled, "Where was that so-called military man of yours when all of this was going on, and why is he letting you wander around town all by yourself now? I don't even know why you're with him if he can't protect you or keep an eye on you. I need to put a bullet in his head for not being there for you. You could've been killed, Keilah. Damn."

Keilah could see that Keytone was starting to draw attention over to their table, so she grabbed his hand and gave it a squeeze. "Keytone, lower your voice. I'm okay. Besides, Michael was in bed asleep when it happened so he didn't even know I had left the room. I always get up early in the morning to work out. Yes, I let my guard down, but I never expected to get jumped in my hotel."

He put his hands over his face and rocked back and forth in his chair, visibly shaken. Keilah could see he was about to explode again in anger, but he restrained himself. "So why is he letting you drive around by yourself now?"

Keilah smiled. "Letting me? I'm a bodyguard, Keytone, and I'm at home. I know this city better than Michael does. Besides, my guard is up now, and you know how stubborn I am. I told Michael I needed some air. He wanted to come with me, but I insisted he stay at the hotel until I got back. What could he do?"

"I guess you have a point. But if he were a real man he would've come with you regardless of what you said. Look, forget about dude. I want you to tell me exactly what happened and what those guys looked like," he asked as calmly as he could.

"I was working out in the fitness room, and they threw a pillowcase over my head. I didn't make it easy for them though. I was able to get it off and kick one of them in the groin. The other one caught a five-pound weight upside the head. They ran out when they heard the security guards coming down the hallway."

Keilah could tell Keytone was struggling to hold his composure.

"So you got a look at them?" he asked.

"Yeah."

Keytone stood and said, "Hold that thought. I need something to drink before I lose it up in here. What would you like to drink?"

"Whatever you get will be fine with me."

Keytone walked up to the counter and ordered two cups of Colombia Nariño Supremo coffee. After returning to the table, he sat their cups down and took his seat.

"OK, Keilah, what else did they do or say?"

Keilah finished telling Keytone what happened in the fitness room and what her assailants looked like. When she was done, she could see Keytone taking mental notes. "So if you see them again you can point them out?"

"I'll never forget those faces."

He took her hand into his and held it there. "Did they hurt you?"

She looked into his eyes and saw a man enraged. "I have a few scratches and bruises, that's all," she said.

Keytone could clearly see the bruising on Keilah's neck. He sat back down and let out a loud sigh. "You do know they're dead once I find them?"

"See, that's why I didn't want to tell you. Don't get crazy, Keytone. I just want you to see if you can find out who they were and what's going on."

Keytone sat there silently for several minutes in deep thought as he drank his coffee. He slowly scanned the room, which was full of patrons, before pulling out his .45 Magnum pistol. He checked the clip, and then quickly slid it back into place. All Keilah could do was sit there in shock. Trying not to draw any more attention, she whispered, "Keytone, please put that gun away before someone calls the police."

He looked at her with glazed eyes and put the gun back inside his jacket. "Keilah, like I said, when I find out who put their hands on you, they're dead. Do you hear me?"

Keilah's eyes widened. "No, I don't want you to do anything like that, just see if you can find out what's going on. Besides, I haven't even told my brothers yet."

Keytone stared at her without blinking his eyes. "Girl, you're crazy if you think I'm going to sit around and do nothing but interview people. We're past that, sweetheart, and whoever did this to you will pay."

Keilah didn't know what else to say to Keytone. He was a man with a ruthless reputation and most people knew not to cross him. Keilah finished off her cup of coffee and stood. "I have to go. I shouldn't have told you."

He also stood. "But you did tell me, and the situation will

be dealt with one way or another. Keilah, you came to me for help, now let me help you."

She couldn't hold back her frustration any longer. "Have you been listening to anything I've said? I came to you to see if you could find out information, that's it."

He stared at her with seriousness and then he laughed. "You know me, Keilah, which means you know I don't operate like that. I love you, and if I sit back and do nothing, what does that say about me?"

"I only came to you because I thought you might know something or could help me find out some information."

"Keilah, you came to me because you know I can help you. If those guys had killed you it would've broken my heart. I got this. OK?"

She looked up at him and saw sincerity. She knew her brothers hated Keytone, but she saw something in him her brothers didn't—a soft side. And once they found out the truth behind their relationship, they would go ballistic.

"Look, you can check into things, but don't do anything crazy," she pleaded.

He smiled mischievously. "Don't worry, sweetheart. I never do anything to someone that they didn't deserve. But I will tell you: When I find the bastards who put their hands on you, they're history."

Seeing that her pleas were falling on deaf ears, Keilah grabbed her purse and placed it upon her shoulder. "Whatever, Keytone. I don't have the strength to argue with you anymore."

Keytone pulled her into his arms and gave her a tender kiss on the cheek. "OK, I'm not going to promise you anything, but I'll try to stay in control. Are you happy now?"

Keilah smiled and before walking off she said, "Yes. Now be careful."

"I will, and you watch your back until we know what's going on."

Keytone watched as Keilah walked out to her car and drove off. As soon as she was out of sight, he pulled out his cell phone. "Yo, it's me. Get everyone together and meet me at the pit. We have work to do."

K eilah's meeting with Keytone was exhausting, but not as tiring as the one with her brothers would be. To try and regroup, she called Michael on her way over to Luke's house. Hearing his voice calmed her and brought her blood pressure back down. As expected, he was worried about her driving around Dennison alone, but she reassured him she was fine. After all, it was her hometown.

It took Keilah about thirty minutes to drive to Luke's subdivision. She didn't call ahead to let him know she was coming, not that she ever did. His house was always the central location of the family and seemed to have a revolving door for family and close friends. When she pulled into his driveway she noticed Genesis' car already there. Luke's wife, Sabrinia, was an excellent chef, and since her brothers were always looking for a tasty but nutritious meal, they always seemed to find their way over.

Keilah exited the vehicle and made her way around to the back of the house where she found Luke and Genesis eating a hearty breakfast beside the pool. They both stood when they saw her walking in their direction.

"Well, well, well, I didn't expect to see you up so early this morning, sis," Luke announced as he gave her a brotherly hug.

Genesis gave her a kiss on the cheek and then stuffed a croissant inside his mouth. Keilah sat down at the table and shook her head as she looked at all the food on their plates.

"I get up early every morning to work out, and it seems like you guys need to join me sometimes."

"Whatever," Luke replied as he sat back down to his meal,

which consisted of strawberry pancakes, sausage links, crois-
sants, eggs Benedict and more.

"Are you hungry?" Genesis asked as he buttered his croissant.

"Not really," she answered as she looked toward the house.
"Where is everybody?"

"The kids are at school and Sabrinia just left for work.
Where's Michael?" Luke asked.

Keilah picked up a fork and stole one of Genesis' sausage
links. She took a bite of it before answering. "He's at the hotel."

Luke and Genesis looked at each other curiously. "What's
going on with you? I don't like the vibe you're giving off,"
Luke said.

"Did you and Michael have a fight or something?" Genesis
asked.

Keilah turned to him and asked, "Why would think we
had a fight?"

"I just thought he would be with you, that's all."

Keilah finished off the sausage and sat the fork down.
"He's still a little tired from last night, so I told him to stay at
the hotel and rest."

Luke nodded and he raised his glass of orange juice to his
mouth. "I see."

Genesis noticed Keilah staring at his plate. "Dang, Keilah.
Let me fix you a plate before you eat up all my food. I know
you're hungry."

She smiled and stood up. "Thanks, but I can get it myself.
Do you guys need anything while I'm in the kitchen?"

"I'm good," Luke said.

"I could use more sausage, thanks to you," Genesis teased
her.

Keilah flicked out her tongue at him just like she'd done
when she was a little girl. Her brothers couldn't do anything
but laugh.

Once inside the kitchen, Keilah saw that Sabrinia had

brunch laid out like a restaurant, making it easier for self-serving. Once she had a couple of pancakes, several pieces of sausage, and some fruit, she rejoined Luke and Genesis poolside.

When she sat down, Luke looked over at her curiously. "What's that mark on your neck?"

Keilah put her hand up to her neck and lowered her head. "That's why I came over here."

"Did Michael do that to you?" Luke asked as he stood and balled up his fists.

"Sit down, Luke, and let me explain." She motioned for them to sit down.

"Explain what?" he yelled. "Genesis, let's go. I'm going to kill him."

Keilah knew that if she didn't hurry up and explain to her brothers what happened they would kill Michael and not give it a second thought.

Keilah's throat was dry, so she took a sip of orange juice before speaking. "OK, you two. There is something I need to tell you, but you have to promise you won't get all crazy on me."

"I'm not promising you anything. Now what's going on?" Luke asked with a strained tone.

She had to be delicate with her news. If she told Luke and Genesis the wrong way, they would turn the city upside down. Keytone was already on the rampage and having her brothers doing the same would be like throwing gasoline on a fire. Keilah got up from her chair and paced back and forth across the pool deck.

"OK, I'll tell you, but you have to wait until I'm finished before you say anything."

Luke folded his arms across his chest. "Get on with it, sis. We don't have all day."

"Will you two please sit down?" she asked before continuing.

Genesis sat down and picked up his glass of orange juice. He leaned back in his chair and waited for her explanation. Luke also sat down and stared at her.

"Well?" Genesis asked. "What's going on?"

"You guys know how I'm sort of a fanatic when it comes to working out, right? Well, I got up at five to work out in the fitness room at the hotel. When I got there, I wasn't alone like I thought I was."

She paused because she knew the rest of her statement was going to set it off. Genesis prodded her by asking, "Who else was there? Michael?"

Keilah nervously played with her hair. "No, he was still in our room asleep."

"Then who was it, Keilah?" Luke asked impatiently.

"Two men were there, and they jumped me from behind by throwing a pillowcase over my head."

Luke and Genesis sat there frozen, as if they were waiting for a punch line.

"What did you say?" Genesis asked as he slowly stood.

"I said I was roughed up by two men who jumped me from behind."

Luke was still frozen in his chair. He couldn't move or speak at first. When he did move, he wiped his mouth with his napkin and also stood. He walked over to Keilah and cupped her face so he could look into her eyes and inspect the bruising on her neck.

"Were you raped?" Luke asked.

Tears fell from her eyes. "No, I just got this bruise on my neck from the pillowcase and a few more scratches and bruises. I was able to fight them off, and I actually left one of them with a limp. I'm sorry I let my guard down."

Luke looked over at Genesis, who seemed to be trembling with anger. Luke led Keilah back over to the table and sat her down in the chair. He pulled his chair closer to her and held her hands.

"You have nothing to be sorry for, Keilah. We're the ones who let our guard down. Did you call the police? Why didn't you call me?"

"The police said they would review the surveillance tapes and get back to me as soon as they knew something."

"Did you get a look at them?" Genesis asked.

"Yes, after I got the pillowcase off of my head."

Luke ran his hands over his face. "Get your things and check out of that hotel right away. You're staying here," Luke demanded.

Keilah picked up a strawberry and took a bite. "Thanks, but no thanks. You and Sabrinia already have a full house with the kids, and so does Genesis and Roman. We'll just check into another hotel."

Genesis intervened by waving her off. "No more hotels, Keilah. I'm sure you guys can bunk with Malachi. It's just him in that big house, and I'm sure he would love to have you over anyway."

Keilah laughed. "I don't think so. You know we don't always see eye to eye."

"Malachi will be fine," Genesis said.

"I'll think about it, and I don't want you guys blaming Michael for me getting attacked, because he didn't even know I had left the room. He feels terrible about what happened and is already blaming himself."

"He should feel bad," Luke replied. "What did these those guys look like?"

"Look, before I get to that, there's more to what happened."

He paused for a moment. "What do you mean—more?"

"The guys who jumped me told me to tell my brothers if they know what's good for them they'd better take the deal. What deal are they talking about? Are you guys mixed up in something?"

Luke frowned. "I don't have a clue, Keilah, but we'll get to the bottom of it. You just get your things and get out of that hotel."

"I don't want you guys to get into any trouble over this," she pleaded.

Genesis held her hand and looked into her eyes. "They touched you, and that's all that matters to me. Luke, I'm out. Hit me up on my cell if you need me."

Luke nodded and said, "Call Malachi and Roman, and fill them in on what happened."

"Done," Genesis responded. "Keilah, do what Luke said and get out of that hotel right away. I'll call Malachi and set everything up."

She released his hand and said, "OK. I'll catch up with you later."

Luke started clearing off the table. "Hold up, Keilah. Help me put this food away and I'll ride with you."

CHAPTER SIXTEEN

Xavier's right-hand man, Romeo, pulled the midnight-blue Escalade into a parking spot at the front entrance of the East-Side Park. As they sat there in silence, the park quickly filled up with people.

"Yo, X, why did you want to come here?"

"I need to think," Xavier informed him. "Momma used to bring me here when I was a kid. She always said it was the perfect place to hear your thoughts, and she was right."

Romeo nodded in agreement with Xavier. "What are you going to do if the Chances don't take you up on your offer?"

Xavier lowered his sunglasses and stared at Romeo. "If they know what's good for them, they'll take my offer. Besides, I won't take no for an answer. This deal is non-negotiable."

Romeo laughed. "You know those guys are not going to let you just walk up in there and take over their casinos."

"They won't have a choice, and if they don't want to cooperate, then I'm sure that fine-ass sister of theirs can help persuade them to."

A couple of young women walked in front of Romeo's truck. One was dressed in a pair of denim shorts that revealed every curve she owned. Her top was lime green and sheer, falling just below her breasts and showing her diamond belly ring. Her braids hung down to her waist, and she had legs to die for. The other woman looked a few years older than her friend and was dressed more appropriately in a pair of jeans and a red spaghetti-strap top. Romeo leaned out the window and smiled at the young women. "Yo, ladies. You gon' holler at me or what?"

The more mature of the two seemed to be irritated by Romeo's outburst. She grabbed the younger woman by the arm and hurried her past Romeo's truck. Romeo burst out laughing. "Did you see that? I think that chick would've hollered at me if old girl hadn't been with her."

Xavier seemed distracted from the conversation. He wasn't looking at the two women nor listening to Romeo. Instead his mind was on the Chance brothers and the multi-million dollar casinos they owned.

"X, are you listening to me?" Romeo yelled.

Xavier sat up in the seat and let out a breath. "My mind is not on any shorties right now. I'm trying to figure out how I'm going to present my offer to the Chance brothers."

"Well, however you do it, they're not going to like it, so I hope you're ready to go to war."

Xavier frowned. "If it's a war they want, I have no problem bringing it. You feel me?"

It was at that time that Romeo's cell phone rang. He reached into his pocket and answered. "Yeah."

While Romeo talked to the caller, Xavier had a million things running through his mind, but his main focus was on the casinos he would soon own. Romeo hung up his phone and looked over at Xavier.

"Yo, X. Keilah just checked out of her hotel. Her brother, Luke, and that other guy were with her. Baby Dee lost them in traffic, so he don't know where Luke took them. If I have to guess, they went back to his house."

Xavier let out a loud sigh. "She'll resurface soon. Take me over to the Lucky Chance. It's time for me to have a little chat with the Chance brothers."

Romeo started up the truck. "Are you sure you're ready to do this now?"

Xavier looked over at Romeo, disgusted. "Why? You act like you're scared. Are you down or what?"

"Don't worry. I'm definitely down," Romeo snapped back.

"All I know is, I can't just roll up on guys like the Chance brothers. They're old school, and from I heard, they haven't always been legit."

Romeo laughed and asked, "Now who's acting scared?"

"Whatever, man. Let's roll."

Romeo pulled the Escalade out of the park into traffic and disappeared around the corner.

Luke pulled up in front of Malachi's house with Keilah and Michael. "Luke, are you sure Malachi is cool with this?"

He looked at Keilah with a smirk on his face and climbed out of the car. "He's your brother, Keilah."

Michael exited the vehicle and helped Luke remove their luggage from the trunk. "Luke, I appreciate everything you guys are doing for me and Keilah, but we don't want to impose on Malachi."

Luke took the luggage out of Michael's hand and smiled. "We got this, Michael. It's okay."

The trio was so deep in their conversation they didn't notice that Malachi had joined them in the driveway. "What's taking you guys so long to come in?"

Keilah walked over to Malachi and hugged his neck. "Thanks for letting us stay here with you."

He hugged her, lifting her off the ground. "You don't have to thank me. I needed a live-in cook anyway."

They all laughed and followed Malachi toward the house. When they got to the door, Malachi turned to Michael and asked, "You're not afraid of dogs, are you, Michael?"

Malachi had two huge German shepherds, but they were well trained, and he took very good care of them.

Michael took a deep breath and replied, "No, it's cool."

"In that case, Michael, you and Keilah are welcome to stay as long as you like."

"I appreciate that, Malachi," Michael replied.

Malachi's dogs, Bonnie and Clyde, met them at the door, curious to see what stranger was entering their domain. Bonnie was jet black and Clyde had the typical black and tan markings. Malachi looked back at Michael. "Michael, they're going to sniff you when you come in. They know Keilah and Luke's scent. Just be cool, and they'll go on about their business."

Michael did as he was told and the dogs did exactly what Malachi said they would. Minutes later, they all met out on the patio. While Michael and Malachi tossed balls to the dogs, Luke and Keilah watched from the railing as they enjoyed a glass of wine.

"Luke, where are the rest of the guys?"

"At the casinos. We rotate our shifts every week. This week, Genesis is running the Lucky Chance and Roman is handling your casino. Next week, Malachi will relieve Genesis, and I'll relieve Roman. It's not so bad, since we usually go by there anyway. Besides, we have good managers overseeing things when we're not there."

She wrapped her arm around her brother's waist. "Can you believe it? Daddy would be so proud of you guys."

Luke looked down at Keilah. "Daddy would be proud of you too, sis. Don't forget, you're doing your own thing, too."

"I know, but the casinos were Daddy's dream."

He kissed her forehead and said, "You were Daddy's dream."

She laid her head against his chest as she finished off her glass of wine in silence.

"Keilah, I don't know what's going on. Maybe it would be best if you went back to D.C. You don't need to get caught up in whatever is going on."

She walked over to the table, refilled her glass and sat down. "Luke, whoever jumped me put me in the middle of it, and I want to find out why."

He walked over and sat next to her. "I guess you didn't understand what I said, Keilah. I said stay out of this and let us handle it."

When Luke raised his voice, it got Malachi and Michael's attention. "Is everything OK over there?" Michael asked.

Keilah sat up in her chair and gulped down the remainder of her wine. She smiled and waved at Michael. "Everything's fine, baby."

Luke grabbed her firmly by the hand and whispered. "Keilah, I'm not kidding with you. If you want to play detective while you're in D.C. then go right ahead because I can't do anything about that, but when you're home, I can. Don't cross me on this, sis."

Keilah looked up into Luke's eyes and knew he meant business. She didn't want to defy or disappoint him, but she had a feeling he knew more about what was going on than he wanted to reveal. If only Keytone could find out what was going on, she wouldn't have to snoop around behind her brothers' backs. If not, she would have to do her own investigation and just pray they didn't find out.

"OK, Luke."

He scooted away from her. "I hope you mean that, Keilah, because I would hate to have to escort you back to D.C. myself tomorrow."

Her head snapped around, and when she looked into his

eyes, she saw red and knew he was very serious. She walked over and refilled his wineglass. "Don't worry, Luke. We're out of here on Monday anyway," she reminded him.

"I wish you could stay longer. Every time we get together we always argue the first few days. I don't like that, sis."

She smiled. "That's what brothers and sisters do. We're a passionate family. That's why we argue, but it doesn't mean we hate each other."

Luke leaned over the railing. "Oh, I know that. We all love very hard. I guess that's why you and Michael are getting along okay. Are wedding bells in the future?"

"I wouldn't say that because we just met. He's a great guy, but I'm not in love with him."

Luke studied his sister's facial expression and said, "I see."

She turned to him and said, "So when I do get ready to get married, are you going walk me down the aisle?"

He leaned against the railing and laughed. "Nothing would make me happier than to walk you down the aisle, but I'm sure your other brothers would have something to say about it."

"You're the oldest. You're supposed to do it since Daddy's not here."

He waved her off. "Traditionally, yes, but we all raised you, Keilah and I'm sure they'll want to be a part of it."

"They will be a part of my wedding. You know I wouldn't leave them out."

Luke put his arm around his sister's shoulder and recited the perfect solution. "How about this? Each one of us can walk you in, starting with the youngest brother. After they walk you down the aisle a few feet, they take their place up front as a groomsman. I would be the last to walk you to the altar and give you away. This way everyone's involved."

"But what about my bridesmaids?" she asked. "They'll need someone to escort them in."

Luke ran off the details like a wedding planner. "Not necessarily. A lot of weddings allow the bridesmaids to walk in alone. The brothers would be there to escort them out when the ceremony is over."

Keilah was speechless. What Luke had said just might work under their unusual circumstances. It would be heartwarming to have all of her brothers walk her down the aisle. "Sounds like a plan to me."

Malachi was out in the yard attending to his pool. Michael walked up on the deck with Clyde following close behind. He was clearly winded from playing with the dogs. "I see you two are making up for lost time," Michael pointed out.

Luke hugged Keilah's shoulders. "Yeah, and it's long overdue."

Michael kissed Keilah on the cheek as Clyde found a spot next to Keilah's chair. "Well, I'm going up to shower. Playing with the dogs got me all sweaty. Malachi assured me that this neighborhood is safe, so after I get dressed, I'm going to ride over to the casino with Malachi and play a little poker if it's OK with you."

"Go ahead, babe, because he's right. The weather is beautiful, so I think I'll just stay out here and enjoy this pool and Jacuzzi. You go and have fun."

Michael looked at Luke and asked, "Are you going to be here with her?"

"No, I have some errands to run, but I can swing back through and hang out with you."

Michael stood there pondering on his decision to leave Keilah alone. "Never mind, I'll stay here with you."

Luke laughed. "She'll be fine, Michael. I wouldn't say it if I didn't know it for a fact."

Keilah plopped down in the chair and stroked one of the German shepherds on the head. "He's right, Michael. Besides I have the dogs with me. You guys go and hang out.

This is a gated community, so no one's coming in that shouldn't be here."

By that time, Malachi had joined them on the deck. He reached for the wine bottle and then noticed it was empty. "What the hell? Y'all drank all the wine."

Keilah took the empty bottle out of his hand and tossed it into a nearby garbage can. "Please, I know you have a fully stocked wine cellar, so don't even go there, Malachi."

She was right. Wine collecting was one of Malachi's hobbies, and most people who knew him were surprised he took up such an unusual hobby because he always portrayed himself as a tough guy. Most fine collectors are usually the total opposite.

"That doesn't mean y'all have to drink it all up," Malachi teased. "Luke, you coming?" he asked.

"Yeah, I guess I could go by there with you guys for a minute but I have some other errands I need to run."

They all looked over at Keilah once more. She threw up her hands and said, "Go. I'll be fine. I hope you jackpot, Michael," she teased.

"So do I," Michael said before disappearing into the house. Malachi looked over at Keilah. "You do remember where I keep my firearms, don't you?"

"You mean your arsenal?" she joked.

"I see you're a comedian now," he responded sarcastically.

"All of that won't be necessary. I'll be fine. Just go. Bonnie and Clyde are here with me. Besides, all I'm going to do is take a swim and then a nap."

Malachi walked off without responding, leaving Luke with their sister. "Keilah, don't leave the house. We're not going to be gone long."

She pulled her sunglasses down over her eyes and said, "OK. I love you."

"I love you, too," he replied before entering the house.

The guys left thirty minutes later, and Keilah was so glad

to finally have the house all to herself. She quickly changed into her bathing suit and eased into the Jacuzzi. As she relaxed, she thought about Keytone and whether or not he'd found out any information. Her next thought went to Ramsey and the fact that she hadn't called to tell him what happened, but before she could dial his number, he rang.

"Ramsey, I was just about to call you. You are not going to believe what kind of day I've had."

He laughed as he putted a golf ball across the room. "All is good, I hope."

"Not at all. I got attacked in the hotel right after I got off the telephone with you this morning."

"Are you serious?" he asked, placing his putter back in his golf bag. "Are you OK?"

Keilah went on to describe her assault to Ramsey in great detail. Once she finished, he sat down in the chair behind his desk, and with his voice cracking he asked, "Did they hurt you?"

"Just bruised up a bit, but I'm good," she informed him.

"Are you sure? I mean two guys manhandling you like that is not good, Keilah. Did you see a doctor?"

"No doctor. I'm good, Ramsey, honest."

"I'm coming out there," he blurted out.

"You don't have to do that," she replied.

"I know I don't have to. I want to. I need to see for myself that you're OK," he informed her.

"Ramsey, I would never lie to you. If I were hurt, I would tell you, so there's no reason for you to come out here."

Ramsey closed his eyes and held the phone without speaking. He had become choked up upon hearing about Keilah's attack.

"Hurry up and come home, Keilah. We have a lot of things to talk about."

"We do?" she asked.

"Yes, and it's long overdue."

Keilah could sense sadness and something else in Ramsey's tone. "You're not leaving the business, are you?"

He chuckled. "No, I'm not leaving the company. Actually I'm trying to start something new and I want you to be a part of it."

"Are you serious?" she asked with excitement.

"Most definitely. No one else could fill the job but you," he answered with a sensual tone.

Keilah's stomach fluttered. "It sounds like the perfect position."

"Oh, you haven't seen anything yet."

Keilah closed her eyes and felt a wave of sensuality sweep over her body.

"It sounds like the perfect offer for me," she purred. "I can't wait to hear all about it."

"I was hoping you'd say that. Now hurry up and get back to D.C. I can't have you out there fighting off-the-clock. You know we're not going to get paid for your little fiasco," he joked.

The truth was, he missed Keilah, and it made his heart ache knowing she had been assaulted.

"I promise. I'll be careful, and this is definitely going on my expense account when I get back," she replied.

"Don't even try it. By the way, I guess Michael's pretty shaken up by all of this, huh?"

Keilah played with the bubbles in the Jacuzzi. "Yes, he was upset."

"I can understand that. So, have you seen Keytone?"

She laughed. "Of course, and he's ready to kill somebody over this."

"I take it you haven't told your brothers about him yet?"

"No, but I'm going to have to do it while I'm out here. I've kept it from them long enough," she replied. "They need to know he's family."

"You're doing the right thing," he assured her.

Keilah took a sip of wine and sighed. "I'm not looking forward to facing all of them though. They hate Keytone because of his lifestyle and over some stuff that went down between them when they were teenagers. He's been nothing but nice to me and I haven't seen him do anything illegal, but I've heard the stories."

"I know, Keilah, but I'm sure your brothers have their reasons, and just because you haven't witnessed anything don't mean it doesn't exist. Just talk to the guys and hopefully they'll understand why you kept it from them. Maybe they'll go easy on you after they get over the initial shock of the news."

"I hope you're right," she said softly.

"You and I both know I am," he responded. "I'm not going to hold you any longer. Good luck with your brothers, and be careful. Try to have some fun, and hurry back."

"Thanks, Ramsey. I'll see you in a couple of days,"

"Have a safe flight home. Good-bye."

"Bye, Ramsey," she replied before hanging up the telephone.

Ramsey hung up and sighed. He had an uneasy feeling in his gut about Keilah's attack, but he also felt confident in finally telling Keilah how he felt about her once she returned to D.C. Her close encounter with death was enough to convince him that he didn't need to wait any longer.

CHAPTER SEVENTEEN

At the Lucky Chance, before Luke could get inside his office, Roman met him at the elevator. "Bro, you're not going to believe who's waiting for you in the office," he said, clearly agitated.

"Who?" Luke asked as he made his way down the hallway.

"Xavier."

Luke frowned. "What is that punk doing here?"

"He said he didn't want to talk to anyone but you."

Their assistant, Toya, walked over and greeted them. "Hey guys. Here's your mail, and if it's OK with you, I'd like to take off for an early lunch."

Roman looked at her and smiled. "Where are you trying to get to so early?"

She turned on her heels and smiled back at him. "I said lunch."

"Sure," Roman teased.

Luke stopped her for a moment and said, "Toya, when you get back from lunch, I need you to contact P.K. Sloan for me."

"If I get him on the line do you want me to send the call through?"

He nodded at her and answered, "If you don't mind, and have a good lunch."

"Thanks, Luke," Toya replied as she grabbed her purse and stepped inside the elevator.

Luke looked at Roman as he placed his hand on the door-knob. "Let's go see what X has on his mind."

Luke opened the door and found X looking down on casino patrons through a one-way window in the office. He turned and said, "Nice place you guys have here. You've come a long way. Business seems to be doing very well."

Roman sat his mail on the desk and joined Xavier at the window. "We make do. Now, what can we do for you?"

Luke stood back and observed X's body language. He was young, cocky, and was trying to make a name for him-self on the streets. X had been tied to several brutal beat-ings and shootings in the area over the past year, and he didn't seem to be letting up anytime soon. X turned around to face Luke. "Roman, I thought I asked to speak to Luke alone."

Roman folded his arms and stood toe-to-toe with Xavier. "You might've requested that, but it's not going to happen. What we have here is a family partnership, and we don't con-duct business alone. Now what is this about?"

Xavier stared at Roman and smiled. "I didn't mean any disrespect to you or your brothers. I know Luke is the head of the family—that's the only reason I wanted to talk to him in private."

Luke walked over to where they were standing. "Xavier, what Roman is saying is that any business that has to be dis-cussed affects all of us, and we won't have it any other way. Now say what you came here to say."

Xavier pointed at a chair. "Do you mind if I sit down?"

Luke made his way around the desk to his chair. "Have a seat."

Roman sat in the chair next to Xavier and listened as he spoke. "OK, I'll get right to it. I want in, and you know I deserve it. Our pops started this shit, and it's only fair that you guys give me an opportunity to invest in the Lucky Chance. I can bring in even more exciting events. We can sponsor boxing matches, concerts, all kinds of events to make even more money."

Luke looked at Roman in disbelief. Yes, Xavier was their father's old partner Graham's son, but Graham died before Joe Chance turned their gambling house into a successful business. For X to feel like he was owed something was ridiculous.

"We're not looking to expand right now, X, and when we do, it will be a family decision," Luke stated.

Could this be the deal Keilah's attackers were talking about? If not, it was ironic that he would waltz into their office the day of her attack and throw them a proposition. But he wasn't the first person who had ever approached them, so for now, Luke would just listen. He decided to play things cool and see what X had up his sleeve.

"Luke, I don't think you realize the millions of dollars you're passing on," Xavier replied.

"Xavier, I don't think you heard me earlier. I said this is a *family business*, and the last time I checked, you weren't family, and for the last time, we're not looking to expand."

X's obvious disappointment showed on his face. He'd tried to approach them the nice way, and it just blew up in his face. "You guys are making a huge mistake."

Roman added, "Don't think we haven't received offers like yours before, Xavier. If we decide we want to make any changes to the way we run things around here, that will be our choice. "

Luke stood and walked over to the door, opening it. "The

best advice I can give you, X, is to go into business for yourself, because this one's off-limits. Now if you don't mind, we
have work to do."

Xavier laughed and stood up. As he buttoned his jacket,
he looked at the pair in disbelief.

"You guys don't know what you're passing up. I have con-
nections that could make the Lucky Chance as hot as any of
those casinos in Vegas."

Roman smiled and said, "We appreciate your interest, but
we'll pass."

Xavier walked out the door, down the hallway to the elevator, and stepped inside. Roman and Luke came out into the
hallway and watched as the elevator door closed. Roman pulled
a radio out of his pocket and told security to keep an eye on
Xavier, especially if he decided to hang around the casino.
Luke and Roman returned to the office and closed the door.

"What do you think about that, Luke? Could he have been
the one to send those guys to attack Keilah?"

Luke sat down behind his desk and sighed. "I don't know.
He was arrogant enough to walk up in here right afterward,
but we can't jump to conclusions, at least not yet. X is trying
to make a name for himself, and I don't want him trying to
do it with us. If he's that connected, he needs to go into business elsewhere." Changing the subject, Roman picked his
mail up off the desk and asked, "Why are you in here today?
It's my week to manage the office."

"I had a couple of letters I needed to get out before the
end of the week. Michael and Malachi are downstairs doing
a walk-through."

Roman walked over to the window and looked down on
the casino floor. "Where's Keilah?"

Luke leaned back in his chair and shook his head. "She's
at Malachi's house. They're going to stay with him the rest of
their trip."

Roman turned and asked, "How's she doing?"

"She's fine, just a little scratched up. She gave those guys a good fight."

Roman sat down in the chair across from Luke. "I hope we can find out who was behind it and soon. I'd hate to think that it was X and we let him walk out of here just now."

Luke looked up at Roman. "No way. I believe she was targeted. A random attack usually involves only one person. Two men jumped Keilah, so it was likely they knew she wasn't going to be easy to take down. No, this was definitely personal."

"Do you think Keytone had something to do with it?"

Luke tapped his pen on the desk and thought to himself. "Nah, that's not his style. Besides, he would never hurt Keilah, even if there's no love lost with us."

"Are you sure about that?"

Luke keyed a few things in on the computer and said, "I'm sure. Now, punks like Xavier don't care who gets in the way."

"Do you think it was him?"

Luke frowned and answered, "It could've been anyone, but whoever it was will pay."

At that moment, security called Roman on his radio to announce that Xavier had left the building. Roman thanked the guard and stood. "Well, I have work to do. Get out of here and enjoy your day. I'm going to call and check on Keilah."

"You might not reach her because she said she was going to get in the pool, but you can try her."

Roman walked toward the door. "We need to have a family meeting tonight to discuss what happened to Keilah and about X coming up in here. I don't think he's going to give up too easily. You know how his dad was, stubborn, hot-tempered, and an alcoholic. I don't know why Daddy ever opened that shack with him in the first place."

Without looking up from the computer screen, Luke replied, "You're right, but it was hard to figure out why Daddy did a lot of things. Graham was one of his drinking buddies, so if he started anything with anybody, it was going to be him. We can meet over at Malachi's tonight to discuss this further. Give everyone a call and set it up."

"Will do," Roman said.

"I'll be leaving in about thirty minutes, so if you need me after that, hit me up on my cell."

"OK. See you later."

Roman closed the door, leaving Luke deep in thought. Maybe it *was* Xavier that had Keilah assaulted. That's something he would have to look into and fast.

A cross town, Keytone walked into a local bar and pool hall. It was a known spot in the neighborhood for finding undesirables to do anything for a buck. Almost immediately, he noticed, sitting at the bar, a known drug addict who kept up with everything that was going on in the neighborhood. Keytone approached him and sat down next to him. "What's up, Pinky?"

Pinky looked over at the person sitting next to him and started trembling. "I don't owe you any money, Keytone. Why are you hassling me?"

"Calm down, Pinky. I'm only here for information. I'll make it worth your while," Keytone said as he handed Pinky a hundred-dollar bill.

Information was what Pinky always had. He held out his hand and smiled. "Thanks, Keytone."

Keytone stood and placed more money on the bar to pay for Pinky's drinks. "Come take a ride with me so we can talk."

Pinky grinned and got off his bar stool, following Keytone out the door. Outside, a couple of guys from Keytone's crew, T. Money and Li'l Mike, waited by the car. When Keytone approached them, T. Money opened the back door of the

Lexus so Keytone and Pinky could get in. Li'l Mike pulled out into traffic and Keytone immediately began to question Pinky regarding the Chance family.

At first Pinky talked about the news of the new casino. Then he went on to say he'd overheard a conversation about someone planning to take over the Lucky Chance Casino.

"Damn, Pinky. Where were you when you heard that?" Keytone asked as he watched the football game on the television above the bar.

Pinky was somewhat full of liquor and did his best to recollect the information Keytone wanted. "I can't remember. I was in a bar somewhere."

Keytone turned to Pinky and asked, "Who was doing the talking?"

"I can't think of that dude's name. I've seen him around. He's a young, smart-mouthed dude."

Keytone felt a little better. He was finally getting somewhere with Pinky. "What does he look like?"

"I don't know. He's a young dude."

Frustrated, Keytone asked, "Did he say anything about assaulting a woman?"

"Not that I can remember. Look, I was drinking a lot that day. I don't even know if what I told you actually happened. I don't remember hearing anything about them doing a female."

"Pinky, do you think you would recognize the guy if you saw him again?"

"Hell yeah. I told you I've seen him around. I just don't know who he is."

Keytone motioned for one of his boys to give Pinky another fifty-dollar bill. "Pinky, if you hear anything else about the Chance family or their casinos, I want you to call me. Do you understand?"

Pinky gladly took the money and smiled. "No doubt, Keytone. Thanks."

Keytone told his driver to pull over and let Pinky out. They pulled over at the next intersection. Before pulling off, Keytone rolled down the window and said, "Go get something to eat with your skinny ass instead of smoking and drinking up all your money."

"I'm going to do that, Keytone. Thanks, man."

Keytone felt good that he was able to get some information from Pinky. There were a few more people he needed to see before coming to a conclusion. Li'l Mike pulled away from the curb into traffic.

Just as Keilah climbed out of the pool and wrapped the towel around her body, her cell phone rang. "Hello?"

"Hey, girl. What are you doing?"

Keilah smiled when she heard Keytone's voice. "Not much, just finished taking a swim. What about you? Did you find out anything?"

"I might've, but I'm not sure yet. I'm still working on some angles."

Keilah made her way over to the chaise lounge and sat down. "Well, aren't you going to share your information with me?"

"Not until I do a little more checking. You just watch your back at that hotel."

She laid back and sighed. "My brothers thought it was best that we check out the hotel, so we're staying at Malachi's house."

"That was a smart move. Look, I'll holler at you later. I have some things to do."

"Keytone?"

"Yes, Keilah," he answered with admiration in his heart.

"Thanks for everything, and I've made up my mind. I'm going to tell my brothers about you while I'm here."

"Do you think now is the time, considering what happened to you? They might think this thang had something to do with me."

She thought for a moment before answering. "No, I think now is a better time than any. Besides, they know you would never put me in harm's way or hurt me. It's time they know the truth."

Keytone held the telephone in silence for a moment. "If you say so. Look, just let me know when you decide to do it so I can be prepared for them, because I know they're going to be in my face."

"They're not going to do anything to you. Besides, I want you there with me when I tell them."

Shaking his head, he laughed. "Four against one is never a good position to be in."

She smiled and said, "Four against two, Keytone. Don't worry, you know I have your back."

"Just as I have yours, Keilah," he replied. "Take care of yourself, and I'll be in touch."

"Same here. Be safe out there."

"Oh, you know this. Later, Keilah."

"Good-bye, Keytone."

Keilah hung up the telephone and thought for a moment. She knew in her heart that her brothers needed to know the truth about Keytone, and putting it off any longer would only make matters worse. She just hoped they would see him as she did and not be angry with her for keeping the secret for so long. Going up against her brothers was never easy, and this time was going to be the ultimate battle.

Keilah rose from her chair and headed into the house for a quick shower. She wanted to go over to her casino and hopefully get her brothers together so she could break the news, but Luke had made her promise not the leave the house alone. On the way to her room, she detoured into Malachi's room, opened the trapdoor in his closet, and pulled out a nine-millimeter handgun. She smiled, checked the clip, and said to herself, "Perfect. I'd like to see somebody come at me now." She also pulled a small .22-caliber handgun out of the small space and tucked it into her pocket as well. Once she had everything she needed, she headed to her room to shower and get dressed.

CHAPTER EIGHTEEN

When Keilah stepped off the elevator on the office floor, Roman was the only person she recognized. She smiled as she walked toward him.

Roman frowned and asked, "What are you doing here? I thought you were told not to leave Malachi's house by yourself."

Keilah kissed her brother's cheek. "I was, but I got bored, so I came down here to get my gamble on. Besides, I'm strapped."

He took her by the arm and hustled her into his office. "What do you mean you're strapped?"

Keilah sighed and raised her pants leg, revealing the small .22-caliber handgun strapped to her ankle. She also removed her jacket to show him the nine-millimeter in her back waistband.

Roman frowned. "It doesn't matter. You were told to do something and you didn't do it. Do you have to be hard-headed all the time, Keilah? How did you get here?"

She sat down in the chair opposite his desk and said, "Lay

off me, Roman. Damn! I drove Malachi's car over here, and correct me if I'm wrong, but I'm twenty-seven years old and I think I can take care of myself. I do it every hour of every day in D.C. without any of your help."

Roman poured himself a glass of V-8 juice and said, "You were assaulted this morning. What makes you think it won't happen again?"

Keilah pulled out her compact, checked her makeup, and said, "I don't know, but if they do, I'm ready for them now. You guys would be surprised at the things I've been through in D.C., and I came out unscathed."

With a smirk on his face, Roman sat down and leaned back in his chair and asked, "Like what?"

Without looking at him, she played with a crystal statue on his desk and whispered, "I had to kill a guy."

Roman spat out his juice and sat up in his chair. Keilah shook her head and got up to retrieve a napkin out of the closet. She handed it to him and softly said, "I told you."

"You killed someone? Who? Why? What happened?" Roman asked as he cleaned the sprayed liquid off his desk.

"I really don't want to talk about it, Roman, but I will say it was in self-defense."

He threw the used paper towels in the garbage and said, "Damn. I didn't know. Do any of the guys know about it?"

"No, I didn't tell them, and I didn't plan on telling you either. I only did so you would know that I can take care of myself."

Roman came around from behind his desk and gave her a hug. "I guess you can, sis. Still, it had to have been a horrible thing to experience."

She looked up into his eyes and said, "It was, but it was either him or me, and I did what I had to do."

He hugged her again and said, "I understand."

Keilah stepped out of his embrace and sat back down in

the chair. She pulled a tube of lipstick out of her purse and reapplied it. "Roman, I know you guys are only looking out for me. I'll try to chill out. OK?"

He leaned against his desk, smiled and folded his arms. "Thank you."

"Look, Roman, I need to talk to you guys. Can you come by Malachi's when you finish?"

"Sure. Is anything wrong?" he asked.

"Why does something always have to be wrong, Roman?"

He looked over at her curiously. "I don't know, Keilah. It was just a thought."

She dropped the tube of lipstick into her purse and smiled. "You guys worry too much. I'm surprised you don't have ulcers."

He let out a loud laugh and grabbed his stomach. "You know, I have been having these stomach pains."

Concerned, Keilah asked, "For real? Have you seen a doctor?"

"I'm just kidding, Keilah, I'm fine. I'll call Malachi to come get his car. You can ride back over to his house with me if you want to."

She interlocked her arm with his. "Sounds good, and on the way, can we grab some lunch or something? I'm starving."

"Let me call the guys first, and then we can stop for lunch on the way."

Keilah pushed the button for the elevator. As the doors opened, Roman told his assistant that he was leaving for a couple of hours. After giving her a few more instructions, he stepped onto the elevator beside Keilah, and they began their descent to the first floor. When they exited the elevator, Roman led Keilah down a back hallway and into a garage to his car. Once inside, he called all the brothers and told them about Keilah's request. As expected, they were just as curious as Roman was about the meeting.

Before pulling away from the building, Roman told

Malachi where his car was, and that he was taking Keilah to lunch before meeting up with everyone for the meeting. All agreed, not realizing Keilah's news would change all of their lives forever.

At the restaurant, Keilah found the opportunity to call Keytone when Roman excused himself to go to the rest room.

"Hey, I don't have much time to talk," she said. "I'm out to lunch with Roman right now. I'm just calling to let you know we're having the meeting at Malachi's in a few hours. I want you close by when I break the news to them so be in the area."

Keytone sighed. "I don't know if this is a good idea, Keilah. I don't think they're going to be able to handle this kind of bombshell."

"You let me worry about them. Just be in the area. I have to go. Roman's on his way back to the table. Good-bye."

Keilah quickly hung up the telephone before Roman got to the table. He sat down and asked, "Who was that on the phone?"

She looked at him in amazement. "Aren't you nosy?"

He picked up his menu and chuckled. "Whatever."

Keilah scanned her menu as well and decided on a grilled chicken salad. Roman selected a sirloin, medium-well, with steamed vegetables. After the waiter left their table, Roman looked at Keilah and asked, "How serious are you and Michael?"

"We're cool," she replied.

"What does that mean?" he asked before taking a sip of raspberry tea.

Keilah took a sip of lemonade and smiled. "It means that I brought Michael out here for you guys to meet him because we're already married."

Roman leaned back in his chair and threw his napkin on the table in anger. "I know you didn't get married without talking to us first?"

"I'm over eighteen, Roman. I didn't need permission from any of you guys," Keilah reminded him.

Roman frowned and pointed his finger at Keilah. "That is about the most asinine thing you've ever done, Keilah. How could you do something crazy like that before discussing it with us?"

Keilah giggled upon seeing her brother's reaction.

"Keilah! Are you guys married or not?" he repeated.

This caused Keilah to laugh even harder. She waved him off, and once she could catch her breath, she answered, "No, we're not married."

Roman picked up his glass of raspberry tea and shook his head. "You play too much, Keilah. That wasn't funny at all."

"Yes, it was. You should've seen your face."

"Seriously, Keilah, what are your plans?"

Keilah folded her arms and thought for a moment. "If you're trying to ask me if I'm in love with Michael, then the answer is no. But, you never know. Things could change."

Roman's studied her. "Michael seems to be a nice guy, but he's a career military man, which means if you two hooked up and had kids, they would be army brats."

Now it was Keilah's turn to frown. "Whatever. I'm not moving my kids around the country. Besides, Michael works at the Pentagon, so he rarely travels."

"Does he have to go to Iraq?" Roman asked.

"Sometimes. He has to also go to cities like New York and Chicago. I don't know where else."

"He's just doing his job. I think it would be cool to have job traveling around like that," Roman pointed out.

"I guess, but going over to Iraq is dangerous," she admitted.

He laughed. "And you don't think what you do is dangerous?"

She leaned back in her chair and giggled, "You're right."

He sipped a little more of his tea, and then the waiter arrived with their meals. After inspecting their selection, they
blessed their food and enjoyed their meals and the time
shared together.

An hour or so later, Roman and Keilah pulled up at
Malachi's house and found the rest of the family, including Michael, already there. When he put the car in park,
he looked over at Keilah and noticed she seemed to be nervous. "Are you okay?"

She reached for the door. "So far so good."

Roman grabbed her arm, preventing her from exiting the
car. "You don't look well. Is there something you want to tell
me before we go in there?"

She looked at him. "I'm fine, Roman. Let's go."

He released her arm and allowed her to get out of the car
even though he believed she was holding something very serious back from him. They entered the house together and
found the rest of their brothers sitting around the pool.
Michael was aware of the family meeting and gave the Chance
family privacy by playing with the dogs in the yard and around
the pool. When Keilah walked out onto the deck with Roman,
Genesis hugged her. "Hey, sis. What's so important that you
had to call all of us together?"

Keilah walked over to the table and took a seat. She put her
hands over her face for a second before speaking. Malachi
walked over and handed her a glass of wine. "Here, you look
like you could use a drink."

She looked up at him with weary eyes and whispered,
"Thank you."

Keilah swallowed the wine down with one gulp. When she sat the empty glass on the table, all eyes were on her. "OK, I can see you guys are anxious to hear what I have to say, so here goes."

She took another deep breath and walked over toward the pool, and then turned to them. "I want you guys to let me finish before you say anything."

Luke stood and said, "OK, Keilah, just get on with it."

With tears in her eyes she said, "I need to make a call first."

She pulled her cell phone out of her purse. With all eyes were on her, she punched in a series of numbers and whispered into her phone. She hung up her cell phone and said, "I would appreciate it if you guys would stay right here. I have to go into the house to get something before I continue."

Once she disappeared into the house, Roman said, "I don't like this. Something's wrong."

Malachi said, "I agree. I feel like Keilah is handling us."

Luke replied, "Let's just wait and hear her out."

A few minutes later, Keilah stepped out on the deck with Keytone following close behind her.

Malachi jumped up out of his seat and yelled, "What the hell is he doing here?"

Keilah put her hands up in defense. "Wait. You guys have to listen to what I have to say, because it's going to affect all of you."

She took Keytone by the hand and led him over to a seat next to hers. "Sit here, Keytone."

Keytone wasn't afraid of any man, but he had history with the Chance brothers and things could get serious.

Luke calmly asked, "Keilah, have you lost your damn mind? Why did you bring Keytone into Malachi's home?"

Keilah not only saw the wrath in her brothers' eyes, she could feel it. "I brought Keytone here because we needed privacy to handle this. We wouldn't be able to get privacy in a club or a restaurant, and I didn't think it would be a good idea to have this meeting at the casino either. Look, I brought Keytone here because he has a place here. What I'm trying to say is that Keytone contacted me a year or so ago and told a story—a story that threw me for a loop, and I didn't believe it until I had the proof in my hands. I found out that Daddy cheated on Momma once and a child was born out of that affair. That child is Keytone. He's our brother."

"That's some bullshit," Malachi yelled. "There's no way in hell Keytone is a Chance."

"It's true, Malachi," Keilah said in defense. "I had DNA tests done. He's definitely our brother, and I think it's only fair that we accept him as part of our family."

"Keilah, why would you drop some shit like this on us?" Genesis asked. "How long have you known?"

"About a year," she admitted. "This was hard for me to accept in the beginning, and I know it's going to be hard for you guys as well, but it's real."

"How long have you known about this, Keytone?" Luke calmly asked.

"My mother told me when I was around sixteen," he admitted.

"Did Daddy know about you?" Luke asked.

"According to my mother, Joe knew about me after he got back together with your mother, but he made it clear that he wasn't going to leave his family. He did provide for us and came around every once in a while to see me. Look, what happened between Joe and my mom was just a one-time thing," Keytone said as he stood. "I'm not here to cause you any problems. I came here because Keilah asked me to, and she felt like you guys needed to know the truth."

"So you knew we were family when we worked for you, huh?" Malachi asked.

"Yeah, I knew. I also knew that you guys were just doing what you had to."

Luke looked Keytone in the eyes. "You've always had a reputation for being hard and not letting members of your crew just walk away from the organization. Did you let us go because you knew we were related?"

Keytone folded his arms. "Isn't it obvious? You had no business working for me in the first place."

"You were wrong for not telling us. We had a right to know," Luke replied.

"I did what I thought was the right thing. Coming here was Keilah's idea. If it was up to me, you guys would've never known, but I'm getting older, and I wanted a relationship with my sister."

Roman asked, "Now what?"

Keytone stared at Roman and replied, "That's on you guys. What I came here to do is done."

Malachi yelled, "Is it? Keytone, guys like you always have an agenda."

Tears began to roll out of Keilah's eyes. "I'm sorry I ever brought you here, Keytone. I thought I was doing the right thing."

"No," Luke yelled. "The right thing would've been telling us about this from the beginning."

Keytone took a step in Luke's direction and in Keilah's defense. "Leave her alone. Joe is the one you should be angry with, not me and especially not, Keilah. Get over yourselves. Not everyone wants something from you. I know I don't."

Malachi, Roman, and Genesis jumped out of their seats when Keytone approached Luke. They were ready to kill if they had to in order to protect Luke. Luke put his hand up to his brothers for them to stand back. Luke knew Keytone wasn't about to get violent with him under these circumstances. All the commotion on the deck got Michael's attention. He walked over to the deck and asked, "Is everything OK?"

Keilah smiled and said, "We're fine, Michael. Why don't you take a dip in the pool or the Jacuzzi?"

"I think I will, Keilah," he replied as he studied everyone's expressions and could see there was some tension, but what was going on was obviously a family matter and he was just a guest. Michael made into the house to change into his swimming trunks.

After he was out of earshot, Luke turned to Keytone and asked, "Well, what do you want, Keytone?"

Keytone ran his hands over his head. "Not a damn thing. Look, we're family and there's nothing any of us can do about it. If you don't believe me, then feel free to order another DNA test, but at this point, I don't give a damn. Keilah and I just thought you guys needed to know. The only reason I agreed is because I didn't want any misunderstandings if you ever saw Keilah and I together."

"So you're saying you're not here to try and muscle in on our businesses?" Malachi asked.

"I could care less about your goddamn casinos, Malachi. I have my own thing going on, so you can relax," Keytone said angrily.

Keilah jumped in. "You guys need to stop it. You have no reason to be mad at Keytone, because Daddy was the one who put us together. We are family, so get used to it."

"As crazy as this seems, Keilah, you're right," Luke replied as he stood and approached Keytone. "Before we acknowledge you're our brother, I want to have our own DNA test done. Agreed?"

"Agreed," Keytone responded.

"Secondly, I'm sure you know that you've made a lot of enemies over the years, and I don't want my family or our casinos associated with you or your organization. And that's nonnegotiable." Luke continued.

Keytone scratched his chin. "I understand you guys did

what you had to do to help your mother when Joe wasn't around. The good thing is that he did come back. Joe was a smart man. He just had responsibility issues."

Genesis jumped out of his chair. "Don't you talk about our daddy."

Roman held Genesis away from Keytone. "Hold up, Genesis. Keytone is right. Daddy did have a problem hanging around when things got tight. We can't ignore the truth."

Keytone shoved his hands inside his pockets. "At least you guys know what it's like to have a dad around. I only saw Joe in passing. Maybe an hour, tops, was the most I spent with him on any given visit. You should be thankful you had him in your lives the way he was."

The Chance siblings listened as Keytone spoke about Joe.

"Where do we go from here?" Roman asked.

Keytone turned and walked toward the French doors he entered through. "We don't have to go anywhere as far as I'm concerned. Keilah, I'll be in touch."

"Wait. Don't leave now," she pleaded as she followed him.

He stopped and gave her a quick kiss on the cheek. "No, your brothers need time to absorb all of this. I'll call you tomorrow."

Keilah grabbed Keytone's arm and said, "Hold up, I'll walk you out." When she returned she faced four angry pair of eyes.

"Don't look at me like that. I did what I thought was right, and the only reason I kept it from you this long is because I was waiting for the right moment to tell you. I knew you guys were going to be pissed, but I was hoping you would understand that Keytone didn't create the problem, Daddy did. Besides, I didn't want you guys to get hurt."

Malachi picked up the wine bottle and threw it against the side of the house, shattering glass everywhere. "Too late," he yelled. "Nothing could be worse than finding out somebody like Keytone is a part of our family, and I still can't believe you brought him into my house."

Keilah lowered her head. "He's not a bad person, Malachi. He's really very sweet. He's even trying to find out who attacked me."

Genesis jumped out his seat. "Well you tell him to stay out of it."

Luke spoke up. "You have to admit that if anyone can find out who attacked Keilah, it's Keytone. He's connected to the streets, and he knows how to get people to talk. He might even find out what X is up to."

"You guys know what this means, don't you?" Roman asked.

"Yeah, Daddy's will," Luke responded. "His will said the casinos are to be left to all his surviving children. That would include Keytone."

"Son of a bitch," Malachi yelled. "Keilah, look what you've started."

Keilah walked over to Malachi and pointed her finger in his face and yelled, "I didn't start anything! If Keytone wanted anything from us, he could've approached us a long time ago! He's known about this for years!"

Roman intervened. "Sit down, Keilah. Look, everybody needs to calm down. Daddy's dirt is not Keilah's fault."

Michael exited the house and walked over to Keilah. "What's going on down here? I could hear you guys yelling all the way upstairs. Keilah, are you OK?"

"She's fine, Michael," Malachi blurted out.

"Stop speaking for me, Malachi!" she yelled as she got in his face again.

"Somebody needs to. You're out of control, sis!" he yelled back at her.

Michael quickly separated the two and said, "Now wait just a damn minute. I can't stand here any longer and let you guys treat Keilah like this. She's your sister for God's sake, so whatever's going on or misunderstanding you have, it needs to get cleared up without all this hostility."

Malachi looked at Michael with fiery eyes. "Stay out of this, Michael. This doesn't concern you."

Michael folded his arms and defensively said, "You're right, Malachi, but whatever is going on, Keilah doesn't deserve to be ganged up on by you guys."

Keilah put her hands up in defense. "Michael, it's OK. I've been going to battle with my brothers all my life. Look, guys, I'm tired. I love you and I don't want to fight with you anymore. What's done is done, so you all do what you want about Keytone because I'm through with the whole thing. I'm going upstairs to lie down for awhile."

Michael took Keilah by the hand and led her into the house and up the stairs to their room. Once they were out of sight, Malachi mumbled, "This is some bull."

Upstairs, Keilah crawled into bed. Michael lay down next to her and pulled her into his arms. Keilah whispered, "I really appreciate you standing up for me, Michael. Not many people would go up against any of my brothers, let alone all four of them."

He kissed her and said, "I love you, Keilah. There's nothing I wouldn't do for you."

Keilah lay there in Michael's arms. She turned to him and said, "You sound like you really mean that."

He linked his fingers with hers and said, "I do, Keilah. If I had it my way, we'd get married right away."

She sat up and said, "Married?"

"Yes, married. I told you before that I knew you were for me. I want children by a woman with your strengths, intelligence, and beauty."

Keilah looked into Michael's eyes. Had she seen him wrong all along?

"What do you say, Keilah? I know we haven't known each

other very long, but I believe in love at first sight. Can't you at least think about it? We can offer each other so much."

Keilah was in shock. Michael was dead serious about marriage but she had always said she would marry for love and nothing else. She knew her heart was with Ramsey, but he'd made it clear that marriage was not in his plans. Feeling a headache coming on, she gave Michael a tender kiss and said, "I'll think about it, Michael."

Michael smiled with satisfaction before pulling Keilah down on the bed next to him. He made love to Keilah and professed his love for her over and over until his body collapsed on top of her. Keilah was overwhelmed at the passion and force of Michael's body as he made love to her. Michael was the only man she'd dated that accepted her career and loved her at the same time. Maybe military life wouldn't be so bad after all, and hopefully she could grow to love him as much as he loved her.

"Keilah, the next time we make love, I don't want any barriers between us."

"What are you saying, Michael?" she asked.

He kissed her neck and said, "I want to feel you . . . all of you. I'm ready to have children, and if that look in your eyes is what I think it is, I would say so are you."

Michael put his finger up to her lips and said, "Don't say anything. The next time we make love, it will be flesh against flesh, skin against skin. I want to enter your mind, body, and soul. I can't do that with latex between us. I love you."

Keilah stared back at Michael. Was he in that big of a hurry to have children? Having unprotected sex with Michael wasn't on her list of things to do anytime soon. Instead of replying to Michael's comments, she turned over and went to sleep.

CHAPTER NINETEEN

Back in D.C. as Ramsey finished up the last of his paper-work, he looked over at a picture he'd taken with Keilah on the firing range. After staring at the picture, he punched up the calendar on his computer and was happy to see that Keilah would be returning soon from California. He missed her around the office, and since she'd been away, he felt like a piece of him was also missing. It was an odd feeling, but it gave him a warm, protective sensation.

Just as he picked up the telephone to call her, his thoughts of Keilah were interrupted when Andria Rockwell walked into his office and closed the door.

He leaned back in his chair and shook his head in disbe-lief. She was sporting a very short silver dress with a plunging neckline and back. It left little of the fabulous body she had underneath her clothing to the imagination. Ramsey frowned and asked, "What are you doing here?"

She strutted over to his desk and leaned over, giving Ramsey a clear view of her breasts. "I came to put you out of your misery."

"What makes you think I'm miserable?" Ramsey asked as he glanced down at her chest.

Andria smiled and then sat down. She crossed her legs slowly and seductively, revealing the fact that she wasn't wearing any undergarments.

He laughed and said, "You're nasty, Andria."

"You like it," she responded as she grabbed a Hershey's Kiss candy out of the bowl on his desk and provocatively placed it on the tip of her tongue before slowly pulling it into her mouth.

Ramsey stood up and cleared his throat. He walked over to his small refrigerator and pulled out a bottle of water. He had to admit that Andria was pulling out all of her antics to seduce him. Instead of answering her question, he stated, "I bet the General would have something to say about that dress you're wearing."

"You know I don't care what my daddy thinks. What I want to know is, how much longer you're going to be working so you can concentrate on me?" she asked with a seductive tone.

"Where's Ripley?" Ramsey asked as he twirled from side to side in his leather chair.

Andria walked around his desk and behind his chair and started massaging his shoulders. She leaned down close to his ear and licked his earlobe. "She's around here somewhere. She said something about making some calls or something."

Sanita Ripley was Andria's personal security agent, and since she'd taken on the assignment, Andria had been more than a handful.

"You haven't been giving Ripley a hard time, have you?" he asked as he typed some information into his laptop.

Andria giggled as she continued to massage his shoulders. "No more than I would anybody."

Ramsey couldn't help but shake his head. "You'd better be

doing whatever Ripley tells you to do. She's one of my best agents, and your daddy's paying us a lot of money to keep you safe. You know there's plenty of people who wouldn't mind snatching you off the streets so they could hold you for ransom."

She played with the diamond necklace around her neck and said softly, "But you already have me, Ramsey."

Ramsey quickly stood.. "Is that so?" he asked.

With her lips within inches of his and her breasts pressed against his chest she blushed and said, "Without a doubt."

He tilted her chin upward and looked her in the eyes. Andria was a beautiful woman, but she wasn't Keilah. He backed away and walked over to the closet and slid into his jacket.

"What's wrong, Ramsey? Are you really over me?" she asked.

He turned to her and said, "We were never serious, Andria, you know that."

She walked over to him, pulled his collar out for him, and whispered, "Maybe you wasn't, but I was."

"Since when?" he asked with a furrowed brow. "It was just sex, and you know it, Andria."

"Wow. I seriously thought we had something special," she responded.

He took her hand and said, "We do, Andria. We're friends."

Andria batted her eyes at him and smiled. "Right now, I'll take what I can get, even though it would nice to get things back to like they were."

Ramsey looked at his watch without agreeing to anything. He was starving, and the least he could do was take her out to dinner for old times' sake. "Have you eaten? Are you hungry?"

She wrapped her arms around his neck and breathlessly said, "What I do want is for you to kiss me. We can talk about dinner afterward."

Ramsey wrapped his arms around her petite waist and whispered, "For old times' sake." He lowered his lips to hers, and within seconds he started feeling sick to his stomach and pulled back.

"What's wrong, Ramsey?"

He backed away from her. "I don't know. I don't feel so good."

She felt his forehead. "You don't feel warm at all."

He gagged again, so he walked over to his desk and took a sip of water. Andria followed him and caressed the back of his neck to soothe him. "Maybe you should get some ginger ale. It works better on an upset stomach."

Ramsey burped. "I think you're right. Listen, maybe we should pass on dinner. I need to go home and lie down," Ramsey suggested.

"What time did you last eat?" she asked as she led him over to his chair to sit down.

"I really didn't eat. I had an energy drink and some dried fruit instead," he revealed.

She cupped his face and kissed him. "No wonder you're sick. Your stomach is empty."

Ramsey felt nauseated again, and this time he pushed Andria out of the way and sprinted to the bathroom to throw up. When he returned to his office, Andria stood up and pulled her purse on her shoulder. "Come on, Ramsey. Let me help you home. You don't need to be alone tonight."

"You don't have to do that. I'll be fine, Andria."

She took his keys out of his hand. "It's not up for discussion, and if you're not any better in the morning, I'm taking you to the doctor."

"That won't be necessary."

She opened the door to his office "Yes, it is necessary. You need someone to take care of you. We'll stop and pick up dinner before going home. You'll feel so much better once you have something in your stomach."

He slowly followed her toward the door. "Andria, you don't have to do this. I can take of myself."

Andria put her hands on her hips. "I want to do it, Ramsey, so let me help you."

Ramsey thought for a moment and decided to let Andria take him home. He did feel terrible and hoped he wasn't coming down with a virus, which wouldn't be ideal with Keilah out of town.

On their way out of the office, Ramsey relieved Sanita Ripley and told her he would see to it that Andria got home safe and sound. Ripley thanked Ramsey and told Andria she would make contact with her in the morning.

Andria stopped at a restaurant near downtown to pick up their meal. As they waited in the bar area for their order, Ramsey noticed patrons staring at the tall, scantily clad, attractive woman accompanying him. This didn't bother Andria at all, but Ramsey knew that if anyone recognized her, it wouldn't be long before the media would show up to snap a picture. The restaurant was known to be a regular dining spot for senators and other high-profile government officials. The last thing he wanted was to have his picture plastered on the front page of the *Washington Post*.

Ramsey pulled a chair out for Andria, and then sat down next to her. She rubbed his arm and asked, "How's your stomach?"

"Better, but not perfect," he answered. "Andria, I don't think it's a good idea for us to be here. We could've gotten something at a fast-food restaurant."

"That greasy stuff? No way. Besides, I love this place. They have some the best food in town."

He leaned over. "I know, Andria, but couldn't you have picked somewhere less military and governmental?"

She interlocked her arm with his and kissed him. "You worry too much, Ramsey. I got this. OK?"

"I just don't want you to get any unnecessary heat from your father," he replied as he wiped more sweat off his brow.

"Let me worry about Daddy," she answered. Andria noticed the sweat on Ramsey's brow. She pulled a tissue out of her purse and wiped it off. "It won't be much longer, baby. Hold on."

Ramsey was feeling sick again, "Excuse me, Andria, I need to go to the bathroom."

Andria watched helplessly as Ramsey held his handkerchief over his mouth and hurried into the men's room. She stood up and walked over to the hostess. "My date is not feeling well. Could you please check to see how much longer it will be for our order?"

"Your name please?" the hostess asked.

"Rockwell," Andria replied.

"I'll be right back, Ms. Rockwell," the hostess said before walking off.

Several minutes later, as Ramsey exited the bathroom and made his way back to Andria, he came face to face with none other than General T.K. Rockwell and several of his colleagues. They were all decked out in their military uniforms, which were covered with all sorts of medals.

"Hello, Daddy," Andria said as she stood and kissed him on the cheek.

"Hello, sweetheart, I believe you already know everyone here," he said as he turned to his friends. "You all remember my daughter, Andria, don't you?" The other men nodded and greeted Andria as well as Ramsey. "This is a friend of hers, Ramsey Stone."

Ramsey shook everyone's hand, including the general's. "Good evening, sir."

The general turned to his colleagues. "You guys can go ahead and sit down. I'll join you in a second. Order me a martini, please."

"Will do, T.K.," one of the men replied as they walked away.

The general had a frown on his face as he turned and shook Ramsey's hand again. "Ramsey, I assume you'll see that my daughter gets home safely since it seems that Agent Ripley is not here."

"Without a doubt, sir," he responded.

"I have faith in you, son," the general acknowledged.

General Rockwell turned back to Andria, who was sitting once again. "Andria, the next time you decide to come out in public, I hope you won't be so careless with your attire. That dress is barely covering your body."

She sat down and crossed her legs. "Don't start, Daddy. There's nothing wrong with my dress."

"Not if you're a streetwalker, but you're my daughter, and you have an image to uphold. I won't let you embarrass yourself or your family."

Andria looked up at her father and boldly blurted out, "Don't you mean embarrass you, Daddy?"

He leaned down close to her and whispered, "We will not have this conversation here. I'll talk to you in the morning."

Andria rolled her eyes as her father joined his colleagues at a nearby table.

"He's such a bully," she said as she pouted.

Ramsey looked at his watch. "Your father loves you, Andria, and you should be past the rebellious stage."

"Are you saying I'm acting childish?"

"I'm saying you need to understand his position, and your antics make his job harder for him. People will see him as less capable of protecting this country if he can't control his own daughter."

She pointed her finger at him angrily. "You men are all alike. It's always about control. Well, I have news for you and Daddy. No one is going to control me."

Ramsey could see that Andria was clearly upset and hurt by his comments, but the truth does hurt sometimes.

"I didn't mean it like that, and you know it," he apologized.

She wiped away the tears that had formed in the corner of her eyes.

"Andria, your father's in a position of power. Stop fighting him. OK?"

She looked over at him and said, "Whatever. Where's our damn food?"

After the hostess finally brought their carryout, the pair headed back to Ramsey's house. When they got there, he was only able to eat half of his food, but Andria gobbled down her food like a wild animal. Once her stomach was full, it didn't take long for her to fall into a deep sleep.

Unfortunately, since Ramsey's stomach was turning flips on him, he was unable to close his eyes. He was still nauseated, but he couldn't understand why. As he lay there losing the battle, he decided to try a little ginger ale to calm his stomach. He felt better after he stepped outside to get a breath of fresh air, but the moment he re-entered his bedroom, he got sick all over again. As he held his head over the toilet, he begged for mercy before crawling back into bed next to Andria. As soon as he pulled the comforter over his body, his stomach started churning once again. He was beginning to wonder if the culprit was Andria's perfume, or her lipstick. Whatever it was, he realized that in order to get some sleep, he had to sleep in one of his spare bedrooms.

As Ramsey's intestinal system seemed to calm down once again, his thoughts went to Keilah. He was thankful she wasn't hurt when she was attacked and was glad she showed them what Keilah Chance was made of. He smiled and wished he could've seen her fight off two men. The thought of her sweating and fighting caused him to become slightly aroused. He closed his eyes and reminisced about Keilah's fiery kisses, the softness of her skin and her sexy sense of humor. He lay there savoring his erotic thoughts of Keilah until they were interrupted.

"Ramsey, are you okay?" Andria asked as she stood in the doorway wearing one of his T-shirts. "Why are you sleeping all the way in here?"

Lying, he said, "I didn't want to disturb you. Besides, I'm not sure if what I have is contagious, and I don't want you to get sick, too."

She walked over, sat on the side of the bed, and caressed his chest. "You're so thoughtful, Ramsey."

As soon as she touched him, he immediately sat up and felt sick once again. He threw the covers back and hurried into the bathroom.

"Can I get you anything?" Andria yelled from the other side of the door.

Ramsey yelled, "No, just go back to bed. I'll be fine."

Andria padded to the kitchen, got Ramsey a large glass of ginger ale, and left it on the nightstand before returning to bed. Once again, Ramsey slowly made his way back to over to the bed. He sat there with his head in his hands. "My God. What is wrong with me?"

Noticing the large glass of ginger ale, he drank it down, crawled back under the covers, and fell fast asleep.

CHAPTER TWENTY

Michael's ringing cell phone at four AM woke him and Keilah, causing him to curse as he reached for it. "Hello?"

"Michael, this is Colonel Bridgeforth. I'm sorry to call you at such an early hour, but there's been a development, and we need you in back in D.C. right away for a meeting in Iraq regarding future deployments."

"Sir, I'm on the West Coast at the moment. Is there any way you could give me at least a week to get some personal business in order?"

"I wish I could, Major, but I can't. We're leaving as soon as we can."

Michael sighed. "Yes, sir. I understand."

"It should only be for a couple of weeks, Michael. Get back here as soon as you can so you can be briefed on the trip."

Keilah listened quietly as Michael talked to the person on the other line. He didn't have to tell her what was going on because she was used to these types of calls.

"Will do, Colonel. Good-bye."

Michael hung up the cell phone and fell backwards onto the bed. Keilah caressed his arm. "How soon do you have to leave?"

He turned and faced her. He put his arm around her waist and pulled her closer to him. "Today—if I can get a flight out. I have to go over to Iraq for a meeting, but I shouldn't be gone more than a couple of weeks."

Keilah closed her eyes and whispered, "I can't believe they can call you at the spur of the moment like that and you have to pick up and go."

He smiled. "Don't worry, sweetheart. I'll be back before you have time to miss me."

She cupped his face and kissed him softly on the lips. "You're a good man, Michael."

He chucked. "I'd like to think I am. I love you, Keilah, and when I get back, I want to make us official. Marry me, baby."

"Are you serious, Michael?"

"You know I would never joke about something this serious," he replied as he ran his finger over her full lips.

Keilah tried to swallow the lump in her throat. "But we haven't known each other very long. How can you be so sure about me?"

"You're the best thing that's ever happened to me," he replied as he nibbled on her ear, causing her to suck in a breath. He smiled with pleasure and trailed kisses from her lips down to her navel, lingering there. He glanced up at her and winked when he heard a soft moan escape her lips. "Now that's what I'm talking about. I can't wait for you to have my babies, Keilah."

"How many do you want, Michael?" she asked curiously.

"If I have my way, you'll be barefoot and pregnant every nine months," he teased.

They both laughed, and then Michael kissed her greedily. Keilah could feel her lower region throbbing as Michael anxiously prepared himself to slide into her hot, moist body. She wrapped her legs around his waist and held onto him as he moved deeper and deeper into her body. Keilah's moans were starting to get louder and louder, and the last person she wanted to wake up was Malachi. Michael didn't care because he loved it when Keilah writhed and moaned beneath him. Seconds later he rolled onto his back, pulling Keilah on top of his body. He pushed her hair away from her face so he could look her in the eyes. "Are you going to be OK out here?"

"I'm only going to be here another day or so. I want to see you off to Iraq, and I'm ready to get back to work. Ramsey's been holding things down for me long enough."

Michael ran his hands over the length of her voluptuous body, resting them on her hips. "Ramsey's a big boy. You know he has no problem running the company while you're away, and vice versa. I'm sure you just miss being at work and at home."

Just then, they heard a knock on the bedroom door.

"Michael, Malachi's at the door," she whispered.

He raised his head and cursed. "I'll get it."

"No, let me because I know he's not going to be happy that we woke him up," she offered as she quickly slid into her bathrobe and made her way over to the door. She opened the door it and came face to face with Malachi, who wore an obvious frown on his face.

"Good morning, little brother. What's up?" Keilah asked in a teasing tone as she stepped out into the hallway.

He folded his arms and leaned against the wall. "You know what's up. Could you guys do me a favor and hold it down in there? I'm trying to sleep."

Keilah smiled mischievously as she tried to smooth down her tousled hair. "I'm sorry, Malachi. We didn't realize what time it was or that we were making a lot of noise. I'll tell Michael not to groan so loudly when we make love."

Malachi's frown progressed even further. "I don't need to know that, Keilah, just keep it down in there."

As he turned to walk away, Keilah called out to him. "Malachi?"

He turned to face her with a disgusted expression on his face. "Yes?"

"Michael has to fly to Washington today. They're sending him back over to Iraq."

He lowered his head. "I'm sorry to hear that, sis, but I'm sure Michael is used to being shipped off at a moment's notice."

"I guess you're right," Keilah replied. "He asked me to marry him."

Malachi's eyes widen. "Are you serious?"

She blushed. "Yes, but I haven't given him an answer yet because we haven't known each other very long."

"That's the main reason you need to really think about this, sis. You shouldn't jump into anything as serious as marriage," Malachi responded.

"I know," she replied as she fumbled with the belt on her robe.

"Personally, I think you should wait and give this more thought. Michael might be cool and all, but I don't think he's the one for you."

Keilah giggled. "Is anyone *the one* for me in your eyes, Malachi?"

Now it was his time to blush. "Not really."

Keilah hugged Malachi and gave him a loving kiss. "I love you."

"I love you too. Now if you don't mind I would like to get back to sleep," he announced.

Keilah opened the door to her bedroom and smiled. "I'll see you in a couple of hours and we'll try to be a little quieter."

"Whatever," Malachi said with a smirk on his face. He disappeared inside his room and hoped his sister and Michael would allow him to get a few more hours of sleep.

Keilah walked back over to the bed and dropped her robe on the floor. She climbed under the comforter and snuggled close to Michael.

"Are we in trouble?" he joked.

She laid her head on his chest. "No, he's cool. I told him I would try to get you to be a little quieter."

Michael wrapped his arms securely around her waist. "I knew you would blame it on me, but that's cool because I'll take the blame for being in love with you any day."

They lay there in silence for a few seconds until Keilah spoke first.

"Michael, I can't give you an answer on marriage right now, but I will seriously think about it while you're in Iraq," she said as she looked into his eyes.

"Don't stress over it, Keilah. The last thing I want to do is make you feel pressured," he said as he kissed her neck. "You're the only woman who's ever made me feel the way I do, so take all the time you need."

"Thank you, Michael. That means a lot to me. No one's ever proposed to me before."

He cupped her face and kissed her slowly on the lips. "All I want is you, Keilah. Nothing else matters to me. You're perfect for everything I want and need in a woman."

Keilah didn't know what to think. Michael was doing a good job convincing her to marry him, but something just didn't seem right. He was saying and doing all the right things, making her decision even more difficult. He seemed to be so sincere and genuine with his expression of love.

A few hours later, Malachi drove Keilah and Michael to the airport. She stood outside the car and tried her best not to cry, but she was not successful. Michael, all decked out in his military uniform, took her left hand and seductively kissed her ring finger before pulling her into his arms.

"Miss Chance, take care of this finger, because the next time I see you, I'll have something very special to put on it. I have big plans for you."

Malachi interrupted the couple. "Keilah, come on. You're going to make Michael miss his plane, and I have to move this car."

Michael looked at Malachi and shook his head. "I have plenty of time, Malachi. Just let me hold my baby a little longer."

Malachi shook his head and then closed the trunk of the car. "You guys need to hurry up, because I don't need any more parking tickets."

Irritated, Michael yelled, "Give me a second, Malachi. Please!"

Malachi stormed around to the driver's-side door and opened it. "OK, I'll be in the car, but if the police come over here it's on you."

Keilah and Michael ignored Malachi completely as he cupped her face and covered her lips with his.

Malachi had had enough, so he blew the horn. "Michael, Keilah, come on, man. I have to move my car."

Michael kissed Keilah a couple of more times before reaching over to open the car door for her. "Stop stressing, Malachi. It's hard for me to leave your sister right now."

Malachi started the engine on the car. "Yeah, man, I feel you, but I have to go."

Michael reached inside his pocket and pulled out a key. He placed it in the palm of her hand and said, "When I get back from Iraq, I would love to have you in my bed waiting on me."

Keilah's throat was dry. She couldn't believe Michael was giving her a key to his house. No man would do that so soon in a relationship. "Are you sure about this, Michael?"

He kissed her on the lips and said, "Yes, I'm sure. Besides,

I was going to ask you to check on my house while I was in Iraq anyway. Would you?"

She slid inside the car allowing him the close her door for her. "Of course I will. Have a safe flight, Michael, and call me when you land."

Michael leaned inside the window of the car and gave Keilah one more kiss before walking away. "No doubt, sweetheart. Enjoy the rest of your stay here with your family and I'll see you in a couple of weeks."

"I will," she said as Malachi pulled away from the curb.

After they drove off, Malachi looked over at his sister. "Are you okay, sis?"

Without looking back at him, she whispered, "I don't know what to do, Malachi."

"You don't know what to do about what? Michael?"

She sighed and said, "Yes. He just gave me a key to his house."

"Don't rush into this, Keilah. If you have doubt, that's a sign to take it slow and really look at this," Malachi replied. "Michael seems to be moving a little fast to me."

She looked over at Malachi and lowered her head. "Can I tell you something without you running your mouth?"

He smiled. "Sure, what's up?"

"I think I'm in love with Ramsey," she admitted.

Upon hearing Keilah's confession, Malachi swerved into another lane of traffic. Keilah and Ramsey had never given him or his brothers any indication that they were romantically involved or even interested in each other. "What do you mean you think? Where is this coming from?"

Keilah looked out the passenger-side window and said, "We've been messing around for several months. It was all my idea, and it was supposed to be strictly recreational at my request, but something happened."

Malachi smiled. "First of all, you shouldn't be having casual sex like that. Secondly, you shouldn't have multiple partners, and lastly you shouldn't have sex with your business partner."

"Don't worry, Malachi. I stopped sleeping with Ramsey once I met Michael. My little liaison with him was only supposed to be a temporary arrangement."

"I don't know what to say, sis. I mean, you know we all like Ramsey and think he's cool. If it's causing you to have some anxiety about your relationship with Michael, you need to find out how Ramsey feels so you'll know where you stand."

She nodded in agreement. "It's hard though. Michael tells me he loves me so much, and even though I don't feel the same way, I have no doubt that I could grow to love him."

Malachi frowned. "Did we grow up in the same house?"

Keilah softly replied, "Yes."

Malachi was angry now. "Then you know as a Chance, we don't settle. Damn, Keilah! You're making this harder than it really is. Does Ramsey have any idea of know how you feel?"

"No, he doesn't know. I mean we tell each other we care about each other and have special places in our hearts for the other in that sisterly-brotherly way, but Ramsey makes it very clear when we talk about relationships that he's not looking for love or to be tied down with marriage. Right now he's dating three different women."

"What you have to understand about men, sis, is that we say stupid stuff like that to keep our options open and to keep women from knowing our true intentions. What most of us are really doing is discreetly looking for Mrs. Right. Not many men are confirmed bachelors for life. We have this instinct to want children to carry on our name and legacy. A bachelor can't do that. Every player eventually wants to settle down, I don't care who they are. Even Ramsey."

"I hear you, but I wish I knew for sure that's what Ramsey's doing," she whispered.

"And you won't know if you don't talk to him," Malachi reminded her.

Keilah fumbled with the buttons on Malachi's CD player and laughed. "You don't know Ramsey like I know him. I had this whole thing planned out, and it backfired just like he said it would."

"What did Ramsey think would happen?"

Keilah slid a CD in and as the music started playing she said, "He predicted it would mess up either our friendship or our business relationship."

"Well, has it?" Malachi asked as he turned the music up slightly.

"No, but I'm afraid it might make things awkward between us."

"Suit yourself, but the way I see it, what do you have to lose? If you love Ramsey, why would you even consider hooking up with Michael?" Malachi asked. "So what if you've had some bad luck with your past relationships? You just don't jump at the first guy that comes along with a smile. Michael might be a cool brother, but the fact remains that you haven't known him very long and you're in love with another man."

She glanced over at him and dapped her eyes with a tissue. "Thanks, Malachi."

"You're welcome, sis."

"Hey, don't say anything about this to the others. OK?" she pleaded.

"Don't worry. I won't say anything," he assured Keilah.

For the next twenty minutes they rode in the car in silence. That was until her cell phone rang.

"Hello?"

"Hey Keilah, are you free for lunch today?" Keytone asked

She glanced over at Malachi. "Yes, Keytone, I'm free. Where do you have in mind?

Keilah noticed the scowl on Malachi's face as she continued to talk to Keytone. His facial expression was typical even on a good day. After she hung up her cell phone Malachi asked, "Why are you doing this?"

"And just what am I doing, Malachi? Keytone's our brother so you're going to have to get used to it."

He pulled into the parking lot of the Lucky Chance Casino and put the car in park. "Dammit, Keilah," he yelled as he jumped out of the car and stormed into the private entrance to the building. When Malachi stepped off the elevator, he bumped into Genesis, nearly knocking him down.

"What the hell is wrong with you?" Genesis yelled.

"Your sister," he mumbled as he walked down the hallway to their office.

Genesis followed behind him, questioning him. "Where is she?"

Malachi sat down at his desk and put his head in his hands. "She's outside in the car."

"You left her by herself in the car? What the hell is wrong with you?" Genesis yelled back as he hurried out the door. When he reached the elevator he frantically pushed the button. "Come on."

When the elevator doors opened, Keilah stepped out and gave him a warm hug. Relieved she was safe, he hugged her and let out a breath. "I was just coming down to get you."

She kissed his cheek. "That's so sweet of you, but I'm fine. I made a few phone calls on my way up."

"You could've made your calls once you got inside. What's going on with you and Malachi?"

"Nothing, really. He's just a little upset because I was on the telephone with Keytone."

Genesis escorted her down the hallway and into the office. He closed the door behind them and found Malachi busy typing on the computer. "Can't you guys try to get along for once in your lives?"

Keilah pointed at Malachi. "He started it. We were having a great morning and as soon as Keytone called he freaked out. I don't know why he has to be so radical all of the time."

Malachi looked up at her from the computer. "You don't have to talk about me like I'm not here, Keilah."

"Malachi, chill," Genesis demanded.

He looked up at them with a smirk on his face. "She owes me an apology."

Keilah folded her arms. "OK, Malachi. I'm going to be the bigger person here. I'm sorry for yelling at you."

He leaned back in his chair and smiled. "Apology accepted."

Genesis frowned. "Is that all you have to say to Keilah?"

Malachi tugged on his earlobe and laughed. "OK. I'm sorry, sis."

She squinted her eyes at him.

"Now we're one big happy family again," Genesis teased.

"Not really. She's getting ready to have lunch with Keytone," Malachi revealed.

Genesis turned to her and asked, "Is that true?"

She pulled out her cell phone and punched in a text message. "Yes, it's true. I want to see him and all of my family members before I leave tonight."

"You're leaving tonight? Where did this come from?"

Malachi continued to type on the computer. "She's leaving because Michael had to fly back to D.C. this morning because he has to go to Iraq."

She frowned at Malachi. "Malachi, may I please answer Genesis' questions?"

"Whatever," he mumbled.

Keilah dropped her cell phone into her purse and turned back to Genesis. "You guys knew I was only going to be here for a couple of days."

Genesis pulled out a chair for her to sit down. "But do you have to leave so soon?"

"Yes, because Ramsey's been running the company by himself. Besides, I want to see Michael off to Iraq."

Malachi made eye contact with Keilah and smiled when she mentioned Ramsey. Keilah discreetly shook her head at Malachi. She didn't want him to reveal anything to Genesis regarding what she told him about Ramsey.

Genesis sat down next to Keilah and said, "I was hoping you would stay a couple of extra days."

"I wish I could, but I really have to get back." She looked at her watch and stood. "And if you don't mind, I have a lunch date."

Genesis also stood and said, "Wait a second, Keilah. I don't think it's a good idea for you to be running around town with Keytone."

She hugged Genesis. "I can take care of myself."

Malachi laughed. "Yeah, just like you did at the hotel, huh?"

Keilah slowly turned around and faced Malachi. "That was cold, Malachi, even for you."

"Keilah's right," Genesis agreed. "That was totally un-called for."

"No. She wants everyone to know how tough she is, let her go on," Malachi suggested.

She walked toward the door. "I'm out of here."

After she slammed the door shut, Genesis turned to Malachi. "Are you ever going to change?"

Malachi leaned back in the chair and said, "No. Keilah needs some tough love sometimes. Y'all baby her too much."

Genesis stormed out of the room and hoped he would be able to catch Keilah before she left the building. Downstairs he found her in the casino playing blackjack.

He sat down next to her and asked, "When are you and Malachi going to stop going to war with each other?"

"Just as soon as he gets off my back. I think he enjoys picking fights with me."

"He does love you, even though he has a funny way of showing it, and you guys are a lot alike personality-wise. That's why you clash so much."

Keilah looked at the cards the dealer gave her and said, "You're delusional."

"Am I? You both have the hottest tempers and are the most stubborn. Do I need to go on?"

She blushed and said, "No. Look, I know Malachi loves me, but he seems to go out of his way to aggravate me."

"Well, Malachi's right about one thing. We do baby you too much, and I'm going to try not to anymore. Deal?"

She leaned over and kissed his cheek. "Deal."

"Now can't I convince you to stay a couple more days?" he asked.

"I'm sorry, Genesis, but I can't," she replied as she picked her cards up and glanced at them.

He sighed and said, "I understand. Look, about you going to lunch with Keytone."

She put her hand up to stop him. "Save it, Genesis. I understand where you guys are coming from, but Keytone would die before he let anything happen to me."

"I wish I had as much confidence in him as you do. If you're determined to go, make sure he brings you back here when you're done."

She smiled. "I will."

"Seriously, Keilah, be careful, and if you're determined to fly out tonight, make your lunch short with Keytone so you see everyone before you leave."

She threw her cards on the table and stood. "I plan to and don't worry, I'll let Keytone know I can't hang out too long."

Genesis kissed her on the forehead before walking off. "Hurry back."

"I will," she replied as she picked up her purse and walked in the opposite direction across the casino floor. As she made her way across the room, her cell phone rang.

"Hello?"

"Are you ready for lunch?" Keytone asked.

"Yes, where are you?"

"I'm standing at the front entrance," he replied.

"I'll be right there."

She quickly hung up the telephone and hurried across the room. It only took her a few minutes to greet him at the door, and as she moved closer she could see Li'l Mike standing next to him.

"Hey, Keytone," she said with a smile.

He took her hand into his. "Good morning, Keilah."

"Hey, sis. I hope you're hungry because I'm starving," Keytone announced as he escorted her to their awaiting car.

When they got outside, T. Money was standing next to the car. Li'l Mike opened the car door so Keytone and Keilah could get inside. Keytone turned to them and said, "I'll catch up to you guys a little later. If you're going to hang out here at the casino, be cool, otherwise I'll see you when I see you."

"So where are we going?" Keilah asked.

Keytone pulled out into a steady stream of traffic and said, "Oh, this little joint that some former residents of New Orleans just opened up a few weeks ago. They settled here after Hurricane Katrina. I can't remember the name of it, but the food is off the chain. I know you're going to love it."

"I'm sure I will," she replied.

"So, where's your man?" Keytone asked. "His name is Michael, right?"

She tilted her head, glanced over at him, and smiled. "At this moment, Michael is on a plane back to D.C. They're sending him back to Iraq."

"Damn. That's messed up. He seems like a cool dude."

"He is," she acknowledged.

Keytone pulled the car into a parking lot and came to a stop.

"We're here," he announced as he looked out the window.

When Keilah stepped out of the car, the Cajun aroma immediately appealed to her senses. "Something smells heavenly."

As the pair walked toward the entrance, Keytone smiled and said, "Just wait until you taste it."

Keilah linked her arm with his. "I can't hang out with you long, Keytone, since I plan to fly out tonight. I want to make sure I get to see everyone before I go."

He nodded in agreement without speaking. A waitress escorted them to their table so they could consume the delicious cuisine of the Louisiana bayou.

CHAPTER TWENTY-ONE

Xavier was still angry that the Chance brothers passed on his offer to bring in more business to the Lucky Chance Casino in return for a piece of the ownership. He knew the casino was a gold mine, and it was the perfect spot for him to extend his power in the city. As he sat behind the desk in his office, he contemplated another way to get the Chances' attention. Luke and Roman were the head of the family, but just maybe he could make Genesis and Malachi see what they didn't.

"Baby Dee," Xavier called out.

Baby Dee walked into Xavier's office holding a piece of barbecue rib in his hands. His huge size and bulging physique clearly showed he was the muscle in the clan. "What's up, X?"

"Have you found out where Keilah Chance is staying?"

Baby Dee took a bite of his rib. "Nah, but I figured she's staying with one of her brothers. After what happened to her, you know they're not going to let her out of their sight."

X nodded in agreement as he tapped his pen on the desk. "Do me a favor."

"What's that?" he asked as he smacked his lips.

"Go over to the Lucky Chance, see who's running the show, and then give me a call. Luke and Roman might not want to listen to me, but I have a feeling Genesis and Malachi will be very interested in my offer."

Baby Dee finished off his rib. "A'ight. I'll hit you up on your cell shortly."

Once Baby Dee was out of the room, X picked up the telephone and made a call, but unfortunately he got voicemail.

"Yo, it's X. I was calling to let you know that our little plan is in the works. If everything goes like planned, everything will be in place by the end of the week. Hit me up on my cell when you can. Later."

Xavier hung up the telephone and picked up the newspaper displaying a picture of the Chance family standing in front of the Special K Casino, and then it hit him. It was the perfect solution to get the Chance brothers to accept his offer, and they wouldn't be able to take no for an answer. He grabbed his cell phone and called Slim and Romeo, who made up the rest of his ruthless entourage and told them to get back to the warehouse as soon as possible. At the moment they were terrorizing one of Xavier's customers who owed X money. They held the man hostage in his own home, and after tying the helpless debtor to a chair and threatening to shoot him in the groin, only then did the terrified man instruct his girlfriend to hand over money to the pair. Before hanging up the telephone, Xavier instructed Slim to shoot the man in the knee as a receipt of payment, and to tell him that next time, he wouldn't be so understanding. Slim did as he was told and the pair exited the man's house leaving him crying out in pain and his girlfriend hysterical.

After lunch, Keytone dropped Keilah off at the Special K Casino instead of the Lucky Chance as she requested. As soon as she entered their office, Luke sighed.

"Keilah, I got a call from Genesis, and he said you went to lunch with Keytone. Are you trying to hurt us on purpose?"

"Well, good afternoon to you too, big brother," she replied as she sat down in the chair. "What are you doing here anyway? You're supposed to be off this week."

"Keilah, don't change the subject."

She waved him off. "I heard you, Luke. I don't want to talk about Keytone, Luke, and while Genesis was running his mouth did he tell you I was leaving tonight?"

Luke sat on the end of his desk. "He mentioned it."

Keilah picked up a framed picture of Luke, Sabrinia, and their children from his desk. "You guys look good together. Sabrinia's perfect for you, Luke."

He folded his arms and said, "Thank you, and I agree."

Keilah continued to stare at the picture and before putting it back in place she said, "I'm serious, Luke. Sabrinia's a great mother and wife. I just hope you realize it."

He smiled with admiration. "She has to be a good woman to put up with me, huh?"

Keilah smiled and said, "You're not that hard to deal with, but you have your moments. I couldn't ask for a better father figure."

She stood and hugged him lovingly. Luke didn't know what was going on with Keilah, but he sensed a little sadness from her. She released him and said, "Look, I hate to leave you guys, but I'm flying back to D.C. tonight so I can spend some time with Michael before he heads off to Iraq. I need to get back to work too. Could you give me a ride over to Malachi's so I can pack my things?"

"I can do that. I only stopped by to pick up my mail. Let me check in with Roman before we leave."

She grabbed her purse. "I'll wait for you in the reception area, and can you please call Genesis and let him know I'm with you? He was expecting me to come back over there after lunch with Keytone."

Luke picked up the telephone and said, "OK, I'll be right with you."

Keilah walked out into the reception area so she could check in with Ramsey. When his cell phone rang, he answered immediately. She could tell he was in his car by the sounds in the background.

"Hey, Ramsey, did I catch you at a bad time?"

A smile immediately graced his face. "No, I'm good. What's up?"

"I was just calling to let you know I'm flying back home tonight. I really appreciate you holding things down until I took care of things out here," she said with admiration.

Ramsey's heart thumped in his chest. That was the best news he'd heard all day. "I thought you were going to stay an extra day or two. What's wrong? Nothing else has happened, has it?"

She picked up a magazine and thumbed through it as she waited on Luke. "No, I'm just ready to come home. Michael's already on his way back because they're sending him over to Iraq for some type of meeting. He left LAX this morning."

"I'm sorry to hear that. So what time does your flight get in?"

She smiled as some of the employees walked by. "I'm leaving late—around ten—so that won't put me back in D.C. until around eight AM."

"Is Michael picking you up at the airport?" Ramsey asked. "Because if he can't, I will pick you up."

"Michael doesn't even know I'm coming home yet. Don't worry. I'm going to grab a cab when I get in, but thanks anyway."

"Keilah, I'm picking you up and it's not up for discussion."

She sighed. "I don't want to put you out like that."

"You're not putting me out. Besides, I need to see a friendly face. I was sick as a dog yesterday, but I'm better now."

"What was wrong?"

"I don't know. I felt like I had food poisoning or some-thing. Look, we'll talk more when you get back. What's your flight number?"

Keilah gave Ramsey her flight, and they discussed a few things regarding their business before they told each other good-bye. When Ramsey hung up the telephone he had to make an effort to keep from yelling at the top of his lungs. Keilah was finally on her way home.

When Keilah tucked her cell phone back inside her purse, she felt her stomach quivering. Hearing Ramsey's voice made her feel that much more anxious to look into his eyes and search for any indication that he felt more for her than friendship. However, Keilah had no idea what lay in store for her . . . no idea.

Later that evening, Sabrinia and Luke hosted a dinner in Keilah's honor before she left for the airport. Since Ital-ian cuisine was Keilah's favorite, Sabrinia prepared a variety of dishes, including lasagna, chicken marsala, shrimp scampi, salad, and a basket full of garlic bread. The kids devoured nearly all of the lasagna before tearing into the cake and ice cream.

Keilah leaned back in her chair and rubbed her stomach. "I am stuffed. Sabrinia, what are you trying to do with me?"

Sabrinia laughed. "I was determined to fix all your fa-vorites."

"Yeah, but I didn't have to try and eat all of it," Keilah joked.

Sabrinia sipped her wine. "I'm glad you enjoyed it."

"That's a no-brainer, Sabrinia. I don't think you're capa-ble of making a bad meal. Now your husband, that's a differ-ent story."

Luke threw his napkin at Keilah. "Speak for yourself. I bet your oven hasn't been used since you bought it."

She threw his napkin back over to him. "That's where you're wrong, big brother. I'm a great cook."

"I'm sure you are, sis."

Keilah looked at her watch and stood. "I hate to eat and run, guys, but I really need to get to the airport."

Genesis stood. "Is Michael meeting you at the airport?"

"No, Ramsey is going to pick me up. I want to surprise Michael."

"Michael doesn't know you're coming home?" Roman asked.

"I told you, I want to surprise him," she explained.

Malachi laughed. "Ramsey's picking you up? That's a good move."

Genesis, Roman, and Luke looked over at Malachi in confusion. Roman asked, "What's wrong with Ramsey picking her up?"

Keilah stared at Malachi and spoke before he did. "Nothing's wrong with him picking me up. Malachi's just saying that because Michael asked me to marry him."

"What?" Luke asked. "Asked you to marry him? When did this happen?"

Roman mumbled, "You're not ready to get married, Keilah."

Genesis asked, "Did you just meet this dude?"

Sabrinia giggled and said, "Y'all are funny."

Luke frowned at Sabrinia and asked, "What's funny about her marrying some guy she doesn't know?"

Sabrinia held her wineglass up to Luke and said, "I'm not laughing at that. I'm laughing at the fact that you guys still don't realize that Keilah doesn't need any of your permission to do anything. She's twenty-seven years old."

Luke turned his attention back to Keilah without responding to Sabrinia's statement. "Keilah, don't you do anything stupid. We'll talk about this on the way to the air-port."

"Wait a minute. I've already called a cab," she announced. "Besides, all of you have had just a little too much wine to be driving right now."

They all knew she was right and agreed they needed to let the wine get out of their systems before they drove home. Keilah gave her nieces and nephews their good-bye hugs and kisses before hugging Sabrinia and her other family members.

Keilah walked back over to her brothers and faced four pairs of eyes like hers. "Well, guys, I guess this is it. I'll call you when I get back to D.C."

"Make sure you do," Luke announced as he hugged her lovingly. "I love you, and I hope to see you soon."

Roman pulled her into an embrace and kissed her fore-head. "Have a safe flight, sis."

"Thanks, Roman."

Genesis was next in line. He kissed her cheek and said, "Be good. I love you."

"I love you too, Genesis."

Last but not least, it was Malachi's turn. When his eyes met hers, they were saddened. He hugged and whispered into her ear. "Good-bye, Keilah. You know I love you and don't worry, your secret is safe with me."

She hugged his neck and whispered, "Thank you. I love you too."

It was at that moment they heard a car horn blaring. Sabrinia announced, "Keilah, your taxi is here."

"If you don't mind, let him know I'll be right out," she replied as she fought back her tears.

"Can we at least help you with your luggage?" Luke asked.

"Of course you can."

All five siblings walked out the door to the awaiting cab

and said their last good-byes before it drove down the street and out of sight.

Later that night, as X and his crew rode around town, he was clearly angry that things weren't going his way. He had hoped to get a chance to pitch his deal to Genesis and Malachi, but they had already left the casino. He turned to Slim and said, "I'm sick of this. It's time for Plan B, and they're not going to like it."

"Are you sure you want to go that route?" Slim asked.

X laughed. "I'll do whatever it takes to get what I want. Let's roll. We have a lot of work to do."

Ramsey felt like having a little fun, so he talked Bradford into meeting him at a local jazz club for drinks. He wasn't planning on staying out late because he knew he had to pick Keilah up from the airport early the next morning. But a little male bonding was something he needed.

"Ramsey, over here," his friend Bradford Hill yelled.

Ramsey made his way through the crowd until he met up with his friend at the bar. Shaking Bradford's hand he said, "Sorry I'm late."

Bradford twirled around on the bar stool and threw a shot of tequila at the back of his throat. "You're not late. You're right on time."

Ramsey placed his drink order with the bartender and said, "You'd better slow down on that stuff."

Bradford laughed. "That was my last one. I want my vision to be clear when I pick out my honey tonight."

The bartender sat Ramsey's Corona in front of him, and he immediately took a sip. "There's a nice crowd here tonight."

"It sure is, and I saw one of your old girls in here, too."

Ramsey took another sip and asked, "Who?"

"Monica," he informed him as he ordered a beer.

"I haven't hooked up with her in a minute. How did she look?"

Bradford looked at Ramsey and just smiled.

"That good, huh?" Ramsey asked.

"Better," Bradford replied.

The bartender sat Bradford's beer in front of him and Ramsey said, "I thought that was your last drink."

"No, that was my last tequila. I'm just getting started on the beer. Oh! Here comes your girl," Bradford announced.

"Ramsey Stone, I can't believe I'm running into you. Why haven't you called me? I thought we had something special going on," Monica playfully reprimanded him.

Ramsey sat his beer down and slowly scanned her body before giving her a warm hug. "I was going to call, Monica. I've just been busy. You can understand that, right?"

She slid her hands down to his backside and pressed her breasts against his chest. Monica was a true Amazon at five feet eleven inches tall, and the dress she had on screamed physical perfection. "You're forgiven, and if you're a good boy, I might let you take me home tonight."

He laughed out loud. "I'll have to remember that. By the way, you're wearing that dress."

She twirled around, giving him a three-hundred-and-sixty-degree view of her shapely curves. "Thank you, Ramsey."

She wrapped her arms around his neck and pulled him close so she could whisper in his ear. "If you give me a kiss, I'll give you the honor of unzipping this dress."

Ramsey smiled and happily leaned in for a kiss, but when he got within a half inch of her lips, his stomach betrayed him, causing him to quickly pull back.

"What's wrong, Ramsey? Don't you want to kiss me?" she asked with her hands on her hips.

He frowned. "I do, Monica. Just hold that thought, and I'll be back in a second."

Puzzled, Bradford looked over at him and asked, "What's wrong with you?"

Ramsey shook his head and made his way to the men's room. It was there his stomach gave way on him. As he held his head over the toilet, he prayed once again for mercy. This went on for a few minutes until he finally felt like he could return to his friends. Before leaving the men's room, he threw some water on his face and popped a breath mint in his mouth. As soon as he stepped out into the hallway, Monica was anxiously waiting on him. "Are you OK?"

He smiled. "I'm fine."

"Good, then dance with me?"

He smiled again and said, "Sure."

But as soon as they stepped out on the dance floor, Ramsey got sick again and had to rush to the bathroom. This time Bradford followed him to see what was going on.

"Ramsey, what the hell is wrong with you? You have that fine-ass woman hanging all over you, and you're spending the night in the bathroom."

Ramsey flushed the toilet and opened the door to the bathroom stall. He walked over the sink and threw more water on his face. "Bradford, something's wrong. Every time I get close to a woman I get deathly ill."

Bradford started laughing and said, "Get the hell out of here. So does this mean you like men now?"

"I'm serious. It happened with Andria the other night, and now with Monica. When I get away from them, I'm okay."

Bradford thought for a moment and then asked, "When did this start?"

"I just noticed it this week," Ramsey admitted.

"Have you eaten anything that you normally don't eat?"

Ramsey grabbed a paper towel and wiped his hands, "No."

Bradford continued to interrogate Ramsey as he relieved himself in the urinal. "Well, have you changed any habits or routines?"

"Not lately."

Bradford flushed the urinal and walked over to the sink to wash his hands. "OK, I'm going to ask you something personal. Who was the last woman you slept with?"

Ramsey frowned. "Why?"

"I don't know, bro, maybe whoever it was passed a little something on to you," he revealed.

"That's some bullshit. I'm very careful," Ramsey yelled.

"OK, who was the last woman you got busy with that didn't make you sick?"

Ramsey thought for a moment, and then it hit him. "Son of a bitch."

"Who was it?" Bradford asked.

"It's not important," Ramsey said.

Bradford threw his paper towel in the trash. "It was Keilah, wasn't it?"

Ramsey reluctantly nodded.

Bradford smiled. "You really are in love with her."

Ramsey said, "This has to be some type of virus."

Bradford opened the door and asked, "Call it what you want, but explain to me why you can't touch another woman without getting sick? You have your confirmation right in front of you, bro."

Bradford exited the bathroom, leaving Ramsey deep in thought. He let Bradford's comments sink in before he decided to call it a night and go home.

CHAPTER TWENTY-TWO

Keilah slept the entire time on her flight back to D.C. When she stepped off the plane, she headed to the closest rest room to freshen up. Her cell phone rang.

"Hello?"

"Keilah, are you on the ground yet?" Ramsey asked.

"Yes, I'm on my way to the baggage claim now. I'll see you in a second," she replied.

"Cool," Ramsey answered before hanging up.

Keilah threw some cold water on her face, touched up her makeup, dabbed a little perfume behind each ear and popped a breath mint in her mouth. She was exhausted, but wanted to see Michael to see if she saw anything in his eyes to convince her he was the man for her. After leaving the rest room, she made her way down the escalator to the ground floor. There she found Ramsey smiling like he hadn't seen her in months.

"It's about time, woman," he teased. "Welcome home."

Keilah gave him a hug and said, "It's nice to be home, Ramsey."

Ramsey looked at Keilah, and her poise and beauty overwhelmed him. He took her carry-on bag out of her hand. "How many more bags do you have?"

"Only one," she answered as they headed over to the carousel.

Luggage was already circulating, and it didn't take but a couple of minutes for Ramsey to grab her suitcase. As they walked out to his waiting car, Ramsey recognized the fact that hugging Keilah didn't make him sick to his stomach. He also recognized how hard his heart was beating in his chest. Just being in close proximity with her was driving him crazy. It didn't help matters that she was wearing a snug pair of jeans and a short-sleeved sweater that hugged her voluptuous chest.

To try and get his body under control, he thought small talk would be the best remedy. "So how was your flight?"

"I don't have a clue, because I slept the whole way," she answered right before yawning.

He frowned. "You need to go home and lie down for awhile. You know your body's jet-lagged."

"My body's fine. I just need you to run me by Michael's house before taking me home, if you don't mind."

Ramsey opened the trunk to his Lexus and piled Keilah's luggage inside. He closed the trunk and opened the passenger-side door for her and frowned. Putting her in Michael's arms wasn't on his agenda for the day. "You want me to take you over there now?"

She climbed inside his car and smiled. "It'll be a nice surprise, and besides, I have a key."

Ramsey closed the door. "He gave you a key?"

Without making eye contact with him, she nodded.

"Let me get this right. You didn't tell Michael you were coming home early?"

"No. He'll be leaving for Iraq in a day or two and I need to see him before he leaves."

"If you say so," he replied. "But you should at least call to see if he's at home before we drive over there."

"If I call him, it won't be a surprise, now will it?" she asked.

Ramsey didn't have a response for her. Instead he climbed inside the car and pulled out of the parking lot. Looking over at her, he noticed what seemed to be tension. "Are you OK? You seem a little tense."

She yawned again and then said, "I have a lot on my mind right now, that's all."

"Is it anything you want to talk about?"

"Maybe later," she replied. "How have things been at the office since we last spoke?"

"Everything's fine. Get that folder off the backseat. It has information in it on a potential employee I interviewed the other day. She used to be Special Forces in the Air Force. Take a look at it and let me know what you think."

"Hmm, a woman, huh?" she teased.

Ramsey chuckled and put on his sunglasses. "Yeah. She looks like a great candidate, too."

Keilah listened to him as she thumbed through the paperwork on the potential employee. She closed the folder and leaned back against the headrest. "I'm sure she is. Can you set up an appointment for me to talk to her tomorrow around one?"

"I don't know, Keilah. I don't want to set anything up unless you're sure you're going to be there. You going over to Michael's house is not a good sign."

Keilah looked over at Ramsey and smiled. "I see you don't have a lot of confidence in me."

"I have more confidence in you than you can imagine, Keilah Chance," he responded with sincerity.

"Just set it up, Stone," she said, giggling.

He laughed. "All right, if you say so."

* * *

It took the pair about an hour and a half to reach Michael's house with morning traffic. Keilah and Ramsey made their way up to the door. She unlocked the door and entered quietly. "I can't believe Michael gave you a key."

She turned and smiled. "He gave it to me so I can check on his house while he's in Iraq."

He grabbed her arm and said, "Well, you're using it the wrong way. I think we should leave."

"No, Ramsey, I told you I want to surprise him."

As soon as she stepped inside the foyer, she froze.

"What is it?" he asked.

Thrown around the foyer were several articles of clothing and shoes, leading upstairs.

"What the hell? Give me your gun, Ramsey," she calmly whispered.

Ramsey sat her luggage down and whispered, "Hell no. I think we should get out of here."

Keilah sat her purse down on the hall table and said, "Hell to the no. Now give me your goddamn gun."

He grabbed her by the shoulders and looked her directly in the eyes. "Have you lost your mind? I'm not going to give you my gun. Let's go."

Keilah pulled her camera phone out of her purse and walked into the family room. There she found several bottles of wine on the table, two wineglasses and two empty containers of take-out food. She quietly snapped pictures of the evidence and cursed Michael under her breath. She returned to the foyer and took pictures of the pile of clothing pitched across the floor. Ramsey ran his hand over his head in frustration as he watched Keilah snap pictures like she was investigating a crime scene. "Keilah, what are you doing?"

She walked over to Ramsey and pulled his gun out of his

holster. "I don't know what went on here last night, but to say this doesn't look good for Michael is an understatement."

With the gun in her hand, she quietly headed up the stairs, but not before Ramsey grabbed her by the arm, stopping her. "I'm not going to tell you again, let's get the hell out of here."

"I'm not going anywhere until I find out what's going on," Keilah replied as she broke from him and headed up the stairs.

He realized Keilah was about to go off on Michael, but he couldn't allow her to do anything that could ruin her life. He decided to follow her up the stairs to Michael's bedroom and be ready to intervene if necessary, but Keilah had a quick temper and could do anything.

In the hallway upstairs, Keilah and Ramsey stepped inside Michael's bedroom and found two bodies cuddled up together. The first thing she did was snap a couple of pictures of the bodies as they lay arm in arm. The next thing she did was something not even Ramsey expected. She aimed the gun at the ceiling and shot off a round, making a deafening sound. Michael immediately sat up in bed and so did his male companion. Keilah's eyes widened, and so did Ramsey's. She immediately aimed the gun at the both of them. "You bastard."

Michael was in complete shock and didn't know what to say. The man in Michael's bed raised his hand and yelled, "Please, don't shoot!"

"You'd better shut your bitch up, Michael," Keilah yelled as her hand steadied the gun right between his eyes.

Michael put his hands up in defense and pleaded with her. "Baby, don't shoot."

"You don't have the right to call me baby, you son of a bitch."

Michael was trembling now. He looked over at Ramsey and pleaded with him. "Ramsey, do something."

Ramsey shoved his hands inside his pockets. "And just want do you want me to do, Michael?"

Michael looked up at Keilah and shook his head. "Keilah, please, I can explain."

"Explain what, Michael? That you're on the down-low, and you've been sleeping with me?" she screamed.

"No, sweetheart, I . . ."

Keilah shot another round off into the ceiling, causing them to shiver even more. Keilah gritted her teeth and said, "Don't you dare 'sweetheart' me, you son of a bitch. I should kill you where you sit."

Ramsey noticed Keilah's body trembling, but her hand was steady as she held the gun. He decided to move a little closer to her just in case. "Partner, he's not worth it. Come on, Keilah. Let me take you home."

The other man pulled the sheet up over his chest and started pleading with Keilah. "Please, I just want to get out of here. I see you two have some things to work out."

Keilah stared at the man. "You're not going anywhere. How long has this been going on?"

Michael tried to answer the question, but she stopped him by yelling, "Shut the hell up, Michael. I'm not talking to you."

The man swallowed hard and said, "We been seeing each other off and on for about three years."

Keilah looked over at Ramsey, and then closed her eyes briefly before whispering, "Why, Michael? Do you have a death wish or something?"

He put his hands over his face. "I can't help it, Keilah. I do love you, but I love spending time with Kevin." He sighed and said, "Keilah, I don't know anything right now. Just let Kevin leave, because this is between you and me."

"Why did you ask me to marry you?" Keilah asked.

This caught Ramsey off guard. Keilah had forgotten to mention that bit of information to him while she was in California.

"I can't answer that while you're pointing a gun at me," Michael replied.

Keilah looked at the man Michael called Kevin and said, "Get the hell out of here."

Kevin jumped out of the bed completely naked and hurried out of the room. Keilah felt nauseated and put her hand over her mouth to stifle the sensation. She looked at Ramsey and calmly said, "Follow him and make sure he leaves."

"Are you cool?" he asked before leaving the room.

She smiled mischievously. "Of course I am, partner. You know me."

"I know. That's why I asked," Ramsey stated. "Are you cool?"

"I'm fine, Ramsey, honestly," she assured him.

"OK, but don't do anything stupid. He's not worth it. I'll meet you downstairs."

Michael looked at Ramsey. "You're not going to leave me alone with her, are you?"

Ramsey walked toward the door. "I'm sorry, bro, but I can't help you with this one. You got yourself jammed up on this one and the evidence speaks for itself."

After Ramsey left the pair alone, she paced the floor anxiously. "Don't worry, baby. You and I are just going to have a little chat."

Once Keilah was alone with Michael, she walked over to his closet and pulled out a pair of jeans and threw them at him. She sat down in a nearby chair and laid the gun on the table. A sigh of relief briefly swept over Michael's body. Keilah folded her arms across her chest and watched as Michael slid into his jeans.

"Michael, I don't think you realize how bad I want to hurt you right now."

He pulled a T-shirt out of drawer and pulled it over his head. He sat back down on the side of the bed. "Keilah, I didn't want you to find out like this. I never meant to hurt you."

"Well you did, Michael," Keilah yelled back.

Michael sat there clueless on what to say or do next. Keilah shook her head. "Have you ever had unprotected sex with this man or any man since you've been seeing me?"

Michael lowered his head. "I wouldn't do that, Keilah."

"Are you sure?"

"I said no, Keilah. I'm not an idiot. I've never had unprotected sex with any man."

Keilah felt like the room was spinning. She had a million thoughts running through her head. One thought was how happy she was that she had the sense God gave her not to have unprotected sex with him. "Then why did you try to do it with me? Why all that talk about having a family with me?"

Michael's eyes filled with tears.

"Tell me the truth, Michael," she begged. "Explain to me how you can proclaim you love me and want to marry me and have a life with me only for me to come back to D.C. and find you in bed with a man."

Michael ran his hands over his face and stared at the floor. "Keilah, when I laid eyes on you, I fell in love. I may have lied about a lot of things, but I never lied about that."

Keilah sat there frozen in her seat, still stunned by what she'd walked in on. She glared at Michael. "Why did you ask me to marry you?"

Michael looked up at Keilah and said, "My plan was to have a child with you, then eventually get a divorce so Kevin and I could be together."

She looked at him in disbelief. "Let me get this straight. You wanted to marry me to give you a child so you and your boyfriend could live happily ever after?"

Michael didn't respond. Keilah picked up the gun and started laughing. "I'm so glad God brought what you were doing in the dark to the light."

Keilah had become unexpectedly composed considering how she'd been minutes before. Michael was severely hung over and the room was spinning. At the time, he didn't know what to think of Keilah's demeanor. She had become calm—too calm.

Without saying another word, she took a couple of steps toward the door with the gun at her side. Michael's voice made her stop in her tracks. "Keilah, I'm so sorry. Where do we go from here, Keilah?"

She turned to Michael and as quick as lightning aimed the gun at him and pulled the trigger. The loud gunshot echoed throughout the house causing Ramsey to sprint up the stairs in sheer panic.

Michael fell to the floor in misery. "Dammit, Keilah. I can't believe you shot me."

By the time Ramsey made it to the room, blood was trickling from Michael's wound. He looked at Keilah and yelled, "Have you lost your damn mind? Get a towel."

Michael continued to moan as Keilah slowly walked into the bathroom to retrieve a towel. When she re-entered the room, she threw it to Ramsey and calmly sat back down in the chair.

Ramsey quickly wrapped the towel around Michael's foot to try and stop the bleeding. "Be still, Michael, and let me put pressure on it. We need to get you to the hospital."

Keilah leaned down toward Michael, who had broken out in a sweat. "Michael, I want you to know that I shot you because I loved you. I don't want you to ever think you got one over on me. You asked me where we go from here? I guess to the hospital. I'll get the car."

When Keilah got downstairs, Kevin was gone. She put Ramsey's gun in the back waistband of her jeans and went outside to start the car.

Upstairs in the bedroom, Ramsey said, "This is your fault, Michael."

Michael was now crying, not only from the pain, but from guilt as well. "I'm so sorry. Oh, God. This shit hurts."

Ramsey helped Michael off the floor. "You know she could've killed you if she really wanted to?"

"Please just get me somewhere so I can get this bullet out of my foot," he begged.

Before leaving the room, Ramsey looked at Michael. "I'm so angry at you right now that I could kill you myself. You're an idiot for putting her life in danger like you did. I should let you lie here and bleed to death."

"Please, Ramsey, help me," Michael begged.

"I'll help you only if you don't press any charges against Keilah, because when we get to the hospital, they're going to ask you what happened. By law they have to report all gun-shot wounds."

The pain caused Michael to grit his teeth. "No, I'm not pressing charges. I love Keilah. I'll just tell the doctor I picked up the gun and it went off."

"Good, now let's get you to the hospital."

Michael put his arm around Ramsey's neck and hopped on one foot out the door and down the stairs to the awaiting car.

CHAPTER TWENTY-THREE

Slim and Romeo sat in the parking lot of the gas station and waited for Luke to leave his gated community. As soon as they saw his Infiniti pass, they fell in behind him begin to tail him. Luke was a routine guy, even though he tried not to be. When Slim pulled up to a traffic light two cars behind him, he noticed Luke had his ten-year-old daughter in the car. Romeo said noticed it too and said, "Slim, that's not good."

"Just hold on, I'm sure he's just taking her to school."

"I thought we were going to be able to make our move on that stretch of highway close to his house," Romeo responded.

"The school is only a few blocks away. He has to come back out on the same road to get to his gym. He goes every morning, so stop bitching, because you're making me nervous. You just be ready."

Romeo pulled a device out his pocket and said, "Don't worry about me, I'm ready."

After Luke dropped his daughter off at school, he continued on to a local gym, just like they said he would. Romeo and Slim pulled into the parking lot a few spaces down from him and were able to approach Luke unnoticed as he opened his trunk and removed his gym bag. In the blink of an eye, Romeo zapped Luke with a stun gun, paralyzing him. They threw him into the trunk of his car, and Slim got behind the wheel and sped off with Romeo following close behind.

Capturing Luke was the easy part. Luring the others would be the challenge, but if they played their cards right and Luke cooperated, everything would go as Xavier planned.

Slim and Romeo were met at the warehouse by Xavier and Baby Dee. When they opened the trunk, Luke had come to, so they stunned him once more to paralyze him again. Baby Dee and Romeo pulled Luke out of the trunk of the car, carried him up the elevator to the second floor, and placed him on the floor of an old cage, which was formerly used to store supplies. Xavier smiled and said, "Well done. He'll be out for a while. Call me when he wakes up and we'll invite Roman, Malachi, and Genesis to join him."

Laughing, Xavier and Romeo walked over to the elevator. "We'll be back once we finish our coffee."

Baby Dee pulled out a deck of cards and said, "Bring me back a cinnamon roll. Come on Slim, and let me kick your ass in some poker."

As Luke laid on the floor, he could hear them laughing. He didn't understand what was going on, but he would sure X would let him know in due time.

Xavier and Romeo returned about thirty minutes later to find Luke screaming at Baby Dee and Slim to let him out of the cage. The moment Luke saw X step out of the elevator he cursed him repeatedly. Xavier laughed and said, "Calm down, Luke. This is only a temporary arrangement. If you do what I ask you to do you'll be home with that fine wife of yours before the sun sets. If not, then we have a problem."

"Go to hell, Xavier. You're never going to get away with this," Luke spouted.

X walked over to Luke and arrogantly responded, "I already have, but how this story ends is totally up to you."

"Like I said, Luke, your wife is fine, and if you can't find it in your heart to cooperate with me, then I have no choice but to send Baby Dee over to that restaurant she works at to escort her home. He would love to tuck her in bed for you tonight."

Xavier's comment infuriated Luke. Just the thought of X or any of these thugs anywhere near his family made his blood pressure rise.

Xavier clapped his hands together and said, "If no one has any questions, let's get this party started."

Baby Dee pulled out a forty-ounce bottle of beer and took a long sip. He burped loudly and said, "I'm hoping Luke don't cooperate. I'm looking forward to spending the night with his old lady."

They laughed again. Luke gritted his teeth and asked, "What do you want from me?"

Xavier smiled and said, "You know what I want. I tried to do this the easy way, but you wouldn't listen. Now you've forced my hand. My daddy's family deserves to have just as much share in the Lucky Chance as you and your family, and I'm determined to get it, with or without you."

"That's some bullshit, and you know it," Luke yelled back. "Your daddy was a drunk and never did anything to help my father build the casino."

Xavier jumped in Luke's face and said, "While we're talking about daddies, why don't we talk about how your daddy treated you and your family like trash. He never worked an honest day in his life. He was a ladies' man and it was all about the hustle."

Luke yanked on the cage violently and said, "Well, your daddy was his best friend so I guess you can say they were two of a kind."

"Romeo, give me the goddamn phone. Baby Dee, get him out of there. Slim, tie him up."

Romeo handed Xavier the telephone. He dialed a series of numbers and while he waited for the person to pick up he watched Slim tie Luke up. The person on the other end of the telephone picked up and Xavier said, "Yo, man. I got him. Do your thang."

Xavier hung up the telephone and said, "Let the games begin."

Back at the Lucky Chance, Malachi and Genesis started their day by conducting a brief meeting with the morning staff. Once everyone was dismissed, they headed downstairs to the restaurant to get breakfast.

Just as they were about to get on the elevator, Roman and their family attorney, P.K. Sloan, stepped out into the reception area. Roman smiled and said, "Look who I ran into."

Malachi and Genesis shook P.K.'s hand and said, "We were on our way to grab breakfast. Do you have time to join us?"

P.K. looked at his watch and said, "I can't join you guys for breakfast, but I'd be honored if you guys would let me take you to lunch around noon."

"Sounds good, P.K. It's about time you spent some money on us for a change," Malachi teased. "Where's Luke?"

Genesis said, "He should be over at the Special K right about now."

"Well, hopefully he'll be able to join us. I have a meeting to get to, but I'll pick you guys up around noon." P.K. and Roman stepped back inside the elevator.

Roman said, "I'm headed over to the Special K. I'll see you guys at lunch."

P.K. smiled and said, "Don't eat too much breakfast and make sure you save room for lunch. I'm taking you guys to a joint you'll never forget. Call Luke and make sure he's able to join us."

"Will do," Genesis replied.

P.K. pushed the button on the elevator, causing the doors to close leaving him and Roman alone. "How's Keilah enjoying her visit home?"

"She's already back in D.C. You know we could never keep her here too long."

P.K. frowned and said, "I thought she was going to stay for a few extra days."

They stepped off the elevator and walked toward the lobby doors. "We thought she was going stay a little longer too, but she said she had to get back to her company."

Roman walked P.K. outside. P.K. opened his car door and said, "I'm sure she's a busy woman. I hope you guys didn't give her a hard time. Wait a minute. I forgot who I was talking to. I bet all of y'all gave her a hard time didn't you?"

Roman laughed.

P.K. started up his car and said, "Say no more. I'll see you at noon."

"Good-bye, P.K."

Roman pulled his keys out of his pockets, walked over to his car and headed to the Special K. When he pulled out of the parking lot he dialed Luke's cell phone. After a series of rings, his voicemail came on. "Yo, Luke, I'm on my way in to the office. Clear your calendar for lunch because P.K. is taking us out to eat. I'll see you shortly."

As Michael was being treated in the emergency room, doctors quizzed him about his injury. Keilah sat quietly in the waiting room while Ramsey made a few calls on his cell phone. When he hung up, he turned to Keilah. "You do know shooting Michael was stupid, right?"

"I let him off easy. I should've killed him."

Ramsey tucked his cell phone in his pocket. "And where would that have gotten you, huh? You have to think about yourself. That kind of ignorance is not worth messing up your life over. Besides, the last time I checked, we had a business together, and you could've put that in jeopardy, too."

With a blank look on her face, she softly apologized, "I'm sorry, Ramsey."

He moved a strand of hair out of her eyes. "Keilah, I'm not saying I don't understand your pain. I'm saying you're going to have to keep your head clear of bullshit like this when it comes to dating."

She interlocked her arm with his, and then laid her head on his shoulder. "I know, but this was the ultimate betrayal."

Ramsey sat there for a moment, and then asked her a question he seriously needed answering. "Keilah?"

"Yes?"

"Have you ever had unprotected sex with Michael?"

She sat up and looked him in the eyes. "No, and I'm so thankful. He claims he never had unprotected sex with any man, but I don't believe anything he says anymore."

Ramsey stared at her and let out a relieved breath. Tears formed in Keilah's eyes when she realized what thoughts were going through his head. It's not like it hadn't crossed her mind, too. "Ramsey, you're the only man in my life I've ever had unprotected sex with and you and I both know it was stupid of us to do that, but I . . ."

A doctor walked up and interrupted them. "Are you two here with Michael Monroe?"

Ramsey stood and said, "Yes, how is he?"

"He's coming along fine. The bullet has been removed, and he's being stitched up as we speak. You'll be able to see him shortly. I just wanted to come out and give you an update."

Ramsey shook the doctor's hand and said, "Thank you."

He sat back down and said, "What were you saying before we were interrupted?"

She sighed and said, "Listen Ramsey, I know this is all too little too late, but while we're on the subject, what about you? Have you had unprotected sex with any of the million women you've dated?"

Ramsey put his arm around her shoulders and smiled. "No way, never in my life."

Keilah cleared her throat and then asked, "Then why did you do it with me?"

He shifted in his seat. This wasn't the place he wanted to tell Keilah that he was madly in love with her and that he wanted to make her his wife, so said the first thing that came to his mind. "I know it was wrong, Keilah but you're special to me in ways you would probably be surprised about."

"That's not an answer, Stone."

"I know, but it's the best I can do under the circumstances. Sitting in the emergency room waiting room is not the place to talk about this," he replied.

Keilah leaned over and whispered into his ear. "Would you be offended if I asked you to go get tested with me? I know it would make us both feel so much better."

He hugged her tighter and said, "Of course I'll go. You and I both know that sex is not the only way to get HIV, and we've both come in contact with some shady people and had our share of scrapes, cuts, and bruises. Getting tested is the right thing to do. I'm glad you brought it up. Look, after we get Michael situated, why don't you come home with me and let me fix you something to eat? You have to be exhausted."

She stood up and so did Ramsey. "I am exhausted, but I'm not hungry. I'll pass, but thanks for the offer. I'm going to catch a cab home so I can decompress."

"OK. I'll check on you later," he said as he walked her to the door.

She hugged him. "Thank you."

Seconds later she disappeared around the corner and out of sight.

Michael was finally moved to a room and was still slightly sedated when Ramsey walked into the room. Michael opened his eyes and noticed Ramsey was alone.

"Where's Keilah?" Michael asked.

Ramsey stared down at the bandages on Michael's foot. "She went home."

"She hates me, doesn't she?"

Ramsey ran his hand over his head. "What do you expect, Michael? You lied to Keilah in every way possible. It's one thing to cheat on her with a woman, but you did it with a man. That's not something that happens overnight. You're lucky she didn't kill you."

Tears ran down Michael's face. "Will you please tell her I'm sorry?"

Ramsey walked over to the window, looked out for a moment and then turned to face Michael. "No, what you need to do is to forget about Keilah and make sure your boyfriend doesn't report the incident. If this ever comes to light it won't only mess up Keilah's life, but yours too, and I'm sure you don't want the Randolphs or your military buddies to know about your alternative lifestyle. But I will promise you this, if Keilah gets into trouble over this then I'm coming after you. You owe Keilah and you know it."

Michael softly whispered, "I love Keilah. I'll take care of her so she doesn't have to worry about getting into trouble over this."

Ramsey walked toward the door and said, "Good, and I trust that you're being truthful with me."

"I am, Ramsey. Thanks for helping me."

Ramsey opened the door and said, "Good-bye, Michael."

Michael closed his eyes and drifted off to sleep.

K eilah felt refreshed after a long, hot soak in her tub. The events of the morning and taken a toll on her, and all she could think of at the moment was some much-needed sleep. As she pulled back the comforter on her bed, her doorbell rang. She cussed before she hurried downstairs and found Ramsey on her doorstep. She opened the door, allowing him to come in.

"You look like you're ready for bed," he noted as he entered the house.

Dressed in some very revealing boy shorts and a T-shirt, Keilah replied, "Something like that."

Shivers ran over Ramsey's body as he took note of her attire. He followed her into the family room and said, "Well, I won't keep you. I just wanted to make sure you were okay. Michael's going to be fine, but they're keeping him overnight for observation. It seems like his pain is more emotional than physical though."

Keilah sat down on the sofa and pulled a pillow into her lap. "Is he going to have me arrested?"

"No. He made that clear before we left his house."

Keilah leaned her head back on the sofa and said, "What about Michael's boyfriend? He could report me."

Ramsey looked over at Keilah and said, "Michael assured me he would take care of everything."

"I can't remember the last time I was that angry, Ramsey. The moment I saw that man in his bed, I knew I was going to shoot him. I just didn't know how many times."

"I would've been pissed too, Keilah, but you jeopardized your whole life over him. Michael wasn't worth it and you know it."

"I know but I lost it, Ramsey. I mean it wasn't like I was in love with him or anything, but the fact that I'd been intimate with him and then found him in bed with a man sent me over the edge. I guess you could say I saw my life flash before my eyes."

Ramsey sat quietly for a second and asked, "Are you going to tell your brothers?"

She curled up on the sofa next to him. "If I do, then Michael will be a dead man. They didn't seem to like him very much. The age difference had a lot to do with it. This whole thing feels like a nightmare."

Ramsey sighed. "All Michael had to do was be honest with you in the beginning."

"Michael told me he was planning on marrying me just so I could give him a child. After that his plan was to divorce me and raise our child with Kevin. You know I would never let him get away with that."

"That's deep. It sounds like he's been planning this for a while. Why didn't you tell me he'd proposed to you?"

She lowered her head and said, "Because I was never going to marry him, so there was no need to tell you. I didn't come home early to be with Michael. I came home early because I needed to talk to you about something very important."

He looked over at her and asked, "What's on your mind?"

Keilah sighed as she reached over and took his hand. "I've been having these thoughts and feelings about me and you, and the only way I can explain it is that you mean much more to me than a friend."

Ramsey couldn't believe his ears. Could Keilah be confessing what he'd planned to confess to her?

"What are you saying, Keilah?"

She let out a breath and gave his hand a tender squeeze. "The heart doesn't lie. I came back to D.C. early to break up with Michael before he went to Iraq. He was moving so fast, and the feelings I had for him wasn't nearly as strong as the feelings he proclaimed he had for me."

Ramsey's felt like his heart was skipping a beat. He couldn't do anything but stare at Keilah. Could it be that his wildest dreams were about to come true? He would just have to sit here and let her finish talking before he would know.

Keilah took a deep breath and said, "Whew. This is so hard for me, Ramsey."

"Take your time, Keilah," he coached her. "You're doing just fine."

"OK, but just bear with me and wait until I finish before you say anything."

"I can do that," he replied with a smile.

Keilah caressed his hand and said, "What I'm trying to say, Ramsey, is that when I'm with you, my heart feels like it's about to burst out of my chest. Just hearing your voice causes me to shiver, and I think about you day and night. I didn't have that with Michael, and because I know your stance on love and being in a committed relationship I tried to make Michael be the one for me, but I wasn't happy. You make me happy, and you make me feel all the things a woman is supposed to feel. I love you, Ramsey, I'm sure of it, and I knew I couldn't let another day pass without me telling you how I feel about you. I don't expect you to say or do anything and I don't want to make you feel awkward. I'm telling you for me. I'm not trying to interfere with your lifestyle or come between you and your lady friends. I'm doing it to clear my conscience and my heart."

Ramsey stared at her in disbelief. He cleared his throat and asked, "Are you finished?"

She nodded in silence. Ramsey then reached over, cupped her face and gave her a hot, passionate kiss. He'd kissed her before but never like this. It was as if the floodgates had been let open and waves of emotion poured in over both of them. Keilah's body felt like she had jolts of electricity flowing through it, causing her to melt at the touch of his hands. Ramsey was in heaven and feeling Keilah's soft body against his sent him into a heated frenzy. Kissing her felt natural and right and his body told what he couldn't deny. Breathlessly, Keilah asked, "I take it that you're OK with what I said?"

He stopped kissing her only to say, "You only said what I was planning on telling you. You just beat me to the punch, as usual, Miss Chance."

Keilah closed her eyes and lay back on the sofa as Ramsey trailed kisses from her lips down to her navel. She writhed beneath him as he kissed his way back up to her lips. He whispered, "I love you, Keilah. I've loved you for several months, but I didn't know how to tell you."

"Really?" she asked.

"Really," he replied. "After you hooked up with Michael, I didn't want to cause any problems. It wasn't until it appeared that you guys were getting more serious that I decided I needed to come clean and tell you how I felt."

"Liar," she joked.

"You think?" he asked. "Remember that job offer I told you about while you were in California and new position I told you that you would be perfect for?"

"Yes," she said softly as she caressed his face.

"Well, the new job offer was you being my wife and the position . . . well, that's something I'll have to show you later."

Keilah lay there in disbelief. "I'm shocked, Ramsey. I had no idea."

With a smirk on his face he said, "You should've known by the way I looked at you, kissed you, and made love to you."

"It crossed my mind a couple of times, but I didn't want to get my hopes up because you were so adamant about staying single. Besides, the reason we hooked up in the first place was for physical reasons only, remember?"

He kissed her softly on the neck and said, "I remember. I told you it would backfire on us."

She blushed and said, "In a good way, though, right?"

He smiled, lifted her top, lowered his head and took her brown nipple into his mouth. Keilah let a soft moan escape her lips. Her lower region throbbed as he feasted on her voluptuous mounds. He finally raised his head and smiled. "No, this backfired on us in a perfect way. I love you, Keilah. I know it's love because I've never felt like this before. So are you going to accept my job offer or not?"

She wrapped her arms around his neck and ran her tongue across his lips before covering his lips with hers. Ramsey's body stiffened as he sucked in a breath. Keilah nuzzled her face against his neck and asked, "What does that tell you?"

"It tells me we need to take this upstairs," he answered.

Keilah could feel the evidence of his love and desire as he lay on top of her. "Lead the way, baby. I'm all yours."

He stood and pulled her up off the sofa. They disappeared upstairs, where Ramsey showed Keilah the new position he'd mentioned to her moments earlier. The couple made love and sealed their union and were not to be seen again until the following morning. Ramsey and Keilah chose this day to go take HIV tests before going in to their office. The results of the tests were now in God's hands.

CHAPTER TWENTY-FOUR

As soon as Ramsey and Keilah settled into their offices for work, Teresa Randolph entered the Stone Chance Protection Agency like a tornado and without an appointment. She charged past Keilah's secretary and into Keilah's office, closing the door behind her. Keilah was with a couple of employees, but as soon as she saw the look on Mrs. Randolph's face she quickly excused them.

As soon as the employees had exited the room, she shook the older woman's hand before offering her a seat. "It's so nice to see you, Mrs. Randolph. How may I help you today?"

Teresa threw her scarf around her neck and said, "I've told you a hundred times to call me Teresa. Now tell me what happened between you and Michael. He's devastated, and I can't have him over in Iraq with the state of mind that he's in. It could put him in a dangerous position."

Keilah sighed, not knowing how much information Michael told his aunt. "It's personal, Mrs. Randolph, and I'd rather not discuss it. I'm sure you can respect my privacy as well as Michael's. Besides, if you want to know, why don't you just ask him?"

"I did, but he refuses to tell me anything. I honestly believe he shot himself in the foot as a cry for help. He's trying to get attention. Keilah, my nephew and his happiness mean the world to me. He is the son of my only sibling, and when he's unhappy, I'm unhappy."

Keilah looked Teresa directly in the eyes. "I'm sorry, but I can't help you, Mrs. Randolph. All I can tell you is that things didn't work out between us, and I wish Michael well."

Teresa Randolph stood. "I see you're just as stubborn as I am. Maybe that's why I like you so much. I see myself in you."

Keilah also stood. "Mrs. Randolph, I'm not trying to be difficult. My relationship with Michael just didn't work out. The experience hurt me, but it showed me that I'm not the one for him. Don't worry about Michael, I'm sure he'll find that special someone for him in little or no time."

Teresa tucked her clutch purse under her arm. "Are you sure there's no hope for a reconciliation between you two? I was really hoping that you would become a part of our family."

Keilah walked her to the door. "I'm sure. Is there anything else I can help you with while you're here? Is everything working out with your agent?"

"Yes, everything is going fine, but she's not as personable as you are," Teresa revealed.

"That's sweet of you to say, Teresa, but I'm sure with time you'll get used to her."

Teresa smiled and said, "Thank you and I wish you well. Please be careful and take care of yourself."

"I will, and I appreciate you caring. Give Mr. Randolph and Arhmelia my regards," Keilah said as she walked Teresa to the elevator.

"I'll tell them, and I'm sorry for bursting into your office like a crazy woman."

"You're welcome here anytime, Teresa. Have a great day."

She stepped inside the elevator and waved good-bye to Keilah before the doors closed.

Later that evening, Keilah and Ramsey shared a quiet dinner together. Before he left to go home, he pulled a small box out of his pocket and placed it in her hands.

Her eyes widened. "What's this?"

"It's nothing, just a little something to let you know how much I care."

Keilah smiled, tore into the package, and opened the box. She pulled out what appeared to be a gold necklace. When she held it up, she noticed it had a bull's-eye symbol on it.

She couldn't help but laugh. "I see you're a comedian now."

Ramsey laughed out loud. "When I saw it in a store, I knew I had to have it. I got it after your incident in California."

She grabbed one of the pillows off her sofa and threw it at him. "You are so wrong."

He threw the pillow back at her. "You've been such a target lately. I had to do something to make you laugh."

"With this bull's-eye, I'm going to be more of a target," she teased as she put the necklace around her neck. She got up and looked at it in the mirror. She turned to him and asked, "How do I look?"

He walked over and stood behind her so he could see how the necklace looked around her neck. "You look fabulous, as always, but this is your real present."

Ramsey put another beautiful package in her hand. It was wrapped in gold paper with a gold-glittered bow on top. She walked over to the sofa and sat down to open the second box, and when she did, tears immediately flowed down her face. She turned to Ramsey and whispered, "It's beautiful. Thank you."

Inside the box sat a three-stone, princess-cut, platinum diamond ring. Ramsey took the ring out of the case and slid it onto her finger and said, "All that I ask is that you don't make me wait too long."

She wrapped her arms around his neck and whispered, "I won't, baby. I won't."

Later that night, as Keilah and Ramsey lay in each other's arms, Keilah was awakened by the ringing of her telephone.

"Hello?" she answered in a groggy voice.

"Keilah, it's Sabrinia. Have you talked to Luke or any of the guys in the last twenty-four hours?"

Trying to gather her senses, Keilah answered, "No. What time is it?"

"It's about ten o'clock here," Sabrinia replied.

Keilah leaned over and turned on the light next to her bed. Ramsey woke up and asked, "What's wrong?"

Keilah was so tuned into Sabrinia she didn't hear Ramsey. She sat up on the side of the bed and asked, "What's going on? You sound worried."

Ramsey eased out of the bed and made his way into the bathroom. When he returned he sat down beside Keilah and asked again, "What's wrong?"

She turned to him and said, "I'm not sure. It's Sabrinia. Hold on a sec."

Keilah listened as Sabrinia continued, "Luke always calls me during the day while he's at the casino. I haven't heard from him since about two this afternoon. When I call his cell it goes right into his voicemail. The same goes for Roman, Malachi, and Genesis. The receptionists at the casinos said they all left at different times between four and six. Something's wrong. I just feel it, Keilah."

"Calm down, Sabrinia. Let me see what I can find out.

Don't worry. I'm sure they're somewhere hanging out and just lost track of time. I'll call you back."

"I hope you're right, Keilah."

Once Keilah hung up, she turned to Ramsey and said, "My brothers are missing. Something's wrong."

"All of them are missing?" Ramsey asked.

Keilah nodded as she immediately dialed Keytone's number. It took a few seconds, but he finally answered. "Keilah, I love you and I always look forward to talking to you, but do you have any idea what you just interrupted?"

"Keytone, I don't care about you getting your freak on. I need your help."

He picked up on the urgency in her voice right away. "What's wrong?"

"Have you seen any of my brothers in the last twenty-four hours? Luke's wife called saying she can't get in touch with him or any of them."

"No, I haven't. Do you think something's wrong?" he asked.

"I have a bad feeling about this. It's not like all of them to be out of touch with the family, especially Luke. He's more responsible than that."

While Keilah was talking to Keytone, Ramsey took the time to get dressed.

"I'll see if I can find them. Sit tight, and I'll get back to you."

Keilah nervously twirled a strand of hair round her finger and said, "Thanks, Keytone."

Keytone could hear her voice quivering and could sense she was beyond worried about her brothers. "Is Michael with you? You shouldn't be alone right now."

"No, he's not with me and don't expect him to ever be again," she replied.

"What happened?"

"I caught him in bed with a man, so I shot him," she revealed.

"You what?" he yelled as he sat up in bed.

"Don't worry, he'll live. I only shot him in the foot, but I felt like killing him," she confessed.

"I figured he must still be alive, otherwise you would've called me collect from jail."

"You're right. Listen, hurry up and get back to me," she requested as she glanced over at Ramsey who was putting on his shoes. "You don't have to worry about me because I'm in very good hands."

Keytone chuckled and said, "I don't know exactly what that means, but I have an idea. Listen, before you go jetting off across the country, sit tight until I get back with you, and try to keep your gun in your holster," he teased.

Ramsey looked up and winked at her. He could tell from the one-sided conversation that it wasn't looking good for Keilah's brothers and she was going to need his help.

Before hanging up the telephone with Keytone she told him to be careful.

Ramsey walked around the bed and hugged Keilah. "It's going to be OK, babe, don't worry. Now get dressed. We have a plane to catch."

She looked up into his eyes and said, "Thank you."

He looked at his watch and said, "I didn't want to interrupt your conversation with Keytone, but there's no way we're going to sit here and wait on news. We're going out there. Now pack."

"I never got a chance to unpack," she pointed out.

He grabbed his keys off the nightstand and said, "Good, now hurry up and get dressed."

She hurried toward the bathroom and asked, "What about you?"

"We can stop at my house on the way. It'll only take me a second to throw a few things in a bag. Hurry up, Keilah."

She ran into the bathroom, took a quick shower, and was

dressed within thirty minutes. On the way out the door, Ramsey said, "Call Keytone and let him know we're on our way."

It was eleven o'clock in the morning by the time Keilah and Ramsey arrived at LAX airport. Keilah yawned as they made their way down to the baggage claim. Sleep was not an option on the plane because she was so worried about her brothers. Even as she walked through the airport, she continued to try and call their cell phones, but just like before, she only got their voicemail.

"Still no answer?" Ramsey asked.

"No," she replied as she dropped her cell down in her purse. Just as she closed her purse, her cell phone rung. She hurriedly answered it. "Hello?"

"Don't hang up, Keilah. It's me, Michael."

"I can't talk to you right now, Michael. It's not a good time. Besides, we have nothing left to talk about."

Ramsey frowned upon hearing Michael's name. He had a lot of nerve calling Keilah under the circumstances. Keilah looked at Ramsey and shook her head in disbelief.

Michael said, "Look, I didn't call to bother you. I just wanted to hear your voice. I'm leaving for Iraq in a couple of days and I wanted to apologize to you again for what I did. I needed to make amends with you before I left. It wouldn't feel right if I didn't."

"As a Christian I have to forgive you, Michael, but everything is too fresh right now for me to even think about what you did to me. I'm dealing with some other issues so like I said, now is not a good time," she said.

"I miss you, Keilah Chance. I miss you terribly, and if I could change what happened between us I would," he replied.

"I sorry, Michael, but I have to go. Have a safe trip to Iraq and I wish you well, but I would appreciate it if you wouldn't call me anymore," she explained.

At that point the phone line went dead. Keilah didn't know if it was a bad connection or if Michael had hung up the telephone. At this point, all that mattered to her was finding her brothers safe and sound and starting a new life with Ramsey.

"What did he want?" Ramsey asked.

Keilah shook her head and said, "He said he was leaving for Iraq and wanted to apologize."

Ramsey frowned and asked, "How did he sound?"

"What do you mean?" she asked when they reached the turnstile.

Ramsey grabbed one of their bags off the rotating belt and turned to her. "You know what I mean. Did he sound angry, depressed, or remorseful?"

Keilah shrugged her shoulders and said, "He sounded a little sad and apologetic, that's all. He was still talking about he loved me and stuff like that."

Ramsey grabbed another piece of luggage off the turnstile and said, "Maybe being in Iraq will help him. I want to know when he comes back to the States. If he's still saying he loves you, he could be a little unstable and I don't want him showing up at the office or your house."

Keilah grabbed the last piece of luggage off the turnstile and said, "I guess you're right."

After retrieving all their luggage, they walked over to the rental-car stations, rented a car, and then headed out to Malachi's house. On the way, Keilah called Sabrinia and Keytone to let them know she was back in town.

CHAPTER TWENTY-FIVE

Across town, Xavier and his crew pulled into the railyard and slowly made their way up to a run-down warehouse. Baby Dee exited the vehicle first and unlocked a large door. After sliding it open, Romeo slowly drove the Escalade inside the warehouse. Baby Dee closed the door behind them as Romeo and X exited the vehicle.

"Baby Dee, watch the door. If anything looks suspicious give me a holler."

Baby climbed behind the wheel of the Escalade. "Will do, X."

Xavier and Romeo made their way to a back room and up the elevator. When they reached the end of the hallway, they came upon a door with a padlock on it. Xavier pulled out some keys and unlocked the door. Romeo pulled out his nine-millimeter and slowly pushed open the door. The pair walked through the door and found Luke, Roman, Malachi, and Genesis inside a caged area. The brothers immediately started cursing at Xavier and Romeo.

"Guys . . . guys. Hold it down in here. I see that P.K. took care of your accommodations and got you here safe and sound."

"Go to hell, X," Luke yelled. "If you don't let us out of here, so help me God, I'll make sure you and P.K. never take another breath."

Xavier laughed and sat down in a nearby chair. "Threats will get you nowhere. Besides, we have some business to conduct. So the way I see it, you don't have a choice but to listen and do whatever the hell I tell you to."

"What do you want from us?" Roman asked.

Xavier flicked a piece of lint off the leg of his pants. "Well, let's see. For starters, I want the Lucky Chance."

"You're not getting our casino, so you can forget that," Luke replied angrily.

"I hate to hear that, Luke, because like I said earlier, I have no problem sending Baby Dee over to your house to get real acquainted with your lovely wife."

Luke was gripping the wire the on cage so hard it cut into his skin. He gritted his teeth and said, "And like I said before, if you go anywhere near my wife or any of our family members, you're dead. Do you understand me?"

Xavier laughed and looked at Romeo. "You're not in a position to do anything about it, now are you?" At that point, Malachi ran as fast as he could and threw his body against the cage in a fit of rage. It was futile, because all he did was hurt his shoulder. Roman and Genesis helped Malachi off the floor. Roman stepped forward and said, "X, this is not the way to do business. I don't know how you got P.K. involved, but I would love to find out how much you're paying him and how long he's been in on it."

Xavier laughed and said, "P.K. is a genius, and for the right price you can buy almost anybody."

Malachi mumbled, "When we get out of here, I want to be the one to put a bullet in P.K.'s brain."

"Count me in on that one, Malachi," Genesis responded.

"Now that we're all together, why don't we get down to business?" X announced.

Genesis stepped forward and pointed at Xavier. "It all makes sense now. I should've known it was you. You're the one who had Keilah attacked at the hotel and your thugs here are the ones who did it."

X put his hands up in defense. "Now, now, now. I'm not going to admit to anything that might incriminate me."

Luke hit the cage with his fist. "X, I swear if I ever get out of this cage, I am going to kill you."

"Ah, come on, Luke. You and I both know that you're not in a position to make threats. Now, let's get down to business. I gave you guys an offer, and you declined, which forced me to go to Plan B and as you see, Plan B is not so pleasant."

Genesis shook his head in disbelief.

"All I want is the Lucky Chance. Like I told Luke, it's just as much mine as it is yours. Joe Chance was a con man, and I'm going to make it right."

"That's some bullshit, X, and you know it," Roman yelled.

X jumped out of the chair. "The hell it is. I know the truth, and I'm going to make things right for my pops if it kills me."

Just then, Baby Dee called Xavier's cell phone. X put the phone up to his mouth and said, "Send him up."

A few minutes later they were face to face again with P.K. Sloan. When he walked in he had a smirk on his face. Malachi yelled, "P.K. you're a dead man."

"I don't think so, Malachi, but what I'm about to be is co-owner of the Lucky Chance and the Special K casinos."

"It'll never happen," Malachi yelled.

P.K. chuckled again. "I disagree. It's a partnership made in heaven, and as soon as I get your sister to sign one more document, we'll be the sole owners of the casinos."

"What do you mean?" Luke asked.

P.K. sat down next to X. "Remember the day Keilah signed the papers for the Special K?"

Luke yelled, "What about it?"

"Most of the paperwork I had you guys sign was legit, but I accidentally left the most important one out of the stack," he revealed. "Now all we have to do is get her signature and my work is done."

Genesis closed his eyes in disbelief. Luke lowered his head and then whispered, "We trusted you. How could you do something like this?"

"Actually, it was easy. You guys were so excited that day, no one took the time to read the fine print. Once I got signatures from all of you, I was home free."

X laughed and said, "It don't feel too good to be left out in the cold, does it? The way I see it, we'll have Keilah's signature in little or no time."

P.K. smiled and said, "Don't be so hard on yourselves. I've enjoyed doing business with you guys over the years. I'm ready to retire and it'll be so much easier doing it with lucrative businesses like the Special K and the Lucky Chance under my belt. I'm sure someone has contacted her, since none of you made it home last night or called. I have no doubt that Keilah is going to do whatever she can to find you guys, and you know what? I made it easy for her. I'm going to lead her right here, so we can get her signature and then our business will be over."

"She'll never sign the papers," Malachi yelled.

X laughed. "If she doesn't, you guys will get to witness your little sister in various compromising positions, and I don't think you want to push me that far."

If looks could kill, X and P.K. would be six feet under, because the brothers had lethal glares.

X looked at his watch. "I'm sorry, but we have to run. I'm going to have one of my girls come by and bring you guys a fish sandwich or something. If my estimates are correct,

Keilah should be getting my message any time now, so sit tight and I'll see you guys a little later."

P.K. and X laughed as they made their way back down to their vehicles, leaving the brothers to wonder what kind of hell they would go through next.

Ramsey and Keilah made it to Malachi's house and took their bags inside. While Keilah fed and walked Bonnie and Clyde, Ramsey looked around the house. When she came back in, he asked, "Does anything look out of place?"

She scanned the room and said, "No, everything looks fine."

"I'm starving, Keilah. Can we see what's in the fridge?"

"You go ahead. I'm going upstairs to check his answering machine first," she said before jogging up the stairs.

Upstairs in Malachi's bedroom, she noticed the blinking light. She picked up the pen lying next to the notepad and pushed the button to listen to his messages. There were several, including ones from her and Sabrinia. By the time she got to the last message, Ramsey had devoured two ham-and-cheese sandwiches and made one for Keilah. When he walked in the door, he froze when he saw the expression on her face. "What's wrong? Did you find out something?"

She put her hands over her face. "A guy named Xavier has them."

Ramsey sat the sandwich down on the dresser. "What do you mean?"

"Just what I said, Ramsey. Listen."

Keilah rewound the message and played it for Ramsey. By the look on her face, he knew that whatever he was about to hear, wasn't good.

"Yo! Keilah, this is Xavier. I know we haven't been formally introduced, but that's cool. We'll see each other soon enough. Anyway, I'm sure by now you're probably looking for your brothers, but you don't have to worry because I want you to know I'm taking real good care of them. Now, you and I have some business to discuss, so if you ever want to see them again in one piece, you need to come to the Dennison rail-yard at Zinc Street, warehouse number three. I don't have to tell you to come alone, and if you don't, you're going to regret it. Send a text to all four of your brother's phones so I'll know you got this message. I can't wait to see you again. We're waiting. Peace!"

"Damn, Keilah. Who is Xavier?" Ramsey asked.

She stood up and said, "I really don't know that much about him. I think they call him X. Luke pointed him out to me at the grand opening and said he was some guy in the area who's trying to make a name for himself on the streets."

"What kind of business could he want to discuss with you?"

"I don't know, but it has to be something about the casinos. Come on. We're going down there to find out and get my brothers," she said as she hurried out the door.

Ramsey grabbed her arm. "Hold on a second, Keilah. You know we can't go charging into a place we don't anything about. This is not the Wild, Wild West anymore. We need to sit down and find out a little more about this guy first."

She angrily pointed at the answering machine. "Was I the only one who heard that message, Ramsey? If we don't hurry up and do something, there's no telling what he'll do to them. For all we know they're already dead."

Ramsey put his arm around her shoulders. "No way. This guy wants something from you, and its obvious he can't get it unless you're involved. Otherwise, he wouldn't have even left you this message."

"Dammit," she yelled.

Ramsey hugged her tightly. "Don't worry, baby, we'll get your brothers back. I promise. Why don't you give Keytone a call, so we can map out a plan of action?"

Keilah wiped a lone tear off her cheek and picked up the phone.

Within forty-five minutes, Keytone was at the door with Li'l Mike and T.Money. She hugged Keytone and stepped back so they could enter the house. "Hey, Keytone. Thanks for coming over."

T.Money and Li'l Mike made their way over to the sofa. Ramsey walked into the room with three glasses of cranberry juice. He sat them on the table. "Hey, Keytone. It's good seeing you again. I just wish it was under more pleasant circumstances, though."

Keytone shook Ramsey's hand. "No doubt."

Keytone introduced Ramsey to his crew, after which Ramsey reentered the kitchen to retrieve drinks for the others. Once he returned to the room they all sat down and Keilah asked, "Are you guys ready to get down to business?"

"Yeah, fill me in," Keytone replied.

Keilah placed the message X left on Malachi's answering machine for Keytone. After he finished listening to it, he shook his head and said, "I don't know what he's up to, but I don't put anything past him. That kid has finally lost his damn mind. He's gone too far this time."

Ramsey sat up. "Do you know your way around that rail-yard?"

"Yeah. I've actually done some business down there myself. Most of it is abandoned, which makes it the perfect setting for things you want to keep private, if you know what I mean," Keytone answered.

"OK, we need some firearms," Ramsey pointed out.

Keilah said, "You don't have to worry about that, Ramsey. Malachi has somewhat of an arsenal, and it's fully stocked. Plus I know Keytone does too."

Keytone rubbed his hands together. "You know me, don't you, sis?"

Ramsey asked, "What does Malachi have?"

"You name it, he has it," she answered. "He can pretty much supply a small army."

Ramsey chuckled. "That's scary."

"You got that right, Ramsey," Keytone added.

Keytone stood up and said, "So, fellows, when are we going to do this? The longer we wait, the harder it's going to be."

Ramsey looked over at Keytone. "What do you think?"

She sat quietly for a second and then she spoke. "I've been thinking. I'm not meeting Xavier at any warehouse and neither are you. If he has business to discuss with me, it's going to be on my terms or there won't be a meeting."

Keytone frowned. "Where is that coming from?"

"It's coming from here," she stated as she pointed to her head. "I know my brothers are in danger, and I know they expect me to do the right thing. They wouldn't want me to put myself in danger over them. They would want me to use my head and not my heart."

Ramsey looked at her and saw the anger in her. "Keilah, are you sure about this?"

She looked over at him and smiled. "I'm sure."

Keytone got up and walked over to the window. "So, how do you want to do this?"

She laid back in her seat. "We're getting ready to shut this city down."

Ramsey and Keytone looked at Keilah and then at each other. They had no idea what she planned to do, but whatever it was, they had no doubt it was going to cause some damage.

"I'm going to have X meet me at the Lucky Chance. Xavier's in for a big surprise, and he's not going to like it."

"How are you going to close the casino on short notice?" Keytone asked.

She pulled out her cell phone. "With one phone call. I'll

have them put on the marquee CLOSED FOR RENOVATION. If anyone wants to gamble they can go over to the Special K."

Keytone held out his fist so Ramsey could dap his. "That's my sister. She don't play. It's on now."

Ramsey laughed. "I'd have to agree with you, Keytone. Keilah is a dangerous woman in more ways than one."

CHAPTER TWENTY-SIX

All four of the Chance brothers' phones received a text message just like X instructed, but when he read them, his smile quickly turned into a frown.

"What's wrong, X?" Romeo asked.

"I underestimated her," he replied.

"Who? Keilah Chance?"

"Yes. She's no ordinary woman for sure. She's not coming to the warehouse tonight. She want me to meet her at the Lucky Chance, and she wants me to bring her brothers or there's no meeting."

"Why?" Romeo asked.

Xavier looked over at Romeo. "I'm sure she's more comfortable meeting in a public place. Nah, she's smooth. Her brothers raised her to be like them, and they did a damn good job."

"So what are you going to do?" Romeo asked.

Frustrated he yelled, "What do you expect? I need her signature, and if I don't get it, all of this is in vain."

"Now what?" Romeo asked.

He hit the dashboard with his fist. "Take me back to the

warehouse so I can have a little chat with the Chance brothers."

Romeo made a U-turn in the middle of the street and sped down the boulevard. "Are you going to let them go once you get Keilah's signature?"

X laughed. "I haven't decided what I'm going to do with them yet. Maybe I should take them out to Runyon Canyon and put a bullet in their heads."

Romeo laughed out loud and gave Xavier a high five. "X, I have to give it to you. You and P.K. played this just right. They didn't know what hit them. I think they're still in shock."

Xavier lit a cigar and blew circles of smoke out of his mouth. He couldn't help but smile to himself. "I'm not worried about meeting Keilah at the casino. It only seems right for things to end where it all started. Victory is just around the corner for us, and we're going to be richer than our wildest dreams. I know my pops is looking down on me, proud as hell. I had to do something to regain his honor. That Chance family has been a thorn in my side for years."

Romeo pulled down a dark street. "Well, you don't have to worry about that anymore. I can't wait for us to have boxing matches there. The money is going to roll in even faster."

"This is just the beginning, Romeo, just the beginning."

The Escalade came to a stop outside the warehouse. Romeo called Baby Dee on his cell and seconds later the warehouse door slid open. Romeo slowly drove the truck into the warehouse and parked. Xavier climbed out of the truck and looked at his watch.

"OK, guys. Keilah has altered our plans a little and changed the location of our meeting over to the Lucky Chance. That gives us about five hours to get things ready. I need to call P.K. and let him know there's been a change in plans. If I know Keilah like I think I do, she's not going to come alone. No matter what, do not take her out until I get her to sign on the dotted line. After that, I don't care what happens."

Baby Dee folded his arms and asked, "Can I have her?"

Xavier started up the stairs but looked back and laughed. "What do you want her for?"

Baby Dee followed close behind him. He smiled. "Have you looked at her? That chick is hot."

"I think you're in love, Baby Dee," Romeo added.

"Maybe I am," he joked along with them.

The trio finally reached the third floor where the Chance brothers were being held. Xavier walked in and clapped his hands together. "I have good news and bad news. The good news is that this whole thing will be over shortly. The bad thing for you is that your beautiful sister has agreed to join our little party."

Luke looked at him angrily. "X, now you listen to me, and I want you to listen good. It's obvious you and P.K. have done whatever it took to steal our casinos from us, but if you put even one finger on my sister, I will kill you."

X, Baby Dee, and Romeo all burst out laughing. X walked over to the caged area and said, "I'm sorry, Luke, but Baby Dee already has dibs on her. I wish I could help you out, but I can't."

Luke leaned forward and whispered, "Please, Xavier. She's our sister. Have a heart, man. Damn."

Xavier could see the agony in Luke's eyes. He cleared his throat and whispered back, "I'll think about it. But if she gives me any trouble about signing this paper or anything, I won't be responsible for my actions or Baby Dee's."

After Keytone and his entourage left Malachi's house, Keilah and Ramsey used that time to catch up on their sleep. They wanted to make sure they were alert and refreshed before they met up with Xavier and his crew. It was nearly eight o'clock before Keilah woke up. She yawned and stretched as she sat up on the side of the bed. As she sat there, she couldn't help but think about her brothers and what lay ahead for them. Why Xavier was holding them hostage was still a mystery, but she wouldn't rest until they were released and back home safe and sound.

Keilah looked at the clock on the nightstand before walking over to her suitcase. She pulled out a few toiletries and headed into the bathroom for a hot shower.

Down the hallway, Ramsey was awakened as soon as he heard Keilah turn on the water. He rolled over onto his back and stared at the ceiling. As he lay there, he wondered what dangers they would be faced with later and then prayed everyone would come out unscathed.

Ramsey sat up and picked up the three fifty seven magnum he got out of Malachi's stash of weapons and inspected it one last time. He heard the shower turn off, alerting him that Keilah would be dressed and ready to go shortly. He stood, unbuttoned his shirt and tossed it on the bed. A hot shower was exactly what he needed to clear his head and adjust his mind set. He walked around the bed to retrieve his luggage and realized he'd left it in Keilah's room. While she was still in the rest room, he padded down the hallway to get it, but when he opened the door he startled Keilah who was standing in the middle of the room in only a black lace thong. She covered her breasts with her hands. "Ramsey, you startled me."

Frozen in his spot, he stood there and admired just how natural her beauty was. "I'm sorry, Keilah, I thought you were still in the rest room. I didn't mean to bust up in here without knocking."

She smiled and dropped her hands to her sides. "Come on in, Ramsey. It's not like I have something you haven't seen before."

Keilah was right. He had seen her in even less than what she had on at the moment, but it had been a while. Gazing at her unbelievable physique caused him to totally forget why he'd come into her room in the first place. He walked past his luggage and straight over to her, where he cupped her face and softly said, "I see your bruises are almost gone."

She wrapped her arms around his body. "I'm glad."

They stood there staring at each other in silence while Ramsey caressed her cheek. "Are you ready to kick some butt tonight?"

"I'm ready to do whatever it takes to save my brothers. It doesn't matter what happens to me. They've looked after me all of my life. Now it's my turn to take care of them."

He lowered his lips within inches of hers and whispered, "And it's my turn to love you like you need to be loved."

Keilah's eyes widened with shock upon hearing Ramsey's confession as he seared her lips with his sultry passion. Ramsey held onto Keilah as tightly as he could while continuing to savor her soft, ample lips. His hands and mouth were all over her body. She could hardly catch her breath, and when his large hand slid inside her lacy undergarments so he could touch her, she gasped and softly said, "Please don't tease me, Ramsey."

"Do I act like I'm joking with you?" His voice was slightly strained. "I love you, Keilah."

She pressed her face against his bare chest and kissed him in various sensitive areas. Keilah could hear the changes in his breathing as he trembled against her lips. "Baby, I don't know how this night is going to end, but right now, all I want to do is feel you in every possible way."

Ramsey tried to swallow the lump in his throat, but it was impossible. Tears welled up in his eyes, because he finally realized that the emotions he experienced were the real thing. He was in love with Keilah, and having her in every way possible was only going to be the beginning for them.

Keilah's hands quickly unbuckled his belt and pushed his jeans down to his ankles. He stepped out of them and did the same with her undergarments. They stood before each other bare, emotionally and physically, and neither of them flinched. Ramsey picked Keilah up, and she wrapped her legs around his body. He kissed her insatiably, and she happily returned the favor. Ramsey gripped her hips and pressed her body against the wall as he dipped his mouth and covered her brown, swollen peaks. He was hungry for her, and he greedily feasted on her round mounds, causing her to pant uncontrollably. He wanted more, and as he carried her over to the bed, he continued his assault on her voluptuous, feminine lips.

As she lay on her back, he slowly ran his tongue from her slender neck, down through the cleavage of her breasts, to her navel and lower to the small triangle patch between her thighs. Before dipping his head into her sweet abyss, he pinned both of her legs to her side so he could feast on her without any obstacles. "Keilah, I'm not going to stop until I have my fill of you. You've been warned."

Before she could mumble a word, his lips were torturing the very essence of her. This was nothing like anything they had experienced between each other before. Keilah felt sensations running up and down her body, which caused her to shudder violently. Ramsey was putting his brand on the most sensitive area of her being, and she felt like she was going to disintegrate. He had control of her body now, and there was nothing she could do but hang on for the ride. Seconds turned into minutes and minutes seemed to turn into hours as he showed no indication that he was nearing the end. If anything, he increased the way his tongue swirled and twirled over her flesh. Keilah gripped the sheets and arched into him while moaning and panting loudly. She knew her body couldn't take much more. Especially when she felt her skin sweltering and her body trembling. She gritted her teeth as her body shuddered causing her to scream, "Oh, Ramsey."

Mission accomplished. Only then did he stop. He smiled

and kissed his way back up to her lips. He whispered, "You can't say I didn't warn you."

She was still trembling, and her skin was hot to his touch. She was on fire, and he was just beginning. He played in her soft, auburn hair as he looked her in the eyes. "You know I love you, right?"

Breathlessly she answered, "Yes."

"And you trust me, right?"

"With my life," she answered.

"Then you know there's no way I'm going to allow anything bad to happen to you, right?"

She nodded in agreement as if she were in a trance. In a way she was, and it was a state of mind beyond anything she had ever experienced. He leaned down, then kissed and toyed with her lips before whispering, "Turn over, baby."

Keilah rolled over onto her stomach and then looked back over her shoulder at him. He gave her one firm kiss on the lips before kissing his way down her back. He kissed her tattoo, causing her to suck in her breath. He pressed his body against her hips and moments later, she felt him inch his way inside her. She bent over farther and prepared herself for his enormous love. He held onto her hips and let the rhythm of their bodies and hearts transport them from the past, to the present, and into the future. Each thrust of his body told her a different story about them, but they all had the same ending, and he whispered it each time their bodies came together. "I love you, Keilah. I love you, Keilah . . ."

Keilah buried her face into the pillow and let Ramsey penetrate her core. His momentum increased when he heard her subtle whimpers. He continued to plunge deeper into her chasm as he inhaled her body and spirit. When she looked at him, he noticed the glazed look in her eyes, and then he felt his body explode, paralyzing him as his seed filled her space. The pair collapsed onto the bed and into each other's arms. Keilah nuzzled her face against his warm neck and murmured, "I have never in my life felt anything even close to what I just felt with you, Ramsey."

He ran his hand lovingly down her back to her round, sexy backside. "That was nothing. When we have more time, I would like to show you how I really feel about you."

She looked at him in disbelief. If that was nothing, she was a little afraid of what he considered something. He looked at his watch and said, "I guess we had better get up and get dressed so we can rescue your brothers."

Keilah kissed him on the chin and pushed back the comforter so she could climb out of bed. Before she was able to put her feet on the floor, Ramsey grabbed her and pulled her back into his arms. "I know you don't think I'm going to let you out of this bed with a weak kiss like that."

She giggled and wrapped her arms around his neck and signed his mouth with her lips. She offered him the sweetness of her tongue as she slipped it inside his mouth, and he happily indulged her. "Now that is what I'm talking about."

Ramsey climbed out of bed behind her, and they showered together before finally getting dressed.

CHAPTER TWENTY-SEVEN

Keytone, Ramsey, and Keilah went over their plan one more time with Li'l Mike and T.Money. Before leaving Malachi's house, Keytone said, "Keilah, I have something for you and Ramsey."

Before she could ask, T.Money opened a box, pulled out two bulletproof vests, and handed them to the pair. Ramsey inspected them. "Where did you get these?"

Keytone laughed. "Don't ask."

Ramsey unbuttoned his shirt and slid into his vest. "I really appreciate this, Keytone. I feel much better now."

Keilah removed her T-shirt and adjusted the straps on her tank top before putting on the vest. Once she had it on, she put her T-shirt back on. She sat down and raised the pants leg of her jeans and slid a .22-caliber pistol into an ankle holster. Ramsey and the rest of the crew did their final weapon check as well before heading out the door. Keytone looked at Keilah and asked, "What else are you carrying?"

She pulled a nine-millimeter out of her back waistband, popped out the clip and slammed it back in. "This."

"I'm scared of you."

She smiled. "You don't have a reason to be scared, but Xavier does. I still don't understand why he's holding everyone hostage."

As if a lightbulb had gone off in his head, Keytone yelled, "Son of a bitch."

Ramsey looked at Keytone. "What is it?"

"I just remembered something a junkie told me right after you got attacked at the hotel. He said he heard some guy talking about a take over. I bet X is trying to take over the casinos."

Keilah yelled, "Well, he's not going to get them. I'll burn them down first before I let X or anybody take our casinos from us."

"I feel you, Keilah," Ramsey replied.

Keytone looked at his watch. "Now that we have an idea of what's going on, let's roll. Keilah, don't forget we have your back, and if it seems like things are getting ready to jump off, give us some kind of signal."

She put on a trench coat and tucked a sawed off semi-automatic action shotgun down in an inside pocket. Keytone frowned. "Can you handle all of that?"

"Do you know who you're talking to?" Ramsey asked. "Just call her Foxy Brown." Ramsey laughed. "That's my girl."

At the Lucky Chance casino, Keilah drove Malachi's car through the private gate and parked. Before getting out of the vehicle she sent a text to Xavier, telling him to meet her near the poker tables. When she walked inside the building, she punched in the alarm code, then made her way downstairs, where she cut off certain circuit breakers. She only wanted the emergency back-up lights on, and she wanted to make sure the surveillance cameras didn't record anything that might go down. After getting everything in place, she made her way over to the poker tables.

It didn't take long for Xavier and his crew along with the Chance brothers, to pull into the parking lot. Xavier made sure the Chances were bound while Baby Dee and Romeo held their guns on the foursome. As they made their way through the casino, Ramsey, Keytone, and his crew held their positions through the building. They cautiously walked through the large room until they found Keilah sitting behind one of the larger poker tables.

The moment she laid eyes on her brothers, her heart thumped in her chest. She walked over to them and hugged and kissed each one. "Are you guys okay?"

Luke said, "We're fine."

Xavier interrupted their family reunion. "Enough is enough. Let's get down to business."

Keilah turned to X and angrily said, "Untie them."

"Hell no. We have business to conduct first."

She walked over to him. "What kind of business do you have to discuss with me?"

Xavier laughed. "Ask your brothers."

Keilah turned to her brothers and they lowered their heads. That's when P.K. Sloan walked into the room. "P.K. What the hell are you doing here?" she asked.

As usual, he was dressed in a very expensive suit and his hands were sparkling with diamonds. He held his hand out to Keilah, and she numbly shook it. "It's good seeing you again, Keilah. I believe I have another document here for you to sign."

Luke stepped forward. "Keilah, what P.K. is trying to tell you is he's just as crooked as Xavier is. He has falsified documents, and because we trusted him, he was able to trick us into signing away our rights to both casinos. All they need now is your signature, and we will no longer be the owners of either one."

Keilah felt lightheaded. "You can't be serious, Luke."

Roman said, "It's true. P.K. has been working with this trash for some time now to steal our casinos. For some reason, he thinks he deserves to own them all because his alcoholic father drank himself to death before Joe made their gambling house."

"What are you talking about, Luke?" she asked.

"It doesn't matter, Keilah," Xavier intervened. "I've earned the right to this casino just like you guys did, and I won't be denied."

P.K. opened his briefcase and placed a single form on the table. He took a pen out of his jacket. "So, Keilah, if you would just sign here, we'll be done."

She frowned. "I'm not signing a damn thing. My family worked hard to make this casino what it is, and you think I'm going to stand here and just sign it over to you? You're crazy."

Xavier pulled out his revolver and aimed it at Keilah's head. She walked directly toward him. Luke yelled, "Keilah, don't."

She ignored Luke and kept walking toward Xavier until the gun was pressed firmly against her forehead. "If you think pointing that gun at me is going to scare me into signing that paperwork, you're mistaken."

Xavier lowered the gun and pointed it at Malachi.

Malachi mumbled, "Don't sign it, sis."

Xavier looked at Malachi and then over at Keilah. He smiled mischievously and said, "Maybe this will change your mind."

Xavier pulled the trigger, and Luke, Roman, and Genesis all dove under a nearby poker table. Keilah ran over to Malachi and held her hand against his wound. Xavier had shot him in the leg. She yelled, "You bastard."

Xavier said, "I guess now you see I'm not playing with you."

Malachi moaned in pain as he lay on the floor.

"Untie him, Xavier," Keilah yelled.

"Not until you sign the paper," he repeated.

"Go to hell," she yelled back at him.

Xavier turned to Baby Dee and Romeo and said, "Go check the perimeter and make sure nobody heard that gunshot."

Keilah pulled a knife out of her pocket and cut the restraint off Malachi's wrists. When Xavier turned back around he said, "Didn't I tell you not do that until you sign the paper?"

She jumped up. "I don't give a damn what you said. Malachi needs a doctor."

Xavier aimed the gun again but this time at Genesis. "Do you think I'm playing with you, girl? This is not a game."

P.K. put his hands up. "Hold on a second, Xavier. Let's not go to the extreme. I'm not looking to get any jail time out of this."

Xavier aimed the gun at P.K. "Are you getting soft on me, P.K.?"

"No, I just don't feel like catching a case and getting a needle stuck in my arm for murder."

"If I didn't need you, P.K., I swear I would shoot your punk ass," Xavier informed him.

P.K. yelled, "Without me, you wouldn't be even close to having any of this shit."

Xavier was getting agitated. "Keilah, sign the goddamn paper."

"I said no."

Xavier raised the gun again and aimed it at Genesis. Just before he pulled the trigger, Ramsey and T.Money stepped through the door with Magnums pointed at X and P.K. "Don't even think about it, because if you pull that trigger you're going to be dead before you hit the floor," Ramsey said. "Now put the gun down."

"Who the hell are you?" X asked as he sat his gun on top of the poker table.

T.Money said, "You don't want to know, partner."

Ramsey winked at Keilah. "Cut those restraints off your brother's wrists."

Xavier seemed somewhat dumbfounded. Keilah cut her brother's bindings before helping Malachi off the floor. "T.Money, get Malachi to the hospital right away."

"A'ight, Keilah," he replied as he tucked his .357 Magnum into his jacket.

Xavier turned to P.K. "Where's Baby Dee and Romeo?"

P.K. shrugged his shoulders. "I don't know."

Ramsey taunted Xavier. "It's hard to find good help when you need it, isn't it?"

Xavier pointed his gun at T.Money. "Nobody's going anywhere."

"I disagree with you, dawg," Ramsey said. "Go ahead, T.Money. Get Malachi to the hospital. I got this."

T.Money put Malachi's arm around his shoulder and helped him out of the building so he could drive him to the hospital. A few minutes later, Baby Dee and Romeo stepped from behind the dollar slot machines with their guns blazing. They eased up on Ramsey. "Drop the gun, player."

Ramsey put his hands up in the air and slowly placed the gun down on the poker table.

"Where the hell have you two been?" Xavier yelled as he retrieved his gun.

"You told us to check out the building, X. It takes a minute. This place is huge," Romeo answered.

"Well, while you and Baby Dee was looking around, y'all let Rambo get up close and personal."

"I'm sorry, X," Romeo apologized. "We're back now. Who is this dude?"

"Don't worry about it. He's with me," Keilah blurted out.

"I thought I told you to come alone," Xavier reminded her.

"Look, X or Xavier or whatever your name is. You might as well shoot me because I'm not signing that paper," she informed him.

X said, "If that's the way you feel, have it your way."

Ramsey looked at Keilah, and she looked over at her brothers. Everything moved in slow motion from that moment on. Gunshots rang out, and poker chips and cards flew everywhere. Luke, Genesis, and Roman dove behind the slot machines while Ramsey tackled Keilah and they fell over a cashier counter.

Ramsey yelled, "Baby, are you hit?"

"No. Are you okay?" she asked as she took her nine-millimeter out of her waistband.

"I'm fine. Where did they go?" Ramsey asked as he pulled a second weapon out of his ankle holster.

"I don't know. I can't see anybody," she replied.

Keilah peeked through a section of the cashier booth and saw P.K. Sloan bleeding on the floor. She quietly moved down a little farther and saw Luke, Roman, and Genesis huddled together behind a row of slot machines. She waved at them to get their attention and motioned for them to get out. Luke shook his head and did charades to find out if she had an extra weapon. She nodded and whispered, "Cover me, Ramsey."

"What are you doing?"

She checked the clip on her gun. "I need to get a gun to Luke."

"OK. Go," Ramsey yelled as Keilah jumped over the counter and ran in her brother's directions. Xavier saw her and immediately started shooting in her direction. Ramsey returned fire, forcing X to take cover. Roman's heart jumped in his throat when he saw Keilah take that unbelievable risk. When she joined them, he grabbed her by the collar. "Have you lost your mind? Don't you ever do anything like that again."

"It's okay, Roman. Here's a nine and a twenty-two. There's one down and three to go. Watch your back."

Genesis said, "No, you watch yours. Thanks, sis."

Keilah pulled the shotgun from under her coat. "We need to take care of this now. Watch the crossfire. I'm going to make my way through the quarter slots until I get over to the bar. Don't let Ramsey get pinned down."

She kissed them and disappeared around the corner.

Xavier yelled, "Keilah, you might as well come out, because you're not getting out of here until that paper is signed."

Ramsey climbed over the cashier's booth and ran toward the rear of the room. Baby Dee aimed and pulled the trigger, hitting Ramsey in the back. Luke leaned over a poker table and shot Baby Dee in the chest. After checking to make sure Baby Dee was dead, Luke immediately checked on Ramsey. "Ramsey, can you get up? I need to get you out of sight."

Ramsey moaned and raised his shirt, showing Luke the bulletproof vest. Luke patted him on the shoulder. "Good boy. Don't move, I'll be right back."

Over the next thirty minutes, the situation intensified when Romeo cornered Roman near the front door. As he raised his firearm, Keilah whistled to get his attention. When Romeo turned, Keilah fired one shot, striking him in abdomen. The force of the blast knocked Romeo completely off his feet and through a glass window. Keytone ran over. "You took my shot, Keilah."

"You're too slow, Keytone. Besides, I had the better shot," she replied.

Roman frowned. "What are you doing here, Keytone?"

Keilah put her hand up to Roman's face. "He's with me. Squash it."

Before Keilah stepped over Romeo's bloody body, she cocked the shotgun and coldly mumbled, "I'm the last Chance and this is our house. Now let's clean it up."

The broken glass crunched under their feet as they walked toward the elevators. Roman turned to them and said, "Thanks, guys. Now give me that shotgun so you can get out of here."

She pulled away from him. "I'm not leaving until this thing is done and everyone's safe. Xavier needs to be stopped once and for all."

Keytone reached into his pocket and pulled out a .45 caliber automatic handgun and handed it to Roman. "Take this, Roman. You might need it."

"Thanks, Keytone." He checked the gun and then turned to Keilah. "You need to get out of here. I don't want X trying to use you as leverage like he did with us."

"I have his leverage, and I'm going to find him so I can give it to him," she sarcastically remarked.

They heard a couple of gunshots, and they took cover behind some slot machines. Keytone peeped around the machine. "Could either one of you tell where those shots came from?"

Roman looked around the corner and pointed across the room. "It sounded like it came from the high rollers' pit."

"You two find out if Luke, Genesis, or Ramsey took care of that other guy while I track down Xavier."

"Be careful, sis," Roman warned before they all walked off in separate directions.

The casino looked like a war zone. Broken glass, bloody bodies, and the fog of gunpowder covered the room. Xavier had found a spot behind the bar in which to take cover. He pulled out his cell phone and tried to call Baby Dee or Romeo, but neither answered. "Damn," he cursed.

Seconds later X spotted Keilah as she moved in his direction, totally unaware of his presence. He smiled and whispered, "Gotcha."

As soon as she approached the bar area, he jumped out and wrapped his arm around her neck. Keilah could feel the cold metal of his gun against her head. "Drop the gun, slim."

Keilah dropped the gun and Xavier tightened his grip around her neck. "OK, this is how it's going to play out. You're going to sign that paper or you're going to get a nine to the head. Are you feeling me? I'm tired of playing with you."

She reached up and tried to loosen the hold Xavier had on her neck. Xavier dragged Keilah across the floor and yelled out so everyone could hear him. "OK. The game is over. I have Keilah, and if you guys don't want to have a dead sister, you need to put those guns down and come on out."

Luke was first to move out from behind some slot machines. He was worried that Xavier was holding the gun against Keilah's head. The slightest movement could cause him to pull the trigger. He put his hands up and said, "All right, X. Just move the gun away from Keilah's head."

"I'm in charge now. You do what I say," Xavier yelled. "Get your brothers out here, now."

Luke yelled for Genesis and Roman to come out from hiding. Genesis pointed his gun at Xavier. "You're not getting away with this, X."

He laughed. "I think I am, Genesis, or you're going to be burying your only sister. Now put the goddamn gun down."

Genesis and Roman lowered their guns as Xavier pulled Keilah over to the poker table where the document was miraculously still sitting. Xavier gripped the back of Keilah's neck and held her head down on the table. He pointed the gun at the back of her head and gritted his teeth. "Sign the paper, Keilah, or so help me God, I'll splatter your brains all over this table."

Tears formed in Luke's eyes. He whispered, "Go ahead and sign it, Keilah."

"No," she yelled in defiance.

Xavier shot a round into the poker table next to her head and said, "The next one is going in your head. Sign the paper."

Roman took a step toward them. "Keilah, please, just sign it. We'll be okay."

Tears were running down her face now. She saw the distressed look on her brother's faces so she picked up the pen and signed away their casinos.

Once the paper was signed, X pushed Keilah over to her brothers and tucked it inside his jacket. "Was that so hard?"

"Go to hell, Xavier," she yelled.

Xavier laughed. "I might go to hell, but I'll be a very rich bastard before I do."

"You're not going to get away with this, X," Luke pointed out.

He pointed his gun at the four of them and smiled. "I already have. I finally got the last Chance to sign the paper, so I guess you all are looking at the new owner of the Lucky Chance and Special K casinos. It's done. Now if you'll excuse me, I have somewhere I have to be. I'm sorry things have to end this way, but I can't have you guys running around Dennison causing me any legal problems. It's too bad P.K. didn't get to hang around for the party, but it was nice doing business with you."

Luke, Roman, Genesis, and Keilah held their breath as Xavier's finger twitched to press the trigger. That's when Keytone stepped out of the shadows. "You're mistaken, X. I'm the last Chance, and I'm not signing a damn thing."

Confused, Xavier said, "What?"

"Joe Chance was my father, too, which makes *me* the last Chance. Now try to make me sign the paper."

Xavier thought for a moment, and then fired his gun in Keytone's direction, but he missed.

That's when Keytone unloaded his clip into Xavier's body, killing him.

Once the dust had cleared, Keytone stood over Xavier's lifeless body and said, "Damn, that was a nice suit he has on. Too bad I had to mess it."

Luke walked over to Keytone. "Thanks, man."

"You're welcome," he replied as he shook Luke's hand.

Keilah looked around and went into a slight panic. "Where's Ramsey?"

Luke said, "Don't worry, he's okay. He took a round in his back, but it hit his vest. I hid him over by the bathroom."

Keilah ran over to Ramsey and found him propped up against the wall. "Ramsey, baby, are you bleeding? Are you okay?"

He grunted. "I'm fine, sweetheart, just bruised up a little. Help me up."

Keilah helped Ramsey off the floor and back over to her brothers.

Roman looked around at the carnage. "What now?"

Luke pulled out his cell phone. "We need to call the cops."

"This is going to be a nightmare," Genesis added.

"Hey guys, I need to get Ramsey to the hospital," Keilah informed them.

Keytone took Ramsey by the arm. "Let me help you. Do you guys need me to stick around?"

Luke held out his hand. "Nah, you can jet. We can handle this."

"Are you sure?" Keytone offered once again.

"You don't need to get mixed up in all of this. Just give me your gun, because they're going to want to match the bullets with the guns. You and your boys were never here and neither were you, Keilah or Ramsey. You saved our lives, Keytone, and I'll never forget that. Now, get out of here," Luke ordered.

Keilah gave her brothers a kiss before helping Ramsey out of the building.

It took hours police to investigate the shooting at the casino. By the time the investigation was complete and they were allowed to go home, it was nearly ten hours later. Preliminary findings by the police interrogation of the brothers helped police determine the incident was an attempted robbery by Xavier and his crew. When the police searched P.K.'s car, they found a kilo of cocaine and other items alerting them to his shady business practices.

When Luke, Roman, and Genesis left the Lucky Chance, they went directly to the hospital to check on Malachi and Ramsey. They found Malachi resting comfortably.

"How's your leg?" Genesis asked.

"Better than it was," he replied.

Luke looked around. "Where's T.Money?"

"Keilah called and told me to tell him to leave, so he left. What happened at the casino?" Malachi asked.

Luke put his hands over his face. "I don't want to talk about it right now. When are they going to let you out of here?"

"Tomorrow," he informed them.

"Did Keilah come check on you?" Roman asked.

"Yeah, after Ramsey got discharged, they stopped in before they headed back over to the house."

"Is Ramsey okay?" Luke asked.

"He just has a couple of bruised ribs. He's lucky he had on that bulletproof vest," Malachi said.

"Do you need someone to stay here with you tonight?" Genesis asked.

"With all these fine nurses around me? What do you think?"

They chuckled. Luke said, "We'll pick you up in the AM.

Call if you need anything. We're going to stop by your house and check on Keilah and Ramsey before going home."

Malachi gave each of them a brotherly handshake before they left his room.

Luke, Roman and Genesis let themselves into Malachi's house to check on Keilah and Ramsey. They expected them to be up, but after the night they'd experienced, they wouldn't be surprised if the pair was asleep. They quietly made their way through the house and up the stairs. When they entered Keilah's bedroom they found Keilah, and Ramsey sound asleep in each other's arms.

"What the hell?" Luke whispered.

Roman asked, "What happened to Michael?"

Genesis replied, "Who cares? Look at them."

Luke motioned for them to back out of the room. When they got back down stairs, they found Keytone at the door. Luke let him in, and they all went out onto the patio.

"Keytone, I want to thank you again for what you did. If it weren't for you, we would all be dead. I'm sorry for ever doubting you," Luke apologized.

Keytone sighed. "We're cool. Look, I just stopped over to check on Keilah and Ramsey. Where are they?"

Roman smiled and said, "Upstairs in bed together."

Keytone started laughing. "I knew it."

"You knew what?" Genesis asked. "Do you know something we don't know?"

Keytone folded his arms and asked, "Did Keilah tell you guys about Michael?"

Luke frowned and asked, "What, about their wedding?"

"No, that she caught him in bed with a man," he revealed.

They all stared at Keytone in disbelief.

"Are you serious?" Luke asked.

Keytone laughed. "Yeah, I'm serious. She didn't tell me the details. She just said she caught him, and she shot him in the foot because of it."

Roman put his hands over his face. "I don't believe this. She shot him?"

Keytone raised his hands. "Yes. Look, don't tell her I told you. I'm just happy she's with Ramsey. He's the one I had hope she would end up with anyway. Besides, no other man will be able to handle her with that temper. I'm sure you all know Keilah's not your ordinary woman."

Luke chuckled. "Yes, we all know too well."

Genesis was still in shock over the information they'd just heard. He mumbled, "So Michael is a down-low brother. I knew something wasn't right with him."

Upstairs, Keilah woke up and ran her hands over Ramsey's bare bottom. He instantly woke up and smiled. He pulled her soft, warm body closer to his. "You know I'm at a disadvantage right now. Don't tease me." Ramsey tilted her chin and kissed her tenderly on the lips. "I don't think I can handle you right now, baby. My ribs are too sore."

She kissed his chest. "I'll do all the work, and I promise I'll be gentle."

He chuckled. "I've made love to you before, remember?"

She kissed his six-pack abs and whispered, "Can we at least try?"

"On one condition," he offered her.

She kissed him lower and was going down even farther, causing him to tremble in ecstasy. She whispered, "I'll do anything for you, Ramsey, because I love you."

"I'm glad to hear that. Now all you have to do is wear my ring, take my name, and have my children," he softly revealed.

She looked up into his eyes and smiled. "What ring? Are you for real?"

He winked at her and said, "Marry me, Keilah Chance."

She seductively answered, "Yes, I'll marry you, Ramsey

Stone. I'll wear your ring, take your name, and have your children."

He cupped her face and kissed her lips until they were scorched and swollen from his love. With tears in her eyes, she straddled his body gently and whispered, "I have to have you right now, baby, and I promise I won't hurt you."

Ramsey gripped her hips and said, "Go for it, sweetheart."

CHAPTER TWENTY-EIGHT

A week later they came together as a family, including Keytone to celebrate the grand reopening of the Lucky Chance. Being accepted by the Chance siblings was something Keytone had always dreamed of, but never thought possible. The night was for family only, and they wanted to make the most of it.

It took a couple of days for workers to replace damaged tables and machines as well as broken windows and bloodstained carpet. The incident at the casino had changed all of them, making them stronger as a family.

As they sat around a large dinner table, eating a fabulous meal, Ramsey stood and said, "I would like to propose a toast."

Everyone stopped eating and gave Ramsey their undivided attention. "First, I would like to congratulate all of you on your success when all odds were against you. I want to wish you continued love and blessings for allowing me to be a part of this wonderful night. This not only goes out to Luke, Roman, Malachi, and Genesis. This also goes out to the strong women behind them. It's been said that every successful man has a strong woman beside him, so ladies, this includes you too. I also would like to thank you guys for having the trust and confidence in me to look after Keilah." He turned toward Keilah and said, "And with your blessings, I want to officially ask your permission to make her my wife."

Gasps filled the room and all eyes were on Keilah as Ramsey leaned down and kissed her lovingly on the lips.

Malachi slammed his cane on the floor. "Wait just a damn minute. When did this happen? What have I missed and what happened to Michael? Not that I care."

Keilah stood up next to Ramsey and blushed as he held her close to his side. "I guess I do owe you guys an explanation."

Unaware that everyone but Malachi already knew what had happened, Keilah began to explain. "Michael wasn't the man I thought he was. I did love him, but I found out some things about him that are unforgivable, so I had no choice but to end our relationship. You all know that Ramsey and I have been close for years. What I went through with Michael was very traumatic for me, and I wouldn't have made it without Ramsey. I love him, and I want to be with him . . . forever. So I hope you guys give us your blessings."

Sabrinia had tears of joy running down her face. Luke stood and said, "Keilah, Ramsey, our prayers have always been for you to be happy and in love. Looking at you two lets us know our prayers have been answered." He looked around the table at his brothers and held up his champagne glass and said, "If there are no objections, I say we have a wedding to plan. Congratulations, and of course you have our love and blessings. Welcome to the family, Ramsey."

The entire family stood and held their glasses high in the air to toast the couple before taking a sip. Next, Keytone spoke as he faced the family he never thought he would have.

"I would like to take this opportunity to congratulate Keilah and Ramsey and to say I appreciate you accepting me. I've always been proud of you guys, and I never wanted anything from any of you but your love and acceptance. If it hadn't been for the love of a sister, we wouldn't be here today. Keilah, I love you, and I'll never forget how gracious and steadfast you were in making your family complete. Tonight I thank all of you, so raise your glass to new beginnings." Everyone did just that as they celebrated.

Once everyone was back in their seat, Ramsey leaned over and kissed Keilah on her shoulder and almost immediately, a nauseated feeling hit him. She noticed his distress and asked, "What's wrong?"

He hurried to the bathroom and threw up. While in the bathroom he was puzzled even more on why his illness had returned. He had started believing Bradford's theory since he hadn't been sick a day since he'd left the other women alone. Keilah walked into the bathroom to check on him. "Ramsey? What's wrong, baby?"

Ramsey exited the stall and said, "I don't know, Keilah. I've been sick off and on for the past few weeks."

She frowned and felt his forehead. "You don't have a fever. Maybe you have some type of food allergy. What did you eat tonight?"

"I had the same thing you did," he said as he threw some water on his face.

"OK, let me get you back to the house because you don't look so well."

Keilah and Ramsey returned to the table and sat down. Luke turned to Ramsey and took a sip of champagne. "Ramsey, you look like hell. What's wrong?"

He picked up a glass of water. "I don't know. I've been having something like a stomach virus for a couple of weeks now."

Roman, Luke, and Genesis looked at each other with worried expressions on their faces. Roman asked, "Does it make you feel nauseated all of a sudden?"

Ramsey nodded in agreement, and he sipped his ice water in hopes of settling his stomach.

"Do you break out in a sweat and feel like your body is on fire?" Genesis asked.

"Every time," he admitted.

Sabrinia started laughing hysterically and so did Roman and Genesis' wives. Keilah stood up and put her hands on her hips. "What's going on? Why are you asking Ramsey all these questions, and Sabrinia, why are you laughing?"

The ladies were laughing so hard they had tears coming out of their eyes.

Luke looked at the couple and said, "I believe congratulations are in order once again for you two."

"What are you talking about Luke?"

Genesis smiled and said, "You're pregnant, Keilah."

Her eyes widened and so did Ramsey's. "I'm not pregnant. I would know if I were pregnant," she yelled.

Roman leaned back in his chair and said, "It's hereditary, Keilah. All of us were sick when our wives were pregnant, and we stayed sick the entire nine months. I feel for you, Ramsey."

"What makes you all think Ramsey and I have even slept together?" she challenged them.

Genesis calmly buttered a piece of bread. "Because we saw you."

Ramsey strangled on his water. Keilah patted him on the back and asked, "What do you mean, saw us?"

"Don't worry about it, just trust us, sis. You're pregnant," Luke replied. "If there's going to be a wedding, we need to hurry up and have it before Keilah starts showing."

Keilah looked over at Keytone and he raised his hands in defense. "Keilah, this is the first I've known about this, and

I'll have to admit, I was pretty sick throughout my lady's pregnancy. Listening to the guys, now I know why."

Keilah laughed nervously and said, "You guys are full of it. You're just trying to scare us. Besides, Ramsey's not connected to you guys by blood, so it doesn't make sense."

Luke smiled. "Listen, Keilah, none of us can't explain this phenomenon, but for some reason, when a person is impregnated by a Chance, the man gets all the sickness involved with the pregnancy. You're the only female Chance, so I can only speculate that the same holds true for Chance women as well."

Keilah took a sip of her champagne and said, "That sounds like some Louisiana voodoo to me. Ya'll are full of it."

Ramsey was speechless. He shook his head in disbelief even though he knew he'd had some wild, reckless nights with Keilah. He couldn't be happier, but now he was anxious to find out if the guys really knew what they were talking about. To prove or disprove their theory, Ramsey and Keilah stopped at the pharmacy, purchased three different pregnancy tests, and then drove back to Malachi's place.

When they got there, Keilah and Ramsey hurried upstairs to the bathroom. Thirty minutes and three tests later, Keilah was too nervous to view the results. Ramsey walked over to the counter and picked up all three of the indicators. He looked down at the sticks and then up at Keilah, and he smiled. "Congratulations, Momma."

EPILOGUE

With the help of her sister-in-laws and a great wedding planner, Keilah and Ramsey were able to put together a fabulous wedding in less than a month. Keilah was a beautiful bride and had the wedding of her dreams. She made sure each one of her brothers, including Keytone had a part in walking her down the aisle to Ramsey, and as expected, the Chances spared no cost. The wedding took place at their childhood church and the reception at one of Los Angeles most luxurious hotels. Ramsey and Keilah couldn't have been happier. Now all they had to do was wait approximately six months for their bundle of joy to arrive.

The couple's wait wasn't long, and on May fourteenth Neariah Amanda Stone arrived at eight pounds, three ounces. The proud parents couldn't take their eyes off her. Ramsey was very emotional during the birth and once he held her in his arms he was in total awe of their creation.

* * *

Hours later while Ramsey slept, Keilah caressed Neariah's soft wavy hair and kissed her chubby cheeks as she breast fed her.

The door swung open and Michael walked in brandishing a pistol. Keilah was so frozen with fear, she was unable to scream. He frowned and said, "Give me my child."

Before she could scream, he pointed the gun at his head and pulled the trigger. Keilah screamed at the top of her lungs and before she realized it, she was sitting up in bed.

Ramsey jumped out of his sleep and hurried over to her. "What's wrong? Are you in pain?"

"No! Where's Neariah?" she asked in a panic.

Ramsey held hand and pointed over to the bassinet. "She's right here, baby. Neariah's okay. See? She's fast asleep. You must've just had a bad dream, Keilah. What scared you so bad?"

A couple of nurses ran into the room to see what all the commotion was about. Ramsey held his hand up and said, "She just had a bad dream. She's OK now."

They nodded and left the room. Ramsey questioned her again. "Keilah, what were you dreaming about?"

"Hand me Neariah. I need to hold her," she explained.

Ramsey eased their sleeping daughter out of her bassinette and placed her in Keilah's arms. As she held Neariah close to her, she tried to get her breathing and the rhythm of her heart back to normal. After composing herself she said, "I dreamed Michael came in here and told me to give him *his child,* and then he shot himself in the head."

Ramsey kissed her on the forehead and asked, "Where did that come from? Neariah is ours."

Keilah touched her heart. "I don't know."

That's when she remembered that she never had told Ramsey about the weird phone call from Michael the night she was attacked outside the restaurant, and she never really gave much thought to it until now.

Ramsey did everything he could to soothe Keilah and to get her to relax. He changed Neariah's diaper and handed her back to Keilah so she could nurse her.

It took some effort, but Ramsey was finally able to get Neariah to go back to sleep.

As he lay there holding his daughter, he decided to catch up on sports and news. One news report caught his attention when they flashed Michael's picture on the screen. He turned the volume up as loud as he could without waking Keilah.

"Major Michael Monroe, a top Pentagon official, was reported missing in Iraq late yesterday," the journalist said. "Sources tell CNN that Major Monroe began suffering from some type of emotional distress shortly before his disappearance. Unconfirmed reports say Major Monroe had made several threats against unnamed parties; however, the Pentagon will only confirm that he was scheduled to return to Washington in two days for a medical evaluation, which is not uncommon for high-ranking officials.

"Iraq is not unfamiliar to Major Monroe, and he has traveled to the country on official military business on several occasions. He was last seen leaving a command post with a group of soldiers in a Humvee. Concern arose when they did not return after their allotted time. U.S. forces are searching for the troops, but so far to no avail. We'll keep you updated on this story as information becomes available."

<u>**Ask Yourself**</u>

Ask yourself a question . . . have you ever had a session of love making, do you want me? Have you ever been to heaven?
—Raheem DeVaughn

February 9ᵗʰ, 2007

She feels like melted chocolate on my fingertips. The same color from the top of her head to the very tips of her feet. Her nipples are two shades darker than the rest of her, and they make her skin the perfect backdrop against her round breasts. Firm and sweet like two ripe peaches dipped in baker's chocolate. They are a little more than a handful and greatly appreciated. Touching her makes me feel like I've finally found peace on earth, and there is no feeling in the world greater than that.

Right now her eyes are closed and her bottom lip is tightly tucked between her teeth. From my view point between her wide spread legs I can see the beginnings of yet another orgasm playing across her angelic face. These are the moments that make it all worthwhile. Her perfectly arched eyebrows go into a deep frown, and her eyelids flutter slightly. When her head falls back I know she's about to explode.

I move up on my knees so that we are pelvis to pelvis. Both of us are dripping wet from the humidity and the situation. Her legs are up on my shoulders, and her hands are cupping my breasts. I can't tell where her skin begins or where mine ends. As I look down at her and watch her face go through way too many emotions, I smile a little bit. She always did love the dick, and since we've been together she's never had to go without it. Especially since the one I have never goes down.

I'm pushing her tool into her soft folds inch by inch as if it were really a part of me, and her body is alive. I say "her tool" because it belongs to her, and I just enjoy using it on her. Her hip length dreads seem to wrap us in a cocoon of coconut oil and sweat, body heat and moisture, soft moans and tear drops, pleasure and pain until we seemingly burst into an inferno of hot like fire ecstasy. Our chocolate skin is searing to the touch and we melt into each other, becoming one. I can't tell where hers begins . . . I can't tell where mine ends.

She smiles . . . her eyes are still closed and she's still shaking from the intensity. I take this opportunity to taste her lips and to lick the salty sweetness from the side of her neck. My hands begin to explore, and my tongue encircles her dark nipples. She arches her back when my full lips close around her nipple, and I began to suck softly as if she's feeding me life from within her soul.

Her hands find there way to my head and become tangled in my soft locks, identical to hers but not as long. I push into her deep, and grind softly against her clit in search of her "j-spot" because it belongs to me, Jada. She speaks my name so soft that I barely hear her. I know she wants me to take what she so willingly gave me, and I want to hear her beg for it.

I start to pull back slowly, and I can feel her body tightening up, trying to keep me from moving. One of many soft moans is heard over the low hum of the clock radio that sits next to our bed. I hear slight snatches of Raheem DeVaughn singing about being in heaven, and I'm almost certain he wrote that song for me and my lady.

I open her lips up so that I can have full view of her sensitive pearl. Her body quakes with anticipation from the feel of my warm breath touching it, my mouth just mere inches away. I blow cool air on her stiff clit, causing her to tense up briefly, her hands taking hold of my head trying to pull me closer. At this point my mouth is so close to her all I would have to do is twitch my lips to make contact, but I don't . . . I want her to beg for it.

My index finger is making small circles against my own clit, my honey sticky between my legs. The ultimate pleasure is giving pleasure, and I've experienced that on both accounts. My baby can't wait anymore, and her soft pants are turning into low moans. I stick my tongue out, and her clit gladly kisses me back.

Her body responds by releasing a syrupy sweet slickness that I lap up until it's all gone, fucking her with my tongue the way she likes it. I hold her legs up and out to intensify her orgasm because I know she can't handle it that way.

"Does your husband do you like this?" I ask between licks. Before she can answer I wrap my full lips around her clit and suck her into my mouth, swirling my tongue around her hardened bud, causing her body to shake.

Snatching a second toy from the side of the bed, I take one hand to part her lips, and I ease her favorite toy (The Rabbit) inside of her. Wishing that the strap-on I was wearing was a real dick so that I could feel her pulsate, I turn the toy on low at first wanting her to receive the ultimate pleasure. In the dark room the glow in the dark toy is lit brightly, the light disappearing inside of her when I push it all the way in.

The head of the curved toy turns in a slow circle while the pearl beads jump around on the inside, hitting up against her smooth walls during insertion. When I push the toy in she pushes her pelvis up to receive it, my mouth latched on to her clit like a vice. She moans louder, and I kick the toy up a notch to medium, much to her delight. Removing my mouth from her clit, I rotate between flicking my wet tongue across it to heat it, and blowing my breath on it to cool it, bringing her to yet another screaming orgasm, followed by strings of *"I love you"* and *"Please don't stop."*

Torturing her body slowly, I continue to stimulate her clit while pushing her toy in and out of her on a constant rhythm. When she lifts her legs to her chest I take the opportunity to let the ears on the rabbit toy that we are using do its job on her clit while my tongue find its way to her chocolate ass. I bite one cheek at a time, replacing it with wet kisses, afterwards sliding my tongue in between to taste her there. Her body squirming underneath me let's me know I've hit the jackpot, and I fuck her with my tongue there also.

She's moaning, telling me in a loud whisper that she can't take it anymore. That's my clue to turn the toy up high. The buzzing from the toy matches that of the radio, and with her moans and my pants mixed in we sound like a well-rehearsed orchestra singing a symphony of passion. I allow her to buck against my face while I keep up with the rhythm of the toy, her juice oozing out the sides and forming a puddle under her ass. I'm loving it.

She moans and shakes until the feeling in the pit of her stomach resides and she is able to breath at a normal rate. My lips taste salty/sweet from kissing her body while she tries to get her head together, rubbing the sides of my body up and down in a lazy motion.

Valentine's Day is fast approaching and I have a wonderful evening planned for the two of us. She already promised me that her husband wouldn't be an issue because he'll be out of town that weekend, and besides all that, they haven't celebrated Cupid's day since the year after they were married so I didn't even think twice about it. After seven years it should be over for them anyway.

"It's your turn now," she says to me in a husky lust filled voice, and I can't wait for her to take control.

The ultimate pleasure is giving pleasure . . . and man does it feel good both ways. She starts by rubbing her oil-slicked hands over the front of my body, taking extra time around my sensitive nipples before bringing her hands down across my flat stomach. I've since then removed the strap-on dildo, and am completely naked under her hands.

I can still feel her sweat on my skin, and I can still taste her on my lips. Closing my eyes, I enjoy the sensual massage that I'm being treated to. After two years of us making love it's still good and gets better every time.

She likes to take her time covering every inch of my body, and I enjoy letting her. She skips past my love box, and starts at my feet massaging my legs from the toes up. When she gets to my pleasure point her fingertips graze the smooth hairless skin there quickly teasing me before she heads back down, and does the same thing with my other limb. My legs are spread apart and lying flat on the bed with her in between relaxing my body with ease. A cool breeze from the cracked window blows across the room every so often, caressing my erect nipples and making them harder than before until her hands warm them back up again.

She knows when I can't take anymore any she rubs and caresses me until I am begging her to kiss my lips. I can see her

smile through half closed eyelids, and she does what I requested. Dipping her head down between my legs, she kisses
my lips just as I asked, using her tongue to part them so that
she could taste my clit. My body goes into mini-convulsions
on contact and I am fighting a battle to not cum that I never
win.

"Valentine's Day belongs to us right?" I ask her again between moans. I need her to be here. V-Day is for lovers, and
her and her husband haven't been that in ages. I deserve it . . .
I deserve her. I just don't want this to be a repeat of Christ-
mas or New Years eve.

"Yes, it's yours," she says between kisses on my thigh, and
sticking her tongue inside of me. Two of her fingers have
found there way inside of my tight walls, and my pelvic area
automatically bounces up and down on her hand as my orgasm approaches.

"Tell me you love me," I say to her as my breathing becomes raspy. I fire is spreading across my legs and working its
way up to the pit of my stomach. I need her to tell me before
I explode.

"I love you," she says and at the moment she places her
tongue in my slit I release my honey all over her tongue.

It feels like I am on the Tea Cup ride at the amusement
park as my orgasm jerks my body uncontrollably and it feels
like the room is spinning. She is sucking and slurping my clit
while the weight of her body holds the bottom half of me
captive. I'm practically screaming and begging her to stop,
and just when I think I'm about to check out of here, she lets
my clit go.

I take a few more minutes to get my head together, allowing her to pull me into her and rub my back. It's moments
like this that makes it all worthwhile. We lay like that for a
while longer listening to each other breath, and much to my
dismay she slides my head from where it was resting on her
arm and gets up out of the bed.

I don't say a word. I just lie on the bed and watch her get dressed. I swear, everything she does is so graceful, like there's a rhythm riding behind it. Pretty soon she is dressed and standing beside the bed looking down at me. She smiles and I smile back, not worried because she promised me our lover's day, and that's only a week away.

"So, Valentine's Day belongs to me, right?" I ask her again just to be certain.

"Yes, it belongs to you."

We kiss one last time, and I can still taste my honey on her lips. She already knows the routine, locking the bottom lock behind her. Just thinking about her makes me so horny, and I pick up her favorite toy to finish the job. Five more days, and it'll be on again.

ABOUT THE AUTHOR

Author Darrien Lee resides in LaVergne, Tennessee with her husband of sixteen years and two young daughters.

Darrien admits that she picked up her love for writing while attending college at Tennessee State University, and it was those experiences which inspired her debut novel. She is a three-time *Essence Magazine* Best-selling Author with six published novels, which includes, *All That and a Bag of Chips, Been There, Done That, What Goes Around Comes Around, When Hell Freezes Over, Brotherly Love,* and *Talk To The Hand.*

Darrien is also in the process of completing several new projects for future releases, including a teen novel and a children's book.

She can be reached at DarrienLeeAuthor@aol.com. You can also visit Darrien's website at:
www.DarrienLee.com and
www.MySpace.com/DarrienLee

LOOK FOR MORE HOT TITLES FROM

Q-BORO
B O O K S

DARK KARMA - JUNE 2007
$14.95
ISBN 1-933967-12-9

What if the criminal was forced to live the horror that they caused? The drug dealer finds himself in the body of the drug addict and he suffers through the withdrawals, living on the street, the beatings, the rapes and the hunger. The thief steals the rent money and becomes the victim that finds herself living on the street and running for her life and the murderer becomes the victim's father and he deals with the death of a son and a grieving mother.

GET MONEY CHICKS - SEPTEMBER 2007
$14.95
ISBN 1-933967-17-X

For Mina, Shanna, and Karen, using what they had to get what they wanted was always an option. Best friends since day one, they always had a thing for the hottest gear, luxurious lifestyles, and the ballers who made it all possible. All of this changes for Mina when a tragedy makes her open her eyes to the way she's living. Peer pressure and loyalty to her girls collide with her own morality, sending Mina into a no-win situation.

AFTER-HOURS GIRLS - AUGUST 2007
$14.95
ISBN 1-933967-16-1

Take part in this tale of two best friends, Lisa and Tosha, as they stalk the nightclubs and after-hours joints of Detroit searching for excitement, money, and temporary companionship. These two divas stand tall until the unforgivable Motown streets catch up to them. One must fall. You, the reader, decide which.

THE LAST CHANCE - OCTOBER 2007
$14.95
ISBN 1-933967-22-6

Running their L.A. casino has been rewarding for Luke Chance and his three brothers. But recently it seems like everyone is trying to get a piece of the pie. An impending hostile takeover of their casino could leave them penniless and possibly dead. That is, until their sister Keilah Chance comes home for a short visit. Keilah is not only beautiful, but she also can be ruthless. Will the Chance family be able to protect their family dynasty?

Traci must find a way to complete her journey out of her first and only failed

LOOK FOR MORE HOT TITLES FROM

Q-BORO B O O K S

NYMPHO - MAY 2007
$14.95
ISBN 1933967102

How will signing up to live a promiscuous double-life destroy everything that's at stake in the lives of two close couples? Take a journey into Leslie's secret world and prepare for a twisted, erotic experience.

FREAK IN THE SHEETS - SEPTEMBER 2007
$14.95
ISBN 1933967196

Librarian Raquelle decides to put her knowledge of sexuality to use and open up a "freak" school, teaching men and women how to please their lovers beyond belief while enjoying themselves in the process. But trouble brews when a surprise pupil shows up and everything Raquelle has worked for comes under fire.

LIAR, LIAR - JUNE 2007
$14.95
ISBN 1933967110

Stormy calls off her wedding to Camden when she learns he's cheating with a male church member. However, after being convinced that Camden has been delivered from his demons, she proceeds with the wedding.

Will Stormy and Camden survive scandal, lies and deceit?

HEAVEN SENT - AUGUST 2007
$14.95
ISBN 1933967188

Eve is a recovering drug addict who has no intentions of staying clean until she meets Reverend Washington, a newly widowed man with three children. Secrets are uncovered that threaten Eve's new life with her new family and has everyone asking if Eve was *Heaven Sent*.

LOOK FOR MORE HOT TITLES FROM

OBSESSION 101
$6.99
ISBN 0977733548

After a horrendous trauma. Rashawn Ams is left pregnant and flees town to give birth to her son and repair her life after confiding in her psychiatrist. After her return to her life, her town, and her classroom, she finds herself the target of an intrusive secret admirer who has plans for her.

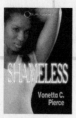

SHAMELESS- OCTOBER 2006
$6.99
ISBN 0977733513

Kyle is sexy, single, and smart; Jasmyn is a hot and sassy drama queen. These two complete opposites find love - or something real close to it - while away at college. Jasmyn is busy wreaking havoc on every man she meets. Kyle, on the other hand, is trying to walk the line between his faith and all the guilty pleasures being thrown his way. When the partying college days end and Jasmyn tests HIV positive, reality sets in.

MISSED OPPORTUNITIES - MARCH 2007
$14.95
ISBN 1933967013

Missed Opportunities illustrates how true-to-life characters must face the consequences of their poor choices. Was each decision worth the opportune cost? LaTonya Y. Williams delivers yet another account of love, lies, and deceit all wrapped up into one powerful novel.

ONE DEAD PREACHER - MARCH 2007
$14.95
ISBN 1933967021

Smooth operator and security CEO David Price sets out to protect the sexy, smart, and saucy Sugar Owens from her husband, who happens to be a powerful religious leader. Sugar isn't as sweet as she appears, however, and in a twisted turn of events, the preacher man turns up dead and Price becomes the prime suspect.

LOOK FOR MORE HOT TITLES FROM

Q-BORO
BOOKS

DOGISM
$6.99
ISBN 0977733505

Lance Thomas is a sexy, young black male who has it all: a high paying blue collar career, a home in Queens, New York, two cars, a son, and a beautiful wife. However, after getting married at a very young age he realizes that he is afflicted with DOGISM, a distorted sexuality that causes men to stray and be unfaithful in their relationships with women.

POISON IVY - NOVEMBER 2006
$14.95
ISBN 0977733521

Ivy Davidson's life has been filled with sorrow. Her father was brutally murdered and she was forced to watch, she faced years of abuse at the hands of those she trusted, and she was forced to live apart from the only source of love that she'd ever known. Now Ivy stands alone at the crossroads of life, staring into the eyes of the man who holds her final choice of life or death in his hands.

HOLY HUSTLER - FEBRUARY 2007
$14.95
ISBN 0977733556

Reverend Ethan Ezekiel Goodlove the Third and his three sons are known for spreading more than just the gospel. The sanctified drama of the Goodloves promises to make us all scream "Hallelujah!"

HAPPILY NEVER AFTER - JANUARY 2007
$14.95
ISBN 1933967005

To Family and friends, Dorothy and David Leonard's marriage appears to be one made in heaven. While David is one of Houston's most prominent physicians, Dorothy is a loving and carefree housewife. It seems as if life couldn't be more fabulous for this couple who appear to have it all: wealth, social status, and a loving union. However, looks can be deceiving. What really happens behind closed doors and when the flawless veneer begins to crack?

LOOK FOR

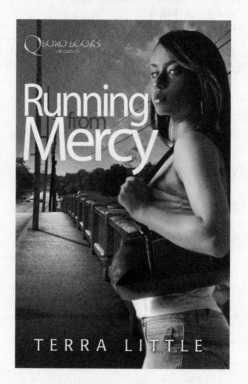

Attention Writers:

Writers looking to get their books published can view our submission guidelines by visiting our website at: *www.QBOROBOOKS.com*

What we're looking for: Contemporary fiction in the tradition of Darrien Lee, Carl Weber, Anna J., Zane, Mary B. Morrison, Noire, Lolita Files, etc; groundbreaking mainstream contemporary fiction.

We prefer email submissions to: submissions@qborobooks.com in MS Word, PDF, or rtf format only. However, if you wish to send the submission via snail mail, you can send it to:

Q-BORO BOOKS Acquisitions Department
165-41A Baisley Blvd., Suite 4. Mall #1
Jamaica, New York 11434

*** By submitting your work to Q-Boro Books, you agree to hold Q-Boro books harmless and not liable for publishing similar works as yours that we may already be considering or may consider in the future. ***

1. Submissions will not be returned.
2. Do not contact us for status updates. If we are interested in receiving your full manuscript, we will contact you via email or telephone.
3. Do not submit if the entire manuscript is not complete.

Due to the heavy volume of submissions, if these requirements are not followed, we will not be able to process your submission.